FOL
2

A Foreign Country

A
Foreign
Country

Fotios Sarris

DUMAGRAD
CITY OF WORDS
TORONTO

A Foreign Country
Copyright © 2020 Fotios Sarris

A Dumagrad Book
Dumagrad: A City of Words
Toronto

info @ dumagrad.com
wordcity.ca

Distributed in Canada by LitDistCo.
Email orders@litdistco.ca
8300 Lawson Rd., Milton, ON L9T 0A4

ISBN 978-1-988887-05-0

Library and Archives Canada Cataloguing in Publication

Title: A foreign country / Fotios Sarris.
Names: Sarris, Fotios, author.
Identifiers: Canadiana 20200193724 | ISBN 9781988887050 (softcover)
Classification: LCC PS8637.A7532 F67 2020 | DDC C813/.6—dc23

Cover design by David Drummond
Printed and bound in Canada

2 4 6 8 9 7 5 3 1

To George and Katina, my parents

A Foreign Country

1

I SEE ME STANDING AT THE WINDOW, looking out on Park Avenue. My life has become so routine, each monotone day leading to another like it, that one starting point seems as good as any other.

So we'll start there: I'm at my window, gazing down on the street. I know just the day, to all appearances a sunny pleasant early-autumn morning not long ago. The awning below is unfurled, muffling the voices on the terrace. These days I can't look out my window without recalling the street as it was. The memories come unbidden. In succession houses rise and fall, crumble, are extended, restored, condofied. Most of the old buildings have been spruced up, remodelled, repurposed. Storefronts have been scrubbed down and gussied up. Even the Hasid across the street has installed a jazzy red neon trim in his window display. And this spring the psarotaverna a few buildings over got a new stucco façade. (No, it's not *that* Park Avenue: I'm afraid our setting is not quite so glamorous.) Striving for colour and specificity, I asked Kostas, the owner, what the flowers in the sprightly new window boxes are, and he said they're geraniums and nasturtiums. He gave me the names in Greek, which I had to look up (like so much else here). The English names are hardly more meaningful to me. While I was at it, I researched the trees on the street. It turns out they're mostly Norway maples and honey locusts. (What did they used to be? Were there even trees on Park Avenue when I was a kid?)

The Hasid's shoe store and the psarotaverna have been around since my childhood; most of the other businesses on the street are new. Some, like the artisan jeweller, the organic cosmetics store, and the pet grooming salon only sprouted up the last couple of years. I can't remember what was there before them. (Why is it every time something new goes up I can't remember what stood there before?) I'm in my father's apartment, on the top floor of an old redbrick triplex. It is I who live there now. There's a second, smaller apartment next to mine and two more on the floor below. On the ground floor is the Symposium Pool Hall (officially, *Le Salon de Billiard Symposium*), which my father acquired in 1985. He put in a bid for the building a few years later, but the owner at the time, a cranky old widower named Rassoulis, refused to sell, not just to my father, but to anyone, or at any price. But Rassoulis passed away just before the Great Real Estate Boom, enabling my father to purchase the building from his daughters, who were eager to get rid of it. (I wonder how they feel now?)

But we need to go further back than this. I just can't decide how far. I've always had trouble with beginnings (not to say I'm any better with endings). For the historian, of course, this is a crucial—perhaps *the* crucial—question: where to begin. Henry James somewhere remarks that relations stop nowhere. But they also start nowhere. As any historian will tell you, beginnings are notoriously difficult to pin down. What are the origins of the Second World War? Of the First? When is the start of the modern age? What are the origins of civilization? When does life begin? Do we go with Matthew or with Luke? Clear-headed Telemachus lamented that no man knows his own begetting. The *Rig Veda* suggests that even the gods are in the dark about the origins of creation. The gods themselves came afterward. Who then knows how creation arose? Perhaps it formed itself. Or perhaps it didn't. The one who looks down on it from the highest heaven, only he knows. Or maybe not.

Meanwhile, I stare out my window. The story of my life. Time to get moving.

So let us go then, you and I.

Yes, let's go.

I know something's up the moment I step out my front door. It's not yet 10 AM and the terrace is almost full. I spot Dzonakis at one of the tables, but he's sitting with Karvelas. I want to speak to him privately, so I make a mental note to find him later. As I round the railing, I'm blocked by a guy in a beige linen suit and a fauxhawk. He pumps my hand and asks how I'm doing. I've spoken with this guy once or twice, but he acts like we're old buddies. He's the cousin or nephew or godson of someone I barely knew in high school, and today he's with an underfed bottle-blonde in a tight white dress. She's chewing gum at the table behind him, wearing giant white hoop earrings and white oval sunglasses. I gather the phony familiarity is for her benefit and meant to show what a man-about-town he is. That's the kind of status I have these days. Total strangers shake my hand, introduce me to their friends. I pretend I care. So intent is the cockatoo on impressing his lady friend that he stands with his ass in her face, so to show what a gentleman I am, I lean around him and introduce myself. She manages a cursory smile amid the strenuous gum chewing and proffers an elaborately manicured hand, fingernails painted purple and edged at the tips with a filar purfling of gold arabesques.

I don't like these shiny types. Perry is of the more-the-merrier school, but I worry they'll scare away our more tousled clientele. I've suggested that it's all about niche marketing and microtargeting and that these Crescent Street types are not consistent with our "brand," but Perry disagrees. This new species surfaced a couple of months ago. One afternoon in April, one of our regulars dropped in with a guy I'd never seen and invited me to sit with them. The stranger started firing personal questions, asking me about the pool hall and growing up in the neighbourhood, and I must have been in a good mood as I answered at some length, dressing things up and perhaps stretching the truth for dramatic effect. Only as he was leaving did he mention that he was a journalist and was thinking of doing a feature on the Symposium. Two weeks later he was back with a camera and recorder, and, sitting Perry and me down for a formal interview, he had me go over some of the territory we'd already covered, with Perry throwing in his own observations and recollections, the both of us, I thought later, playing up the working class ethnic angle almost to the point of caricature. Yet when the article appeared, I was stunned to see our stories had been even further embellished, the author or one of his editors presumably having judged the original versions insufficiently colourized. It was such a shabby piece of journalism, it made me wonder about everything else I read in the papers. Perry mocked me for taking the thing so seriously. It was a puff piece, he said, and I should be grateful for the publicity. And, indeed, the effect on business was astonishing. We were swarmed with new customers, including the likes of the cockatoo and his girlfriend. And it hasn't let up. Which makes me nervous. Our success is too sudden. It feels unwarranted, illusory. And I fear it will vanish as suddenly as it came.

As the cockatoo jabbers on, I nod and grin. Bonhomie doesn't come easily to me: I find it dreary, gut-grinding work. It may be the hardest part of the job. I am not my father. I'm also distracted by what I'm seeing through the window, and at the first chance I grab the cockatoo's hand and, giving it a parting shake, tell him to say hello to his cousin or uncle or godfather (whose name, mercifully, comes to me in the nick of time). I head for the door, but I've no sooner reached it than I'm blocked by François, who is on his way out. François is one of the oldest of our new regulars and is here almost every day, the Symposium functioning for him as a second office. He's in his mid-fifties, but dressed in an unbuttoned grey V-neck cardigan, white Henley undershirt, faded black jeans, and black canvas slip-on sneakers with white Jolly Roger polka dots, he's barely distinguishable from our other customers. These days we attract a young crowd, university students and fledgling professionals in their twenties and thirties. We also get a lot of media types and "creatives," including minor local celebrities—radio announcers, DJs, musicians, journalists, that sort of thing. But then these are the people who live in Mile End these days. As Perry likes to put it, the neighbourhood is going to the poodles.

Mile End—that's what this area is called. *Quartier Mile End.* I've read the name goes back to the nineteenth century, though I don't remember hearing it until the eighties. Before that, I don't think any of us knew we lived in Mile End. Now you hear and see the name everywhere, always accompanied by its trusty sidekick—*trendy.* Sometimes I long for the old days. I don't much like the poodles. I resent their presence. I know this is sheer hypocrisy and sentimentalism. Where would Perry and I be without the poodles? Or guys like Fausto Zappavigna and Petro Kourkoulas, and all the others in the neighbourhood who, with their shitty jobs or with no job at all, can afford to live here only because they inherited their parents' properties? Where would this whole neighbourhood be if all that money hadn't poured in? Do I really want to go back to the squalor and decrepitude, the alkies and junkies, the hoodlums, biker gangs, street crazies? Perry sometimes speaks of us as though we're a couple of con men while characterizing our customers as dupes and simpletons. Talk like this reminds me of our fathers' generation, the diner and pizzeria owners before us who expressed a similar disdain for their customers. I recall how my father used to say, "What does the Frenchman know about food? All he knows is hot dogs and french fries." But much as I hate such talk, I sometimes think Perry may be right, that we're part of some great scam.

François wants to rib me about the turmoil inside the pool hall, and he recounts a conversation he just had with one of the *kobolóya*. But his *rigolo* feeds my anxiety, and I keep glancing past him, trying to see the commotion. He doesn't notice. François prides himself on his knowledge of world affairs and is intent on sharing his take on the Balkans. I don't want to hear it, so, lying that I'm urgently needed, I promise to pick this up with him later and break away.

Just inside the entrance, I stop. I can't believe what I see. I can't remember the last time I saw so many kobolóya here (the term is Jimmy's, referring to the worry beads so many of these guys are forever twirling between their fingers). I see faces I haven't seen in years. I didn't know there were so many kobolóya still alive. The truth is I feared something like this might happen. It was my first thought when I heard on the radio that the Canadian government would be officially recognizing the Republic of Macedonia under that appellation. I just never imagined this kind of turnout. That's why all the poodles are out on the terrace. Do they fear a countercoup, the return of the ancien régime? At the counter, Perry steams milk behind the espresso machine. He stands stone-faced while a couple of kobolóya bark at him. At the other end is Arjun, assembling orders on the back counter. No one has noticed me, and I consider going back upstairs.

But I head toward the counter and sidle up beside Perry. "When did they get here?" I ask him in English. Eyeing me acidly, the kobolóya who've been shouting at him turn their backs on us.

Perry gives me an aggrieved look and holds up two fingers. "Two minutes," he says, also speaking English. "They started coming in two minutes after I opened. I'm not exaggerating, I checked my watch, I'm surprised they weren't waiting at the door." He turns off the steam valve, swabs the spout. "They're swelling my balls."

"How was breakfast?"

He bobbles his head, gestural Greek for "Don't ask."

"You should have called me," I say. Noticing some bagel slices on the toaster tray, I step over to the back counter. "What are these?"

Perry turns. "Ah, shit," he says, glancing over at Arjun.

"I got it. What are they?"

"Two lox and cream...." He thinks. "One no onions. And one egg salad."

I hang up my blazer and wash my hands.

"Aren't you seeing your father today?"

"Not till later."

"We can manage, don't worry. It's not like these fucking *remálya* order anything."

As Perry lifts his loaded tray and heads for the terrace, Arjun comes over to help me garnish the sandwich plates. He shakes his head and grins at me. "It's been crazy, man," he says. "I've never seen it like this." Arjun is a recent hire, recommended to us by one of our regulars. He's smart, hard-working, great with the customers. He's doing electrical engineering at McGill. He won't stick around long.

"You know why they're all here, I suppose," I say to him.

"Perry sort of explained. Sounds like the Punjab."

I don't know enough about the Punjab to comment.

"So these guys used to be your regulars?" he says.

"Yup." My name rings out behind us. "This is what the place used to be like all the time."

"Aleko!"

"Well, maybe not quite like this."

"I think someone wants you," says Arjun.

"*Reh*! Aleko! I'm talking to you!"

I turn to face the magnified glower of Leftheris Asikis. He stares at me through big rectangular eyeglasses, the lenses thick enough to broil ants on a sunny day. "I hear you, Leftheri. You don't have to scream."

"We've made a decision. That flag goes back up today."

I turn to Arjun. "Could you finish this?" I turn back to Leftheris. "Sorry...who made a decision?"

"We had a discussion this morning."

"Who did?"

"All of us. We discussed the matter this—"

"*Kathiyité*!" shouts Dzonaras, coming up behind Leftheris with reinforcements. "That flag is going back up right now," he says, pointing an arthritic finger above my head. "You know what's happening. You've read the news. We have to get organized! Think what your father would say if he heard you still refused to put that flag up."

"And how exactly would he hear that?"

Dzonaras stares at me mutely.

I lean in closer. "Dzonara, are you the one putting these fleas in my father's ear?"

"What are you talking about?"

"Dzonara," I say, maintaining an even tone, "my father in his condition doesn't need things like this to be bothered about. If you were a real friend, you wouldn't be putting these worries on him. And I would be grateful if you kept your nose out of my personal things." My Greek is even more garbled than I've rendered it here, but the message is clear. In any case, I doubt Dzonaras is one of my father's informants. The two were never that close and don't have much contact. But he goads some of the others.

Dzonaras glances at Perry, who has returned from outside. "What do *you* have to say about this?" Perry scowls incomprehension. "With everything going on, don't you agree that we should hang that flag back up?"

Understanding dawns on Perry's face.

"We have to get organized like last time," says Leftheris. "It's your generation's turn to take command."

"If Andreas were here," says Dzonaras, "he'd be leading the charge."

"But he's not here," I say. "And this is not his place anymore."

"You haven't buried him yet," Dzonaras says. "This is still Andreas's place. And everyone knows he's not happy with some of the things the two of you have been doing here."

"How does everyone know this?"

"We know."

"Listen Dzonara," I say, losing my patience, "this is not a social club. Things have changed. You see those people out there? They're our customers. They're what keep us here. And I can assure you most of them couldn't find Macedonia on a map. Or give a flying fuck what its name is." (Again,

I'm taking liberties with the translation.) "Nor should they. That's not what they come here for. This is a business. It has no nationality." In English, I say, "This is a flag-free zone."

Dzonaras visibly seethes. Leftheris's gecko eyes get even bigger.

"That's the trouble," Dzonaras sputters. "That's the trouble with the world today, right there," he says, walking away. Glancing back at us, he says, "Shame. Shame on you both."

"Shame," Leftheris echoes, following behind him.

Perry and I exchange a quick glance, and he turns and walks away. It's hard to know what Perry thinks of my behaviour, but if it were up to him, the flag would have gone back up a long time ago. It wouldn't have come down in the first place. He probably sees me as lacking in solidarity and fellow-feeling. Perhaps he sees me as a traitor.

The flag in question is the Sun of Vergina, which my father hung behind the counter back in 1991, when this name dispute first erupted between Greece and its newly independent northern neighbour. He became heavily involved in the protests and demonstrations, including the big one on Parliament Hill, and the Symposium functioned as a kind of war room. Gazing at the faces around me, I recall what they looked like then. Already most of these guys were well into middle age. Now they're old men, these clamorous warlike sons of the Achaeans, stooped, shrunken, slow-moving in their rumpled pants, nylon windbreakers, and oversized spectacles. Most couldn't even lift Odysseus's bow, let alone string it. These days they mostly talk about their aches and pains and the pills they have to take. Leftheris is right: it's time for the next generation to take up the fight. And I have no doubt many will. But I won't be among them.

Spotting Nick Karvelas in the crowd, I remember Dzonakis and look around for him. But he's nowhere in sight, and I throw on my blazer and head out to the terrace. He's at the same corner table, reading a newspaper. I drop into the seat opposite him and he glances up at me.

"Why aren't you inside with the others?" I ask.

He folds his newspaper and puts it with those on the table. He reads them all, from *Kathimeriní* to *Rizospástis*, whatever he can find. "The stillborn schemes of sad old men," he says as he removes his glasses. Is this a quotation? This is often the case with the Greeks: they sound as though they're quoting an old saw or proverb, which half the time I don't understand. Sometimes it's in the ancient tongue or regional dialect, making it even harder to decipher.

"How's your father?" he asks. "I'm sorry I haven't been by." He holds his folded glasses in his fist. A small man, he has large hands, worker's hands, digits thick and hairy. In Canada, he washed dishes and drove a cab. In Greece, he worked on tobacco farms and in construction. He's from a village near Thessaloniki, not far from my father's, though they only met in the eighties, when my father worked as a cabbie.

"Don't think about it. You visit him more than anyone."

"Tell him I'll be by soon. How is he?"

I shrug and reach for the envelope in the inside pocket of my blazer. "I want to show you something."

He watches me apprehensively, as if he knows what's coming. I remove a Polaroid from the envelope and slide it across the table toward him like a TV detective. Heaving a sigh, he slips his glasses back on and picks it up. I give him a few seconds.

"Do you recognize the woman?"

He turns down the corners of his mouth.

"Tell me the truth."

He throws me a reproachful look above the rims of his glasses. "I always tell you the truth," he says and glances down at the Polaroid again.

"Who is she?" he says finally.

"Come on. Are you serious?"

Before he can answer, a customer stops at our table. I have to do more grinning and glad-handing. When he leaves, I turn back to Dzonakis.

"It's the same woman as in the other photographs," I say. "The ones I showed you last time."

"You mean five or six years ago? You expect me to remember?" I slide over a second Polaroid. He studies it a moment. "Is this you?"

"Come on."

"Doesn't it look like you?" He turns the photo toward me.

"No," I answer without looking at it. "That looks nothing like me."

"Don't get angry," he says, examining it again. "I don't know what you looked like at that age."

"That's the same boy as in the other photographs. Just older."

"I don't know why you expect me to remember." He slides the photos back to me and asks where I found them.

"I found another stash of his papers..." An ambulance is tearing down Park Avenue, siren wailing, so I pause a few seconds. "I was going through them yesterday. These were with them, some others too."

Dzonakis shrugs. "And so? What do you want me to tell you? Your father had a *gómena*. We know this already. Everybody knows it. Your father played around. You've known this for years."

"And the boy?"

"Don't start that. We know all that too. The woman had a boy. So what?"

"But look at them." I push the photos back toward him. "Look at their faces."

Dzonakis won't look down. He keeps staring at me.

I pick up the photos and give them a quick glance before putting them back in the envelope. By now they're practically burned in my memory. One shows my father and a slim attractive blonde woman side by side on a park bench. She's in her early thirties. My father must be in his forties. Both are smiling at the camera, genuinely happy. The other shows my father standing with a small boy in front of a tree. The boy is nine or ten. He and my father are holding hands, the boy gazing at the camera with his head tilted, a scrunched, one-eyed squint on his sunlit face.

"There's no proof of anything in those photographs beyond what we already know," Dzonakis says.

I know not to push the matter. I like Dzonakis. He's an honest, upstanding guy, which is why I consult with him. But I still don't trust him completely. He has an inexplicable loyalty to my father, and I suspect he withholds details that might upset me or make my father look bad. Unlike my father's other friends, Dzonakis doesn't lie and invent, but I can't always count on him for the truth.

"Alex, I hope you're not planning to show those to him," he says as I slip the photos back in my pocket.

"Why not?"

"Aleko, please. Promise me you're not going to show him these."

I don't answer.

"Aleko...what's the purpose?"

"I have a right to know."

He sniffs.

"Don't I? Don't I have that right?" The word sounds odd even to me. I'm not sure it's appropriate in this context. It has a different ring in Greek, different connotations. But I don't know what other word to use.

Dzonakis smiles at me disdainfully. "That's the problem with you Canadians. You think you have rights. You keep hearing the word from politicians and journalists and you come to believe it. There's nothing to know. All the stuff you hear is gossip and slander. Which, I hope you'll forgive me for saying, comes mostly from your mother. And your uncle. But even if it's true—let's say it's true. All of it. The worst of it. Let's say you confirm that everything your mother and uncle have been saying is true. What then? What do you gain?"

"Knowledge. Certitude. So I can stop thinking about it and go on with my life. I just want to stop worrying about it."

"Then stop. What's there to worry about? Your father wasn't perfect. He made mistakes. Who hasn't? No, he wasn't the best husband or father. But, Alex, listen to me...your father is a good man. He's one of the finest men I've ever known."

I shake my head in disbelief.

"Maybe I haven't known your father as long as the others, but I know him better than most people. I know him maybe better than you do."

"I'm *sure* of that."

"Listen to what I tell you. Your father isn't any of those things you've told me. Those are malicious lies. Your father is a kind, generous, decent man, one of the most decent people I've ever known. Like everyone, he has enemies. Yes, there are people who will say things about him, your uncle chief among them. But look in there." He points at the window. "See all those guys? Talk with any of them and see what they have to say about your father. That crowd alone is testament to his standing in this community. Talk to any of them. See what they have to say."

"I have talked to them. They're liars. They cover for him."

"No one's covering anything."

"Explain to me how no one can remember her name."

"Who?"

"Santál," I say. The name is Chantal, but I pronounce it the Greek way.

"How is it no one can remember her last name? It smells of conspiracy." There's a fancy Greek word I know. "They're covering up for him. They don't want me to track her down."

"I've never heard anyone mention her name. If I did, I promise you I would tell you. And I can also tell you this. If that boy was your father's, you would know. Everyone would. He would own up. He would have done what was necessary. Your father was always an honourable, responsible person. I know what you're thinking. But you're wrong. Your father, deep down, where it counts, your father is a good man."

I stare in bewilderment when Dzonakis talks like this. I wish I could see what he sees. And he's not alone. It's true: my father is beloved. He has more friends than I can keep track of. And they're doggedly loyal to him. It's incomprehensible to me. They see something I don't, something I can't. Deep down my father is a good man? An *honourable* man? What do these things mean here? And how deep does one have to dig to find them?

It's close to two when I arrive at St. Paul's (officially, *Le centre d'hébergement Saint-Paul*) and the second-floor dining hall is almost empty. Mrs. Tooby and Mrs. Reed sit facing the TV, their walkers parked by their chairs. They have their backs to me, but judging by the tilt of her head, Mrs. Reed is asleep. Mr. Landry is at the corner table working at his jigsaw puzzle. Lunch still lingers in the air, mingling with the usual odours of the place, including some chemical deodorant or sanitizer that's about as effective as potpourri in a cow pasture. Turning a corner, I come upon Mrs. Hawley trembling in her wheelchair, her scarecrow frame barely discernible inside a bulky knit cardigan. Beneath the hem of her skirt dangle her scaly grey legs, thin as a stork's. I say hello and she regards me with a mixture of curiosity and suspicion. She asks if I will take her to her room.

"I can't do that, Mrs. Hawley. I'm a visitor. Only staff members can take you to your room."

"Who are you visiting, dear?" she asks in her thin, crumbly voice.

"I'm Mr. Doukas's son."

"Well, aren't you a good son."

I nod. I can't count how many times I've been through this exchange.

"Will someone take me to my room soon? I'd like to go to bed."

"It's still early, Mrs. Hawley."

"What time is it, dear?"

I look at my watch. "It's just before two."

"Is it only that? Two in the *afternoon*?"

"Look," I say, pointing toward the windows.

She turns and looks with effort, as if trying to locate the daylight. "But I'm so tired," she says.

"I'm sure one of the nurses will come along soon."

"Do you think so, dear? I'd like to go to bed."

"I don't know if they'll put you in bed at this time of day, Mrs. Hawley. It's still early."

"What time is it?"

"It's just before two."

"Two? Two in the afternoon?"

"That's right."

"Is that all?" She shakes her head. "I feel so tired."

During such exchanges, I wonder why I could never be this patient with my parents. I still can't, even after all these years, after all the knocks and lessons. Why can't I be with my father the way I am with this stranger?

So many of St. Paul's residents are like this—polite, reserved, deferential. The home has Scots Presbyterian roots and most of the residents are Anglo. These are people who suffer without noise or drama, some Protestant sense of propriety and stoicism seemingly proof against even the failings of the flesh. I admire them. I gather this is the other side of Anglo repression, the bright side, this genteel grit and quiet rectitude. Greeks are impresarios of pain. We showcase our suffering. We wield it like a weapon.

On the way to my father's room, I run through my litany of prompts and mantras. Just be the same way with him, I tell myself. These pep talks and reminders have been a long-standing ritual, and though they've borne little fruit, I keep at it. Remember, he's your father. He's old and sick and may not be around much longer. He may be gone even now. He may be lying dead in his bed. Remember the past. Be patient. You're here to help. Don't lecture, don't reproach. Be kind. *Be kind, be kind, be kind.* These days I seem constantly to be in the midst of some such monologue. Often it's more like a dialogue, an ancient quarrel I've been rehearsing and trying to put to rest for decades. I'm still playing out grievances going back to my childhood, working on rebuttals and defenses, refining arguments, still trying to win battles lost and finished ages ago. I come up with new formulations and provocations. I often catch myself talking aloud. It's a kind of hysterical esprit de l'escalier. As a boy, when I saw adults talking to themselves, I assumed they were insane.

Even before I enter my father's room, I can hear the ball rattling in the roulette wheel. I drop my knapsack into the chair and unzip it. "*Kaliméra*," I shout out. My father keeps staring at the wheel. "I've brought you grapes," I say while he continues to ignore me. He's seated at the desk by the window. He's got on the black cotton track pants I brought him, along with a grey long-sleeved polo shirt. In the photos I have of him, he's nattily attired. Even after he'd fallen out of step with fashions in the late sixties, he remained a fussy and dapper dresser. He wouldn't have been caught dead in track pants or jeans. I never even saw him in shorts, not even at the beach. I try to get him track pants that don't look it. Essentially, they're cotton trousers, either black or dark blue, with an elastic waistband. All the same, he's embarrassed to be seen in them, even in this place. It's probably one reason he confines himself to his room. Though St. Paul's is part of the provincial public system, we pay a premium for a private room. Angry at being put in a nursing home, he would not put up with shared accommodations. As far as he was concerned, he was perfectly capable of living at home. If I were a good son, that's where he would be, even now, instead of in this prison. His friends give me flak too: a good son would have his father at home with him. And they may be right. But this is as good as I get.

I wash the grapes and put them in a bowl on the bedside cupboard. "I brought you those undershirts," I say. I pull out one of the packages from my knapsack and hold it up. "Undershirts," I repeat more loudly. My father keeps staring at his wheel, lost in the ball's orbit. I thrust the package before him just as the ball comes in for a landing. He growls and pushes me away. The ball is sitting in the fifteen pocket. He stares at it as if trying to comprehend the meaning of this. With his left hand, he picks up the pen by the wheel and in a small flipover notebook scrawls a large jagged 15 at the bottom of a long wiggly column of similar figures. There are numerous notebooks in a drawer of the bedside cupboard, their pages filled with such columns, two per page, each page numbered and dated. Occasionally he will take them out and pore over the figures.

He puts down the pen and picks up the ball. With his left hand, he nudges the wheel and launches the ball in one fluid motion. It's impressive. You'd think he'd worked as a croupier all his life. The wheel is a portable job, about half the size of the real thing and housed in black Bakelite. I haven't been able to find out who gave it to him. Everyone at the Symposium pleads ignorance. I brought the wheel to the staff's attention, hoping they might get rid of it. I thought there might be a house policy about gambling paraphernalia. I was told the visiting doctor had been delighted by it. It would provide a form of occupational therapy.

"But he only operates it with his left hand," I pointed out to the young nurse with whom I had raised the matter.

"So make him use his right."

"I can't make my father do anything. He doesn't listen to me. And when I'm around, he conceals his infirmities. I don't know what he does when he's alone, but I doubt it's any different."

"This might help his left hand."

"But I thought we were supposed to be discouraging him from neglecting his right hand."

The nurse looked confused, so I tried again:

"Won't this just encourage him to keep on neglecting his right hand?"

"Then get rid of it."

"Can't you get rid of it?"

"No," she said. "If the doctor says the toy is good for him, we're not going to take it away. But if *you* want to, that's your business."

Thus the toy remains, set permanently on the desk by the window. Standing over my father, I watch the ball as it starts to drop. After some bounces and ricochets, it lands in the nine pocket. Is this good? Is it bad? I have no idea. There are no chips, no layout. If any wagers have taken place, they're in my father's head, and nothing in his reaction provides clues. His expression is blank. He picks up the pen and enters the number in the notebook. Has he won, lost? Does he even know? He picks up the ball and goes again.

I head to the bureau and remove the undershirts from their packaging. I refold them and store them with his underclothes. I toss the packaging in the wastebasket and take another look at my father. His gaze seems sharper, clearer, his movements livelier, more certain. There appears to be improvement. I'm of two minds about that. It was only three months ago he was rushed to the hospital after another stroke, his second, and this time it looked like he wasn't going to make it. I was advised to start making preparations. A night or two later, when the phone rang after midnight, I caught myself: there was no denying it, a sense of expectation; or after I'd picked up the phone and heard Perry's voice, the dim but unmistakable sense of disappointment. I don't know what that says about me, but I can't pretend the feelings away. A few days later I was informed that my father was much improved and would likely be returning to his residence in a week.

I remove my blazer, and as I hang it up, I feel the breast pocket for the pictures. I don't know why I've brought them. Even if I were to show them to my father, I know what he'd say. What's the point? Spite, and nothing more. I recall my prompts and mantras. I pull up a chair by the desk and sit facing him.

Though he looks better than he did at my last visit, how different the man I gaze at is from the one in the photos. The same strong angular features that once gave him his good looks, the high, sharp cheekbones, prominent chin, large dark eyes, now give him a wasted, grim, almost ghoulish appearance. His face has developed a disconcerting asymmetry, one cheek drooping lower than the other. His eyes have dulled. Inside their dark purple cavities, they have a waxy, stupefied cast. The cheeks are drawn and sunken and his dentures appear too big for his mouth. Sometimes when he speaks they look as though they're about to pop out. He's retained much of his hair but it's sparse and wispy. And his bare upper lip still jars me. Hospital staff shaved it clean six years ago, after his first stroke. Until then, he'd worn the same pencil moustache his whole adult life. Even now, six years later, his face seems incomplete and distorted without it.

Watching him watch the wheel, I try to imagine what's inside his head. I'm practiced at this, having done it all my life, but in the last few years my father has become more inscrutable than ever. I assume he's making bets or predictions of some sort—otherwise what's the point? The few times I've asked him to explain what he's doing, he's refused to answer. He won't let me in on his modus operandi or objectives. Launching the ball, he stares at the wheel as at a hypnotist's watch, the absorption in his eyes reminiscent of those Zen states in which space and time dissolve in a perpetual now and subject and object become one. Is this what he's experiencing? Eyes fixed on the wheel, he seems removed from his surroundings, his entire being encompassed by the tiny orb's tight revolutions.

He plays another couple of rounds and then pushes his chair back and reaches for the wheelchair. With some difficulty, he transfers himself into it. He refuses my help. As he settles into the wheelchair, a slipper drops and I bend down and put it back on. One of his socks is inside out.

"You asked me to bring you grapes," I say as I sit back down. "There's some on the bureau. Should I bring them over?"

He shakes his head as he adjusts the chair's angle with the joystick. The expert consensus is that he doesn't need a wheelchair and indeed would be better off without one. Even after this latest stroke, the doctors and therapists have maintained that, with the support of a cane or walker and the proper exercises and effort, he could regain a good portion of his strength and mobility. But my father was so uncooperative in his rehabilitation that everyone concerned, myself included, eventually lost patience and abandoned him to his mulish infirmity. There appears to be for him more dignity in a wheelchair than in a walker, perhaps on the premise that it is better to admit defeat than to persist in a losing battle. Better to break than bend. Even now I believe it's not too late for him to regain some of his mobility, but I don't have the strength to fight him.

I ask about lunch but get only grunts. I fall silent and my father stares at the floor. This is how we spend much of our time together. It's fine with me. I always bring something to read. After a lengthy silence, he raises his head. I brace myself, wondering whether he's going to bring up the flag. It wouldn't surprise me if they got to him already. Does he know about yesterday's announcement? He still watches TV and listens to Greek radio, but I don't know what he takes in or retains.

"So...tell me," he begins. I run through my mantras. "Did you call ." He pauses several seconds. "Did you call..."

He can't locate the name, but I'm pretty sure I know who he has in mind.

"Niko," he says at last. "Did you call Niko about...about that thing?"

He can't remember who gave him the roulette wheel, but a detail like this sticks in his brain like a tumour.

"Yeah, I called him," I lie.

There's a silence, giving me what turns out to be a false sense of hope.

"When?"

I maintain an air of nonchalance. "After I saw you." We stare at each other. "It's all taken care of," I say. "Everything's fine. It's taken care of."

My father says something that I hope I've misunderstood. These days, his speech is slurred and choppy, and I can't always make out the words.

"What did you say?" I ask him.

"Nikos said you never called."

I should have seen this coming. A week earlier, one of the second-floor tenants had a plumbing emergency and, being the handy type, dealt with it himself. The next day he came down to the pool hall to tell me about it, and suggested I call in a plumber to be on the safe side. Unfortunately, he did this in the presence of several kobolóya, and on my next visit, my father asked me what was happening on the second floor.

"Nikos said you never called," he repeats. "I spoke to him yesterday."

I remain silent.

"I spoke to him and he said...he never heard from you."

Nikos Papoulias, my father's plumber, is also a good friend. They've known each other thirty years. I don't like Nikos, however, and have found a plumber who is both more competent and more courteous. But he's not Greek, and for my father it is a first-order principle that we give our business to Greeks.

"I couldn't find him," I reply, "so I called someone else."

There is another misleading silence.

"Who?" my father says at last.

I get up. "How about some War?"

Grabbing the wheeled tray table, I place it between his chair and mine. I fetch the playing cards and sit back down. My father stares at me through hooded eyes. I can tell he's fixing to say something. I see him herding the words. The fingers of his left hand twitch the way they do when language resists him. As one of the therapists explained it, sometimes the words are there but beyond reach. He can make them out but can't quite get at them. He knows what he wants to say but can't grasp the requisite terms, as if meaning had been knocked from its vessel and was flailing in the waves.

Giving up, he says simply, "You're lying." It's the best he can manage.

I shuffle the cards. "You want to cut?" I set the deck on the table.

He continues to stare at me, his eyes vacant and menacing at the same time. My father never had much confidence in me, but since learning that I'd made Perry a partner, he's become more distrustful than ever. I explained my reasons and that Perry only has a small share, but it made no difference. He was livid. He said I had duped him, I lied to him. He called me a traitor and a fool.

"You never called Nikos," he says.

I cut the deck myself and deal out the cards in two stacks. I turn over my top card to reveal the three of diamonds. This is no doubt the dullest card game ever invented, but it's one of the few my father can manage.

I wait for him to turn over his card but he stares down at his stack as if unable to understand what to do with it. I reach across and flip his top card. It's the nine of diamonds. I put the two cards face down on his side of the table and play my next card. Another three.

My father stares at the card a moment and then lifts his head. He's trawling for words again. I see it in his eyes.

"I heard...I heard you've taken the flag down...at the pool hall."

They got to him after all. At least we're past Nikos. But is this any better? I recall my mantras.

"That was six years ago. We've covered this. Turn over your card."

His eyes are still fixed on me.

"We already talked about this," I say as I reach across and turn over the six of clubs. I place the two cards on top of the previous two. I turn up my next card, the jack of hearts.

My father's fingers are twitching. "You didn't...I don't..."

"We settled this a long time ago. Just because you don't remember doesn't mean we didn't talk about it."

"Why?"

"Jesus! Why do you care? What difference does it make at this point?"

He glares at me.

"*I'm* running the place now," I say. "Just let me run it."

He snorts. "You can't even... If I didn't... If you...I can't..." Tangled up in his ganglia, he falls silent. I know what he wants to say anyway and don't need to hear it again.

"I've told you a thousand times," I say, "the pool hall is doing better than ever. Way better than when you ran it. We bring in more money in a month than you did in a year."

"Pumpkins."

"It's true."

"You're driving our customers away."

"Where did you get that? Maybe I'm driving *your* customers away. And thank god. You should be grateful. They're cheapskates. They sit around all day not even ordering a coffee. If we relied on them, we would have closed down years ago."

"I know what's going on."

"What are you referring to exactly?"

"You've turned it into a drug den. It's full of hoodlums and dope fiends."

"Who tells you this stuff?"

"I know what goes on."

"You don't know what fucking day it is," I shout, my voice carrying down the corridor. "You can't even wipe your own fucking ass. But you want to tell me how to run the store. The man who almost sank himself into bankruptcy twice! Why is it you believe everyone except me? Why do you trust your old demented friends more than your own son? I'm running the place now. You're here, I'm there, and that's the way it is. Why can't you just trust me to do my job? It's like you can't let yourself believe I've turned the place around, that I've made a success of it. It's like you *want* me to fail." I reach across the table and turn up the king of diamonds. I drop it, with the jack, on top of his other winnings. I show my next card, the nine of clubs.

My father is staring at me, bobbling his head. "Success," he says. "When have...when ever have...make success of anything?"

"Do you want to play or not?"

He raises a trembling hand. "Me," he says, jabbing his chest. "If not for me..."

"OK. Turn your card over."

We stare at each other grimly.

"Nothing," he says.

We keep staring.

"Are you going to turn your card?"

"You are nothing."

He's old, I remind myself. He's demented. Let it go. He doesn't know what he's saying. What does any of it matter now?

I'm about to reach for his card, but I'm suddenly on my feet. "Fuck you!" I hear myself shout in English. My father continues staring at me blankly. Did he even hear me? "Fuck you!" I repeat even more loudly as I head to the closet. Putting on my blazer, I feel the envelope in the breast pocket and I reach in for it. *I know things too*, I hear myself shouting. But I let go of the envelope and head out the door. I know some things too, motherfucker! I'm not as ignorant as you think! The woman behind the reception desk is staring at me. I realize I'm muttering to myself.

Leaving St. Paul's, I bike to the McLennan Library and spend the afternoon going through microfilmed issues of the *Gazette* and the *Star*. I sign out some books, and by the time I pedal back to the pool hall, it's after six. As I cross the terrace, I'm hailed by Maxime, who's sitting with an aspiring starlet. She's about nineteen and wearing a tight grey vest over an even tighter black V-neck T-shirt. Maxime is in his early forties and sports a few days' growth of stubble. He directs French-language movies and TV shows and he wants to know whether he can shoot some scenes in the Symposium. We agree to speak again after he's worked out his budget. Turning around, I come face-to-face with Stéphane, a kitchen hipster at a slow-food restaurant on Bernard. He wears a do-rag and has a column of Chinese script tattooed on the side of his neck. I've never bothered to ask him what it means. As we make small talk, I keep glancing over his shoulder at Jimmy, who's speaking on his cell. He's standing in a corner of the terrace, a tray tucked under one arm. He doesn't notice me. Detaching from Stéphane, I'm buttonholed immediately by a guy in a Castro cap. He shoves a flyer at me and asks if he can post it inside. I stare at a crudely designed black-and-white playbill for an upcoming Zulu Proust concert. I give him back the flyer and direct him to the corkboard.

Things are back to normal inside. Apart from Odysseus Maroutsis alone at a table scratching lottery tickets, the kobolóya are gone. Seated at the counter are Nino, Cuzzy, and the De Melo brothers. I pause at the doorway and eyeball Jimmy through the window. Seeing me, he turns away. I remain by the door. He flips his phone shut and, slipping it into a pocket of his Adidas tearaways, swaggers in. Jimmy is Perry's nephew and lives with Spiros's ex in Cartierville. A tall, lanky nineteen-year-old with a taste for oversized athletic gear and running shoes like parade floats, he dropped out of CEGEP a year ago and works at the Symposium full-time. He says he plans to go back to school after he's made some money and gained "life experience," but I don't believe it. Jimmy is never going back to school. Which is fine with me. He's not a bad employee. He's energetic, will work long hours, and will come in with little notice. Most important, he's family, and in a business like this, nothing beats family. Whatever his faults, Jimmy can at least be trusted not to rob us. He can be lax and ill-mannered, but as my father used to say, better the known faults than the unknown merits.

"What have I told you about the fucking phone?"

"I promise you, it was *crucial*."

"All your phone calls are crucial. You're a very important man."

"Come on, bro, what about you and Perry? You're on your cells all the time."

"That's ridiculous."

"Shah, I seen you."

"That's bullshit. Anyway, we own the place. You just work here, remember?"

"Oh!" he finger-snaps. "Cold, bro."

"You do like we tell you. No fucking phone on the job. And especially not in front of customers."

"That bites," he says as I head to the counter.

"That's life."

"That *giga*bites!"

I can't stand Jimmy's lingo. A pastiche of skater, hip hop, Greeklish, and god knows what else, it strikes me as ersatz. Even Jimmy and his friends use it with a kind of winking self-consciousness, as if they're playacting, as if they themselves can't take themselves seriously. Their speech sounds to me manufactured, synthetic. But was it any different in our own day? As kids what did we speak but TV American—the English of the Fonz, the Sweathogs, J.J. Dynomite? Yet something has changed. Our idiom was more rooted. Though we didn't know it, a good part of our speech was bequeathed to us by the Irish, Scots, and Jews who'd occupied these streets before us and whose voices we echoed with no more awareness than a canyon. Much of our language came from the street itself, which has its own memory. Those ghosts remain—I catch traces of them even among Jimmy and his friends—but they're fading. Even ghosts pass away.

As I swing around the counter, only Fernie notices me and he gives me one of his crooked smiles, a habit he's adopted to hide his bad teeth. The others are busy arguing about the upcoming NHL season. Fernie and I observe them silently. Fernie is one of the few people I know who has no interest in professional sports. He didn't care for them even when we were kids. He's here for the cards. Tonight is poker night, and I assume, given these guys are still here at the counter, they're expecting more arrivals. Nino has come straight from work and is in one of his suits, his tie hanging from a side pocket, his collar unbuttoned. Nino's an accountant at a bank, where he's known as Tony. The only people who still call him Nino are his family and us. Cuzzy (short for Cosimo) owns the bakery that supplies our breads and desserts. He started working there when he was fifteen, and ten years ago he purchased the place. Next to him is Jose (the J pronounced as in John, not Juan) and, as always, he's got on his Expos cap. Fernie jokes that he wears the cap to bed. Today he's also in his oversized Galarraga jersey and board shorts, which make him look like a hypertrophic schoolboy or helium mascot. Three years ago, when it was announced the Expos would be moving to Washington, he donned a black armband, which he wore every day for a year. Jose is a hundred and fifty pounds heavier than Fernie, but you can tell at a glance they're brothers. Fernie is as wiry and twitchy as ever, though today he's especially wan and desiccated, which is worrisome. There's speculation he hasn't entirely given up some of his old habits, though I can't imagine how, on his wages and with the alimony and child support, he can possibly afford them, unless he's fallen back on some of his old ways of making money. Both De Melo brothers still work at the envelope factory where their father got them jobs as teenagers, and they also still live with their parents in Chomedey. For a couple of years Fernie lived on his own, but after returning from prison, he went back to his parents' place. That's usually where these poker nights are held, but a few months ago Perry was talked into hosting the occasional one here. Some of us still live in the city and this would even out the travel burden a little. I was opposed. Given the lengths Perry and I went to reassure the local constabulary that we were on the up-and-up and they need not worry about any louche activities resuming at the pool hall, it didn't seem wise. But Perry has made more than his share of compromises over the years, and I decided not to fight him on this one. Still, I made it clear that at the slightest hint of gossip or police snooping, the poker nights would cease immediately.

At the counter stats fly back and forth like mortar fire. The statistical arcana these guys hold in their heads is staggering—the dates, names, plays, scores, averages. I'm reminded of a remark by Noam Chomsky that, if the depth of knowledge and analytical acumen the average American brought to sports were applied to politics, the world's ills would have been solved ages ago. If I listen in now, it's largely from a sense of occupational duty. Working at the Symposium, I've learned there are many people out there for whom a lack of knowledge about sports is a form of stupidity. To reveal you don't know who the NHL scoring leader is or who won the Super Bowl is to invite suspicion and disdain, which I can't afford in my line of work. Conversations like this one keep me current, furnishing just enough information that I can maintain face when the need arises.

After tempers at the counter subside, I ask Perry who else is coming.

"Just Carlos. As far as I know." He glances around at the others for confirmation.

Jose looks at his watch. "Shouldn't we get started?"

Perry looks up at the wall clock. "Let's give him another few minutes. He's just over on Waverly, I think."

"Doing what?" Cuzzy asks.

"He's looking at another property. He said he was going straight after work and might be a bit late."

"He's still looking in this area?" Cuzzy says. "Is he looking for something to flip?"

"No, he wants something long term. With an income."

Cuzzy is shaking his head.

"What," Perry says irritably.

"I wouldn't be looking in Mile End anymore."

"Mile End's hotter than ever," says Jose. "The guy next to my uncle on Clark just sold his triplex for four hundred something. The place is a fucken dump. And it's on *Clark*."

"That's my point," Cuzzy says. "This turkey's cooked. You know where I'd be looking if I were Carlos?"

We watch Cuzzy. He's gained a certain authority on this subject.

"Two places," he says, raising a thumb. "Villeray..." Next comes his index finger. "St. Henri."

"St. Henri?" Jose says skeptically.

"I guarantee you what's happened here is going to happen there. It's even going to happen in Point St. Charles and Little Burgundy, though there it might take a little longer."

"I don't see that happening," says Nino. "I don't."

"Why? Look at Harlem."

"Montreal's not Manhattan," says Jose.

"Exactly. Harlem was worse. I'm telling you, it's happening everywhere."

If sports has always been the main topic of conversation with these guys, lately real estate has been coming in a close second. It appears to be a hot topic with everyone. The rising prices in our neighbourhood have made us giddy and ravenous. And this being 2007, everyone is convinced the process is unstoppable. If you want to get rich, the thinking goes, buy up all the property you can as fast as you can. A man without real estate is nobody. Among us, no one has pursued this logic as aggressively, or successfully, as Cuzzy. He's on his fourth property, the latest a duplex on Rivard he and his brother Joe bought a few months ago and are now in the process of renovating.

"I guarantee in a few years," Cuzzy says, "St. Henri is going to be hotter even than here. Think about it..." The digits start going up again one by one as he itemizes the area's virtues. He has to bring in his other hand. He muses a moment. "You got everything, basically. And you got these beautiful old houses, perfect for restoration. There aren't many houses like that left in the city, at that price."

Jose looks at his watch again. "I think we should get started."

"Let's give him another couple of minutes," Perry says.

"Hey," Nino says to me, "I hear the paisanos are rebelling."

I groan.

"How come you won't put that flag up?" he asks.

"I'm not going to talk about that."

"Why, what's the big deal?"

"He's more pig-headed than *they* are," Perry says.

"Really?" I say to him. "Is that what you think?" He grimaces, gazes down at the floor. "You think I'm being pig-headed?"

"These guys are your oldest customers, man. They've been coming here how long? They're your father's friends."

"So you think we should cave."

"How's it caving? I mean, you're Macedonian yourself."

"I'm not Macedonian."

"Your father is. You're fucking Greek, man. We both are. You don't care these pricks are stealing our name? And now the Canadian government is going along with it, the fucking pussies."

"I can't believe all this is over a name," Jose says.

"It's not just a name, bro!" booms a voice. Elbowing past me, Jimmy heads over toward Jose. "It's Greek property, bro. We're talking about identity theft. What if tomorrow Spain started calling itself Portugal?"

Jose nods pensively, apparently conceding the logic of this.

"That's not quite analogous," I can't help interjecting.

"Why not?" Jimmy says, wheeling around. "Portugal is Portuguese and Greece is Greek. These fuckers are trying to steal our name and history so they can steal our land. But Macedonia is Greece, bro, and Greece is Macedonia."

"I've read the bumper stickers, Jimmy. Try reading a little history."

"I know the history, bro. What are you gonna tell me, Alexander the Great was a *wooronomítis*?"

"All right," Perry says, stepping in between us as if we might come to blows. "Don't you have work to do? The terrace is full."

Jimmy keeps staring at me past Perry's shoulder.

"Enough!" Perry says. "Go!"

Jimmy gives me a hard backward glance as he heads toward the terrace.

"What's a wormidis?" Jose asks.

"Don't worry about it," Perry says.

"That's Jimmy's quaint name for Bulgarians," I explain.

"What does it mean?"

"Pig nose."

Jose frowns. "Why—"

"All right," Perry says, "let's go. Game time."

Everyone gets up eagerly.

"Tell Carlos we're in the *thomatiáki*," Perry says to me. Greek for "the little room," the thomatiáki is what everyone, non-Greeks included, calls the smaller of the two stock rooms at the back of the pool hall. "You joining us?"

"Just let me do a couple of things and I'll be right there."

"You and Jimmy gonna be okay?"

"Give me a break."

As he heads to the back with the others, I take off my blazer and wash my hands. I check the condiment jars and coolers and wipe down some tables. As I load the dishwasher, my cell vibrates.

It's Perry. "We're going to order pizza. You want some?"

"You want me to make some burgers or something?"

"They want pizza. I'm going to call Omonia."

"You need drinks?"

"We got everything. Just let me know when the pizza comes."

Jimmy returns and I help him prepare sandwiches. Neither of us speaks. While he delivers the orders, I replenish the coolers. Carrying a crate of soft drinks, I notice a couple of guys at one of the pool tables and recognize Brian Manley. Luckily, he's lining up a shot and doesn't see me. As I crouch by the cooler with my back to the tables, I try to determine how I might make a quick escape. I don't know when Brian came in and wonder whether he's already spotted me. But wouldn't he have come over to say hello? Maybe he's embarrassed on my behalf and wants to spare both of us.

As I straighten up, I see him heading toward me with his friend. "Hey!" Brian calls out. I stare at him blankly, as though I don't recognize him.

"Brian," he says. "Brian Manley. From Toronto."

"Brian, right," I say. I reach across the counter and we shake hands.

"This is Eric," he says and I shake his friend's hand. "I know Alex from Toronto," Brian explains. To me, he says, "I was over at Eric's place   he lives around the corner—and we thought we'd shoot a few games."

I don't recognize Eric and suspect he's never been here. Even though Brian doesn't live in Montreal, it wouldn't surprise me if it was his idea to come. The Symposium is the sort of place he would know about.

"So..." he says, glancing about. "You work here?"

"I own the place."

His eyebrows lift.

"It used to be my father's."

"Right," he says, looking around some more. "Your father owned a pool hall." He nods to himself, though it's impossible to know what he's thinking. "Hey, you still in touch with Laura?"

"No. You?"

"I never really—I only knew Laura through Nicola, right? And I'm not in touch with her either. You know how it is. Over the years, you just... Oh, I bumped into Lucas a few months ago. At a film festival in Amsterdam. He was screening one of his docs. You know he makes documentaries?"

"Really?"

"Yeah, he's won awards. You should google him. Are you in touch with Martin or Liz or anyone from that crowd?"

"No. What about you?"

"No, no... You know I'm living in New York now."

As it happens, I do know this. What's interesting, though, is that Brian assumes I would know it. I resume my dumb show.

"I've read some of your articles in *Esquire*," I tell him, "but I didn't know you were living in New York."

"It's just easier. Plus..." He reaches into his postman's bag and hands me a business card. "I got a really cushy gig."

The card has a university logo on it. *Brian Manley, Lecturer, Media Communication Arts*. "Nice," is all I can think to say.

"I've got a new book out. I'm doing a reading tomorrow at Concordia. That's why I'm here, in Montreal. It'd be great to see you."

"A book," I say, sounding duly impressed.

Brian gives me a précis. The book is about what he calls "Web Two-Oh" and how it's affecting culture and politics around the world. In a few weeks he'll be starting a promotional tour through Europe and Australia. To everyone's surprise (he inserts with the requisite modesty), the book has turned out to be something of a bestseller.

I already know most of this. I own the book, though I haven't read it. But I've read the reviews and heard the interviews. I've also read Brian's previous book. That one looked at topical cultural and political issues in light of the work of philosophers like Aristotle, Machiavelli, Hobbes,

Nietzsche, and a few others. The publisher regarded it as a niche item and promoted it as such, but, for unaccountable reasons, the book created a stir and, creeping its way onto the bestseller lists, made of Brian a member of the commentariat.

"You should come," he says, pulling out a pen. On the back of the card he writes the time and location of the reading. "I'm going to talk about some of the research I had to do. There's some good stories." He explains that he visited places like India, China, the Middle East, and Africa.

I only catch a part of what he's saying, as I keep glancing past him at Carlos Medeiros, who's standing at the doorway, chatting with Jimmy. As Brian returns his card to me, Carlos steps inside and heads straight toward us. I put my whiteface on again, making as if I'm in the midst of important business, and signal to Carlos that the others are in the back. But he ignores me and steps up beside Brian. "They're waiting for you," I say, then add for good measure, "I'll see you there in a minute." Carlos glances at the two strangers and, with a silent nod to me, makes his way to the back. Somewhere I hear a cock crow. I doubt Carlos is offended. I doubt he even caught what happened. But I'll have to sound him out later and provide some explanation, just to be on the safe side.

"Sorry, what were you saying?" I ask Brian.

"I was just saying maybe we could have a drink. If you have the time."

"Yeah," I reply, staring at the card. "No, that would be great. I'll have to change my schedule, but...I'll see if I can get someone to replace me."

"That'd be great," Brian says.

"Yeah," I say as we stand there nodding a few seconds.

"Well, hopefully see you tomorrow."

"Yeah," I say. "Nice to meet you," I say to Eric.

As the two head out the door, I glance again at Brian's card. I have no intention of going to the reading, or of ever getting in touch with Brian, yet I put the card in my back pocket. I look around, trying to figure out what to do next, but already I'm spiralling.

For several minutes I putter around pointlessly. I can't believe Lucas is making documentaries. About what? Comics and video games? *He's won awards*. I'm sure I'll end up googling him.

While I'm helping Jimmy with an order, the pizza arrives and I carry the boxes to the back room. Through the closed door, I can hear the voices on the other side. They're arguing about hockey again: Who's the better goalie, Luongo or Brodeur? Suddenly I feel tired and want to lie down.

I return to the counter and call Jimmy over. "Could you take these to the back?"

"Sure," he says as I hand him the boxes.

I scan the hall. The few customers have moved indoors. It's chilly out now. "Can you manage on your own from here?" I ask Jimmy.

"Of course."

"Sorry about ragging on you earlier."

"Pff. I can handle you, bro. Don't worry."

Outside, I pause and breathe in the cool air. The street lamps are on and the terrace is empty. A squat *yayá* in black waddles by balancing a pair of shopping bags in either hand like a water carrier. A few paces behind her, two young women walk side by side staring at their phones. Toward the north, where the sun sets in Montreal, the sky is an opalescent wash of pearl and violet. It's the violet hour. There's a foretaste of winter in the air. Across the street, the shoe store has gone dark, its owner at his Shabbos prayers. The neon trim in the window burns a bright popsicle red. Next door, in the cosmetics shop, the young clerk is arranging items on a shelf. I can smell the place all the way from here. I'm told it's the organic soap. I resent that it's become a feature of the street.

Upstairs, I go straight to my bedroom and spread out on the bedcovers. As I stare at the ceiling, my cell lights up the room. Looking at the caller ID, I hesitate to answer.

"Where are you?" Perry says. "I thought you were going to join us."

I tell him I'm not feeling well and came upstairs.

"What's wrong?"

"Nothing. I'm just tired."

"You coming later?"

"I don't think so."

"You want me to bring you some pizza?"

"Oh no, thanks. I got food here."

There's a brief silence.

"Come just for a while," Perry says. "After you've eaten."

"We'll see."

"All right. You know where we are."

I manage to get up and change into my night sweats. I heat up some leftover pasta. After I've eaten, I sit at my desk. I'm exhausted, but I have to get back on track. I've grown lazy lately. Turning on the lamp, I see my reflection in the window. I sit amid a farrago of books, notebooks, papers, magazine and newspaper clippings. A white cardboard shoebox by the computer monitor spills over with letters and photographs. More photos and papers are strewn on the sofa and floor. I see the physical disorder as a reflection of my life in general. If I tidy up the apartment, will my life improve as well? It would be a start, anyway. I try not to think about what a waste my life has been. This summer I turned forty-five, and what do I have to show for it? I've done nothing, seen nothing, been nowhere. Last year I told Perry that in the summer, come hell or high water, I would take some time off and go to Greece. My plan was to spend a few days in Athens and then head north to my father's village. In April I bought a plane ticket. I bought books, maps, a backpack. I bought a pair of hiking shoes. Then, a week before I was set to fly out, my father had a stroke, his second. Of course I had cancellation insurance. Such has been my entire life, an endless succession of false starts and failures, of numbing triviality, cravenness, and inanition. The same mistakes over and over, the same offenses, cruelties, stupidities, lies, evasions. In the words of Freud and Devo: We must repeat. Why *is* that? Why *must* we? Marx said that historical events occur twice. But if the first time it's tragedy and the second, farce, what is it the third, the fourth, the tenth time? Eight years ago I fled to Toronto in the hope that I might end the cycle, that I might escape my own existence. But having ruined my life here, in this small corner, I had ruined it everywhere on earth. So, returning to my corner, I decided I must learn to live within my limitations. I gave up my higher ambitions. I was what I was and what I was was a bush-league businessman, an *entrepreneur* as we like to say these days. It wasn't how I'd imagined my life turning out, but that's how it was, and all I could do was try to make the best of it. And I did very well indeed, as it turned out. Who would have thought? The first success of my life.

Yet what difference has it made? I feel as much a failure and fraud as ever. I'm still waiting for my life to start. But at forty-five there's no starting over. Nor do I have any illusions left about myself. I know I'm no Prince Hamlet, am an attendant lord etcetera. And I can certainly start a scene or two. So I decided to take stock, see if I can get it all down in words. Why? Who knows? But what else is there for the likes of me? I read somewhere that failure in art can only be compensated by a life in action, and I'm hoping the reverse might also be true. What's likelier is that, having made a mess of the one, I'll do the same with the other. I don't even know what it is I'm trying to do, what I'm working on. I envision a history of some sort, or perhaps a memoir, if not a confession. I have this notion that by giving a frank account of all the waste and folly, I might, by some verbal alchemy, transform a portion of this base metal into something of value, I might shore the fragments against my ruin. If the unexamined life is not worth living, does it follow that self-examination will make it so? That's the wager.

This too may prove another fool's errand, another Sisyphian push up the hill. Shall I awake in a few months, a few years, broken, deceived again, in the midst of new ruins? Is this just more dross for the waste pile? Only the passing days, and words, will tell.

2

I GOT WORD ABOUT MY FATHER'S HEART ATTACK from Dzonakis. I knew there was trouble the moment I heard Greek on the phone.

"Are you aware your father is in the hospital?"

He sounded accusatory. I hadn't spoken with my father for almost two years, since Easter of 1999 when I'd told him I was leaving Montreal. But Dzonakis didn't know this. No one at the pool hall knew. When anyone asked about me, my father would boast of my progress and accomplishments, make stuff up. I found all this out later. Visiting my father in the hospital, Dzonakis noted my absence and pressed him for an explanation. He insisted I should be notified immediately, but my father refused. So Dzonakis tracked down my uncle and was shocked a second time to learn that my uncle too was not speaking with me. He was happy, however, to give Dzonakis my number.

"He's too proud to admit it but your father needs you," Dzonakis said on the phone. "He has no one. You can't rely on friends at a time like this. You're his only family, Aleko. You have to come back. I don't know why you two aren't talking and it's none of my business, but it doesn't matter anymore."

I was worried about how Laura would react, and I put off telling her about the call. Things were tense between us, and I wasn't in the mood for another fight. I gave her the news while she was getting ready for work the next morning. I was on the edge of the bed, and she shot me a look in the full-length mirror.

"Why are you telling me now?" she said, trying on a blouse.

"I thought I wouldn't say anything until I'd figured out what to do."

"And what is that?"

"I don't know. Except obviously I have to go to Montreal."

"Obviously?"

"I know, I know. But it sounds serious."

"You find out yesterday..." She walked over to the bureau and rummaged through her jewelry boxes. Turning to me, she tilted her head to insert an earring. "You find out yesterday your father had a heart attack, but you don't say anything until today. I find that a little strange." Already she was fuming. But this was my father we were talking about, so what could she say? *You can't go*? Actually, she could say that. That was what worried me. "Here's the part I'm trying to understand." She returned to the closet. "Why didn't you tell me yesterday? You got the call in the morning, right?"

"Despite everything I've told you, I was shaken. He is my father. I guess I needed time to digest it. And I decided not to say anything until I was clearer in my own mind about what I was going to do."

"Which is?"

"I don't know. All I know is I need to go to Montreal."

Laura stared at me while strapping on her watch. "For how long?"

"I don't know. I don't know what shape he's in. I'm thinking, hopefully, maybe three, four days."

She snickered derisively, slipping on a navy-blue jacket. She examined herself in the mirror. Seeing her in these getups, I always flashed back to our first meeting. More astonishing than her transformation was the speed with which it had transpired. Lately she had even started wearing makeup and getting her legs and armpits waxed.

Still barefoot, she exited the bedroom and padded down the corridor to the bathroom. When she returned, her hair was gathered up in a tight bun. The look was a little severe and didn't suit her face, but it was businesslike and gave her an air of braininess and authority.

"I don't know what to tell you," she said, walking over to the mirror. "I guess you gotta do what you gotta do." She gave me a stern look in the glass. "And for once it'd be nice if you stuck to your word. Three or four days, you said."

I thought it best not to reply.

After one last check in the mirror, she was out the door, no kiss, no goodbye. All in all, it had gone better than I'd expected.

In Montreal I stayed with Perry and his brother Spiros. A few months earlier they'd taken over the middle apartment of their parents' triplex. Spiros had moved back home and settled into his old room two years earlier, after Angie finally dumped him. She kept the house in Cartierville, where she remained with their two kids. But with Spiros having custody part of each month, his parents' place proved too small, so he and Perry had claimed the second floor. They would have preferred the third floor, but as their mother still did their laundry and housekeeping and was now in her seventies, they decided to spare her the extra climb.

I stuck to my promise and remained four days. I called Laura every evening and filled her in on what was going on, though some details I left out. The situation had grown more complicated, and on the train back, I practiced what I would tell Laura. She'd said she would prepare dinner for us, which I regarded as a tactical manoeuvre, and she was in the kitchen when I got home. The counter was crowded with dirty bowls and dishes, empty cans, spice jars, and vegetable scraps. By the cutting board lay a Chekhovian carving knife. As we kissed I knew that, behind our pretense of unconcern, we were both braced for battle. By now we could read each other pretty well. We talked about Montreal and I elaborated on what I had already explained on the phone. Only later, while we were eating, did I mention my plan to return there.

Laura chewed silently and stared at me.

"I imagine it doesn't come as a complete surprise," I said. "Given the situation."

Straightening her spine, she performed a series of neck and shoulder stretches. "A bit of a surprise."

"Really?"

With forced composure, she said, "Why do you have to go back?"

I ran through my explanation, though it didn't come out quite as I'd rehearsed it. I'd anticipated the questions she followed up with, and if my answers were vague or equivocal, it was partly because I was still feeling things out. I was not lying when I told her I wasn't sure what my plans were in the long term. Still, I expected to hear that this was a deliberate, if unconscious, stratagem. I'd be told that, by keeping myself in the dark about my motives, I could convince myself that I was not being duplicitous. I would hear yet again about how we often deceive ourselves so that we can better deceive others. But Laura mentioned none of this. She only asked how long I planned to stay.

"I don't know." I had given up any pretense of eating and was pushing my food around with my fork. "I can't say for sure."

"What's the longest you're likely to be there? Worst-case scenario?"

"I don't know. It all—"

"A week? Two weeks? A month? A year?"

"Obviously not a year."

"Obviously?"

I stared at the remnants of ratatouille on my plate.

"So less than a year," she said. "Six months?"

"No, I don't expect it'll be six months."

"So not six months. Can we say less than six months?" Laura was done with eating too. She glared at me, arms folded.

"Yes, I would say it should be less than six months."

"Let me ask you this. What if—just for the sake of argument—what if the doctors are wrong? Just for the sake of argument. What if, for whatever reason, your father can't go back to work? Or let's say he has another heart attack. He's getting old. And, from what you say, he doesn't have a healthy lifestyle."

"What is it you're asking of me?"

She smacked the table. "The truth!"

"Jesus," I said, glancing over at the patio door, where the curtain hung open. In the gathering dusk, I could see lighted windows on the other side of the alley.

"That's all I'm asking for."

"OK, but calm down."

"Where are you in all this, Alex? That's what I want to know. Where are your commitments? Can you answer me that? Do you *know* the answer to that?" She regarded me silently. "Here's what I find interesting. Given your history with your father, and all you've told me about him, I find it interesting how it's only now, after we've started making plans for the wedding, that you suddenly have this urgent need to go back to Montreal. It's an odd coincidence, don't you think?"

"What are you suggesting? That I've made all this up?"

"No, I believe your father had a heart attack. Of course I believe he's in the hospital. But what I don't believe..." A kind of giggle escaped her. "What I don't believe are any of your bogus explanations about why you need to be with him. Or that you *feel* you need to be with him. I don't buy that for a second."

"My father just had a heart attack," I said, struggling for composure.

"So what? He's old! What did you think was going to happen? Did you not know this moment would come?"

"The man is alone, he's broke—"

"Until today you've been telling me he could rot in hell for all you cared. And this is Canada. We have resources. We have doctors and nurses and social workers. And what about all his friends? He's Mister Popular, isn't he? Your father doesn't need you, Alex, and you know it."

"My father is in a very weak state right now. He's in the hospital. He has no money and he's—"

"I don't care about any of this!"

"He's entirely dependent on the pool hall, which—"

"I don't care!" she said, putting her hands over her ears.

"—if it remains closed—"

"I DON'T CARE I DON'T CARE I DON'T CARE."

I fell silent and waited until she stopped and lowered her hands.

"Look," I said, "it's your prerogative not to care, but unfortunately—"

"Alex," she said, slapping the table hard enough to rattle the dishes, "it's like this: I'm not going through this shit again. When you came crawling back to me last year, you made a commitment. Remember? *You* did. Not me. It wasn't my idea, remember? It was you who begged me to take you back. You're the one who forced that decision on me. Remember? I wasn't the one who proposed."

I would have disputed this characterization of events, but it was not the time. "Laura, I beg you," I said. "Please try to see the situation from my point of view. I have to do this. For my sanity and peace of mind."

"*Now* we're getting closer. So this isn't about your father. It's about you."

"The two are not divisible."

"Yes, they are!" she screamed. "Oh my god, are we going to start all that again? I will not go through that same old shit again, Alex!"

"It's not the same old shit."

"It is! It's exactly the same. How fucking stupid are you? This is the same old fucking story. New act, same play. Of which, by the way, you... *you* are the sole author. Do you even recognize that? Alex, you can't change the past."

"What are you talking about?"

"If this was really about helping your father, I'd be a hundred percent behind you. But that's not what this is. Can you admit that much? But, no, of course you can't. Because you don't have the fucking balls. Because you're a child. Not even a child. You're a fucking infant. You complain your mother infantilized you, but the reality is you don't know anything else. You don't *want* anything else. You *like* sucking on that big fat milky titty. It's where you're most comfortable, isn't it?"

"I thought we were talking about my father."

"Don't you see, you idiot? With all your talk about Socrates and Sophocles you are the most *un*reflective, self-ignorant person I've ever known. You talk about the unexamined life but you have no interest whatsoever in self-examination. Because you have no interest in *changing*. You're in a state of suspended animation. You say you want an adult life, you want a wife and family, but you don't really. Because you're terrified of all those things. You're terrified of adulthood. And I'm not interested in being married to a child. I want a father for my children, not a child for my husband. If you really want to be an adult, Alex, then you need to understand that your duties now are here, to *me*. Not to daddy. You're almost forty. Your duty now is to finish your degree and get a job and raise a family. But you're terrified, of marriage and adulthood and everything that goes with it. And I'm sick of it. I will not be your fucking yo-yo. There's no more in-between. I'm not going to be part of some eternal compromise formation. Which is what all your relationships have been. Do you even realize that? Do you realize your entire life has been nothing but an orgy of ambitendencies? Yeah, I know, you hate that kind of talk. You know why? Because you know it's true, and you're too fucking chickenshit to face it.

You're too chickenshit to do the work the truth demands. But I've done that work. I've spent my life doing it, and it's not easy. It's damn hard. It takes courage and stamina and determination. All of which you lack. But to repress, Alex, is to repeat. I've said it a million times. To repress is to repeat. To repress is to repeat. Do you really believe if you go back to Montreal you will change anything? That this time it will turn out differently? Alex, I promise you, I *promise* you, that if you go back—I don't care what you think your reasons are—you will end up playing out the same old fucked up bullshit you've been playing out your whole life. You won't be fixing the past. You'll be running away from the present. Which is what you've always done. It's what you're best at."

She fell silent and glowered at me. Calmly as I could, I said, "Laura, if we can focus on the facts for a moment. My father had a heart attack. It's true he and I have been on the outs for a while, but he is still my father. And I'm the only family he has. And at the moment, he's in the hospital and his business sits closed because—" With a single swift motion, Laura swiped a hand over her dinner plate and flung a fistful of cold ratatouille at my face.

I took a breath and, cautiously opening my eyes, reached for the paper napkins. Again I glanced at the patio door.

"No more lies, Alex," Laura growled as I wiped my face. She leaned in toward me. "No. More. Lies!"

The stains on my shirt would not come off and I grabbed more napkins and dipped them in my water glass.

Laura leapt up. "You want to go to Montreal? Go. But don't expect to come back." She stomped from the kitchen, and I hurried to the patio door and shut the curtain. Down the corridor she started pulling my things off the coat rack and flinging them to the floor. I crossed the kitchen and entered the hallway.

"Alex doesn't live here anymore," she said.

I kept some distance between us. "Could we talk about this calmly?"

She kicked at a pair of my shoes. "You leave now, Alex, you don't come back. That's all there is to it."

"Laura, please. All   "

"This is *my* house," she yelled. "You're just a tenant! You understand?"

"Yes. I understand, but—"

"No, I don't think you do. I don't think you do understand. I want you out. I want you out of here now! Right now!"

I reached a hand toward her.

"Don't touch me!"

Slithering past me, she raced up the stairs to my study. The next instant, she was on the landing with my suitcase. I pasted myself to the wall as the suitcase thundered down. I considered running up after her. Seconds later, more items from my closet came sailing and tumbling down the stairs. I went to the basement. Quickly gathering all my luggage, I returned to the ground floor. The stairs and corridor were strewn with clothes and other articles from my closet. I stood by the staircase, watching more items fly— shoes, blankets, books, video cassettes, my clock radio, an electric heater I'd never seen before. I retreated to the kitchen, where I could hear Laura pounding about overhead. I parted the curtain at the patio door and peeked out. It was almost night, the sky turning a dark metallic blue. I glanced at the small patch of garden in the backyard. In the spring Laura had planted it with herbs and vegetables. I remembered the previous summer. I remembered hawthorn and hydrangeas and trout lilies. I tried to remember what they looked like. I thought of oaks and elms and gingko biloba, also known as maidenhairs. I thought of purple hydrangeas and blue guitars. I thought of Richard Feynman. I heard footsteps.

I pulled the curtain shut and turned around. Laura stood at the doorway, staring wild-eyed. "So tell me," she said, stepping forward. "Has it all unfolded according to plan?" She came around the kitchen table. "Is this how you imagined it?" She stopped by the counter, her eyes the windows of a house on fire. "Has it all gone according to script?"

"I honestly don't know what you're talking about."

"Honestly? What do you know about honesty?" She let out a snort. "What a coward you are," she said, taking another step forward. "You don't even have the guts to walk out on me like a man. Do you think I'm one of your Silvanas or Soulas?"

"I think we both need to calm down."

"Listen to me, Alex," she said, coming closer. "You're not going to Montreal."

"I'm not?" I said, back pressed up against the curtain.

"No. You're staying right here. As you promised."

"But I thought you said—"

"You go back to Montreal now," she said, "I don't care what's going on with your father...it's on you."

We stood staring at each other in silence like a pair of prizefighters.

"What's on me? What are you trying to tell me?"

Without answering, she turned to leave. But I grabbed her wrist.

"*What's* on me, Laura?"

She bent and twisted, trying to pull free.

"Are you going to kill yourself? Is that what you're telling me?"

"Let me go!"

"Are you going to kill yourself again?"

"Let me go!" she yelled, kicking at me. I bent at the blows but held on to her. She elbowed the side of my head. I grabbed her hair and pushed her up against the table. She spat in my face. I put my hand over her mouth but she jerked back and, opening wide, bit down on it. I let out a cry and she pulled free and headed toward the door. I wheeled my arm round and struck her open-palmed on the side of her head, watching in murderous ecstasy as she tumbled to the floor. *So this is how it happens.* How long had it been? Not even a year. Less than a year and here I was at it again. Gazing down at her, I wished to get hold of myself, but I was already gone. I was a rig hurtling downhill, brakeless, pulled by a force greater than gravity. I could see the wreckage at the other end, the smashed glass, the mangled metal and flesh, yet the sight only pushed me harder. Falling on top of Laura, I grabbed her neck and shoved her up against the cabinet, her face and my hands smeared with our blood.

"You want to die? Is that it?"

"Doot," she grunted as I squeezed her throat.

"You want to die?"

"Yes. Do it. Show...show the world...man you are."

I eyed the knife on the counter and the next thing I knew it was in my free hand, Laura following it with her eyes as it descended toward her neck. "At last," she gurgled as I pushed the tip experimentally, watched it dimple the soft underbelly of her jaw, "the real Alex Dooks..." I squeezed the handle tighter, poised to push, when, by some grace, some merciful subliminal intervention, light broke, and letting out an animal howl, I hurled the knife across the floor and charged out of the kitchen.

"Bastard!" Laura shouted behind me. "Motherfucker!"

I searched through the debris in the corridor.

"Coward!"

I could hear her footsteps as I put on my jacket. I raced out the door, slamming it shut behind me, but an instant later she was out on the porch.

"Come back here!" she yelled.

I wasn't running, but I moved quickly.

"Come back here, pig!"

I couldn't tell whether she was coming after me. I didn't look back.

"This is assault, you fucker!" I kept my head down and kept going. "I'm calling the police!" she cried, her voice growing fainter. "I'll have you arrested!" A porch light came on and I picked up speed. "You can't run from this one, motherfucker! You're done! You're going to prison." Now I was running. "Murderer!" she cried. "Murderer!" she called out again and again, the verdict echoing through the darkened street.

I hoped to avoid going to a hospital and stopped at a pharmacy and then a toilet in a pizza shop and managed to patch up my hand. I headed east, walking block after block aimlessly. I spent the night in an odoriferous flophouse eerily similar to the place I'd stayed in a year ago. It had the same dank smells. Or was it a trick of memory? I felt I was losing my mind. I went straight to bed, but even with the pills I took, my hand throbbed and I barely slept. In the morning, I cleaned and rebandaged it and went to a car rental agency. I rented a van. I parked by a payphone a couple of blocks away. Though Laura was scheduled to work, I wasn't going to take any chances. At the sound of her recorded greeting, I hung up and called a second time, then a third. Getting back in the van, I drove to the house.

I rang the bell several times before opening the door. The house was in order. My things were back in place and the kitchen was tidy. What did this mean? With Laura you could never know for sure, but I took it as a good sign. It also confirmed me in my decision.

As I was loading the van, the elderly Portuguese couple next door came out and sat on their porch. After our usual perfunctory greeting, they watched me silently as I went back and forth. It didn't take long. Some of the larger items, like my old futon and frame, my desk, and my bookcases, I had to leave behind. When I was done, I placed in the mailbox the sealed letter I had written at the hotel; then, settling behind the wheel, I waved to the Portuguese couple and drove off. What were they thinking? What had they heard the night before?

The whole drive to Montreal, I worried I was a wanted man. Had Laura really called the police? What would she have told them? I scouted for squad cars. Stopping for gas, I became nervous when I saw the cashier at the window looking at me and dialling the phone. I paid and drove off, making sure to stay within the speed limit.

By the time I reached Montreal, I had settled down somewhat, though I still tensed up at the sight of a police car. I found a parking space not far from the pool hall. As I climbed the stairs to my father's place, I could hear his phone ringing. Again, my first thought was that it was the police. It was still ringing when I got inside. I stared at it on the end table by the sofa. It kept going. This wasn't the police.

I unplugged the phone and toured the apartment. The air smelled of mildew and cigarettes, and I opened all the windows. I'd been inside my father's apartment no more than three or four times. It was plainly furnished, without the frills and bric-a-brac you found in most Greek homes. There was hardly anything on the walls. Above the living room couch hung a painting of a forest waterfall, and in the kitchen, taped to the side of the fridge, was a colour illustration of Pavlos Melas cut out of a magazine. On the bookshelf in the living room stood a couple of framed photographs, both of me. One showed me in high school graduation regalia, the other, as a *tsoliás*, age two.

Returning downstairs, I looked around the pool hall and then unloaded the van. I carried a few essential items upstairs; everything else I stored in the basement crawlspace. When I was done, I reconnected the phone. It resumed ringing. At least I knew she was still alive. Unplugging the phone again, I crawled into bed.

When I tested the phone in the morning, the silence came as a shock. I wasn't planning on answering it, so I left it unplugged. After a quick breakfast, I dropped off the van and went to the hospital. My father wasn't in his room. I was informed that he'd had a stroke and was in intensive care.

The intensive care unit consisted of a large curtained-off area with a row of eight or nine beds. My father lay amid a jungle of tubes and wires. His eyes were shut but his chest rose and fell beneath the covers. A tube was taped to his nose, and on a monitor by his bed coloured lines arranged themselves in shifting peaks and valleys. I went to the desk and introduced myself. Some minutes later, a youth in a lab coat informed me that my father was in serious but stable condition. He spoke of ischemic cascades, embolic infarcts, atrial fibrillation, and atherosclerotic plaque. I tried to commit what he said to memory so I might look it up later. He explained that, while it was still too early for a reliable prognosis, I should be prepared for "lasting damage to motor functions" and "acute mental deficits." In the meantime, I was to rest assured that "all measures were being taken to prevent future strokes or coronary episodes."

What I had gotten myself into? Sitting by my father's bed, I could hear Laura's cackle. *What if the doctors are wrong? What if there are complications?* I felt snookered, the butt of some prank. Already the anger was welling up, the old resentments and terrors. How quickly I found my stride. I had just arrived and already I wanted to run. But I was out of track. There was no going back to Toronto. I wasn't going to make that mistake a second time.

It was an exaggeration to say I had gone crawling back to Laura last year and that I had forced her into a decision, but there was no denying I was the one who'd proposed marriage. At the same time, though, she hadn't played fair. My mother had just died and Laura had preyed on my desolation and vulnerability. She could barely hide her glee confessing that she'd slept with some guy in Paris. She had to let me know how handsome and charming and smart he was, and how fabulous in bed. She didn't spare any detail. But at the time I was so addled and heartsick and desperate, I couldn't think straight. And I couldn't bear the thought of being alone. I had needed Laura more than ever and I asked her to forget the Frenchman and give us another chance. I told her I was a changed man, and at the time I meant it, I believed it. With my mother gone, Laura need not fear she would ever play a subordinate role again. She was the most important person in the world to me. I swore up and down I was fully committed to her, and as proof I proposed marriage.

And even as I was doing it, I knew I was making a huge mistake. I feared that in a few months I would come to see things differently again. All the old problems, doubts, and anxieties would be back. It didn't even take *that* long. It was like opening the door to expected guests. But I had made a vow. In fact, I had made two. I had also promised myself that I was done running. I would stick this one out. For better or for worse, in sickness and in health. And I remained committed to that promise even after I learned of my father's heart attack. Laura could tell herself what she liked, but until she had started issuing her ultimatums, I had every intention of returning to Toronto. There had been no ulterior "plan," there had been no "script," but when she started with the veiled threats, something snapped in me. Hinting that she would harm herself was crossing an uncrossable line, and she knew it.

I kept watch on my father's chest rising and falling and the indecipherable activity on the monitors. He might be dead in a few days, or even hours. One had to laugh. It would be the perfect finale, the crowning irony. And what would I do then? Would I stay in Montreal? What was there for me here? Perhaps I should return to Toronto, if only to finish my PhD. But how did that make any sense? That was as much a sham as everything else in my life. It had been a sham from the outset. I never had any intention of researching the history of Greek immigrants in Canada, which I had put on my application strictly for tactical reasons. Even then my plan was to declare a different research area once I was in the program.

I was done with the whole charade. I needed to stay grounded, not panic again. I was here to stay. There was nowhere further to go. I gazed at my father and thought how for years all I'd wanted was for him to be gone from my life, yet now the thought of his dying filled me with terror. There was too much unfinished emotional business. They may fuck us up, our moms and dads, yet we have no choice but to repay them with whatever love and forgiveness we can muster. Anything less and we fuck ourselves up worse. This was perhaps the lesson of the last few years. This was what Laura did not understand, the one insight that, with all her years of "work," she had yet to achieve. We don't choose our family and we might not even like them; yet we have no choice but to figure out how to live with them.

I returned to the desk and gave the administrator there my contact information. I walked downtown and stopped for lunch at a diner. As I waited for my order, I continued to brood. If my father survived, he was not likely to return to work any time soon, or ever. So where did that leave me? And what about the pool hall? I should speak with Tom. Searching for his card in my wallet, I saw the two cheques from my father. Why did I still have them? Were they even still cashable? After I'd eaten and paid my bill, I stopped in the vestibule to use the payphone.

Tom Petropoulos was not just my father's notary but an old friend of his, and after the heart attack, he'd paid a couple of visits to the hospital, the first to see how my father was doing, and the second to have my father and me sign the mandate documents he'd recommended.

Tom answered the phone and I gave him the latest about my father.

"Fuck their Christ," he said in Greek. "What happened?"

I told him what I knew.

"They should cut their throats, the wankers."

I explained that I needed to speak with him in person, and he said I could drop by that afternoon.

The offices of Mtres Athanasios Petropoulos & Stephan Assadourian were on the third floor of a drab highrise on de Maisonneuve. When I arrived, the waiting room was empty and the receptionist's desk unoccupied. Tom's door was open, and seeing me from his desk, he waved me in. He was speaking loudly on the phone, explaining in Greek how to obtain a *certificat de localisation*. Swivelling this way and that, he would occasionally glance my way and roll his eyes. Tom was an exotic to me. He had come to Canada as a child and spoke French and English fluently. Yet in many ways he was indistinguishable from my father's other friends. Short, square-set, with a wide fleshy face and a gruff hobnail manner, he would have fit right in at the Symposium. It was hard to believe he was university-educated, though the evidence was up on the walls. Also on the walls were photographs of Mtre Petropoulos L.L.B., D.D.N. in the company of assorted worthies, including the Metropolitan Archbishop Sotirios, Exarch of Canada. In the largest photo, Tom was shaking hands with former mayor Jean Doré. A row of smaller photos on the window sill showed members of the Petropoulos clan. Mrs. Petropoulos was a severe woman lacking the fleshiness I associated with Greek immigrant wives. This alone marked her in my eyes as a member of a different social order. You could tell Mrs. Petropoulos had never worked in a factory or cleaned homes.

When he hung up, Tom asked me again how my father was doing. As he transferred piles of folders and binders from his desk to the floor, I elaborated on what I'd told him on the phone.

"*Kathíkya*," he grunted. "So what are you going to do?"

"About what?"

"Somebody has to be held responsible."

"For what?"

"For what? Your father just had a stroke while in the hospital."

"What am I supposed to do? Who knows what happened? It's no one's fault."

"No one's fault? What's the matter with you? Your father has a stroke in the hospital and it's no one's fault?"

"He's sixty-seven. He smokes, he drinks."

"You're in the hospital so they can make you better, not kill you. *Malákehs*."

Was he trying to drum up business? But if he was, I'd need a lawyer, not a notary. Maybe he got a finder's fee. Or maybe he was indulging the Greek passion for blame. With Greeks, every wrong had a traceable source or cause, and every wrongdoer must be identified and held to account.

"What happened to you?" Tom said, pointing at my hand.

Glancing down at the bandage, I relived my battle with Laura two nights earlier. The same hand had held a knife to her throat. Had all that really happened? I had possessed the heart of a murderer. I felt a chill now to think how close I'd come. I flashed back as well to my mother, who had also been much on my mind the last two days. What was this demon that lurked inside me and that could overcome me so quickly and seize the controls? I had let myself believe he was an aberration and had been permanently exorcised. But what if he could not be purged?

"I cut myself," I said.

"It looks like half your hand's come off. Who bandaged it? The same malákehs who tried to kill your father?"

"It's not as bad as it looks."

"Close the door," he said in Greek and wheeled around. "Jacqueline's gone for the afternoon, but..." He slid open the window behind him and held out a pack of Rothmans. I shook my head.

"Not like your father, eh?" An ambiguous comment, its range of reference indeterminate. He opened a drawer and produced a porcelain ashtray. Lighting a cigarette, he swivelled to one side, crossed his legs, and stared at me. It was time for me to explain why I was there.

"So, the reason I wanted to see you—I hope you don't mind if I speak in English."

Tom shrugged.

"It's easier for me with stuff like this."

"Whatever you like."

"I was hoping you could clarify some of the things we talked about at the hospital."

Rounding his lips, he pumped out a pageant of smoke rings.

"As you recall," I continued, "the plan was for me to run the pool hall till my father got better, but with his condition now...well, I don't even know if he's going to come out of this alive."

Tom frowned through the lengthening and collapsing loops. "Is that what the malákehs said?"

"No, not exactly..."

The phone rang. Tom ignored it but I waited anyway. When it stopped, he motioned to me to continue.

"When I agreed to run the pool hall, it was supposed to be for three or four weeks, but now no one can say how my father is going to come out of this, or how long it's going to take, and as you know, I need to be back in Toronto by the end of August, so if he's incapacitated for an extended period...or permanently...I'm trying to figure out—"

"Why don't you sell the place?"

This brought me up short. The remark was so abrupt and matter-of-fact, I wondered if it was a trick. Was I being probed for some hidden agenda or ulterior motives? Was this a test of my loyalty and good faith?

"I've been telling your father to sell that shithole for years," Tom said. "Or shut it down. He'd make more money renting the space."

I remained silent, still trying to figure out what Tom's intentions were. The phone rang again. Tom glanced at the display and we both waited till it stopped.

"Look," he said, "the doctors are telling you they don't know whether your father's going to recover, or how long it's going to be. And you say you have to be back in Toronto. So what are your options? If your father can't run the place and—"

"No, I understand, but...can I actually sell it? I mean, even if I wanted to?"

"You can do whatever you want. You have power of attorney, plus the mandate of incapacity should that become necessary." He took in an extra-long haul of smoke and stubbed out his cigarette. "You can do whatever you want."

I still hadn't abandoned the notion that this was a test. Tom had been friends with my father for thirty years, but he didn't know me from Prometheus. We'd met a total of four or five times. What was he up to? He seemed oddly nonchalant about the whole matter. Did he have my father's interests at heart? I hesitated to ask my next question.

"Can I transfer the business over to my own name? Or somehow sell it to myself?"

He scowled. "Why would you want to do that?" he said, opening a desk drawer. He pulled out an aerosol can and started spraying. "My partner will kill me if he knows I've been smoking in here." He swivelled around and sprayed toward the window. "The business is yours anyway," he said, putting the can back in the drawer. "You're sole executor and heir in your father's will. So why would you sell the business to yourself?"

I was so blindsided by this, I was stunned into silence.

"You're still in school, right?" said Tom.

I nodded.

"Philosophy, philology...?"

"History."

"I thought it was philosophy or something like that."

I shook my head.

"How old are you?" he asked.

"Thirty-nine."

"And what are you doing, a Master's?"

"Doctorate."

He gazed at me with undisguised disdain. "And when are you going to be finished all this?"

"I don't know. A few years."

He raised his eyebrows incredulously. "All right, so obviously you can't run the poolroom. You can't run the poolroom while doing a Doctorate in history or whatever it is in Toronto. So we wait a few weeks. Maybe the doctors are wrong. They usually are. Maybe he'll recover. Unless they manage to kill him for good. In which case you've got the will. If he's not getting any better...well...I don't know. You'll have to make a decision. In the meantime, see what you can get for the place. If we need to petition the court for the mandate, you need to tell me as soon as possible, because that'll take time. But if you keep your mouth shut, you can act on the power of attorney until the homologation comes through."

I wasn't sure what all this meant, or what I was supposed to keep my mouth shut about. But I didn't ask. I was consumed by thoughts of the will. When would my father have had it made? It couldn't have been after I'd moved to Toronto. And if he'd made it before, might it not have been supplanted by a later one Tom didn't know about? But that seemed unlikely. My father wouldn't go to a notary other than Tom. I needed to see this will for myself. But I wasn't going to ask any questions about it yet. I didn't want to let on that I didn't know about it.

Back at the apartment I ransacked the place. I searched the closets, drawers, cupboards, knowing the whole time it was probably in the steel file cabinet in the living room. But that was locked and I hadn't been able to find the key. Then I remembered that Cuzzy's brother Joe was a locksmith and I called Cuzzy for his number. Joe said he'd be over in a couple of hours.

It had been twenty years since we'd seen each other, but I retained a vivid memory of him. Being six or seven years older, he didn't have much to do with us when we were growing up. I only ever saw him from a distance, usually getting in and out of his Z28. At sixteen he'd dropped out of school to work in construction, and he'd married five or six years after that. In those days he was lean and athletic and he sported a high back-swept bouffant and was always dressed up in tight polyester disco duds and roach killers. The guy who appeared at my door was paunchy, balding, and dressed in jeans and a black leather jacket much too tight for him. But had I passed him on the street, I would have recognized him. Even with the added weight and subtracted hair, he retained something of his old Latin swagger, though he spoke with a heavy goomba accent that either I'd forgotten or I hadn't found as jarring as a teenager. He claimed to remember me and forced upon us a prolonged and awkward prelude of reminiscences that never got very far given how little our pasts overlapped. When I finally got him to the file cabinet, he opened it easily, and he refused to take any money. I insisted, though in the end I had to forcibly shove some bills in his jacket pocket. I invited him to have a drink, but he declined, explaining that he had to pick up "the old lady."

As soon as he was gone, I started on the file cabinet. I worked my way down from the top. There were four drawers, and the first two contained legal and business documents. There were bills and invoices, order forms, government notices, tax statements, but no will. In the third I found a stack of bookkeeping ledgers filled with page after page of narrow serried columns of figures and computations. None of these drawers contained anything personal or sentimental. My father was not the sentimental type. Among his possessions were few of the mementos and keepsakes that accumulate over the course of most people's lives. Hence my surprise upon opening the last drawer.

Its contents were laid out as in a chest drawer and covered by old Greek newspapers. I removed a couple of these and scanned their pages. When I removed the rest, my insides twisted at the sight of a stack of porn magazines. I took a long breath and pulled them out one by one. To my relief, all were the garden-variety sort of smut you found at any dépanneur.

I continued my search. I found more newspapers, loose clippings, notebooks, some brochures and pamphlets. The notebooks were filled with my father's handwriting. The two largest contained English-language exercises and vocabulary lists. The others were filled with extended diary entries interspersed with observations, aphorisms, and quotations. The two smallest contained long crowded lists of figures, numerical tables, and cryptic equations, formulas, and calculations. Among these were also some short verbal entries, but they were written in a kind of shorthand or cipher I have yet to crack.

Finally, tucked away at the back of the drawer, was a cardboard shoebox. In it were two string-tied bundles of letters, most still in their original airmail envelopes, and piles of photos and postcards. Many of the photos were in black and white and taken in Greece. In some I recognized my father as a young man. I was tempted to go through them right then and there. Old photographs, even of strangers, mesmerize me. Their harrowing message is always the same: Life is fleeting and you too will soon be dead. But now was not the time. I needed that will

I searched the apartment again, and this time I unearthed a black pebbled plastic briefcase behind some old boots in a corner of the bedroom closet. In it were various deeds and legal documents, including my father's will. I unfolded it with trembling hands. And there I was on page two, named as sole beneficiary and universal legatee. I was also identified as executor. Even with the will in front of me, I remained incredulous. I still couldn't be sure there wasn't another updated one lurking somewhere.

I had to have another talk with Tom. I called and made an appointment for the following week. While retrieving Tom's card from my wallet, I'd found my father's cheques again, and after I hung up the phone, I ripped them up and tossed them in the kitchen bin. I went down to the pool hall and spent much of the day taking inventory and cleaning up.

Dzonakis had warned me about the state of the place, but it was worse than I'd expected. Since my departure two years ago, my father had been running the pool hall on his own and he'd let the place go. Even business hours had become erratic. The space would need a lot of work if I was going to hang on to it, which was beginning to look like my best career option. And for that, I would need money, which I didn't have.

Several times over the course of the day the phone rang and I didn't answer. Sometimes the calls came back to back. Toward evening, I went by the hospital. My father was conscious and deintubated, but he still couldn't speak and we spent the visit in silence. It was hard to gauge how lucid he was, though he seemed to recognize me. I stayed a couple of hours and then went to an internet café. I hadn't checked my email since leaving Toronto and found six messages from Laura. The first four vilified me in the usual terms. In one she even threatened to hunt me down in Montreal, though she didn't specify for what purpose. In some ways, the two that followed these were even more disturbing. The first had a conciliatory tone, with Laura admitting she'd been rash, even unreasonable, though she defended her behaviour on the grounds that she'd been ambushed and made reference to my criminally actionable conduct and my cowardly and sleazy letter. She ended with a request that I call her as soon as possible and assurances that I would receive a fair and civil hearing. The final message was even more genial. She dropped the threats and accusations and contended that we owed it to each other to resolve the situation like mature and reasonable adults.

I read all six emails repeatedly and began to compose a response. But after a few days I realized it was pointless. I knew what needed to be said to placate Laura—I'd said it countless times—but why continue the duplicity? Alternatively, a truly frank discussion between us at this point seemed futile, if it was even possible. It would only add fuel to the fire and worsen the pain all round. I needed to put this thing to bed as quickly and quietly as I could. I never sent a response, or even finished it (though I still have it archived). In trying to compose one, though, I found myself confronting unpleasant truths about myself. I was able to see commonalities between my relationship with Laura and all my other relationships with women. Most of us are convinced that we're meant to couple, that it's our purpose and destiny. We are programmed by both biology and society to believe this. But perhaps some of us belong alone. Not all of us are cut out for this difficult business of intimacy. In my case, it seemed to bring out the worst in me, to activate tendencies and capacities best left unrealized and unknown. It's a truism that we only complete ourselves in another, but perhaps some of us should remain unfinished.

I had my meeting with Tom, and he clarified some things for me. As soon as I left his office, I called Perry and invited him for dinner at one of his favourite restaurants. I had a proposal to make. Perry still worked for his uncle Stathis. He'd started as a busboy in the late seventies, when Stathis had a small restaurant on Prince Arthur. Now there were four and the original had doubled in size, and Perry was second-in-command of the whole operation, shuttling among the locations as needed. But he was bored and tired and he thought he wasn't making the kind of money he could be. For years he had talked about going into business for himself and had even begun making noises about the two of us starting something together. So I'd decided to call him on it. But it wasn't going to be easy. I would have to offer him generous terms. For one thing, I needed a sizeable lever against his native immobility. He was a hard worker, yet he suffered from a kind of indolence and inertia. He was risk-averse in the extreme, possibly even worse than me. I was also going to be demanding a lot from him, money being the least of it.

I acknowledged as much during our dinner. I was honest about everything, including the Symposium's current revenues. For the first couple of years, maybe longer, he'd be taking a salary cut. I was candid as well about my situation with my father, explaining that we wouldn't be able to legally formalize our partnership right away, and that we would have to keep the details of our arrangement to ourselves. In short, I was demanding a level of trust from him that would have been inconceivable with anyone else. But Perry and I went way back. We had known each other since we were kids, and there remained between us an almost brotherly bond. Nonetheless, I was asking for a lot, and I reflected on my father's ill-fated partnership with my uncle. There was a tendency in my family for history to repeat, and I wondered whether I was making a terrible mistake. But what choice did I have? I laid out my proposal and let Perry take it from there. He said he would need to think about it. He wanted to consult with his parents and uncle. I couldn't have hoped for a better response. I told him to take his time, I wouldn't need an answer till the end of August.

"And what if I say no?" he asked.

"Truly? I'll probably sell the place. I don't say that to pressure you, honestly. But I can't see running it on my own. I'm not like my father. I don't know how he did it. And I can't see having anyone else as a partner. But you have to do what's right for you. I mean that. I know I'm asking a lot, and I don't want you to do this unless you're a hundred percent certain it's right for you."

Perry gave his answer in less than a week. He was in. I felt enormous relief. I'd had no idea what I would do if he had said no. But as we began to discuss plans, I found myself thinking about my father and uncle again. Though Perry had raised no concerns when I'd described my vision for the Symposium, he now floated some suggestions that contradicted my own plans. His idea was that we entirely redo the place and turn it into one of those swishy salons with the tiffany lamps, wall-to-wall carpeting, and lacquered wood. I couldn't believe my ears. Besides running counter to what I'd proposed, such places, as I pointed out to him, had already seen their day. Also, we didn't have the money for such a makeover. Perry said he could get it from his parents. I told him I didn't want us to go into even greater debt. More to the point, I felt strongly we should preserve the Symposium as it was. Its datedness and shabby antiquity, the sense of its being frozen in time, were precisely what we needed to capitalize on. I believed we could be the next Café Napoli.

The Napoli, a pool hall a few blocks away from us, was at one time the Italian equivalent of the Symposium. Toward the late eighties, however, it began to attract a species of customer not common to these parts, a species that, neither Italian nor much interested in billiards, had a taste for quality espresso, urban exoticism, and "gritty authenticity." As these itinerants multiplied there would be even more startling transformations, and we locals would watch with wonder as select neighbourhood businesses that had been teetering on the brink of extinction were suddenly granted not just a new lease on life but a level of success their owners would have never imagined. I was convinced we could lure some of these life-giving boulevardiers our way. I had urged my father to make some changes toward that end, but he'd ignored me. Now I was determined to put my ideas to the test, and I wasn't going to let Perry get in the way.

He didn't put up much resistance and I won him over. As our building was set further back than most others on the street, one of the ideas I'd pressed on my father was that we install a terrace. Now Perry and I applied for a permit. Perry agreed with me that, while our Greek coffee might appeal to a few outliers, it could never compete with espresso, so we purchased a La Cimbali machine and signed on with a supplier of gourmet beans. The Symposium's menu had never included much more than burgers and hot dogs, and we agreed this needed to change. Perry, however, believed we should shift to healthier fare. I thought this was a lousy idea: people didn't go to pool halls for tempeh and soba. The menu was an integral part of our image and should be consistent with the setting. We needed to retain our authenticity. Perry, reasonably, countered that we were already compromising our "authenticity" (those are his hooked fingers), so why balk now? I said we had to strike a balance. Our current problem was an excess of authenticity. We were too much an ethnic establishment of a bygone era and we were frightening people away. That was also part of my argument for taking down the Sun of Vergina. The Symposium could not survive in its current incarnation. But in remaking it, we had to apply a light touch. We were trying to create a kind of illusion. We wanted a Symposium that was a sanitized and upgraded replica of itself.

He was unconvinced; I rephrased my argument, telling him we needed to leverage our existing assets and reputational capital and make small but strategic modifications that conformed to emerging trends and market demands while still offering an authentic heritage experience. (With Perry, it was sometimes necessary to resort to such language.) Again I won him over. We kept the burgers and dogs, adding sandwiches and panini, some salads, and a selection of pastries and desserts. To the place itself, we made few changes. Perhaps the most significant was removing the venetian blinds on the front window. It was amazing what a difference such a detail could make. Presumably the blinds were there to provide privacy and anonymity, but they shut out the sunlight and hinted at activities unfit for public view. Without them, the place opened up and looked bigger, brighter, more welcoming. We got rid of the video games and the lottery and poker terminals, which also lent the place an air of seediness, and the carambole table, which wasn't seeing much action. This gave us space to install a couple of vintage pinball machines (which Perry nabbed at a discount through a connection of his uncle's) and to expand the front seating area. There were protests. The loudest were over the thomatiáki, which we reconverted to a stock room. Some of the guys threatened to complain to my father, and many stopped coming. We had reckoned on this. To grow into our new skin, we would have to shed the old. But (as I kept repeating to Perry) we needed to be patient.

Unfortunately, some of the guys did speak to my father, and he believed the wild exaggerations and outright lies they told him about what we were doing to his business. Nursing his own resentments, he was prepared to believe the worst about me. Given how he was recovering and what I was told by medical staff and his social worker, he needed to be in a nursing home, and following a bureaucratic purgatory of musical beds, I was finally able to settle him at St. Paul's. He was furious. He'd assumed he'd be returning home and living with me. But I was having a hard enough time dealing with the pool hall without having to take care of him as well. He said I was a selfish unfilial ingrate.

I didn't have the time or energy to deal with the apartment either, and a year after my return, it remained as I'd found it. I knew I should donate his clothes to charity, but despite his slow progress, such a step felt presumptuous. So I stored most of the clothes in the basement, leaving in the closets a few items he might still be able to wear.

In the summer, I finally tackled the file cabinet. I sorted the top drawers quickly, but the bottom drawer was as time-consuming and emotionally complicated as I'd expected. I expected the notebooks and letters would present the greatest challenges, so I started with the photos.

It is said that a picture is worth a thousand words, but these ones belied

that maxim again and again. I sorted them into categories and sub-cat-
egories. Like the notebooks, many would require exegesis from my father,
and I gave careful thought to how I might wheedle him into providing it.
One day, having chosen a few of the most benign, I took them to St. Paul's.
I'd begun to do something with my father I hadn't done since childhood:
ask him about his life. He tended to become suspicious when I did this,
so I stuck to unprovocative material—his jobs in Greece, life in the village
before the war, his impressions of Canada when he'd first arrived. Mostly I
got grudging, curt, and not terribly enlightening responses.

That afternoon, after my father had finished his lunch, I pulled out the
photographs and braced for the worst. I decided to show them to him in
the dining hall, hoping the setting might temper his reaction. The photos
themselves aside, I didn't know how he'd respond to learning that I'd
breached the file cabinet and snooped through his personal belongings. I
placed a photo before him, a small square scallop-edged monochrome that
showed three dapper young men in a city square. My father stared down at
it. Looking up at me, he said, "What is this?"

I found this encouraging. I explained that it was one of several old
photos I'd found in the apartment—I didn't specify where. Did he even
remember the shoebox or what was in it? Did he remember any of the
other things in the bottom drawer? Did he remember the file cabinet?

He looked back down at the photo and I asked him who the men in it
were. He gave no response. I asked again. Still nothing. I pointed at the
man in the middle and asked if he recognized himself. He gave me a look
of affronted disdain but did not answer.

I showed him more photos, one by one. He maintained his granite
stare. I asked him if he recognized any of the faces or locations. Occasionally he would say, "He was a friend," or "I knew him from the plant," or
"She was the cousin of a co-worker." If I pressed for more details, he would
grow irritable. Finally he exclaimed, "I can't remember what I had for
breakfast this morning and you want me to recite to you ancient history?"
I figured we'd done enough. I didn't want to push my luck.

On my next visit, I brought more photographs, and his reaction was
the same. I waited a couple of weeks before I showed him the next batch. I
selected four from among the riskier ones and again showed them to him
after lunch. The first was a studio portrait of a blond fair-skinned boy of

five or six. Given the boy's clothes and hair, I guessed it to be from the early seventies. I caught something in my father's eye that gave me hope. But then he looked up from the photo with the usual blank expression and said, "Is this you?"

If this was bluffing, the man was a virtuoso. He should have been a millionaire.

"You think that's me?"

He gazed at the photo again. "I don't have my glasses," he said.

"Where are they?"

He didn't answer.

I went to his room. The glasses were by the roulette wheel. When I got back, the photo was still on the table. I placed the glasses in his hand. "Put them on," I said. I jiggled the photo to remind him it was still there. He slipped on the glasses with his left hand. As I took my seat, he picked up the photograph and scowled at it. He held it further away.

"Who is this?" he said.

"You really don't know?"

He removed the glasses and held the photo closer. I slid another over, and he gazed down at it, still holding the first in his hand.

"Who's this?"

"It's the same boy as in this one," I replied, taking the photo he was holding and putting it on the table beside the other. "You can't see?"

What I showed him next was a half photograph, the left side ragged where part had been torn away. The remnant showed a young blonde woman in a dark coat. She stood with her head turned, casting an arch or skeptical gaze at whomever had occupied the voided portion.

He kept staring at the photo blankly.

"Who is she?" I said. "Please. Talk to me."

"Who is it?" he said flatly.

"Oh, come on. It's *your* photograph."

"How is it *my* photograph?" he said angrily.

"It was in the apartment, with all the others. Why would you have a photograph of a woman you don't know?" I traced a finger along the photo's ragged edge. "And why is it torn? Was there someone standing next to her? Do you remember? Who was standing next to her?" He gazed at the photo as though only now realizing it was torn.

"I don't know what this is," he said.

Was there a part of the brain responsible for lying? Why couldn't that have been knocked out by the stroke?

I slid the next photo between the others. This must have been the oldest of all the photographs in the shoebox. A stiff cracked sepia portrait surely dating from before the war, it showed a young woman in her early twenties, with round wire-rim glasses, short wavy hair parted on the side, and sombre Levantine features that could have as easily passed for Semitic as for Greek. She gazed unsmilingly, stolidly, almost morosely, past the camera.

"Do you know who *she* is?" I enquired. "I assume she's a relative."

A long time passed.

"No."

I waited.

"You must know who she is."

My father raised his head. "Who is she?"

There was another long silence.

"You're such a fucking liar," I said in English.

My father's expression remained unchanged.

"You're very good." I couldn't tell whether he even understood me. "Nothing will ever change you," I said, still speaking English. "Not a heart attack, not a stroke, nothing."

He regarded me with the same vacant, inscrutable gaze.

I switched back to Greek. "Why can't you talk to me? After all these years. Who knows how much time we have? Why can't you just be honest?"

Something flashed in his eyes. "It's midnight in here," he snarled. "What do you want me to tell you?"

"Just the truth," I said.

He gazed at the photos again. I turned the last one over. On the back was a short handwritten inscription in Latin script. I had typed it into an online translation application, but the results were inconclusive, the language detected wavering from Esperanto to Swedish to Romanian.

"Do you know what that says? Can you read it?"

I waited.

"Do you know what language that is? Can you at least tell me that?"

Silence.

"Do you speak this language?"

More silence.

I swept up the photographs. But as I returned them to the envelope, I noticed another I'd left inside and pulled it out. It too showed a beautiful young woman with dark eyes and a grave expression. The photo had once belonged to my uncle and for a few years sat on the credenza in his dining room. I'd brought it along thinking I might use it as a test. Thrusting it before my father now, I asked, "Do you know who *that* is?" He barely glanced at it. And I could tell from the way he peered at me that he knew what it was. A shadow fell upon him. I myself could barely look at this photo without feeling heartsick. As we held each other's gaze, the space between us dropped away and something passed between us. For a brief moment, it seemed we were united in a shared penitence. I thought he might even say something, that we might begin to speak. But it was fleeting, perhaps illusory, as the next moment he'd slipped back into his unsoundable abyss. I continued to watch him, but I knew nothing further was coming and got to my feet. As I gathered my things, he gazed at me with his usual empty slack-jawed expression. Slinging my knapsack over my shoulder, I told him I'd be back in a couple of days and headed toward the elevators. I wasn't sure what had just happened, but at least, for the time being, my rage had subsided. What remained in its place, however, was even harder to bear.

3

My mother never tired of talking about her life in Greece, about her childhood, her parents, her brother and sister, her uncle, the wars. This was the literature of my childhood, these tales of loss, hunger, misery, and heartbreak. In later years, my university friends would be surprised to hear I didn't know the Narnia series and *Winnie the Pooh*. But I wasn't read such books. I wasn't read to at all. Instead I was crammed full of my mother's reminiscences, these tragic tales of hardship and grief. My father, no stargazer himself, would say, "What are you telling him? He's seven years old, he doesn't need to hear about such things." When my father spoke about the past, it was more like history, abstract and remote. Often it was hard to understand. If he spoke to me about his own life, it was to tell me tales of my grandfather. On this subject he could be positively effusive. If my mother was the tragedian in the family, he was the bard and balladeer. "There's no person in all of Macedonia," he would say to me, "who doesn't know the name of Alexander Doukas. Ah, Aleko, who knows what your grandfather might have been had he been born in a different era. We are all prisoners of our times and circumstances. Which is why you, *you*, my boy, with all your advantages and opportunities, can achieve what your grandfather only dreamed of."

My grandfather had been a natural prodigy, an untutored genius. He had no formal schooling but knew everything about everything. Having worked as a cement-layer, stonemason, and auto mechanic, he was good with his hands and could fix or build just about anything. He could also name every herb and flower, and such was his knowledge of natural remedies that people in the village trusted him more than the town doctor. In the evenings, the men would gather in the *taverna* to hear him read the newspaper aloud. He would recite his own poetry or play songs he'd composed. "Given the opportunity," my father would say, "your grandfather could have been one of the great poets of Europe." Unfortunately, he had none of his poems to show me. Proficient at numerous instruments, my grandfather had jammed with the likes of Yiorgos Mitsakis, Markos Vamvakaris, Rita Abatzi, and Vassilis Tsitsanis. According to my father, the latter had even cribbed some songs from my grandfather. (Having heard my father's Tsitsanis records, I wasn't impressed. It would be some time before I developed an ear for Greek music.)

What my grandfather was most renowned for, however, was his heroism. During the war, he'd worked as an intelligence operative in the resistance, running escape networks and smuggling supplies and information to the British. But he'd been exposed by collaborationist informers and had fled to the mountains, never to be heard from again. For years, rumours circulated about his whereabouts, and there were even reports of sightings. Some said he was living on the island of Lemnos under an assumed identity, others that he was in Albania or Yugoslavia. My father dismissed such stories. Alexander Doukas was not one to run and hide. And he most certainly would not have settled in a foreign country. "These are the ways of a coward," my father would say. "Alexander Doukas was a patriot, a Greek down to his toenails. He would never have abandoned his country, or his family, like that." According to my father, his father was shot by the British on Vitsi Mountain. This caused me no end of confusion. Why had the people my grandfather helped shot him? My father never explained it. Nor did he explain why he was so certain this was how my grandfather had met his end. He just knew. Television and teachers taught us that the British and the Americans were the heroes of the war, Europe's liberators, yet my father loathed both of them. The British were as much the enemy as the Germans, Churchill no better than Hitler. It was all extremely confusing. The history of Greece was confusing.

I was flattered to know that I resembled my grandfather. "Look at him, look at him," my father would say, catching a familiar mannerism or gesture in me. "It's uncanny, that's just like my father." "His sap is in you, my boy," he would say to me. "You are the spitting image." I wished we had pictures so I could see the resemblance. But my father had no pictures of his family. They'd been destroyed in a fire. I was of course named after my grandfather, following Greek custom. I was also named, however, after Alexander the Great. This was what my father told me, which made no sense. I could be named after one or the other, but not both. How could a single name derive from two sources? It wasn't logical. It didn't seem *physically* possible. "Who do you think your grandfather was named after?" my father said when I raised the matter with him. I guessed it was his own grandfather. "And who do you think *he* was named after? The Doukas name is an ancient and noble one. You come from kings and warriors. The Doukases once ruled the Byzantine Empire, and there have been *many* Alexander Doukases. But ultimately they all go back to the original. So of course you can be named after both your grandfather *and* Alexander the Great. You might say you're named after all the Alexander Doukases who have come before you." This I found not just workable but rousing (though I wasn't sure what the Byzantine Empire was).

My father hardly ever spoke about his mother and sister. It was a painful subject, so I never asked him about it. Most of what I knew about them, I'd heard from my mother. After my grandfather's flight to the mountains, my grandmother had herself fled with my father and his sister to Thessaly, where during the civil war my father's sister was killed by sniper fire. At the end of the war, my father and grandmother returned north, settling in Thessaloniki, where my grandmother would perish in that house fire that devoured their possessions. My father moved to Athens and eventually applied to immigrate to both Canada and the US. Canada came through first and he set sail for Halifax in the fall of 1956. When I asked him why he chose Montreal, he told me he liked the sound of the name. This seemed to me impossibly frivolous but he wasn't kidding. I would hear him tell people that if the US had accepted him first, he would have gone to New York City, and I told him that I would much rather have been born in New York than in Montreal. He pointed out that if he'd gone to New York, I would never have been born at all. I could follow this reasoning to a point, but not to the point that it stopped me from indulging my fantasies of growing up a New Yorker. How would my life have turned out? I would have been a different sort of person. How galling to think I'd been consigned to this drab inconsequential region of the planet because of a trite aesthetic fancy. Nor was there any comfort in considering that, given the variables of my birth, there was no alternative, that, as my father suggested, I could only have come into being here or not exist at all.

Such metaphysical preoccupations caught hold of me early and never let go. To this day I remain preoccupied with gardens of forking paths and divergent roads in yellow woods. Nor is it only, or even primarily, the big, dramatic turning points that most exercise me. More troubling in some ways are the inconsequential events of our quotidian existence, the failure of the alarm clock to go off, the decision to walk to work rather than take the bus. Don't even such trivial decisions have long-term consequences? Don't they, too, alter the course of our lives, perhaps as radically and irrevocably as the seemingly more signal ones? As a teenager, I took to intentionally producing forks and fissures. Walking down a street, I might abruptly slow down or come to a stop or break into a run, and for no reason other than to cause a breach in the unfolding of being, to create a blip in the existential continuum, after which, in my mind's eye, I would watch my discarded double, my sloughed shade, the person I had been seconds earlier, continuing up ahead of me or lagging behind, but now a mere spectre, a wraith, a hypothesis, an abstraction remaining a perpetual possibility only in a world of speculation. I envisioned multitudes of such aborted, discarnate duplicates, a vast scattered procession of them, all making their way toward their respective destinies. Did their paths ever cross, or maybe even merge again? Some, I imagined, might be dead, others crippled from horrible accidents. Who could know? Then again, some might be living fabulously glamorous and exciting lives. Maybe some had a girlfriend.

Or could it be they were all converging toward one terminus? Was it possible that, after detours and deviations, their paths ended up in the same place, what might have been and what has been pointing to one end? This would have been my mother's view.

I was playing a dangerous game, messing with fate. I feared I might be punished. Eventually the games stopped, but not the preoccupations.

They just assumed a different form. After reading *Herzog* and *The Adventures of Augie March*, I became obsessed with their author's origins. What would have become of that boy prodigy, Montreal born, had his family not moved to Chicago when he was eight? What if he had stayed? Would there be a Saul Bellow? Upon what did Saul Bellow depend?

It was around this time too that I came across a passage in the *Pensées* of Pascal: *When I consider the brief span of my life absorbed into the eternity which comes before and after, I take fright and am amazed to see myself here rather than there: there is no reason for me to be here rather than there, now rather than then. Who put me here? By whose command and act were this time and place allotted to me?* Until I read these words, I had naïvely assumed only people like me, sprung from imported seed, were plagued by thoughts like these. I conceived of the autochthonous as plants or trees, as sprouting straight from the soil like pines and oaks, with roots deep in the ground. Whereas I was a space castaway, an alien who had dropped from the sky, crash-landing on the planet like a Robinson Crusoe on Mars, or Charlton Heston on the Planet of the Apes.

My father's application to the US eventually came through, but by that point he was settled in Montreal and reluctant to pack up and start again. He liked Montreal. He was also of two minds about the US. Whatever the country's undeniable advantages and opportunities, he despised its politics and bullying ways. Canada seemed a more civilized and companionable place, a less frenetic and vulgar America.

He worked in restaurant kitchens, washing dishes, peeling potatoes. He regularly held down two and three jobs at once, and put in as many hours as he could get. He boarded with a young Greek couple, occupying the small back room of their five-and-a-half on Napoleon Street. Having no closet, he divided his small wardrobe between a wheeled metal rack in his room and his steamer trunk from Greece, which he kept by the oil furnace in the shed. Even with his work schedule, he maintained an active social life and quickly acquired a wide circle of friends, almost all of them Greek immigrants. Of restricted means and frugal habits, these were not people to frequent clubs and restaurants, but they were young and liked to enjoy themselves, so there was no end of parties and dinners and picnics, not to mention all the engagements, weddings, and baptisms. Handsome, gregarious, open-handed, he made friends easily, attracting both men and women to him. Because he was smart, witty, and well-spoken, people assumed he was educated, that he had gone to high school. He was a man much in the heart of the world.

One person who took an instant shine to him was my uncle Tasso. The two met at an engagement party, and discovering they had (at the time) similar politics, as well as uncanny commonalities in their histories, they formed an immediate, if (as it turned out) fragile, bond. Still childless, my uncle and aunt lived in a small apartment on Clark Street, where my father was a frequent visitor. My uncle had recently purchased a television, and the two men would stay up and watch the news. The TV sat in a corner of the dining room, next to an oak display cabinet and a credenza crowded with family photos, among which were two that showed a woman with dark handsome features, a lush mane of hair, and a proud, severe gaze. According to my uncle, but for these photographs, he and my father would have never become friends. The photos drew my father to the house. My father told a different story, claiming it was my uncle who brought the photos to his attention and who insisted on talking about their subject at every opportunity. It was my uncle as well who, one evening, while my aunt was cleaning up in the kitchen, made the *proxenió*.

Initially, my father expressed reservations. My uncle assumed it was because of his sister's age, though my father never mentioned that detail. There was, after all, something unseemly about an older bride, even when, as in this case, the difference was no more than eighteen months, and my uncle had worried it might prove a hindrance. When he tried to address the matter, however, my father cut him short, assuring him that he had no doubts about the young lady's physical charms, which were amply evident in the photographs, or about her numberless other virtues of which his friend had given him a full inventory. What made him hesitate were his own shortcomings, the belief that it was he himself who was not worthy of such an excellent and deserving young lady. Reminding my uncle of his current straitened circumstances and long-term business plans, he declared that, until he'd realized his ambition of acquiring his own restaurant, he regarded all talk and thought of marriage as idle and premature. In his view, until a man had a solid financial foundation in place, he had no business taking on a wife and family.

My uncle, while commending my father for his prudence and honesty, wondered whether he might not be taking things too far. Under such requirements, he observed, no one would ever marry but the wealthy. He tacitly understood that what was going on was no more than a negotiating tactic on my father's part, a sly attempt to draw my uncle out on his own finances and those of his sister. It was only natural. But my uncle didn't wish to beat around the bush, and for the first time that evening the word *príka* was uttered. Telling my father that he wished to be equally candid, he admitted outright that his sister had virtually nothing to her name. Apart from a few liras she had squirrelled away and a modest hope chest she'd built from her own earnings and consisting of the standard quota of bedding, towels, napery, linen, hosiery, china, and other such staples, she had no money or property. Nonetheless, he believed he could throw something into the mix to sweeten the deal.

My uncle had himself only the year before purchased a restaurant, taking over the hot dog joint where he'd worked since his arrival in Canada. It was a tiny place on St. Lawrence Boulevard consisting of an L-shaped lunch counter with six stools and two compact four-seater booths. But it did a steady business, attracting not only locals but also cabbies, truckers, policemen, salesmen, and other commercial and professional itinerants from across the city. Montrealers can grow misty-eyed for steamies, smoked meat, and bagels, and to this day I meet people who recall the Galaxy Snack Bar with reverent nostalgia. Being a regular, my father had seen with his own eyes the crowds at the Galaxy, but he was surprised by the figures he heard that evening. Who would have thought there could be such profits in hot dogs and french fries? My uncle said he would be happy to show him the books. If anything, his problem was that he was *too* busy. Running the place on his own for over a year, he was worn out, and if he and Christina were going to have a child, he could not continue like this much longer. He would need help. He could hire someone, but it wasn't easy finding a person you could trust. He knew my father to be a smart, hard-working, honest, and reliable person, and he trusted my father thought the same of him. Thus, if my father were willing to make of the two of them family, he was prepared to make my father a partner. He could only give him a minority share, but those details could be worked out after the *logothósimo*. First he needed to know whether my father was interested. He didn't need an answer right away. My father could think the matter over, take his time.

My father played it cool. This was his way, always the poker face. (This is my uncle talking.) He said he would have to mull it over. It wasn't the reaction my uncle had expected. Did my father consider the Galaxy beneath him? Or did the age difference matter to him after all but he didn't want to admit it?

My uncle would grow more confused and vexed with the passing days. He had expected an answer within a week or two, but a month later there was still no word. Though my father came by with the same regularity, he never mentioned the matter. My uncle was too proud to bring it up himself. How much time did the man need? Was he having his sister investigated by people he knew back home? Years later, he would come to understand that this was my father's way, that he liked to cloak himself in mystery and keep everyone guessing about his motives and intentions. It was a part of his character my uncle would come to hate, this shiftiness and manipulation. At the time, though, he felt confused and regretted he'd ever made the proposal. He felt embarrassed, deceived, betrayed. He could understand if the man was not interested, but just say so outright, whatever the reasons. Why pussyfoot around like a woman? Perhaps he'd had his friend all wrong. Eventually he assumed the thing was dead and he resolved never to mention it again. He also turned his mind to how he might bring the friendship to a swift and tactful end.

My father noticed none of this. He remained his usual gregarious self, keeping up his visits at the house and the restaurant, oblivious to his friend's changed demeanour. Then, one evening, he showed up at the Galaxy just before closing time and placed a large manila envelope on the counter. With no one else in the place, my uncle turned off the outside light, locked the door, and finished cleaning up. As he removed his apron, my father grinned at him and said, "So *Tassouli mou*, I have happy news." Putting on his blazer, my uncle approached the counter warily. His friend removed several photographs from the envelope. There were nine or ten of them, and my father laid them out on the counter so they faced my uncle. They were all black-and-white studio shots of my father in different poses, soigné and debonair in a light-coloured summer suit and tie. A few of them were close-ups. Most were wallet size, with two the size of a postcard.

"I had them done the other day over at Wiseman's," my father said, still grinning. "I thought I should have you look them over. Get your opinion which you think is best."

Baptized Eleni Anagnostopoulos (or, to give it its proper genitive form, Anagnostopoulou, reflecting a woman's status as a dependent), my mother was born in Athens on an uncertain date in the spring of 1931. Her papers show her birthday as November 7, but she said this was the day she was baptized. Being the second daughter, she received a cold welcome from her parents. During the *Dekemvriná*, her neighbourhood was held by rebel forces, and one day, while her mother and brother were out foraging for greens, her neighbourhood was shelled by the British. Her house had two rooms and she was in the bedroom. Immediately she sought cover under an icon of the *Panayía*, but no sooner had she pressed her back against the wall than a voice directed her to crawl under her parents' bed. She obeyed, and seconds later the corner she had vacated was a pile of rubble. She lay under the bed waiting for the shelling to stop while her father and sister silently haemorrhaged to death in the other room. She would find them lying side by side amid the debris and blood. Whenever she spoke of these events, she would describe the voice as that of the Panayía, the all-holy mother. Who else could it have been?

She remained with her mother and brother in the half-ruined house, until one afternoon men in uniform showed up and seized her mother. She and her brother were put in a children's shelter. A few days later, her uncle, a retired and unmarried army colonel, collected her at the shelter and took her to live with him. Her brother, two years older, was transferred to a shelter outside Athens, but after a few weeks he escaped and made his way back to the city. For a while, he squatted in abandoned buildings and scrounged out a living on the streets. Lying about his age, he enlisted in the navy. Then, getting himself on a merchant ship, he sailed about the world until he jumped ship in Montreal.

Their mother was put in prison under an indefinite sentence, and for a while there was talk of execution. Her husband, who had been active in the resistance, was said to have collaborated with the *andártes* after liberation, and she was charged as an accomplice. She was given numerous opportunities to sign a recantation, but she refused and remained in prison until she died in 1950. The cause of death was given as tuberculosis. What kind of woman *was* this, God forgive her? What kind of mother would willingly orphan her children and abandon them to a life of servitude and beggary? This was not a mother but a monster, the mutant product of a brutalizing indoctrination. Such thoughts as these would run through her daughter's head for the rest of her life. She loved her mother—how could a child do otherwise?—but she could never understand or forgive her. In prison she had never written her children or conveyed any wish to see them. She was a hard, bitter, heartless woman. The colonel said his sister loved the Party more than she did her own family.

My uncle told a different story. He claimed it was the colonel himself who had ensured there was no contact or communication between his sister and her two surviving children. When I asked him why he was so sure of this, he said the facts spoke for themselves. His mother was a kind and loving woman devoted to her children. She had no interest in politics, and what involvement she'd had in her husband's activities was purely incidental and unwitting. She was a simple, uneducated, naïve woman caught between the two sides. She'd had the ill fortune of marrying a man whose republican leanings marked him as a traitor in her eldest brother's eyes. A career army officer and royalist, her brother had regarded her marriage as an act of treason and had tried to stop it. Failing at this, he'd found his opportunity for recompense with the outbreak of civil war and had his sister arrested on phony charges. Thirteen years her elder, he was in declining health and lame from a war injury, and disposing of his sister in such manner had the added advantage of providing him with free live-in help in the person of his niece.

It was like one of those black-and-white melodramas I watched at the Regency. Still, my uncle made a strong case. He pointed out that, as things worked in Greece in those days, having an army officer in the family should have all but ensured his mother's release or, at worst, a lenient sentence. That she instead received the most severe punishment possible was itself proof that her brother was behind it all. My uncle swore his mother would have had no qualms signing a recantation (not that there was anything to recant), so the colonel's claim that she had repeatedly declined the opportunity served as further proof. Nor did my uncle believe his mother had died from tuberculosis. She had been killed or had committed suicide.

But my mother would have none of this. She couldn't bear even to hear it, and she forbade my uncle to discuss these matters in her presence. The two had such contrasting conceptions of both their parents, you wouldn't have known they were talking about the same people. But my uncle seemed to have no inkling of how differently he'd been treated from his sisters. On the other hand, I couldn't understand why my mother was so hostile to his account of their mother's demise. It seemed not only more plausible but more palatable than her own. After all, she herself described the colonel as a selfish, egotistical tyrant, claiming that in all the years she lived with him, he never showed her any affection and treated her more like a servant than a niece. Yet she was also strangely grateful to him. He had rescued her from that horrid shelter, where she would never have been consigned but for her mother's heartlessness. When she was sixteen, he'd placed her as an apprentice with a seamstress and, a few years after that, found her a steady job in a military garment factory.

When she wasn't at work, she kept house and tended to the colonel. With few friends or liberties, she rarely went out on her own except to run errands. Sundays, she accompanied the colonel to church. Now and then he took her to a restaurant. Occasionally she would walk in the park with girls from the factory, or they would go to the cinema or a *zakharo-plastío*. She wrote to her brother twice a week and spoke of her loneliness and sadness. He wrote less frequently and spoke about his own sense of isolation living *stin xenityá* (a very Greek and untranslatable expression meaning roughly "foreign parts"). He spoke of how hard life was in Canada, of the long dark brutal winters and the short damp summers. Ignoring the hints, she continued to express hopes of one day reuniting with him, her tone growing more disconsolate and pleading with the passing years. She understood he had his own troubles, but her life in Athens was so cramped she feared that, if something were not done for her soon, she was destined for spinsterhood. She would send pictures of herself, which he would study with a mixture of pride and regret. A woman so lovely and refined shouldn't be alone. And time was passing. She was already past her prime. Even more than the letters, the pictures made him feel what a poor brother he was.

In fact, his sister didn't lack for suitors. The problem was that, after their initial meeting with the colonel, they would never be heard from.

She rarely knew about these men. For one reason or another, each was inevitably judged unsuitable and told not to call again. They were too old or too young; some had dubious pasts, pastimes, or politics; some seemed unhealthy; some lacked proper manners; and all were without sufficient means or connections. Once, as she and her friend Maria wandered the National Garden, they were approached by a short man in a grey suit who, visibly colouring, said to her, "Please forgive me, I don't wish to intrude, but I believe you are Eleni Anagnostopoulou." Her heart raced with terror, and had she not been with a friend in a crowded park in broad daylight she would have put her head down and kept going, but on this occasion, before she could even decide how to react, Maria said to the stranger, "And who are you?" She was familiar with Maria's brashness, but in this instance it struck her as especially presumptuous, and she flushed with embarrass-ment and anger. The young man, crimson himself, bowed stiffly and intro-duced himself. His name was Yiorgos Kanellopoulos, and something in his voice and manner calmed her a little. He had a courteous, gentle, and unthreatening way about him that she found reassuring. Still, she intended to have a word with Maria later.

Mr. Kanellopoulos was the cousin of Ariadne, another girl at the fac-tory, and ever since he'd arrived in Athens the year before, his cousin had not stopped talking to him about her friend Eleni. He admitted she'd even shown him a picture. Asking Ariadne how he might be introduced to her friend, he was informed that he would have to arrange a meeting with the lass's uncle. Reluctantly, he sent a request in writing and was pleased to receive an invitation to the apartment, where he and the colonel had what seemed a most amicable conversation. They had ranged over many serious topics and spoken for two hours, and he was given every indication that the colonel was pleased and that he would be hearing from him again. But two weeks passed without a word, and when he sent a respectful query, he received a terse admonition never to write again. This had been a couple of months earlier, and since then he had succeeded in putting the mat-ter out of his mind. But having now had the good fortune to encounter Miss Anagnostopoulou in person, he hoped he might be forgiven if he presumed to enquire whether she could shed some light on the situation.

Miss Anagnostopoulou, cheeks still burning, though now for different reasons, found herself at a loss for words. Surprisingly, she felt sorry for the young man. He seemed so sweet and sincere. But he had also roused in her a repressed anger, and she found herself responding in a more forthright manner than was her wont. "Don't take it personally," she said. "No one in the world is good enough for my uncle. Stavros Niarchos himself would be found wanting." Mr. Kanellopoulos laughed politely and enquired whether the colonel might have mentioned him. She confessed she'd never heard his name and knew nothing of his interview with the colonel. Her uncle was not in the habit of keeping her informed on such matters.

At work the next day, she said to Ariadne, "How could you not tell me about your cousin? I had no idea he'd been to the house."

"But I did tell you. I even showed you a photo of him. And you insisted he had to speak to your uncle. Remember? You're the sort of girl, you said, who sticks to the rules."

It came back to her. She remembered being unimpressed by the photo, which was probably why the incident had faded from memory. "But why didn't you tell me he'd been to the house and spoken with my uncle?"

"I was waiting for *you* to say something. And when you didn't, I felt too awkward to bring it up. I didn't want to put you in a difficult situation. And Yiorgos told me not to say anything, and I felt I had to respect that. He was upset. He's not the kind to do such things, you know. He's very shy. So what did you think of him? Isn't he a darling?"

"He seems very nice."

"He's a saint. You won't find a better man, on my word. I don't say that because he's my cousin. But because he's my cousin, I know him. I know what he's really like, and I can tell you there's no better man in the world. He is what he seems. On my word. The most agreeable man you'll ever know. You say, *Yiorgo, sit*, he sits, you say, *Yiorgo, stand*, he stands. You wouldn't believe what he's done for the family. One day we'll sit down and I'll tell you everything. The man is a saint. And he's a looker too, don't you think? If he weren't my cousin, *I* would marry him."

She nodded. What could she say? He wasn't *un*attractive, but he wasn't to her taste. He was short and had an undistinguished face, a little soft and feminine. She'd always imagined her husband as tall. She was short herself, and Yiorgos stood no more than three or four centimetres taller. But she'd grown curious and in the coming days she would ask Ariadne to tell her more about her cousin. She learned that he'd come to Athens with his two brothers after the death of their mother. Being the oldest son, and their father already dead, he was now head of the family and felt responsible not only for his brothers but for all his relatives still in the village. A tailor by training, he currently worked at a garment factory, but he planned to open his own shop one day. "Let me set up a rendezvous," Ariadne pleaded. "In the name of God, you're twenty-five. How long can you wait? I know you have to respect your uncle and all that, but he has to be reasonable. He has obligations to you too. You admit yourself he's never going to approve of anyone. So what are you supposed to do? Times have changed. It's a different world. We have full rights now under the law. Your uncle is from another era. You can't let him ruin your life. You have to think about your future. What are you going to do, spend the rest of your life looking after an invalid? And when he dies...what? You could be an old lady by then."

It wasn't as if she hadn't thought about these things, yet she couldn't bring herself to defy her uncle. But Ariadne kept at her until, after a couple of weeks, she relented. She agreed to meet Yiorgos at a zakharoplastío after work one afternoon, with Ariadne as chaperone. When they took their seats at one of the outdoor tables, Yiorgos clumsily produced a small gift-wrapped box. She thanked him and left it sitting on the table. Despite his bold conduct in the park, that afternoon he was shy and tongue-tied and Ariadne did most of the talking, with Yiorgos following her cues and responding to her prompts. She liked that he was shy. He wasn't like most men. As an Athenian, however, she detected something of the hick in him. He had a slight but noticeable countrified accent similar to Ariadne's, but in a man it was somehow more off-putting. He dressed well, though, and he had nice manners.

They met again during the August holiday, the three of them rambling through the National Garden. She dabbed on perfume from the bottle she had found in the gift box from their previous rendezvous. Yiorgos recognized it and said, "I hope you didn't put it on just for my sake." She replied, perhaps a little too bluntly, that she wouldn't have put it on if she didn't like it. He told her it was from Paris.

On their third visit, they met without Ariadne. Yiorgos suggested they go to the cinema, but she worried this might be a ploy. She knew the sorts of things men did in darkened theatres and she wasn't going to take any chances. Yiorgos didn't seem that type, but you could never be sure. She doubted there were many exceptions. Besides the stories she heard from the girls at the factory, she'd had enough of her own experience merely navigating the streets of Athens. In public, she had learned to keep her head down and never look at a man. But even with these precautions, they were constantly accosting her and making catcalls. They would accompany her for blocks though she ignored them. She would threaten to shout for the police and it didn't make a difference. They would laugh at her. Buses were even worse as it was harder to make an escape. Men would sit beside her and sweet-talk her and even touch her. Sometimes they would place a hand on her thigh. She would get up and move to another part of the bus. When the bus was crowded, men would paw her, press their bodies against her, whisper the most indecent things in her ear. It was sickening. There were times she would flee the bus in tears.

Every young woman had stories like this, but some found them amusing. They regarded the catcalls and sweet talk as a kind of game, a harmless flirting, and they advised her to play along. They said she should feel flattered. The best thing to do was offer a witty reply, make a cutting remark, show them you couldn't be ruffled. And if a guy crossed the line, firmly put him in his place. Men liked that. They respected a woman who stood up for herself. Acting genteel and demure invited more harassment. But she was not acting genteel and demure, she would protest. She simply did not approve of such games, even if she had been capable of playing them. To respond to advances as the girls advised would be to condone them, to participate in one's own debasement. She knew some saw her as a goody-goody and a prude, and that was fine; she wasn't ashamed of her scruples and sense of propriety. Women were not animals. They deserved the same respect and dignity accorded men. That was what it all came down to, and she pitied and disdained women who couldn't understand this.

As an alternative to the cinema, she suggested a *vólta* in Kolonaki and, to her surprise, Yiorgos raised no objections. She was impressed, but also a little confused and suspicious. They met at the main square, and as they walked the swanky tree-lined streets, she kept an eye out for familiar faces. She had told her uncle she was meeting friends and even had Ariadne phone the house and pretend to confirm plans. Never having taken part in such deception, she felt underhanded and anxious. She was worried someone might see her. Yiorgos didn't mind that she kept an inordinate distance between them. He understood her concerns and respected them.

They stopped at a hotel bar and ordered drinks and *mezéthes*. It took several minutes for her nerves to settle. She had never been to such a place, let alone in the company of a man. She surveyed the faces around her. Yiorgos spoke about his family and about life in the village. She was impressed by his seriousness and probity, but she could see why her uncle had denied his petition. He was simple, unsophisticated, rustic. He appeared to be everything Ariadne said he was—gentle, considerate, honest, loyal, responsible—but he was also a little dull. And he had nothing to his name—no money, property, connections. He knew nobody in Athens. And everything he earned went to supporting his family. Besides his younger brothers, he still had a grandmother and a couple of cousins in the village who depended on his remittances. How would he ever manage a wife and children, let alone realize his silly dream to open a tailor shop? And having nothing herself, what could the two of them possibly build together? He was untroubled by her own lack of means. He was a simple, decent person.

On their way to the bus stop, she became anxious about how he planned to take leave of her. She had insisted he not escort her home, and when they reached the stop, she worried he might try to make an advance. But he only wanted to talk about when they would see each other again. And when the bus arrived, he did no more than lift her hand clumsily and kiss it. It was an embarrassing and touching gesture that summed him up. She liked him, but she could not imagine him as her husband. At the hotel, he had asked her how long she was prepared to wait. He imagined he would have his business set up in two or three years, and seemed to believe that his owning a tailor shop would turn her uncle around. She had to set him straight; she wasn't joking when she'd told him her uncle would never approve any man. "He wants me for himself and he'll see to it I never get married." Yiorgos asked whether she was prepared to defy her uncle, and she admitted she didn't have the nerve. "But he gives you no choice," he said. "Under the circumstances, you have an *obligation* to defy him." She spoke again about her brother in Canada and explained how it was her fondest hope they would be reunited. Yiorgos replied that he would love nothing better than to move to Canada. He himself knew people in Montreal, and of the opportunities and wealth that could be had there. He didn't see her desire to rejoin her brother as an obstacle: if she were willing to take him as her husband, he would move to the North Pole with her. She had to fight back the tears. No one had ever spoken to her like this. "And what about your own brothers?" she enquired. "And your grandmother and cousins in the village?" "Don't worry about any of that," he said. "Everything will work itself out as long as I'm with you." "But you don't even *know* me," she said, colouring. "I know as much as I need to know," he replied. "I see perfectly what you are. And I can't imagine a better woman to spend the rest of my life with." She had only ever heard such talk in the movies and it made her lightheaded. She didn't know what to think. She was grateful for his words and would have liked nothing better than to reciprocate, but she didn't share his confidence. She still wasn't even sure about her feelings for him. It felt wrong not to like him, but she couldn't get rid of her doubts. And she could not forget about her uncle. So why did she continue to see Yiorgos and give him false hope? This could not go on. And what if they were discovered? She could not imagine what the colonel would do.

A few days after her afternoon in Kolonaki, she received an unusual letter from her brother. It was bulkier and heavier than usual. Tearing the envelope open, she saw more than the usual two or three onionskin sheets and her first thought was that something terrible had happened. Then, among the sheets, she found a couple of photographs. They showed a handsome young man with wavy greased-back hair and a pencil moustache. She didn't know the face, but she felt her heart racing. She had an intuition of who he might be. Her heart pounding harder and harder, she read the letter. She knew the next time she saw Yiorgos would be the last.

His own first letter to her was dated the day of the Nativity of the *Theotokos*, which she took as a good sign. But it arrived on a Tuesday, which was a day of ill omen. I found it after her death among the other letters my father sent in their extended epistolary courtship. She'd kept them all. Of the letters she wrote to him, my father kept only a small portion. Most were long and meditative, revolving around the subjects of marriage, family, virtue, God, and fate. My father's letters were short and matter of fact, their tone of levity and humour verging on the flippant. For someone who hadn't gone past elementary school, my mother had an impressive prose style, and even my father thought the letters she wrote him eloquent and intelligent, if a little lugubrious and naïve. But naïveté was not undesirable in a wife, and he didn't mind the extravagant piety. Who wanted a worldly bride? In hindsight one cannot but see in them the trouble to come. At the time, though, my father found them charming.

It would be over a year before they met, and the moment he laid eyes on her at Windsor Station he knew he'd made the right decision. She was, as her brother never tired of telling him, even more beautiful in person, a *koúkla*, as he once described her to me in a rare moment of fond recollection—a doll. She was everything she seemed in her letters—smart, shy, serious, courteous, well-spoken—and he felt an immense pride showing her off to his friends. She had a cultivated, almost aristocratic, air, though she could come across as humourless. This was not surprising in someone of such moral sobriety and high-mindedness. And, in any case, she wasn't some gómena; she was going to be his wife. He could hardly imagine a woman better suited. While he himself had little affection for the Church, he didn't expect his wife to share this view. Indeed, what may have been appropriate and elevating in a man was often unseemly and deleterious in the weaker sex. The mother of his children should be a devout Christian.

Her letters left no doubt that she was a woman of stern virtue and laid out her priorities, habits, and expectations in detail. In her small and elegant handwriting, she had explained there were few things she despised more than extravagance and wantonness, and that what she most wished for in a marriage were not expensive clothes and jewelry and fancy things but love, honesty, constancy, and understanding. She wanted four children, two boys and two girls, so none would be without a companion, and she expected her husband to be honest and honourable and to fulfill his duties with cheer and tenderness. Among such duties were regular attendance at mass and strict observation of the canons of the Church. She conveyed these expectations and injunctions with an almost childlike bluntness and assurance that my father found amusing and endearing. In one of the letters he kept, she confidently asserts that she is not in the dark about men's needs and appetites, boasting she has read an advice manual for prospective brides authored by a renowned medical doctor, and warns that, while fully prepared to perform her wifely duties, she in turn expects her husband to abide by the strictures laid down by both God and basic decency, including keeping the Sabbath and all major holidays unsullied by physical defilement. I imagine he shook his head at this, but it seemed not to have raised any alarms. Indeed comments like this tended to confirm him in his decision. How well it spoke of his country that, in this day and age, it could still produce women of such character and virtue. He'd come to know many single Greek girls in Montreal and had seen for himself how even a few years' exposure to Canadian ways could spoil a woman. He was right to have chosen a girl from home.

But things changed with my mother's arrival in Canada. She began to carp about his way of life, decrying the endless merrymaking and frivolity, the drinking and dining and reckless spending. It must come to an end. She was especially shocked by all the single women he knew and declared that these friendships too must be terminated forthwith. Such relations, platonic or not, might be fine for a bachelor, but they were scandalous in a man engaged. She wasn't terribly fond of most of his male friends either, but these she knew she couldn't do much about and she expressed the hope to him that, after they were married, they would socialize only with respectable married couples. My father paid no attention to her admonitions, merely replying now and then that he was getting married, not entering a monastery. My mother wondered what her brother made of his friend's ways. Surely he couldn't have been ignorant of them. A disciplined, hard-working, and clean-living man, he shared none of his friend's dissolute habits. But what did she really know about her brother? They were children when they had last seen each other. And he was a man. Men had different views about such things. And they stuck up for one another. They all belonged to a confederacy of turpitude and licentiousness. But she was his younger sister and he should have looked out for her. He should have given her warning. Perhaps he didn't know. Was that possible?

My father was permitted to invite few of his friends to the wedding, and certainly none of the unmarried women. He and my mother spent their wedding night at a motel on the city's outskirts. This constituted their "honeymoon." By this point, my father was under no illusions about what awaited him in the matrimonial bed, but he was unprepared for the tribulations of that night. His bride was repelled even by her own body. She was not just diffident and awkward; she seemed terrified and revolted. He'd never seen anything like it. He attributed her behaviour to her strict upbringing and lack of experience and expected she would loosen up over time. He would loosen her up. But over the coming weeks, the restrictions, aversions, compunctions, prohibitions, and superstitions kept piling up, and she continued to insist they make love with the lights turned off and under the sheets. When they kissed, she refused to open her mouth, rubbing her closed lips against his like a child. It was anything but erotic: Was this a technique she had picked up in one of her manuals? He tried to teach her how to relax her mouth and kiss properly, but she had absolutely no tolerance for such efforts or discussions. And when once or twice he had dared to give his tongue license, she had recoiled with violent disgust.

The proceedings were cursory and mechanical, and she wished them performed with dispatch. Physical contact between them was actuated by a dreary will to procreate and therefore ceased when she learned that she was pregnant. Oddly, however, she became at the same time more affectionate and physically demonstrative. Though there was less sex, their intimacy deepened. She shed much of her sullenness and insularity and became a nicer, warmer person. Even while deprecating his physical advances, she was in every other way more indulgent and tolerant of him. They went out more often, had friends over, fought less frequently. Pregnancy affected her as drink did other people: it loosened her inhibitions, sharpened her wit, made her more outgoing and convivial. For the first time, she showed a capacity for fun.

But then, in her third month, she "lost" the baby. That's how she described it, the word she always used. And in less than a year's time, she would lose the next. The reasons were not hard to figure out. In her universe, there were no random or arbitrary events; everything had its cause, and every cause, where the event was of sufficient moment, had to be named. Where these miscarriages were concerned, this wasn't difficult.

The first befell her on a cold Sunday morning in November of 1959. The night before, my father had dragged her to a Greek nightclub with a group of his friends. She had told him she wasn't feeling well but he'd protested that the others had gone to a lot of trouble to make the arrangements and he wasn't going to cancel on them now. He promised they would come home early. At the club, their table was near the band, right by the loudspeakers, and the music shook my mother's insides. During the first intermission she asked my father to take her home, but he paid no attention and they remained for the next two sets, everyone at the table except her drinking and smoking. In the end, they didn't get home until after one, and she felt tired, sick, and angry. He had broken his promise, and she mentioned this to him, remarking as well that he'd been disrespectful and demeaning to her throughout the evening. He had ignored her all night, dismissing her complaints, and he had flirted shamelessly with the other women at the table. Well used to such reproaches by now, my father tended to ignore them, but on this night—perhaps he was especially drunk or tired—he lost his temper and told her he was fed up with her paranoid hectoring. Raising his voice and gesticulating in a physically threatening manner, he pointed out that all the women at their table were married, and that, in any case, they were even bigger hags than she was. And if she thought that *that* was flirting, it was because she was a dried-up prude. He said she was so sexually deformed by her priest-induced fears and neuroses that she would not be satisfied until she'd chopped off his balls and hung them on a gold chain around his neck. A few hours later, she awoke in bed with a terrible pain in her stomach and found the sheets covered in blood.

She was pregnant again a few months after that. Determined this time to take every precaution to protect the life inside her, she ruled that, for the duration of this pregnancy, she would be refraining from all forms of physical exertion. Where, with her first pregnancy, she had occasionally submitted to my father's advances, this time she would be off-limits until after the birth. My father told her she was insane. She was being irrational. He said her worries were without basis and the dangers she feared, entirely in her head. He begged her to speak to her doctor, who would confirm what he told her. But she said she didn't need to speak to anyone. She understood her body better than any doctor. And what about *him*, he said, what was *he* supposed to do the next seven months? Suppress all his urges? And why not, she said. What had he done all the years before they were married? Monks and bishops did it their entire lives. My father had some predictable retorts to this and suggested that, if he were expected to make such a sacrifice, then, in all fairness, my mother was obliged to overcome her inhuman inhibitions and allow for some obvious and reasonable alternatives. As always when urged to such degenerate acts, she reacted with anger and disgust and reminded him yet again that what was ordained by nature could not admit of compromise. Every part of the body had its purpose and function, she said, and to ignore and pervert these was a sin against nature and God. He pleaded and wheedled, telling her that she had put him under a cruel and impossible sentence. She said that she had lost the first child because of him and she was not going to let him kill this one too. He called her a prig, a peasant, a barbarian. He bought her gifts and made her promises. He begged and bargained. Then one night, he came home late and drunk and cantankerous and, waking her up, demanded satisfaction. When she refused, he tore away the covers, pinned her to the bed, and forced himself inside her. A few hours later (as she told the story) she would bleed into the toilet bowl.

For weeks she could not stop crying, and she would not let my father near. He slept on the living room couch. Her health deteriorated and she complained of headaches, dizziness, nausea, body aches, asthma, and much else. She stopped going to the factory and then quit. My father took her to several doctors and they all said they could find nothing wrong with her. After four or five impossible months, he decided, on the advice of two of the doctors, to have her committed. It was a difficult decision and affected him in profound and unexpected ways. Alone in the house, he became forlorn, anxious, even frightened. He was filled with pity and remorse and recognized that he was a bad husband. He had contributed to his wife's collapse. Maybe for the first time since their wedding, he remembered how much he loved and admired his wife and recognized how dependent he'd become on her. He saw again how fortunate he was to be married to such a woman, and one sleepless night he vowed that, if she returned home healthy and strong, he would be a better husband. He would spend more time with her, help more with the housework. He would drink less, be more respectful, attentive, patient. He told her as much. These were not private resolutions: they were stated promises, assurances.

When she returned home, he was true to his word. He was so grateful and delighted to have her back. He was loving and patient and kind. He never raised his voice. She regained her strength and confidence and found a job at another factory, and he felt hopeful again. In her prayers, she thanked God for His beneficence. *Megáli ih khári tou*, she would mutter over and over. Great and unfathomable was His grace. Only He knew why the path must be so circuitous and painful. But if such was the suffering necessary to save her husband and marriage, she would have endured worse. Maybe it was the effect of the electroshock therapy, or the Imipramine, but she felt at peace. She might be falling in love again. Her husband was a changed man. Soon they were touching and kissing again. They were going out, visiting friends, dancing, singing. In bed they would hold each other. One night she signalled her willingness and, reaching up, turned off the lamp. From there things proceeded as usual, every word and gesture following one upon the other in the familiar, predictable pattern, except that on this night, every word and gesture, every grunt, kiss, moan, caress, and thrust, and every last cell, cellule, and corpuscle proceeding from them, followed one upon the other and arranged themselves in such a manner as could have but one issue.

On my birthday, my mother would always say to me, "This is the day they knifed me open to bring you into the world." There had been complications. I never understood what they were, because my mother herself didn't know. No one at the hospital bothered keeping either of my parents informed. Because of these complications, I came into the world in the manner of Julius Caesar. But I assumed all babies were delivered like this. I had been given to understand that babies grew in their mother's stomach, and when they were ripe, they were removed surgically. It made perfect sense. How else could you get them out? When I was six, I heard about the two lost babies. My mother told me she lost them inside her stomach. I wasn't sure what this meant. In school we were told about a place called Limbo, but my mother explained that our Church did not believe in Limbo. So where did the babies go? Did their souls survive? Where would these vanished, abstract siblings be today had they not disappeared inside my mother's stomach? Who would I be? Would I even exist? Would my parents have had another child if the previous ones had lived? My mother said she had wanted four children, but was there any guarantee I would have been the one to succeed the first two? The evidence seemed against it. Was my own existence predicated on their negation?

The years after my birth were the happiest of my mother's life. That's what she said. Again and again. It came to sound like an accusation. *Why can't you make me as happy now as you did then?* For four years she stayed home, spending every moment with me, finding in the monotonous round of feedings, cleanings, burpings, washings, and all the other dreary domestic chores that filled her days a bliss she would never have dared imagine. Look at any picture of my mother from this period and you can't miss the joy in her eyes. The poor woman couldn't understand where all this good luck had come from. Was this really her life? Sometimes it frightened her and she would cross herself. Megáli ih khári tou. It was a reminder that you can't judge anyone's fortune until the final tally, how even the worst misery could be redeemed by just a little light and love. In the balance of our earthly existence, a grain of happiness outweighed a mountain of misery. But how could it be otherwise? Most people would not be able to live out their lives. Maybe all the hardship and privation had been necessary, had not just prepared her for marriage and motherhood but also given her the capacity to appreciate its pure and simple pleasures. When she looked at other women she had come to know in Canada, she was amazed by how little they understood about life and marriage. It might be because they hadn't suffered as she had. Perhaps the years of strife and misfortune had been a blessing.

We lived in a five-and-a-half rental on the top floor of a stone triplex on Esplanade. Directly across from us was Fletcher's Field, a great green triptych that extended from Mount Royal Avenue on the north to Hôtel-Dieu hospital on the south. The north section consisted of a row of tennis courts and two baseball fields, the south, a football field and children's playground, and in the middle, an enclosed soccer field with bleachers. On the western verge ran Park Avenue, cutting between the park and the mountain. Today it's *Parc Jeanne-Mance*, but I know people who still call it Fletcher's Field, just as there are people who say St. Lawrence Boulevard and Dorchester and Esplan*aid*. When I was growing up, everyone said Esplanaid. Even the street signs were in English.

I believed Esplanade was the best street in the city, maybe in the world. Apart from the park and the mountain, the houses on the street, with their tall, stately facades, deep leafy lawns, and ornate *couronnement* and ironwork, had a distinct charm and elegance. They were not like the rent barracks in the grubby couloirs east of us. I felt sorry for the kids who lived there. I felt above them. Ours was one of the smallest houses on Esplanade, but I wouldn't have traded it for any other. With its greystone façade, rounded turret, and battlement roof, it resembled a miniature castle. As we were on the top floor, we had a clear view of the cross on Mount Royal. I could see the it through my window. It served as my personal night light, filling my room after dark with its comforting glow. I had a charmed life.

The cross figures in my earliest memories. In one, I'm with my parents on a park bench on a sunny day. I'm seated on my mother's lap and my father is slumped over a newspaper. We're facing the mountain, and my mother is explaining the meaning of the cross. She's talking of Golgotha and the afterlife. Decades later, I will set her straight, tell her about the settlement of Ville Marie and of Chomedey, Sieur de Maisonneuve and the floods of 1643. But sitting on her lap at the age of three or four, I am given an account of Christ's passion and His sacrifice for humanity. I gaze at the monument at the foot of the mountain, and when she's done, I point at the statue at the base of the monument and ask who it is.

"That's an angel," she says.

"No, *there*," I say, indicating the statue of the man below the angel. "Who's that?"

"An angel," my mother repeats. "It's an angel, my love."

"No. At the bottom."

Glancing up, my father stares a moment at the figure I'm pointing at. "Some swindler no doubt," he says and goes back to his paper.

Cycling along Park Avenue one afternoon twenty years later, I will stop to read a newly installed plaque and learn that the monument is in fact a tribute to George-Étienne Cartier and the Great Coalition. The billowing figure atop the obelisk is not an angel but Nike, goddess of victory, the monument an allegory of confederation, a creation myth in verdigris. Every boy in the neighbourhood had a picture of himself astride one of the lions crouched sphinx-like at each corner of the terrace, yet how many of us knew we'd been perched on one of the four corners of the British empire? Or that the draped female figures we pitched stones and snow-balls at for target practice were personifications of Justice, Education, and the Provinces of Confederation? Had this been Boston or Philadelphia, and the monument dedicated to a Benjamin Franklin or Thomas Jefferson, would we have been equally ignorant? Would I have reached my twenties without knowing who these figures were? In fact, even born in Canada, I knew from an early age who Franklin and Jefferson were, well before I ever heard of George-Étienne Cartier.

Was it simply this country and my schooling that were to blame? Partly. But I felt some of the responsibility fell on me. As a child, I had lacked a certain sensuous alertness and curiosity. I was oddly insensible to my surroundings. On those rare family excursions when my father would take us to the beach or the countryside, I would stare out the windows of the car with a kind of indolent stupefaction, the names on the road signs going by—Rigaud, Lachute, Saint-Jérôme, Saint-Jean-sur-Richelieu—as meaningful to me as if we'd been driving through Normandy. I would gaze at the passing farmhouses with utter incomprehension, not bothering to imagine the lives that went on inside them because I knew they were unimaginable, and at the water towers, silos, power stations, freight yards, and other ciphers that dotted the landscape, accepting them in all their muteness and mystery. I never asked, *Hey, what is that? What's that for? What goes on in there?* I never sought answers from my parents or any of the other adults around me, partly because I assumed they had no more knowledge about such things than I did. I was comfortable in my incomprehension. The world did not belong to me; it was full of other people's property. The Cartier monument was one more piece of the world's vast furniture that had no connection to me and that I could therefore safely ignore.

No doubt language played a crucial role. It wasn't till my late teens that I learned such words as *sieve, ladle, doily, dresser, duvet, foyer,* and many other common English nouns that, denoting ordinary household objects as they do, I would have had little occasion to use outside the house. Conversely, there was the stuff of the world, the things beyond our doorstep, for which I had no name at all, in any language. The eye is not independent of the tongue. What we see is not separate from how we speak. But between world and word, we regard the first as solid, the other as abstract, and privilege the former. As Nabokov liked to point out, however, "reality" must always stand inside quotation marks. Perception is already cognition. If it weren't, there would be only a meaningless wash of sensory stimuli. We would be babies again. Perhaps there are yogis and arhats who can regain this primordial preconsciousness, but most of us householders are bound to a world of our own conception. World minus word dissolves into incoherence. And given how, for the first years of my life, the world existed in my mother's tongue, is it any surprise so much of it was a blur?

My mother was also preoccupied with such matters. More specifically, she was anxious about how, having almost no English, I would manage in school. She endeavoured to teach me the alphabet and simple words from her limited vocabulary, which for years afterwards I would pronounce with her accent. She also began questioning my father's plan to put me in Greek school. She feared I would be at a disadvantage. But he wouldn't credit such objections. With TV and radio and all the other surrounding influences, there was no danger of my failing to learn English. But how was I going to get a solid grounding in my own language and culture? No, it was imperative I be put in Greek school. He wasn't going to raise a foreigner. My mother remained silently unconvinced. She believed I should be educated in the language of the land, that I should be able, first and foremost, to communicate with the people among whom I would be making my way in the world.

But this was the mid-sixties, and this was Quebec, and matters were more complicated than my parents realized. Historically, efforts to deal with disparities between the province's French and English had concentrated on ethnic rather than linguistic imbalances, the critical question being not where and by whom French was spoken but rather how Francophones might gain greater access to the upper reaches of power. Now language and education came to the fore, and calls for reform were focusing not so much on Anglo oppression as on rising immigration. The Quebecois had put their trust in demographics, believing their strength lay in their numbers and cultural cohesiveness, but by the early sixties, their birth rate was in decline while rates of immigration were on the rise, and most immigrants put their children in English schools. In the past, this had suited Francophones just fine: many of these foreigners weren't even Catholic, so how were the French schools, administered on religious lines, supposed to deal with them? But with these newcomers now posing an existential threat, something had to be done. According to official history, the first rumblings of unrest were felt in the general populace before making their way up to the political class—hence the term "quiet revolution."

It did not take long, however, for things to get noisy. One of the earliest convulsions occurred in the suburb of St Léonard. Against the prevailing trend, the Italians of St. Léonard generally enrolled their children in what were supposed to be bilingual schools with a curriculum divided between

French and English. In practice, however, English dominated, and in 1967 the Saint Léonard School Board ruled that English would be phased out entirely. Incensed, the Italians created the Saint Léonard English Catholic Association of Parents to maintain the English curriculum, and ran a good portion of the Association's classes in people's homes. The French retaliated with the *Mouvement pour l'integration scolaire*, whose mandate was to ensure the integration of Italian children into the Francophone school system. Soon speeches, petitions, and rallies gave way to violence and riots. For the Italians, English was the language of opportunity and mobility. Why come to this hibernal Land of Nod if not to give your children a chance at a better life? To have some petty meddling bureaucrats get in the way of that seemed like nothing but enmity and spite. The French were no less dismayed to find themselves attacked merely for requesting that these strangers they'd welcomed into their home learn their hosts' language. And throughout it all, the Anglos rolled out their usual fustian about individual rights, freedom of choice, and the rest of the colonialist cant they used to keep the recalcitrant frogs under their heel. Thus it was that the Italians of St. Léonard, along with all the other immigrant groups that would soon join them, entered the fray between the province's French and English not so much as a new set of combatants as a fresh piece of contested territory, and a kind of weapon.

All this was worlds away from Fletcher's Field, where my mother was mired in her own pedagogical struggles. Having had to go back to work the previous year, she'd put me in nursery school. The long stretches of time apart from me would have been hard enough to endure, but her anxieties were compounded by my eating habits. My mother would tell people she had never once heard me complain of hunger or ask for food. She stated that if she didn't regularly force-feed me, I would have perished by now. I was also exasperatingly slow in taking food down. Rather than spit it out or purse my lips and resist as other children did, I would uncomplainingly accept whatever she spooned into my mouth and then hold it there for minutes at a time. She expressed her frustration to friends, and she was astonished by the things she heard. People advised her to ignore me until I cried, or to feed me only as much as I was willing to take in. Some told her to hit me. She couldn't believe her ears. What kind of person would hit an infant? And what possible good could it do? It was amazing what savagery nested in the human heart. Even when I was old enough to feed myself, meals remained a battle of wills. My mother nagged and cajoled and often still had to feed me forcibly. It was an exhausting job, and she couldn't imagine anyone but a mother having the patience for it. Even my father couldn't bear these contests and would remove himself from the kitchen to avoid quarrelling with her. He belonged to the school of neglect and believed my mother was spoiling me. No living creature, he would tell her, will let itself starve. Nature forbids it. But my mother wasn't going to rely on nature.

The closest Greek nursery school was on Park Avenue, and she visited numerous times before enrolling me. She issued stern instructions and warnings to staff and closely monitored their compliance. My father continued to assume I would be going to Greek school when the time came, but my mother was already devising alternative plans. There was only one Greek day school, and one afternoon she visited it and spoke with the principal and some teachers. She told my father of her visit afterwards and informed him that I would not be going there. The staff could not provide what I required. She would need to preside over my noontime meal herself, and the school was too far for her to be able to do that. I would have to be put in a school near her factory. For my Greek education, I could be enrolled in one of the weekend or afternoon programs available.

My father was furious. He couldn't believe my mother had taken such action behind his back, and he was certain she was giving him an exaggerated and misleading account. She had no right to hold such a meeting without him, and he insisted he speak with the principal himself before any final decision was made. My mother told him he could do whatever he liked, but she had made up her mind. I was not going to that school. "What's wrong with you?" he said. "What do you think will happen? The boy will eat. You think they're going to let him starve? You're forgetting what counts here. This is about his education. You're so preoccupied with what they put in his stomach you forget about what they feed his mind. There's no telling what they teach in these foreign schools."

But my mother would not be swayed. One day, during her lunch break, she explored the factory area for schools. The closest she found was on St. Dominique Street. The ages of the children in the schoolyard indicated it was an elementary school. That they were speaking French didn't register in her ear. Nor would it have mattered. All that concerned her was location. When she told my father about the place, he made one last plea, to no avail. It didn't occur to him either to ask about the language of instruction.

A few days later, my mother picked me up at the nursery school and we walked to St. Dominique. I remember a wide brick building, a schoolyard with a basketball court, a heavy wooden door, a long bright corridor, and, on the walls of a bright office, a big round clock, a wooden crucifix with a bronze Jesus, and a photograph of a man in a white robe and a Jewish beanie (a piece of headgear that would remain a source of confusion for many years). I remember, as well, a pretty young blonde lady seated behind a desk. She enquired where we were from, and my mother produced her Greek passport, her Canadian citizenship card, her marriage certificate, and my baptism certificate, explaining that while she and my father had been born in Greece, I was born in Montreal. The young woman asked if we were Catholic.

"Greek Orthodox."

The woman nodded. Smiling at me, she said something in French.

"He no speak frents," my mother said.

"He speak English?"

"Leet beet."

The young woman said that this was a French Catholic school and gave my mother back her documents. She scribbled on a notepad and, tearing off the sheet, handed it to my mother. This was the school we wanted, she said, and she gave my mother directions. Gazing at the name and address, my mother would not have known they belonged to a school run by the Protestant School Board of Greater Montreal. Nor would it have mattered. But, evidently, it mattered to this anonymous administrator. Even in 1968, when the French and Italians were hurling insults and folding chairs at each other in St. Léonard, there were still French schools in the city unwilling to accept the children of non-Catholic foreigners. Or was it just this particular woman? What if we'd gone on a different day and been met by someone else? And what if I had been accepted? Who would I be today? Who would my friends be?

We found the school, though my mother had to stop twice to show passersby the sheet of paper. We paused on the sidewalk and gazed up at the big brick building while frowzy boys in the schoolyard eyed us suspiciously through the chain-link fence. We stood there for a very long time. Then, taking my hand, my mother led us back the way we'd come. I was relieved. I had not liked the look of those boys or the way they'd stared at us. I assumed my mother had had similar thoughts.

But she had other things on her mind. She didn't like how far the school was from her factory. On the way there, she had spotted another school and wanted a closer look. The boys in this schoolyard were no less odious than those in the previous. Motioning to one of them, my mother pointed at the building and said, "Inglees?" The kid turned, studied the building a moment, and said, "Yeah, it's an English school. Bethlehem Elementary School."

We went inside. It made no difference to my mother that this school also turned out to be Catholic. Nor did it matter to the people who registered us that we were Greek Orthodox. My mother was relieved. She had no beef with the Catholics. Indeed she was mystified by the antipopery she encountered among some Greeks. She admitted she had no understanding of what the schism was about. She liked to say that we all worshipped the same God and observed the same commandments; everything else was politics and money. She didn't know that non-Catholic immigrant parents tended to enrol their children with the Protestant board because, notwithstanding its name, it had a secular curriculum. When she learned of this, she was even more pleased that I'd ended up in a Catholic school. Christian instruction of any sort was better than none at all. In any case, what mattered to her most was that my school was a mere six-minute walk from her factory.

Lunch break at Bethlehem was from 11:30 to 1:00, so I would usually get to the factory before my mother's started at noon. People would be hunched over their machines, eyes downcast and riveted, arms moving with rhythmic regularity and efficiency, and I would pull up a chair by her side and read or colour or play with one of the toys she kept at the factory. When the noon bell rang, the buzz and clatter would cease instantly, spines would straighten, and there would be a happy murmur of sprung voices. Some workers would disappear, going home to tend to children or down to the cafeteria, but many would return to their machines after clocking out and eat lunches there from paper bags and tin foil. If the weather was bad, I might stick around till the bell summoned everyone to work again. But most of the time, I rushed back to the schoolyard to play.

The sewing machines in the factory were laid out in facing double rows, and my mother's machine was at the end of one of these. She faced a wall with large grille windows, and on sunny days the sunlight would slant through their cross-hatched panes in dust-bright beams. In the summer heat, a panel at the centre of each window would be propped open with a metal bar. Opposite my mother worked a man she called Zazák. I was used to strange names, so I never questioned this one. Men were uncommon in this part of the factory. The sewing machines were mostly worked by women. The few men ran the big steam presses or leaned over wide wooden tables cutting fabric with giant scissors. You also saw them pushing around wheeled carts loaded with enormous spools and bolts of fabric or repairing machinery. Then there were the ones in the glassed-in offices, dressed in shirts and ties, even in the summer. This was the only part of the factory that was air conditioned.

Zazák had long dark greasy hair and a thick moustache and was always drinking tea. He kept a large white teapot by his side. To my mother's left sat a French woman whose name I don't remember. Neither she nor Zazák spoke much English, and as I knew no French, I didn't feel comfortable speaking with them. I wouldn't begin to receive French instruction until grade three. Next to the French woman sat a young Italian woman. She didn't speak much English either, but she often came over to play with me and give me chocolates and cookies, and sometimes she sat me on her lap and shared her lunch. My mother was thrilled to see me eating, it didn't matter what. The more I ate, the happier she was. I liked all the Italian women at the factory. They were warm and easy to get along with even though they didn't know much English. The Italians seemed to me like Greeks who spoke a different language. From my mother, I learned the expression "*Una fatsa, una ratsa.*" The French were hard to get close to. They had different ways and beliefs, and you couldn't be sure what they thought of you. Though Zazák and the French woman were always nice to me, I didn't trust their smiles and pleasantries. The French believed that immigrants were stealing their jobs, and they didn't like that we all spoke English. I avoided Zazák and the French woman because I didn't want them to feel obliged to speak a language they hated. I felt bad I didn't speak any French and didn't want them resenting me. I much preferred their silence to their feigned affability.

My mother's shift ended at five, but school let out at 3:45, so most afternoons I was on my own for a brief interval, which I usually spent playing with friends. My mother had gone over the dangers and proper uses of electrical outlets and appliances and cautioned that I was never to use the oven or open the door to strangers. I could let friends into the apartment but we had to confine ourselves to my room and the foyer. She'd also provided instructions on how to handle myself at school. She'd warned me of the temptations and dangers I would face, of the miscreants and ne'er-do-wells I was sure to encounter, the boys who chewed gum in class and who didn't pay attention to the teacher and who juked school and smoked cigarettes and whose main mission in life was to corrupt boys like me. She'd warned me about girls as well. If anything, they posed even greater, though hazier, perils.

But I had scant contact with girls at Bethlehem. The school was segregated, with girls occupying the opposite wing of the building. Even the schoolyard was bisected by a chain-link fence. Bethlehem was meticulously and pitilessly arranged to keep the girls apart from us, which made them all the more mysterious and alluring. What *were* these exquisite creatures in black pinafores and Mary Janes? If you put me on a spaceship and flew me across the universe, I would not encounter a sight as wondrous. One day I would marry a nice Greek girl and have my own family, but until I had completed my schooling and earned my medical degree, I was not even to think about them. I knew from the age of six that girls were *xemialístres*—de-brainers, brain removers. "*Klévoun to mialó*," my mother would say, they steal your brain. She didn't go into detail, but I had some sense of what she was talking about. Already I had fallen under their spell. Whenever they were within sight, I couldn't keep my eyes off them. At recess, on the street, in the park, everywhere, I would watch them furtively, obsessively, deliriously, taking in their lilting, ropeskipping, hopscotching, paddleballing figures and their high-pitched shrieks and laughter like a raving Odysseus tied to the mast. My mother made me vow I would keep away from girls. When I was older, in high school, she would instruct me on the sanctity of female virtue and how it must never be violated. There was no greater sin a boy could commit than to sully a girl's honour to satisfy his own base impulses. Even as an adult, I retained a notion that merely to show a woman I liked her was to dishonour her.

Another of my mentors on the subject of girls was Socrates, under whose tutelage I fell in grade one. Socrates Polychronopoulos lived a few houses over from me and was the only other Greek boy my age on the street who went to Bethlehem. He was as fascinated with girls as I was and would constantly talk about them. He was not shy. I remember one conversation in particular the summer before grade two. It was a late August evening, so the crickets would have been buzzing and the air full of the humid brown and green scents of the park. Socrates's yayá would have been in the front yard, listening to the Greek program on the radio, while the voices of the men in the park would have been wafting out of the darkness and mingling with those of the women and children on the porches and balconies behind us. Socrates and I were talking on his stairs, when, a few houses down, Anna Pantelis came out to her front yard. Anna had strict parents who never let her out on her own. She was the cutest girl on the street, and every boy had a crush on her. Socrates and I fell silent as she crossed her yard and, standing at the curb, shouted toward the park that her father had a phone call. A few seconds later, he emerged from the darkness, and as he crossed the street, Anna turned and hurried back into the house.

Socrates turned to me and made some remark. What he said, I can't recall. Nor do I recall what I said in return. All I remember is that it had something to do with Anna's dick. And this I remember only because of Socrates's reaction. Even before he could speak, I knew from the look on his face that I had committed a terrible blunder.

"Are you joking?" he said.

"About what?"

"You know girls don't have dicks."

I was too confounded to speak. Socrates threw his head back and started yelping.

"Holy Jesus," he shouted, "he thinks girls have dicks!"

"Shut up," I said, looking around.

Socrates's yayá was hard of hearing. And, in any case, she understood no English. But there were other people around who did.

"You really think girls have dicks?"

I kept quiet, knowing I had exposed myself.

Socrates leaned in and whispered, "Girls have a hole."

What could this possibly mean?

He pulled back and stared at me. "Girls have a hole," he repeated unhelpfully. "They have a hole between their legs."

"Don't scream."

"I'm not screaming. I just can't believe it. You must be the only person in the world who doesn't know this. Girls have a *cunt*. You never heard of a cunt?"

If I had, I didn't know what it meant. But I probably hadn't heard the word until that night.

"Where do you think babies come from?" Socrates asked me in what seemed a non sequitur. "How are babies made?"

I feared that if I answered I would get into bigger trouble.

"How are babies made?" he repeated.

Hesitantly, I told him what I knew. I said that when a man and a woman got married, a baby formed in the woman's stomach and nine months later a doctor cut the woman's stomach and took the baby out.

"And how does the baby get in there, in the woman's stomach?"

"They get married."

"What are you talking about? How does the baby get inside the stomach?"

I didn't know what to say. I'd never much thought about the matter. I just figured, you get married, you get a baby.

"How come *my* parents have four kids and yours have only you?" Socrates said.

I had to chew this over. Should I tell Socrates about the lost babies? He might have an explanation for that too. He seemed very knowledgeable. But I couldn't. It was my mother's secret. I would be betraying her.

"I don't know," I said. "Why?"

Socrates explained that, deep inside the hole girls had between their legs, there was an egg, and when the man stuck his dick inside the hole, cream came out of his dick and covered the egg and the egg grew into a baby, and nine months later it slid out of the hole.

It was I who shouted now. "Cream? Cream comes out of the man's dick? You're crazy!"

"You're ignorant."

"And how big is this hole? How does a baby come out of it?"

"It stretches. It's made to stretch."

"That's crazy! Who told you this?"

"Everyone knows this except you! Ask anyone!"

He seemed very sure of himself. His confidence alone was persuasive. But cream coming out of a dick struck me as fantastical a notion as a genie coming out of a lamp. And the thought that my parents would have engaged in such a depraved act was insupportable. But Socrates had older brothers. He told me the things they told him and the things he overheard them telling each other. And he had a younger sister. I couldn't bring myself to ask him if he'd seen her hole. It seemed obscene.

"You know what?" he said. "I can show you. Tomorrow. If I can find it."

"Find what?"

"I'll show you tomorrow."

"What?"

"You'll see."

I was full of anticipation. The next morning, I kept watch for Socrates, but he didn't emerge until eleven. I found him crouched in his front yard singeing ants with a magnifying glass. As soon as he saw me, he leapt to his feet and, grabbing my arm, led us into the park. Some of the other guys were watching a game at the baseball field, and he steered us toward Duluth. We pulled up behind a tree and he took something out of his pocket.

"It's naked pictures like I bet you never seen."

He unfolded a page ripped out of a magazine. "They're from Germany or somewhere." My heart was racing. The few naked pictures I'd seen were on calendars and postcards on the walls of service stations. The women in them always had on bikini bottoms or shorts or were strategically clutching a beach ball or large hat. This picture was not like those. There was something sinister and frightening about it. It was in black and white and the woman in it was gaunt and unattractive. The models in the calendars and postcards resembled the housewives in Duncan Hines commercials. This woman was angry. She lay propped on her side on a couch with her knees touching.

"I don't get it," I said after studying the photo. "I don't see anything."

Socrates turned the page over, and now the woman was standing. He stabbed a finger at the middle of the page.

"That's a cunt," he said.

I stared, transfixed. There was no hole. What there was, however, was even more disturbing and implausible: a thick triangle of dark, kinky, manly hair. While I may have been prepared to accept that girls didn't have a dick, *this* was unthinkable. It went against the laws of nature. Even a hole was easier to comprehend.

"That's *hair*," I said.

"It's a bush."

"You're telling me women have *hair* down there?"

"It's called a *bush*."

"You said there's a hole."

"It's in there. It's *inside* the bush. This isn't a good picture. I couldn't find the ones I wanted. Angelo must have hid them. He has some where the girls have their legs open and you can see it clearly, but I couldn't find them. Anyway, you can see there's no dick."

He was right about that. But now that he'd put it in my head, I needed to see this hole. I needed proof. I asked him about those other pictures.

"I don't know where they are. Maybe Angelo found out I found them and he moved them, I don't know."

In the ensuing weeks, I would keep asking Socrates about the pictures, but he couldn't find them. I needed to see this mythical hole with my own eyes. Did it even exist? Others confirmed Socrates's story, but I still couldn't believe it. What could it possibly look like? I couldn't even imagine. It became a constant preoccupation. It became like my own private Sasquatch, my Loch Ness Monster, my Moby Dick.

In grade one, Socrates and I both had Mrs. Peacock. But in our second year we were put with different teachers. Socrates got stuck with crabby Mrs. Labarre while I got Miss Hoobin. Everyone loved Miss Hoobin. She was friendly and class was fun. I had a good year, but for one incident.

One morning in early April, there was a knock on the classroom door and Miss Hoobin stepped outside. When she returned, she told us to rise and led us down to the auditorium. We were joined by the other grade two classes and were made to stand single file from tallest to shortest. I couldn't see Socrates anywhere. I was near the back of the line, but Socrates was about my height and should have been nearby. I didn't understand what was happening and hoped we were being taken on a field trip. For a long time, we stood around doing nothing. Then, hearing footsteps and voices in one of the stairwells, we all turned. To judge by the uproar, I was not the only one roused by the sight of the grade two girls streaming into the auditorium. Teachers had to go around telling boys to settle down.

In short order, the girls were also arranged in a queue beside our own and paired up with us. A small fair-skinned blonde with pigtails now hovered at the edge of my vision. I was too terrified to look at her. I stared at the boy in front of me. Meanwhile, Mr. Donnelly, the principal, had entered the auditorium and, standing way over at the front, began to address us. No doubt he was providing the explanation I'd been waiting for, but I could barely hear him, and given the state I was in, I couldn't focus anyway. I just stared at the back of the head of the boy in front of me while my brain whirred like a sewing machine. From the corner of my eye, I could see my partner crane her neck to look around the girl in front of her. Then, after a few minutes, the pairs ahead of us interlocked hands and my heart leapt. Was I supposed to take my partner's hand? I turned to her for confirmation and saw she was a knockout. Without looking at me, she presented her hand, and I resumed staring at the back of the head of the boy in front of me. Mr. Donnelly talked for another minute, and then, for the next half hour, we were led through a sequence of marching drills. I still had no idea what was going on and what all the marching was about, but I wished it would never end.

A few days later, we were taken down to the auditorium again for what Mrs. Hoobin described as "another rehearsal." Again I was paired with the pigtailed beauty, but this time no sooner had our palms joined than I felt a hard grip on my shoulder and I was yanked from the line. As I was borne toward the stairwell, I glanced up into Mr. Donnelly's vast hairy nostrils. "What did I do?" I whimpered as we went up the stairs, his hand fat and hot on my neck. I racked my brain. Had I touched my partner improperly? Had she complained? Did she know what I was thinking about? Was that possible? Could girls tell?

We went into Mr. Donnelly's office and he put me in a chair facing his desk before he sat in his own. I had never been in the principal's office before. It was vast and dark and windowless. But can this be? Surely the principal's office would have had a window. And yet I remember the room as not just sunless but almost without light entirely. I remember two large gilt-framed photographs on the wall behind Mr. Donnelly, one of the Queen, the other of the old man in the white robe and Jewish beanie. Mr. Donnelly searched through his desk drawers, and I assumed he was looking for his strap. Usually he kept it in his jacket pocket.

"What did I do?" I said again, and again he ignored me.

I searched his expression for clues to the gravity of the situation. He had a broad pink fleshy face and small pink-rimmed eyes that appeared even smaller behind the thick lenses of his square black-framed eyeglasses. On his head was a sparse thatch of pale-yellow hair through which glistened the pink of his scalp. Mr. Donnelly's main duty and pleasure were tracking down and censuring troublemakers. He stalked the corridors and lurked in corners on the lookout for schemers and recreants. He would pop into a classroom unannounced, and if he failed to spot any mischief, he would turn to the teacher with a look of disappointment and ask if there were any schemers or recreants in need of disciplining. The standard punishment was the strap, with a minimum of three lashes per hand and up to ten for grievous offences. Cono Vertucci was said to hold the record at thirteen, though it was Cono Vertucci himself who made this claim.

Mr. Donnelly gazed at some papers and then began to speak in a low monotone. After a few seconds, he glanced up at me and said, "I trust you understand."

By this point, I was barely holding back the tears.

"Alexander?"

He put down the papers in his hand and leaned in toward me.

"Do you understand what I just said?"

I hadn't even heard what he'd just said.

He straightened up. "Alexander, do you know what religion you are?"

I couldn't speak. He watched me silently a moment and handed me a couple of tissues.

"Alexander? Do you know what religion you are?"

"Greek Orthodox."

He almost seemed impressed. Or maybe he was relieved I could speak. "That's right. But as I just explained, these rehearsals are for the Catholic children. For first communion. And as you just pointed out, you're Greek Orthodox."

"My mother says they're almost the same."

Mr. Donnelly's eyebrows rose. "Your mother sounds like an enlightened woman. Still and all, these rehearsals are for the Catholic children. You may have your own first communion, I don't know, but...really, Alexander..." He handed me another tissue. "This is nothing to be upset about. It means a free period. From now on, when there are rehearsals, you'll go to Mrs. Neuheimer's class with the others. You're not alone. We have many children here who aren't Catholic."

"But I don't mind. Why can't I just do the rehearsal?"

Mr. Donnelly fell into a pensive silence. The way he gazed at me, I thought I may have persuaded him.

"Alexander, do you go to church?"

"Yes."

He seemed pleased by this. "What do you think the priest at your church would say if he knew you were rehearsing for a Catholic ceremony?"

"He doesn't have to know."

This was the first time I saw anything resembling a smile on Mr. Donnelly's face. Again I thought I might be making progress. But the next instant, he was on his feet and sternly motioning me to follow him. We walked down the corridor and entered a classroom with a dozen boys. They were seated in pairs or groups playing games. At the teacher's desk was Mrs. Neuheimer, grading workbooks. She and Mr. Donnelly spoke briefly, and then Mrs. Neuheimer introduced me to the class and told me to join whichever group I liked. I sat with Socrates and Ronnie Wu.

That evening, I told my mother about this cruel debarment and pressed for an explanation.

"The principal is right," she said.

I stamped and cried. "But all you have to do is tell him it's okay. If you tell him, he'll let me do it."

"Darling, we're Orthodox. You can't be part of a Catholic ceremony. It wouldn't be right for us or for them."

I was unyielding and demanded she write a note giving me permission. She calmly explained why she wouldn't do that. I would sulk for days.

Some weeks later, as my mother and I were walking home after church, we came upon a small crowd at Rachel. St. Urbain Street was closed to traffic and a procession of children was marching down the middle of it. We stopped with the other onlookers and watched the two columns approach, the boys dressed in navy blue suits and white shirts and bow ties, and the girls dressed like little brides. At the intersection, the procession turned east on Rachel while the onlookers, my mother included, clapped their hands. The mere sight of so many children lifted my mother's heart. She didn't know who they were, and I didn't tell her. I slunk back so they wouldn't see me. I had difficulty spotting my erstwhile partner, as I had only seen her those two times in her pigtails and now her hair was gathered up and crowned by a white tiara. She looked majestic. Next to her was a swaggering Serafino Bastone, who had been behind me in the rehearsal. At least they weren't holding hands. Everyone had their palms pressed together in a posture of prayer. But this was slight consolation.

The last day of school ended with fireworks. How better to start the summer? But the fireworks were not about school. They were in celebration of St. Jean Baptiste, and were launched from the field by the stone perimeter wall of the Hôtel Dieu hospital, which formed Esplanade's southern terminus. Some kids called it the Berlin Wall. I seem to recall that most Greeks on the street lived north of Rachel, away from the wall, but why would this be? Can I trust my memory? Toward the wall there were mostly Frenchies and Anglos, along with a couple of Black families, who to us were just Anglos of a different complexion. Most of my friends lived north of the Armoury. Below it, the street took on a scruffier, less welcoming feel. The people seemed rougher, less sociable, surly. Beyond the wall was downtown, still largely unknown—and, in my mind, mythic—territory.

The eve of St. Jean Baptiste, the park filled up early. People climbed into the trees and onto the backs of the lions to secure a clear view. Watching from our balcony, I felt the whole city was converging on us. Fleur-de-lys flags waved above the crowd or were worn as capes, and now and then people burst into song. The songs were in French and made the rest of us nervous. For us, the night's festivities were not about sovereignty or nationhood; they were about summer, sunshine, and freedom.

And what summers they were, those lush lavish amber summers of my boyhood. How they stretched on and on. How they glowed. I have not seen sunlight like that since. I catch glimpses of it now and then, but they're fleeting, illusory, wishful, mere echoes. I will never know such happiness again. Back then, we spun happiness out of nothing.

Weekdays I was usually on my own. My father was at the restaurant, and my mother never got home before 5:30. By the time I was eight or nine, she had sufficient confidence to let me feed myself at lunchtime, and I no longer had to go to the factory. Those rare occasions my father was home, he might prepare something for the two of us, but usually I would heat up the previous night's leftovers or make myself a sandwich and a can of soup. Still, it wasn't as though I was entirely unsupervised. Most households had older kids or grandparents or stay-at-home mothers with preschoolers or layabout uncles and aunts and other relatives who for one reason or another did not have jobs, not to mention the parents who worked nights, so there were always adults around. There were always eyes watching from the front yards and balconies and park benches, always someone around to feed you or bandage you if you fell or give you a scolding if you misbehaved.

Every morning, the first thing I did was go to my window to check on the weather and see if anyone was out. A few kids on the street had cable and they wouldn't emerge until after lunch, when the soap operas began. Even on nice days, they would spend the morning inside watching American game shows and sitcom reruns, which they would afterward talk about among themselves, partly to let the rest of us know what we were missing. Those of us without cable had four local stations to choose from, only two of which were English, and whose morning programming was aimed at housewives and preschoolers. Usually Socrates and I were the first kids out, and until the others showed up, we'd pass the time playing cowboys on our bikes, kicking or throwing a ball around, catching flies and grasshoppers, zapping ants with our magnifying glasses, practicing with our slingshots, watching the tennis players, horsing around in the playground, or reading comics. Socrates liked to hunt bees, catching them in a glass jar with a lid he'd pocked full of holes. I was afraid of bees and would watch from a distance. When it rained, we would put on our raincoats and race popsicle sticks on the ribbed currents of the gutters.

As a kid, I heard a lot of talk about the *katokhí*. "How I would have loved to see you in the katokhí," my father liked to say whenever I behaved in a manner he regarded as pampered or privileged. If I whined about the beets or fish or boiled weeds my mother had made for dinner, he would tell me about the nights during the katokhí he'd gone to bed hungry. Bobbling his head, he would say, "If this was forty-one, you'd be licking the plate and asking for seconds." "But this isn't forty-one," I would, predictably, retort. "There's other stuff I can eat." But my parents had strict rules about food, and I had to eat whatever my mother cooked, whether I liked it or not. If Anglo kids were lectured about starving children in India and Africa, I had to hear about the katokhí and forty-one. We all knew this number. You heard no number more often. It was like a talisman, invoked by Greek parents when they wished to point out to their children how good they had it. But what did we know about forty-one? I didn't even know what the word katokhí meant exactly. I understood it to mean something like hunger or suffering. It wasn't until my late teens that I realized it was the word for *occupation*. And it wasn't until even later that I would learn about the famine of forty-one. At the time, this was no more than a number to me. What could I know about occupation and famine, of privation and loss? What could a coddled, contented, well-fed Canadian boy understand about such things as war and want and the fickleness of fortune?

In the twentieth century, 1974 hardly ranks with 1914 or 1939, or even 1989. Ask people what they know or remember of it and they'll mention Watergate, the oil crisis, maybe Patty Hearst or Ted Bundy. Yet 1974, in its own way, was a momentous year, a year of milestones. There was Willy Brandt, Golda Meir, Juan Peron, and Haile Selassie; there was Portugal, Angola, and Malta; and of course there was Greece and Cyprus. Most of all, there was Greece and Cyprus.

But that's not what I remember of 1974. What I remember is the end of summer, a hot, cloudless, radiant afternoon in August. Socrates and I are watching a Sun Youth little league game in the bleachers. It's in the late innings and the Mets have just retired the Dodgers when we catch sight of three figures running at top speed above the soccer field.

We leap off our seats and run to meet them. Yanni Economides sees us from his balcony and disappears into his house. Seconds later he's racing down his front stairs. Leading the trio of runners is Mike Maheras—aka, the Knife—and, even before he can catch his breath, we know we're in for something big.

"You're not gonna believe it," he says as Victor Kowalchuk slows to a stop behind him and doubles over. Earlier in the day, a few of us wanted to set up a baseball game for the afternoon, but Mike and Victor announced they were climbing the mountain. They urged the rest of us to join them, but this is essentially a taunt. Climbing Mount Royal is for the most brazen, and that afternoon only Billy Stavropoulos took up the gauntlet. Like many of my friends, I'm forbidden to climb the mountain. I can roam the park free as Adam, but I'm not allowed to go further than the lions. Some of my friends aren't even allowed to go into the tunnels below Park Avenue, which are reputed to be a haunt for pushers and muggers. I avoid the tunnels because they give me the creeps, always crossing Park Avenue at Mount Royal. The kids who climb the mountain and who go into the tunnels are the bold and rebellious ones, the bad kids who won't listen or whose parents aren't strict. Periodically, these firebrands will get together and bait the rest of us, taunting and cajoling us to climb up to Beaver Lake or the cemetery with them and knowing full well we won't. Then, on their return, they'll recount their adventures, describing in hair-raising detail how they'd spent the day hacking through jungle growth, scaling towering cliffs, leaping over depthless gorges, and scraping through one near-death experience after another. On this particular afternoon, however, we hear a tale like none before. There are gasps, there are wails of disbelief.

"I swear, I swear!" Victor replies.

"Swear to God!" says Mike.

"We all saw, we all saw!" pipes in Billy.

"But couldn't they see you?" asks Socrates.

"He just told you. We were hidden behind the bushes."

Yanni shakes his head.

"What?" Mike says to him.

"I don't believe it," answers Yanni.

"We all saw!"

"It's true, it's true! I swear to you!"

What Mike, Victor, and Billy say they saw was a guy and girl screwing.

They caught sight of them in the scrub just minutes earlier, on their way down.

"Bullshit!" says Yanni. I wonder at his assurance, though I do want him to be right.

"I'm telling you," Victor says.

"I swear on my mother's life," says Billy.

This silences us. One doesn't swear on one's mother's life casually. That's one way to catch someone out: "Swear on your mother's life," you say, and if he won't, you've nabbed him. There are reckless and shameless types who'll swear on their mother's lives even when they're lying, but Billy's not one of them.

"I don't believe it," Yanni says.

"So don't," says the Knife, pulling out his black three-diamond yo-yo.

"We could see her tits," Billy says.

"No way!"

"I'm telling you."

"Did you see her hole?"

"The guy was on top of her," says the Knife, throwing a sleeper. "But she had her shirt off."

"How old were they?"

"I don't know. Old. Twenty, thirty."

"You shoulda seen, man," Billy says, cupping his hands at his chest.

"How could you tell, if the guy was on top of her?" asks Yanni.

"You could see."

"You're full of shit," Yanni says, turning away. "I don't believe it."

"So don't," Mike shouts. "It's a free country." He throws a hard sleeper, rocks the cradle. We follow behind Yanni toward Esplanade.

"We're gonna go back tomorrow," Billy says. "You should come and see for yourselves."

"Right, like they're gonna be there again tomorrow," I say.

"You never know," Victor replies. "Maybe that's where they have to go to do it."

"When you going, what time?" Socrates asks.

We divide around some girls playing hopscotch.

"Same time," Victor says. "Right after lunch."

In bed that night I can't stop thinking about what Mike and the others described. I arrange it a hundred different ways in my head. Already I have discovered the palliative affordances of my anatomy, and I manage to calm myself sufficiently to sleep. But the images are back in my head as soon as I wake up in the morning.

When I get out of bed, I go to the window. I spot Socrates under a tree and quickly get dressed and run downstairs. He's lying on his stomach, reading a comic. I sit beside him and grab the comic book. It's a black-and-white Green Lantern pocket digest I've already borrowed.

"Are you going?" he asks as he sits up.

I toss the digest onto his lap. "Are you?"

"I think I'm gonna go," he says in a tone suggesting long deliberation.

"Are you serious?"

"Yeah, why not? You should come."

I feel betrayed somehow.

"What are you worried about?" says Socrates. "Your parents?"

I shrug, pull up a clump of grass.

"How they gonna know?"

But it's not just my parents. I'm small and light for my age. I'm not strong or athletic, and given all I've heard about these climbs, I don't think I'm up to it. But I can't tell Socrates this.

"What if those people are there again?" he says.

"Don't be an immigrant."

"You never know."

"What are the chances?"

"I don't know. I wanna go anyway. I never been, man. Don't you just wanna *go*?"

We walk to his place and he drops off the comic. He comes back out with his mother's double-sided makeup mirror, and we bedevil dogs and squirrels with deflected sunbeams. When Petro Marinos and Billy show up, we head to the playground and horse around there while talking more about yesterday's incident. At noon we break up, and I go home and put leftover lamb chops in the electric broiler. There's a serving of boiled dandelion greens in the fridge. My mother says throwing out food is a sin, and when fruit or bread or yogurt go bad, she removes the mouldy parts and eats what remains. But I can't stand *hórta* and we've had them three days in a row. I flush them down the toilet. It's like drowning a litter of kittens.

I pray God will let this one go. I take the chops from the broiler, cut the meat into small pieces, and lay them out on a slice of packaged bread, adding mustard and two Kraft singles. I go to the living room and eat cross-legged on the floor in front of *The Flintstones*.

When the show ends, I go out to the balcony and see some of the guys huddled across the street. There's Billy, Socrates, Petro, Tony Cabral, Dennis Leacock, and Jimmy Kavalas. Word is out. By the time I've put on my running shoes and raced outside, they're already up by the soccer field. As I cross Esplanade, Yanni comes up behind me.

"Don't tell me you're going with them," he says.

I quicken my pace. "What's it to you?" The truth is I still haven't made up my mind.

At Park Avenue, Mike stops near the tunnel's entrance and, seeing Yanni and me, gives a look of surprise. "What are you doing here, *kourátha?*" he says to Yanni.

Yanni's parents are among the strictest on the street. He doesn't have it as bad as Anna Pantelis, but of the boys he's the most fettered. His mother doesn't work and keeps a jailer's eye on him. Until he was seven, he couldn't leave the house on his own, and he would watch all the other kids on the street and in the park from his balcony. Kids mocked him. Once he took out his dick and pissed on Nick Tsoukalas's head. Even now he can't stray beyond the reach of his mother's voice, and as we stand around the mouth of the tunnel, he keeps glancing back across the park.

"Go home to your mother," Mike says to him.

"Fuck you!" Yanni snaps, but Mike has disappeared down the tunnel.

I follow behind the rest, Socrates two steps ahead of me. I take guarded breaths, testing the odours. I hold the banister and stare at the ground, concerned as much about rats and dogshit as about muggers and perverts. The air is cool and dank but so far inoffensive. Caged bulbs on the walls emit a weak yellow light. The voices and footsteps of the others echo around me. As I reach the bottom of the stairs, everyone breaks into a run, hooting and shrieking. I chase after them, legs and arms pumping. I visualize the cars racing above us. What if there were an earthquake? I bound up the stairs at the other end, surfacing into sunlight with a surge of exaltation. Yanni is still on the other side, gazing across traffic at us. Mike and Victor give him the finger. He returns the gesture, with sauce on top. The others cluck loudly and strut about with their hands in their armpits and arms flapping. Yanni shouts out something that disperses in the traffic. He turns and vanishes below the embankment.

"Fucken immigrant," Victor says.

"You think he's gonna tell his mother?" asks Socrates.

"He wouldn't do that," says the Knife. "He knows he'll get a fucken beating if he does."

We turn and go past the lions. On one of the benches, an old man drinks from a brown paper bag. Sun worshippers are scattered on the grass like corpses. Near the gazebo, a hippie couple are having difficulty getting a kite airborne. Behind them, the downtown skyscrapers. Up ahead, trees. Above everything, the sky. The mountain is gone, invisible behind the trees. As we keep going, the trees crowd around us, the sunlight breaking into shards. The air is moist and fragrant, the traffic noise softens. We walk along a narrow gravel path, Socrates and I bringing up the rear. From somewhere comes a distinctive smell, which I have not yet learned to identify as marijuana. In the distance a couple of hippie girls sit on a blanket. Behind them, a girl sits alone under a tree, reading a book. The path is lined with high green stalks clustered with spiky burrs. Among them hover squadrons of bees. Dennis snaps off some burrs and the rest of us run and duck as he hurls them at us.

We come to the wide gravel path that snakes up to Beaver Lake. This is the easy way up, the route most people take. We wait for some joggers to go by and we cut across the path. We're going up the hard way, pushing deeper into arboreal darkness. The terrain becomes rougher, the grass and weeds thin out. The soil is dark and sticky, covered with sodden leaves. The air is thick with birdsong, the hum of traffic receding. There's a rustling and crackling overhead. Something snaps and from the corner of my eye I see movement. I look but there's nothing. A moment later, I catch sight of a striped creature, something like a squirrel. It wriggles under a fallen trunk. I gaze up at the scraps of sky visible through the leaves and branches. I find it reassuring and keep looking up periodically.

We tramp on and the grade steepens. Up ahead there's a layered rock shelf. Mike crouches and signals to us commando style. We halt and crouch behind him. He waves us over, motioning for us to keep low. He puts a finger over his lips and points at the rock shelf.

"It's all Germans behind there," he whispers loudly.

We look.

"Our mission is to take that hill."

"We'll spread out and circle around them," Petro says.

"Hold on," Victor says, "I'm the Sergeant."

"Says who?"

"I'm the Captain," says Petro.

"I'm the General," says Victor.

"Shut up," Mike says. "The Germans will hear us. *I'm* the General. Victor's the Sergeant."

"I said General first," Petro says.

Victor pushes Petro over and they wrestle in the dirt.

"Stop or you're both court-martialled," Mike says.

Petro gets up and slaps the dirt off his shorts.

"Get down," Mike orders.

Petro remains standing, brushing his shorts. "I thought we were here to see people screwing."

"Shut up and get down," Mike says. "First we gotta take that hill."

Without warning, Jimmy Kavalas breaks into a run. With both hands cocked, one behind the other, and arms shaking, he machineguns noisily.

"Hit the dirt!" Dennis shouts and rolls toward a tree. "They've seen us."

We all pull out our automatics and, spitting and spluttering, scurry from tree to tree. Down on his stomach, Mike elbow-crawls through the dirt. Raising a fist to his mouth, then jerking it away, he hurls a grenade over the rock shelf. A few seconds later, he sounds the explosion. "Chaaaaaaaaaaarge," Victor screams and we rush forward, guns blazing.

A few feet in front of me, Billy stops, clutches his chest. "I been hit!" He falls to the ground. He moans and writhes in the dirt. "I been hit bad. Get the medic."

Dennis drops to one knee beside him. "General," he shouts, "we got a man down."

"Fuck him," Mike shouts back. "We gotta keep moving."

Dennis rises and chases after the others. Billy jumps up and rushes after him. I follow behind Billy, swerving right, where the grade is less steep. As I gain the elevation, the others crouch behind trees. Every few seconds they wheel out and fire their guns. To my left, Billy runs toward a tree, then abruptly stops. Calmly he walks toward a clearing, indifferent to the bullets whizzing around him. "Hey, isn't that it?"

"What?"

"Where we saw them yesterday."

Abandoning their redoubts, everyone gathers around Billy.

"Not there, stupid," says Mike. "You can see the path. It was further up," he says, pointing. He heads off. The rest of us follow. I'm amazed by the Knife's ability to read the terrain. I have no idea where we are, where we're headed. The mountain has become immeasurably huge, shapeless, boundless. I am relieved when the winding path at last reappears, even moreso when we turn onto it. Secretly I pray we'll stay on it.

But then, in the distance, we see a group of guys coming our way. There are four of them. We can hear them speaking French. One of them has a pack of cigarettes inside the sleeve of his T-shirt. They're a little older and bigger than us and they eye us toughly. The Knife stares back. But we pass without incident. My heart pounding, I glance back and see one of them looking at us. He flashes me the finger and I turn forward.

Where the path curves, Mike veers into the woods. "It was up here," he says. We follow. I pause at the margin and peer through the shrubs and trees. The ground is rough and steep.

"Socrates," I call out.

He turns around.

"I don't wanna go," I say quietly.

He urges me on with a wave.

"Let's go back," I say.

He glances ahead. Mike turns and sees us. "Get a move on," he shouts.

"Come on," says Socrates.

"I'm going back."

"Why?"

"I don't wanna go."

"What if they're there again?"

"Don't be stupid."

"But what if they *are*?"

"I don't care. I'm going back."

Socrates turns and runs to catch up with the others. The climb looks terrifying. It's impossible to tell where it leads.

I turn around and stay on the winding path, praying it will take me back to the lions. Coming around a bend I spot the Frenchies up ahead. They're standing around, smoking cigarettes. I duck behind a tree. I hear footsteps and voices. I lope slowly toward the woods, taking long, light strides. I hear something behind me and break into a run. Suddenly the ground is muddy and bumpy with rocks and roots. Behind me there's a rustling, and glancing back I see a movement. "Please God," I gasp as I try to gain speed, "I promise I'll never do this again." On a sudden dip, I fall. But I'm back on my feet instantly. My knees and right hand sting. I glance down to see my hand is scraped, but I feel the Frenchies bearing down on me and I keep running. Coming into a clearing, I turn around and see no one. I slow to a stop. I'm winded but I try to restrain my breathing so I can hear. I hear birds, the rustle of leaves, the comforting sound of traffic. I look about in all directions and examine my limbs. There's blood on my hand. I rub at it and suck on the wound as I resume my descent.

I can see the street. What joy! The sun is hot on the back of my neck. I go past the monument, heading north, and walk down to Mount Royal. I cross at the traffic light and make a diagonal across the softball field. In the distance, Nick Tsoukalas and Lambros Arvanitis are tossing a baseball. As I near Esplanade, a reedy voice calls out my name. Maria Sevapsidis is waving at me from the other side of the street.

"Your mother wants you," she shouts.

"What?"

"Your mother was looking for you. You have to go home right away."

I don't understand. My mother is at work. Nick and Lambros are running toward me. "What happened? Where's everyone?"

"Where did you see my mother?" I ask Maria.

"She's at your house. She was calling you."

My heart is racing again. This makes no sense.

"What happened?" Lambros asks. "Where are the others?"

"They're still on the mountain," I say as I run across Esplanade. "I have to go."

Yanni is on his balcony, smirking malevolently. "Your mother wants you," he shouts.

Is this a prank? Does Yanni have something to do with it? "You're full of shit," I yell at him.

"I swear," he says, his tone suddenly serious. "She's been calling you for twenty minutes."

I bound up my stairs and reach for the key on the string under my T-shirt.

"Did you see them?" Yanni shouts.

I unlock the door and go in.

"Where's everyone?" Yanni yells as I shut the door.

I stand at the bottom of the stairwell, listening. I climb the stairs softly. My mother's black flat-heeled shoes are on the top step, the ones she wears to work. I stand in the foyer motionless. There are sounds in my parents' bedroom. What does this mean? Did Yanni squeal? But how did word get to my mother?

I creep toward the bedroom, wiping my hand on my shorts. I stop a couple of feet from the doorway and listen. There are hurried movements back and forth. I inch closer and hover at the doorway, arrested not so much by what I see as by the sheer inscrutability of it. The room is in a strange, heart-sickening disarray. Drawers are sticking out, their contents disinterred and piled on the bed and chairs. The closet door stands agape. My mother is bent over a large suitcase spread open on the bed. She is so absorbed in what she's doing, she doesn't notice me. There's a frantic, haunted look in her eyes as she arranges the clothes in the suitcase. A white blouse lies in tatters on the floor. I can't make sense of any of it. All I know is I'm in deep trouble. The enormity of my defiance and degeneracy is greater than I'd imagined. I don't know what the scene before me means or portends, but as I take in the disorder and the horrible stricken look on my mother's face, I keep thinking, *Oh my God, what have I done, what have I done...?*

4

On my desk there's a colour photograph of my parents in a neighbour's backyard. My father squats on a low stack of cinderblocks, behind him, a grey weathered plank fence. It's Easter Sunday and he's turning a spit, the spinning lamb a brown blur. He's staring at the camera, a wry smirk on his face. He has on grey dress pants and a blue shirt, the sleeves rolled up. In his free hand there's a cigarette. Behind him my mother, arms folded at her stomach, is staring grimly at the back of his head. She has on a green floral dress, red open-toed slippers, dark socks. In my eyes, this photograph captures their marriage.

But I wonder what other people would see, people who didn't know my parents. Would they even guess the two figures in it were husband and wife? Can one be sure that it's really a mix of arrogance and preening licentiousness we see in the man's face? Smouldering rage and resentment in the woman's? What if the viewer were told that the woman was about to sneeze, or that the man had delivered the punchline to an off-colour joke? Would that change what we saw? Or what if the photo had been snapped three seconds later? Would we see the same things in it?

I have two other pictures of my parents together, taken by my aunt Voula at my father's restaurant. They're side by side at a table crowded with bottles, glasses, and dishes. In one, my father stares glumly at an empty beer glass while my mother regards him with naked hostility. In the other, his arm is around her and the two gaze into each other's eyes with smiles radiating love and mutual delight. The two pictures were taken seconds apart.

I didn't see my father much when I was growing up. He was always at the restaurant and didn't return most nights until after I'd been put to bed. The rare evening he was home, he would sit on the couch and read his papers, watch TV, and listen to the Greek programs on the radio. In the nice weather, he would sit with the men in the park. On warm summer nights, they collected around the benches and picnic tables and talked and argued into the late hours. They came from all over the neighbourhood, from as far as Durocher and Drolet and St. Viateur and further still. When my father was with them, I would sometimes sit with him after all the other kids had been summoned home. My mother didn't like my staying out so late, but he overruled her on this. I imagine he thought it a kind of education.

The men came from all parts of Greece and spoke with different accents and dialects. They would reminisce about their hometowns and villages, their recollections filled with strange sensuous details—the smell of the sea or mountain thyme, the taste of well water or freshly picked figs—that I found impossible to imagine. I had never seen a fresh fig and had been given to understand that the packaged kind from the grocery store (which I didn't like) bore no resemblance to the real thing. I gathered that much of the world I lived in had this second-rate or ersatz quality. Yet the world the men spoke of was abstract and unintelligible to me. Even the words they used were often unintelligible, though they still managed to evoke, by their obscurity and meaninglessness, wondrous and inconceivable landscapes. Frequently, the men would invoke the names of Socrates, Homer, Aristotle, Hippocrates, and such, and they would quote proverbs and sayings in the ancient tongue. Once, during a discussion about Praxiteles, Mr. Maheras pointed at the statues across the street and said, "Look, from us they took those, the thieves. They have no culture of their own, so they steal ours." I wasn't sure what he was pointing at or what had been stolen.

I often heard about how great we Greeks were and from an early age developed a skeptical attitude toward such claims. I saw little evidence of it. While I accepted that we'd given the world philosophy, medicine, democracy, and so on, it didn't look like we'd done much since. On TV and radio we had almost no presence. Meanwhile, the Italians, whom I considered the group closest to us (*una facia, una razza*) were everywhere. They were in movies, TV shows, sports, music. They had Frank Sinatra, Dean Martin, Sophia Loren, Gina Lollobrigida, Rocky Marciano, Phil and Tony Esposito, the Fonz, and on and on, while we had Nana Mouskouri and the two Aristotles (Onassis and Savalas). My father was one of the most vociferous champions of his homeland's achievements and beauties. He mentioned and quoted our ancient forbears more than anyone and believed that anything of importance, whether material or conceptual, could be traced back to them. At the same time, he railed constantly about Greece's barbarism, denouncing it as a primitive backwater, a cesspool of corruption, avarice, and mendacity beyond redemption. He had even vowed he would never step foot in the country again. I gathered this had to do with Greece's recent history, a subject I found impenetrable. The men talked about it constantly, with certain names coming up again and again—Veloukhiotis, Zervas, Papagos, Tsaldaris, Tsortsil. I had a hard time keeping track of who was who and what they'd done and telling the good guys from the bad guys. The men themselves were unable to agree on these things. One day you'd hear someone praising some politician or military leader for his courage and patriotism and the next he'd be denouncing the same person as a coward and traitor. It was all very confusing.

One thing the men agreed on was the Junta. Even here, though, there were rumours of closet sympathizers, not to mention such oddities as Kostas Kalamakis and Miltiades Gekas, who, open in their support of the colonels, were ostracized by most of the other Greeks on the street. The men my father hung out with believed the Americans had put the regime in power. They referred constantly to *skotinés sinomosíes* and *ta symféron* (dark conspiracies and vested interests), and, listening to them, you would think nothing happened in Greece—or anywhere in the world—that wasn't the CIA's doing. It had its hand in everything. Listening to these conversations, you came away with a sense that the world was a treacherous and illusory place and that behind the placid everyday world of school, work, family, and friends lay another, hidden realm, a region of shadowy schemes and intrigues where the important decisions were made and to which only a privileged few had access. My father liked to say there were no more than a dozen men in the world who knew why events unfolded as they did, though to hear him pronounce on these events, you'd think he was one of them. He was up on everything, everywhere. He followed the news obsessively and would read whatever Greek papers he could get his hands on, regardless of their leanings. He would even browse the English papers, though he couldn't read the articles. Now and then, he would ask me to translate.

Those evenings he was home, he watched both the six o'clock and eleven o'clock newscast. For dinner, my mother knew not to set the table until the weather came on. From an early age, I would join my father for the six o'clock news. I would sit beside him on the couch, gazing at the bleak black-and-white images on the screen in rapt incomprehension. Much of the time, he would mutter to himself, and intermittently he would shout at the TV. Certain faces set him off on sight, and he would flash his palm at the screen and shout *Liar! Swindler! Hypocrite! Thief!*, or *Na, maláka! Na, pousti!* My mother would shout back from the kitchen, "Please, Andrea! Not in front of the child!" "The child needs to learn," he would say. "He needs to know what a dirty, crooked place the world is." "At seven he needs to know?" my mother would reply.

Increasingly I was called upon to act as interpreter, and by time I was nine or ten I could cobble together something halfway coherent and credible, even if I barely understood what I was saying. Sometimes my father feigned incomprehension only to test me. Occasionally he was overt about it. "Who is that?" he might ask, pointing at Anwar Sadat's face behind the anchorman. "And what continent is Egypt on?" he might continue. "And what is its capital?" "And who is the Prime Minster of Egypt?" "And what is the difference between a President and a Prime Minister?" Often he would ask me a question I couldn't answer, and I never knew how he might respond. One of his more common reactions was to shake his head pityingly and say, "What do they teach you in these Canadian schools? Why are we even bothering? We should send you to the factory right now." But he could be harsher.

One evening, when I was seven or eight, I was so stirred by a story that, without any prompting, I reported breathlessly that somewhere in one of those remote and horrible parts of the world where the bizarre and abominable were commonplace, gorillas had broken loose and killed several townspeople. My father, seated as always beside me, turned a look upon me that made me want to say, *Yeah, I know! Can you believe it?* The truth, though, was that I had no trouble at all believing such a story. I had no trouble accommodating the inexplicable and believing the unbelievable. The distinction between the bizarre and the normal was yet unclear. The news had taught me that the world was a more varied, unpredictable, and mysterious place than one could ever imagine, and that there were parts of it where the extraordinary and grotesque were routine. That apes might run amok and kill townspeople struck me as no more unusual than many other stories I saw on the news.

My father, though, upon receiving this bulletin, promptly slapped the back of my head. "What gorillas, you idiot?" he said. "Don't talk nonsense!"

I turned away so he wouldn't see the tears. What I'd thought was a look of astonishment and incredulity was in reality contempt and disgust. But why take it out on me? I was only repeating what the man on the TV had said. I was just translating. If there were parts of the world where gorillas ran loose killing people, what fault was that of mine?

My father's disapproval was unbearable to me, and following such incidents, I would retreat to my room, seeking answers and armature among my encyclopedias and desktop globe. What would have become of me without these aids? How benighted might I have remained, had the providential wayfarer bearing these wares not rung our bell on one of the rare evenings my father was home? It is a certainty my mother would have sent him packing. Seeing a man in a trench coat and fedora holding an enormous briefcase, she wouldn't have even opened the door. But my father, my curious father, needed at least to know the stranger's business. And then, hearing the word "encyclopedia," he needed to know more. "What kind encyclopedia?" he asked.

Five minutes later, the stranger was laying out his brochures and samples on the coffee table, while my mother was dispatched to the kitchen for refreshments. My father poured out glasses of ouzo (with a few drops for me) and taught our guest how to toast in Greek. He proved a genial and chatty fellow, and my father liked him. He knew a lot about the Greeks and even knew some words, which delighted my father. With his limited English, he instructed our guest on the etymology of *encyclopedia* and *pedagogy*, along with *pediatrics*, *cyclical*, and *cyclops*. Over the course of the evening, the two men would discuss the origins of the alphabet, the genealogy of Christopher Columbus, the influence of ancient Athens on American democracy, and a great many things besides, and it wouldn't be until long after I'd been put to bed that our guest, loaded up on cookies, nuts, *kourabiéthes*, *melomakárouna*, and quantities of ouzo and whisky, would shamble down our stairs carrying in his enormous briefcase a signed order for not only the standard twenty-volume encyclopedia but also the five-volume children's set, the ten-volume encyclopedia of science and technology, and the two-volume dictionary. The desktop globe, he threw in as a gift.

I still sometimes wonder how my life might have turned out had that salesman never come into our home. How many more humiliations and slaps to the head would I have received? How would I have learned about the continents and capital cities of the world, or of the difference between a president and a prime minister, or between a *gorilla* and a *guerrilla*?

But even these resources could only take me so far. The range of what I didn't know was vast. Worse still was what I thought I knew but knew only partially. Long before Donald Rumsfeld came along, I knew about "unknown unknowns," having been instructed in the varieties and perils of these by, among others, my grade five teacher Miss Quigg.

Several times a week, Miss Quigg would declaim a word from our speller and ask a student to spell out and use the word in a sentence. One morning, she called my name and assigned me the word *communist*. (This may strike some as an odd choice for a grade five speller, but the year, recall, was 1973.) I had no difficulty spelling it or thinking up a sentence, though the moment I was done, I sensed impending disaster in the look on Miss Quigg's face.

"Pardon me?" she said, bending her head and peering at me under knit brows.

I scrambled for a revision that might persuade her she'd misheard. But I couldn't think of anything. I repeated what I'd said at a lower volume. "Jesus was the first communist," I murmured, this time giving the sentence a vaguely interrogative inflection.

For several seconds, Miss Quigg appeared to lose the capacity for speech.

"Wherever in the world did that come from?" she said at last.

I wasn't sure I understood the question.

"Alexander, I'm speaking to you. Where did that sentence come from?"

"I heard it on TV."

"On TV?"

"Yes, Miss."

"Heavens. What kind of person would say such a thing on TV?"

I assumed the question to be rhetorical.

"Alexander?"

"Yes, Miss?"

"Who was it who said that on TV?"

"I don't know, Miss."

"What was the program?"

"I don't remember. It was a long time ago."

"A long time ago? And yet you remember the remark. You don't remember the program, you don't remember who said it, but you remember the remark. It seems to have made quite an impression on you." Miss Quigg's eyes dilated. "Tell me, Alexander...do you understand what you just said? Do you understand its meaning?"

I shook my head.

"Sorry?" said Miss Quigg.

"I don't know."

"You don't know? You don't know whether you understand, or you don't know the meaning of what you said?"

I wasn't sure I understood the distinction. My head was swimming. "I don't know," I repeated desperately.

"You don't know. And yet you went ahead and repeated the remark. Do you know what we call people like that?"

I had no idea.

"You understand, Alexander, that the point of this exercise is to demonstrate knowledge of the words in our reader, not merely that we know how to pronounce them. Do you know what happens, Alexander, if you go around mindlessly mouthing words you don't understand?"

I had never considered the question.

"That way tyranny lies," said Miss Quigg and fixed me with a look as if challenging me to contradict her.

"You know, Alexander...I should send you down to the principal for this."

"Oh no, Miss, please.

"Oh yes."

"No, Miss, please, I didn't mean anything."

"Didn't *mean* anything? But that is precisely my point, Alexander. The words we use, the words we utter in public, have *meaning*. Whether we ourselves know what it is or not. This is the problem with the world today, isn't it? The words you just uttered *mean* something. They have meaning and consequences. That's what I'm trying to get through to you. What you just said, young man, is what is known as *blasphemy*. Do you know what blasphemy is?"

"Yes, Miss."

"And do you know what happens to blasphemers?"

I remained silent. I didn't want to put any ideas in Miss Quigg's head.

"Alexander, do you know what happens to blasphemers?"

"They go to the principal's office?"

"No!" Miss Quigg thundered. "They go to hell! Forget the principal's office. They go *straight to hell*."

Until now I'd been managing to hold back the tears. "I'm sorry, Miss. I won't say it again, I promise."

"Say what?"

"I'll never say that sentence again."

"Say it? Young man, you must not even think it!"

"Yes, Miss."

"I cannot imagine what TV shows you are watching, or where your parents are. Is there no one at home monitoring your activities?" She shook her head. "And who would say such a thing on TV? For the life of me I cannot imagine what sort of person would make such a pronouncement."

The person, of course, was my father. I'd heard him make the pronouncement many times in the park. Though most of the men appeared to be religious, some were critics of the Church, the fiercest of these being my father, who would denounce the clerisy for bowing to dictators and plutocrats and putting the interests of the privileged above those of the masses. "And what was Jesus?" he liked to say. "Was he a friend of the rich and powerful? Do our clerics even understand the words they dribble through their beards? Read the New Testament. Before the *Communist Manifesto*, there were the gospels. Do our clerics believe that if Jesus came back today, he would be a champion of capitalism? Do they even understand Jesus's model of a Christian society? Jesus was a communist. He was the first communist."

I wasn't sure what exactly a communist was or how I was supposed to feel about them. At school and on TV we learned they were bad. You got the impression communism was a kind of crime or scourge or illness. But my father and some of the men in the park spoke favourably of it. Some even called themselves communists. My father was not so clear about this. He was slippery on the subject. One day after my run-in with Miss Quigg, I asked him outright: "Are you a communist?"

He gave me a look of annoyance. "Of course not. God forfend."

"But *papoú* was a communist."

"What? Who told you that?"

"You said he fought with the communists in the war."

"He fought against the fascists and royalists. Your grandfather fought for freedom and democracy and justice. He fought for *Greece*."

"But Jesus was a communist?"

This gave him pause. "That's true. Jesus is the only true communist who's ever lived. Because communism can only exist in heaven. On earth it turns to hell. I'm a democrat, like your grandfather. I believe all people are equal and no one should be abused or exploited for the benefit of others. But I also believe in freedom, and I believe you can only have both under socialism. I'm no communist."

To some degree, this was reassuring, but it was also confusing given my father's behaviour the previous summer. That September, only a few months earlier, Canada's best hockey players had battled the Soviet national team in what has since come to be known as "the Summit Series." One of the more benign proxy wars of the Cold War era, it was a huge deal in Canada. Even my father and the men in the park got caught up in the excitement. In the weeks leading up to the series, they could hardly talk of anything else. It was odd to see these middle-aged immigrant men so animated about hockey. Odder still, a good portion of them sided with the Russians. Among these was my father. He'd never shown the slightest interest in hockey, but that September he borrowed a portable TV to install at the Galaxy so he and my uncle could watch the series at work. My father didn't know the first thing about hockey and when we watched the games at home, he was constantly asking me to explain things to him. At the same time, he delivered his own running commentary, honing in on the grace and virtuosity of the Soviet players and the brutishness and dirty tricks of the Canadians. He would rail at the referees, who consistently failed to call out Team Canada for what seemed to him clear infractions. He decided they were biased and the series was fixed. I kept having to explain that bodychecking was perfectly legal, but he didn't believe me. "If it's legal, why don't the Russians do it? Why don't the Russians play like that too? The Canadians can't keep up, so they hit and bully them. Look at them. They're thugs. Look! Animals!" The lowest point came at the end of the series, when, after Henderson's winning goal, the players and coaching staff of Team Canada could be seen directing profanities and obscene gestures at the Moscow fans. Appalled and disgusted as he was, though, he kept silent for fear of provoking the jubilant mob crammed inside the Galaxy.

I watched that final game at school. Classes were cut short and all of us, boys and girls, were herded into the basement auditorium, where we sat on the floor cross-legged before one of the four TVs that had been wheeled in on high chrome trolleys. When Henderson scored his fabled goal in the final seconds, it was bedlam. The building shook as everyone in the place, including teachers and staff, shrieked and leapt and hugged one another. I was as exultant as anyone, but when I got home that afternoon, I resolved to maintain a mature and sportsmanlike dignity. I knew my father would be having dinner with us, and when he arrived, I remained in my room until summoned by my mother's call. He was at his usual place at the kitchen table, a bottle of Export in front of him. My mother was at the stove, stirring a steaming pot. I rounded the table in regal silence while my father watched me with a faint, sardonic smile.

"Look at him. The victorious barbarian. Are you happy, my little capitalist?"

He'd never applied this epithet to me, and though I wasn't sure what it meant, it was no compliment. I shrunk back as he patted my head.

"I am *not* a capitalist," I said.

"No?" he replied, his grin even more sardonic. "What are you, then?"

"I'm a *Canadian*."

He retracted his arm and took a swig of beer. "That you are," he said, which I suspected was even less of a compliment.

In my earliest years, my father would usually get home when I was already in bed, though if I awoke during the night, I could sense whether he was around. The house was charged with his presence. If I heard him and my mother in the kitchen, I would get out of bed and go to them. On the other side of the door, the air was always thick with steam and tobacco and the transistor radio was tuned to the Greek program. The kitchen looked different at this hour, the electric light blazing brighter and harsher, the night outside deeper and blacker. I was entering an adult world, a world of sobriety and obligation and worry. Even my mother, usually at the stove or sink, appeared different, more wife than mother. If my father was hunched over the transistor, listening to the news, she would run over and swoop me up so I wouldn't disturb him. But I knew not to disturb my father when he was listening to the news. There were serious adult things he had to stay abreast of. Sometimes he would let me sit on his lap and listen with him quietly. What came from the radio was a meaningless babble but one imbued with the gravity and mystery of the world, the vast world outside our blackened windows.

As I grew older these nocturnal visits became less frequent. More and more, when I heard my parents' voices in the middle of the night, I would try to shut them out and get back to sleep. If my parents were in their bedroom, which was next to mine, that could be harder to do. I would catch the occasional word, and even if I was not able to figure out what they were talking about, there was no missing the asperity and jagged-ness of their tone. Much of the time they seemed to be talking about how my father spent money, or his time. Sometimes he would raise his voice and my mother would say, "Please, Andreas, the child, the child." In the morning, though, everything would be back to normal, as if the voices I'd heard had been a dream. My father would still be in bed or, more often, already at work, and my mother would go about her duties with her usual quiet efficiency. I grasped from an early age that I was part of a larger drama, that there were serious things going on I couldn't fathom, import-ant events taking place in the wings, out of sight, like the dreadful doings of ancient tragedies. I caught hints and intimations—a look in my mother's eyes, the curve of my father's mouth, a silent exchange of glances at the kitchen table, the voices through the wall—but the deeper meanings eluded me.

I began to conceive of the world as a multiplicity of horizons laid out as concentric circles. My life occupied the smallest circle at the centre. Then came the world of my parents, one circle up and encompassing my own. My father's domain extended beyond my mother's. She inhabited the familiar world of home, domesticity, and children. My father's world was that of men, of money, business, striving, and survival. That world terrified me, partly by its vastness and mystery, but mostly because one day I would have to join it. Its horizon extended far beyond my father's own, beyond indeed that of most people we knew. My father himself would allude to these remote regions, and I would get glimpses of them on TV and later in books and newspapers, their signals as abstruse and intelligible as the data of radio telescopes. How would I ever manage? I had enough trouble making sense of what was going on right under my own nose. I was nine or ten, for instance, when I realized my father and uncle were not speaking. It turned out they hadn't been for a couple of years. Though they still ran the restaurant together, apart from their business affairs, they had nothing to do with each other. Years later, my father would claim they'd fallen out over politics, my uncle having become a *khoondikós*, a fascist. By this point, though, I was well aware of my father's promiscuity with such labels. I had lost track of everyone he'd called a "fascist." The list included not just Ioannis Metaxas, Konstantinos Karamanlis, Winston Churchill, and Henry Kissinger, but also Manos Hazdzidakis, Brian Mulroney, Ronald Reagan, the priest and the cantor at our church, the baker on Laurier Street, the dance teacher at my Greek school, and so many more. Which was why I had no trouble believing my uncle when he told me he never came close to supporting the Junta or embracing anything resembling fascism. He wouldn't, however, provide me with an alternative explanation. He just kept saying, "Ask your father," even though the only reason we were talking about the matter was that I'd already done that and he was now denying what my father had said about him. Was he protecting me? I didn't want protection. I just wanted the truth.

Nor could I get any reliable information from my mother. She had no shortage of explanations and theories, but they kept changing over the years. Despite her certainties, as rigid as they were variable, it was clear she herself didn't really know what had happened. For years she had kept up a feverish campaign of shuttle diplomacy in an effort to bring the two men back together, until, one night in 1972, my father announced out of the blue that he had acquired his own restaurant. He was leaving the Galaxy. My mother was aghast. How was this possible? How could we afford such a venture? Where had the money come from? And what about her brother, the partnership? There had been an agreement. My father had debts and obligations. My father coolly assured her that he and Tasso had settled their affairs amicably, and he had discharged his debts with honour and even magnanimity. Tasso had nothing to complain of. She could ask him herself. My father never wanted it said by anyone that he had taken advantage of his relations. As for our finances, everything was in order. If she liked, he would be happy to sit down and explain the numbers to her.

The restaurant was on Bernard, near Park Avenue. Previously called the Miss Bernard Restaurant, it was now the *New* Miss Bernard Restaurant, as proclaimed by the new illuminated box sign above the entrance, which featured an illustration of a busty waitress in a frilly white apron balancing on fingertips a tray with a giant burger and soda glass. The New Miss Bernard was bigger than the Galaxy, and classier. It was a *real* restaurant, with soaring leatherette triplefold menus showcasing a pageantry of burgers, submarines, brochettes, pizzas, pastas, pies, cakes, sundaes, shakes, and things I'd never heard of. There was a bar near the entrance, four large booths along one wall, and tables enough to seat twenty-four. Each booth was outfitted with a wall-mounted jukebox that offered a selection of English, French, and Greek pop songs. I loved the New Miss Bernard and felt proud to say my father was the owner.

My mother, however, would not set foot in the place. A couple of times, my father drove her by it, and she turned her head in the opposite direction. She also forbade him to bring home food from its kitchen, even though it would mean less cooking for her. She couldn't tolerate mere mention of the place, and when friends or neighbours brought it up, she would grow sullen and visibly uncomfortable. Though she never tried to prevent or dissuade me from going there, I knew to avoid telling her about my visits.

In the summer, I would drop by at least once a week, as it was around the corner from the Regency Cinema. The Regency on Park Avenue was one of the city's last old picture palaces, a place abounding in brass, velvet, gilded festoons and garlands, and bas-relief gargoyles, though I was more aware of the crumbling plaster, ripped upholstery, dank smells, and sticky floor. However grand it may have once been, it was now reduced to a scruffy ghetto establishment, screening Greek or Greek-dubbed movies. We knew families who went almost on a weekly basis. Ours was not among these. My father worked most nights, and my mother considered it unseemly for a married woman to attend public events unaccompanied by her husband. She also hated war movies, which was what most of the dramas at the Regency were. My mother liked love stories with a happy ending. "I don't see why people pay money to be reminded of how horrible life is," she would say. On those rare occasions when we did go, it was always a last-minute decision, and leaving the house heedless of showtimes we'd arrive mid-film and spend the remainder whispering questions and hunches in an effort to puzzle out the story. But no one was bothered by this. Everyone did it. There was constant traffic in the aisles, as the concession lobby at the back was a smoking area, so during the screenings, patrons (men, mostly) would station themselves at the low wall behind the last row of seats and watch the movie while having a cigarette.

But while I rarely went to the Greek movies, by the age of eight I was a regular at the Saturday morning matinées. The matinées let out around noon; after my father acquired the New Miss Bernard, my friends and I would troop over there en masse. There might be four or five of us, but everyone, whatever our number, was free to order anything he wanted, on the house. My father made sure the orders came piled high with fixings and extras, and if he was in an especially good mood, he would supply us with dimes for the jukebox. He was a popular man with my friends.

Much as he cajoled and pleaded with her, however, he could not win over my mother. She maintained her boycott and would never have darkened its doorway but for that fateful visit from the Trifonopouloses in the summer of 1974. Voula Trifonopoulos, née Tsapalou, was my mother's cousin, though my mother spoke of her almost as if she were a sister. The two had been close as children, but at sixteen Voula had moved with her family to Chicago. Voula was married to a second-generation Chicagoan named Bobby (short for *Kharálambos*, and in Greek pronounced *Bábi*) and they had two sons, Gus and Tom (Konstantinos and Athanassios). On their previous visit, when I was three, they had stayed with us, but this time they insisted, against my mother's impassioned protests, on staying at a hotel. They made sure, however, to come during my mother's summer vacation so she would be free to spend as much time as she could with them.

My father was not as enamoured of the Trifonopouloses as my mother. He liked Voula well enough, but he didn't have much regard for Bobby, whom he routinely referred to as *ton Amerikáno* or *ton bakáli*. In Greek, the latter (meaning grocer) was a common pejorative and seemed to denote someone uncouth and illiterate. In fact, since their last visit, Bobby had expanded his single grocery into a chain of four and appeared to be very successful. But my father hadn't changed his opinion of him. Bluff, boastful, loud, chauvinistic, Bobby was in my father's eyes the quintessential American philistine. These were also Greek traits, but in Bobby they had a distinctly American tinge that got under my father's skin. Bobby's Greek was badly pronounced, ungrammatical, and heavily interspersed with bumbling pseudo-Hellenic Anglicisms. I got the impression he hardly ever spoke it in Chicago. With his family he used English, which he spoke with a rubbery nasal squawk that at the time I would not have been able to identify as midwestern or Chicagoan but nonetheless sounded American. Even though he'd been to Montreal before, he was bemused by the widespread use of French and treated it as an affectation. To the great amusement of his sons, he would do a snooty imitation of Francophone Montrealers, and we could never pass a brasserie without his shouting, "Look, another one. I've never seen so many bra stores in all my life." In stores and restaurants, he always asked clerks and wait staff whether they spoke "American," even after my father had repeatedly pointed out to him that the language spoken in Canada and the US alike was English. And he insisted on paying for everything. Protest and parry as my father might, Bobby would not capitulate. As soon as he saw the bill coming, he was on his feet, pulling from his pocket his fat green roll like a frontier duellist. There were times he physically knocked my father out of the way and I worried the two might come to blows. "He acts like the big tycoon and we're some charity case," my father would grumble privately.

Still, my father went out of his way to be hospitable. He was proud of being a good host and took time off to show the Trifonopouloses the sights. We made the standard stops: Notre Dame, the Oratory, Beaver Lake, St. Catherine Street, St. Hubert Street, the Botanical Gardens. Normally a fervent debunker and derider of all things Canadian, he now sang the city's praises. I couldn't believe how knowledgeable he was. Shepherding us around, he would reel off facts and statistics and point out architectural details as though he were leading a tour of the Acropolis. Bobby remained doggedly unimpressed. No matter what you showed him, he could point to a bigger, taller, older, or newer equivalent in the US. There were few things my father loathed more than American hubris and chauvinism; such an attitude in a Greek, however, even a Greek-American, seemed to him downright perverse. In my father's eyes, Bobby was a traitor to his race. He marvelled Bobby hadn't truncated his surname, like the odious and recently disgraced US Vice-President.

That summer, Greece was much in the news. Days before the Trifonopouloses' arrival, Turkey had invaded Cyprus and the Junta had fallen. My father and the men in the park talked of nothing else. Bobby had little knowledge of the situation and even less interest in it. He had little interest in politics generally. Whenever my father tried to engage him, he would take on a look of weary boredom and return one of his stock aperçus or aphorisms, which included "What do you expect? He's a politician," and "It's the same everywhere: the big fish eats the little fish," comments whose effect was to cut discussion short rather than extend and enrich it. My obsessive father, however, would not be deterred. One afternoon, as he and Bobby were having a smoke outside Notre Dame while the wives completed their tour, he again brought up the recent events in Greece and Cyprus. Bobby barely seemed to be listening but my father persisted. Running through Henry Kissinger's malign involvement in the politics not only of Greece but numerous other countries, my father demanded of Bobby whether he didn't agree that Kissinger should be locked up as a war criminal. Bobby stared at a couple of miniskirted hippie girls sauntering by. "I don't know," he said, shrugging. "He's probably done some bad things. But who hasn't? If we lock up Kissinger, then we'll have to lock up all the politicians. And then who would ever run for politics?"

"You think Kissinger is like any other politician?"

"Kissinger has to do what he thinks is best for America's interests," Bobby said, gazing at one of the church's towers.

"And what about Nixon? You think he's worked for America's interests?"

Bobby took a last pensive haul of his cigarette and crushed the butt under his shoe.

"You don't think Nixon should go to jail?" said my father.

"Nixon's no different from the rest. He just got caught."

Comments like this infuriated my father. They confirmed there was nothing in the world stupider than an American. But Bobby was a son of the Hellenes as well, which made him something of a freak, a grotesque socio-historical mutation or aberration. He was the cultural equivalent of a two-headed cow or goat-faced boy. And for my father, he may have been a portent of how his own Canadian-born son might turn out if he wasn't careful.

In my eyes, there was something exotic and glamorous about Bobby and Voula. The Trifonopouloses gave me my first direct sense of how different the US was from Canada, of its power and sway over its citizens, its ability to mold them in its own image. The Greeks I'd known, whatever their personal differences and idiosyncrasies, were cut from the same cloth. The Trifonopouloses suggested to me that this might have less to do with the Greeks than with Canada, or more specifically Quebec. To me, the Trifonopouloses bore an astonishing resemblance to the families you saw on American TV. Bobby reminded me of the fathers on shows like *The Brady Bunch* and *My Three Sons*. He had an ease and camaraderie with his boys I'd never seen outside of television. The three interacted almost like equals. They even had similar tastes and interests. I'd never seen such a thing. In my universe, parents were autocrats and disciplinarians. They occupied a realm of their own and spoke from on high. At the same time, they had little access or insight into our world. Their children were, quite literally, foreigners to them. There was between us, parents and children, an abyss that could never be bridged, and we, the children, knew it. It was the natural order of things. But the Trifonopouloses revealed it could be otherwise, that not all immigrant families were necessarily and inevitably like the ones in my neighbourhood, that even Greeks could look and sound like the people on TV.

But the Trifonopouloses were American. I couldn't imagine there was a Greek family in Montreal like them. Indeed I had never encountered any immigrant family like them. Gus and Tom were the first immigrant children I'd ever met who couldn't speak their parents' language. I found this astounding. To my father it was a scandal. Whenever he heard Voula address her sons in English, he would say, "For the name of God, speak to them in their own language," to which she would reply, "English is their language. They don't know Greek." And he would say, "Of course they don't. Because you never use it. Even with Bobby, the two of you only speak English. It's shameful. You're robbing your children of their heritage. Surely you have Greek schools in Chicago. Put them in Greek school. And *speak* to them. Speak to them in their mother tongue."

I loved that Voula spoke English. It was one of the things that made her exotic—a woman born in Greece who spoke good English. I especially loved it when she spoke English with me, which also drove my father crazy. "He speaks Greek, you know," he would say to her. Speaking English with Voula created a kind of intimacy between us. It made her seem younger. I loved bumping into friends and having them hear us. When they caught up with me later, they would ask who that woman was, where she was from, how we were related. I would tell them she was my aunt, not going into particulars. They would sometimes enquire how old she was. It was hard to believe Voula was the same age as my mother. She didn't look like any of the mothers on our street. She was thin and fairly nice looking and wore tight-fitting bellbottom jeans, floppy broad-brimmed hats, and platform shoes. My mother made her clothes herself or bought them at dusty discount shops on St. Lawrence Boulevard. Next to Voula, she looked like an old lady.

Two days before the Trifonopouloses were set to leave, my father announced he would be hosting a farewell dinner the following evening at the restaurant. It was clear from my mother's reaction that she had not been consulted, but with the event publicly declared, what could she say? She had no room to manoeuvre. It had been bad enough having to explain to the Trifonopouloses about her husband and brother; she wasn't about to reveal that she refused to go into her husband's restaurant, not even to Voula.

The next day was a Sunday so the restaurant was fairly quiet. My father nonetheless had an extra waitress on hand. He was determined that every-thing go off without a hitch. He'd set a couple of tables together for us, and he had prepared a special bill of fare that included some traditional dishes that were not on the menu. Throughout the night, he kept an eagle eye on everything and twice sent back dishes for deficiencies apparent only to him. He was uncharacteristically attentive to my mother, solici-tous of her approval even more than that of the Americans. My mother was stiff and silent amid the boisterous Americans, tossing about glances of displeasure and disapprobation. Whenever he could, my father broke from his hosting duties and sat next to her, taking her hand or draping an arm around her shoulder while chatting with the Americans. My mother remained unresponsive.

I assumed she was still furious about how my father had tricked her. In truth, though, the situation was more complicated than I realized. My mother was secretly pleased about how things had turned out. The Tri-fonopouloses had given her cover. Whatever her suspicions and resent-ments, she'd been curious about the restaurant and would have liked nothing better than to have a look at it, if only to see how it measured up against my father's descriptions. The Trifonopouloses had enabled her to go back on her word without losing face. What most preoccupied her when we arrived that evening was Voula's impending departure. The joy-ous week had passed so quickly. She wished the Trifonopouloses could stay forever. She loved having them in the house, waiting on them, cook-ing for them, cleaning up after them. How she wished they had stayed with us rather than at a hotel. She had loved the bustle and crowdedness of the last few days and wished all days were like that. Why couldn't Voula live in Montreal? And what a change there was in my father. Throughout the previous week, he had been kinder and more gallant than he'd been since their earliest days. With one or two minor lapses, he had been the exemplary host and husband, and she had felt for him a tenderness and admiration she hadn't felt in years. Yet, while pleased and grateful for this, it also rankled. Why did this side of him come out only in the company of strangers? Why was he always so much more genial and gracious when there were others around? Why only then was he so open, patient, cheer-ful, considerate, affectionate? Why did he need others present to be kind to her?

Throughout that evening, she watched him closely as he shuttled between the dining hall and kitchen, attending to everyone, carrying dishes back and forth, pouring drinks, managing the staff. She watched him with the customers, noted how they greeted and addressed him. She could see their affection and respect. She watched how she handled the waitresses and delegated tasks, the calm efficiency with which he juggled everything. She realized how impressive what he did for a living was, this running of a restaurant. She was sure *she* couldn't have done it. It took a certain personality and talent. She felt a grudging admiration, even pride.

But then, in a flash, her mood changed. She was gloomy and anxious again. Something had happened, and it had registered on her face. There was a hardening in her expression, a clouding over, a look of suppressed alarm. My father noticed it too, but only some minutes later, when he returned from the kitchen. Taking his seat beside my mother, he clasped her hand and she stiffened and pulled it away. The gesture didn't escape him. He leaned toward her and whispered in her ear. She sat cold as a cary-atid. He stood to return to the kitchen, exasperation on his face.

Over the next hour, my mother withdrew even further into herself. She spoke with the others intermittently and distractedly. Her mind was elsewhere. All evening she had felt oddly alert. Everything jumped out at her and she absorbed the surroundings with unusual lucidity. Outlines were sharper, colours more intense, the world glowed. As it turned out, the place was nothing like my father had described. She was not surprised. Listening to him, she'd imagined something resembling a banquet hall in the Grand Bretagne. But the place was small and dingy. Seated facing the bar, she had perceived details that would likely have escaped her notice any other night: the scuffs and grime on the linoleum, the crack in a corner of the mirror behind the liquor shelves, the exposed plywood under the broken faux-terracotta tiles of the bar's canopy.

From the start, she had paid particular attention to the two waitresses. They were young, in their late twenties or early thirties. One was dark-haired, the other blonde, and both were slim and pretty. She imagined this was not a coincidence. They didn't wear a uniform but they had on identi-cal white waist aprons. They both wore skirts that stopped well above the knee. Was this a requirement? Both women had nice legs. She noted their makeup and hair, their easy manner with the male customers. She watched how they spoke with their boss. What kind of women were these? My father's waitresses tended to be French Canadian, and French-Canadian women made her uneasy. She knew of their reputation. When my father spoke of them at home, it was usually to complain, but she knew how men really felt about such women. She observed closely how he interacted with them. He always spoke in English and addressed them in a matter-of-fact manner. Sometimes he was a little sharp and aggressive. She wouldn't have liked it if he spoke to *her* that way. But these women didn't seem to mind. She noticed that he interacted more with the brunette, who had been assigned to our table. The blonde focused on the customers. She thought she detected a difference in the way he treated them. With the brunette, he was relaxed and direct, more himself. With the blonde, there seemed to be tension. There was between them a cool formality, something forced and self-conscious. Something *false*. She'd noticed the difference right away but hadn't given it much thought. But after the last of the main dishes had been served, he and the blonde had crossed paths at the bar and the world lit up. The heavens shook. She saw what had been in plain sight all along, as if her guts and bones had understood before her eyes could see. Now it was all crystal clear. The façade had cracked. She could see through the pretense.

But what was it she had seen? What had given it all away? In the coming days, she would return to this question obsessively.

In the first instance, there had been the two of them standing side by side mixing drinks, my father speaking in a low, business-like tone and the blonde nodding solemnly, as if noting instructions. But then he'd leaned over and whispered in her ear, and what he said caused her to break into a smile that transformed not just the cast of her face but the whole tenor of their interaction. Then, as she turned to look at him, there passed between them something fleeting but vivid, something delicate, a kind of intimacy, a history, a confidence, a confederacy. And the veil was torn. Embarrassed, overcome, my mother had dropped her gaze, wondering whether she had not imagined the whole thing. But when she glanced up again, she saw the waitress watching my father as he made his way to our table with drinks, and the look on her face confirmed her initial impression to the point of certainty.

She could hardly look at them the rest of the night. Yet she could hardly look away. The next morning, she was able to hide her panic behind the tears and rituals of farewell, but it didn't take long after the Trifonopouloses had gone for my father to realize something was eating her. He thought he knew what it was, but he wasn't going to be lured into another confrontation. He was tired. He was tired of fighting about the same old crap. Nor was he going to apologize for wanting his wife to take an interest, and, yes, even some pride, in his business. He was proud of what he'd accomplished, and he wanted her to share that feeling. What was so terrible about that? But she was clearly still angry and wanted to have a fight about it. Well, he wasn't going to give her the satisfaction. She could sulk all she wanted.

But my mother in fact softened over the coming days, though he was now too angry himself to notice. Shortly after the Trifonopouloses' departure, she began to doubt herself. She knew she had a tendency to jump to conclusions and think the worst of every situation, and now when she tried to recall what she thought she had seen at the restaurant, she couldn't bring it to memory. Was it possible she'd imagined it all? Contrary to my father's supposition, what she was longing for was not a fight but evidence she'd been wrong. She wanted a word or gesture to reassure her. Instead he reverted to his old ways, behaving in a manner that could only exacerbate her suspicions. She was upset, maybe even on to him, yet rather than enquire about what was troubling her, he avoided her. Why? Was he afraid of having his own suspicions confirmed? He began spending all his time at work again, and the brief intervals he was home, he would keep his head buried in his newspapers or lie on the sofa and stare at the TV. What game was he playing? And what did he make of her own silence? Did he see it as a kind of submission or tacit acceptance? Did he think they had settled into one of those arrangements wherein the docile, cooperative wife turns a blind eye to her husband's indiscretions and carries on her duties with quiet dignity? From all she heard, this was how many a marriage and wife endured. But she was not like other women. Back home, such transgressions were a criminal offence, and she could have gone to the police and had him thrown in jail. But they were in Canada, where the laws and mores were more permissive. Nonetheless, Canada was a Christian country and must provide some recourse. Surely not even Canada would permit such behaviour to go unpunished.

But first she would need proof. At the moment, all she had was an intuition. She wished someone could give her advice or guidance. She wished she could speak to her brother. Not for the first time she wondered whether it had been something like this that was behind his rift with Andreas. Whenever he was around, she scrutinized my father for a sign or clue that would give him away. But he was like a master card sharp. He revealed nothing. She came close to asking him straight out, but always pulled back; she would be putting herself at a disadvantage to speak before she had evidence. Then, one night, she caught a whiff of something as they brushed past each other, a scent or perfume. Later, while he was in the bathroom, she opened the closet and sniffed through his clothes, and there it was again: an alien, feminine smell. It resembled nothing of hers. She went through his pockets and sniffed his handkerchiefs. She stuffed one into a pocket of her apron.

The next day, she went through the bottles and canisters in the bathroom, uncapping them one by one and comparing their scents with those of the handkerchief. After a while, everything blended together and she wasn't even sure what she was searching for. She combed through every drawer and closet in the apartment, burying her nose in his shirts, hats, ties, even his socks and underwear. When he was home, she would sniff at him behind his back. There was no doubt about it: there was something there—something flowery and womanish and foreign. She began detecting it at the oddest moments, catching traces of it even when he wasn't around, or when she was sleeping. Occasionally the scent seemed to be wafting off her own clothes, and there were times she even smelled it at work.

Near a state of frenzy one morning, she told the foreman she was not well and needed to go home. She could not believe she was doing such a thing. The foreman got permission from the bosses, and she gathered her things and left. The day was sunny and warm, and St. Lawrence Boulevard was crowded. Trucks stood double-parked on the street and the traffic grunted along at a snail's pace. She walked past the five-and-dimes, the delis and snack bars, the fabric shops, the uniform store with mannequin nurses and chefs, the button shop with its forlorn judy and scattered spools, past the Greek barbershop, the Portuguese bakery, the Slovenian butcher with the steaming sausages in the window whose smell filled the street. Not that she noticed any of these things. Her brain was aflame and she walked without seeing. She avoided the eyes of the passersby, fearing they could tell she was up to something, that she was shirking work to pursue devious ends.

North of Mount Royal Avenue, the crowd thinned out and trade gave way to industry. Behind the windows now lay dusty tools, appliances, and machine and auto parts. Some windows were covered over with newspaper or cardboard. There was a sense of desolation. With no clear idea of what she was doing, she turned onto Bernard toward Park Avenue. She walked several blocks until, a few minutes later, she could make out the restaurant in the distance. She recognized the silhouette of the waitress on the box sign. As she passed the restaurant on the opposite side of the street, she glanced toward it quickly and saw only her own reflection in the sunbright window. Facing forward, she picked up her pace.

What the hell was she doing? She might not be able to see in, but those inside could clearly see out. What if she'd been spotted?

At the next corner, she stopped and turned around. She was relieved to see no one chasing her. Why was she here? What had she hoped to discover? My father and the blonde in a passionate embrace? She had sacrificed half a day's pay, which she would now have to justify to my father. And for what? What a fool! Perhaps it was not too late to go back to work. But as she was gazing at the restaurant half a block away, she saw the door open and a woman step out. It was her, the blonde waitress. She was sure of it. She started after her. Why? She just wanted to see where she was going. Passing the restaurant, she turned her face away. The blonde crossed to her side of Bernard and then crossed Park Avenue. She observed the way she walked, noting the wiggle of her hips, the slender legs, the macramé shoulder bag hung low. The waitress broke into a run and she panicked. She had been found out! But then she saw the yellow light. The waitress just wanted to beat the red.

She had to pick up her pace now and didn't wait for the green. She ran across Park Avenue to avoid the oncoming cars. Up ahead, the blonde kept going. At Clark, she turned right. When my mother reached the corner, she was gone. Then, a second later, she saw her on the other side of the street, climbing a staircase. My mother kept going, past children playing on the sidewalk. When she turned around a few seconds later, the woman was nowhere to be seen. She stood and stared at the house the woman had entered. In the distance loomed a massive industrial building with its familiar black water tower, a neighbourhood landmark, visible from distant points all around. Returning the way she'd come, she passed the shouting children again and stopped at the corner. Across the street was a restaurant. She crossed Bernard and peered through the window, but it was hard to see past the reflected sunlight. Across the lower half of the window was a wire hung with cardboard beer logos. She recognized the Molson Export brand my father drank. Right by the window stood an empty table. Girding herself, she went to the entrance and pulled the door open.

There was a smell of beer, burnt grease, and cigarettes. At one of the tables sat two men, eating. Behind them sat another man, alone. Three more men were perched at the counter, and they all turned to look at her. She kept her head down and sat at the table by the window, facing the door. She hung her handbag on the back of the chair next to her, but then she removed it and put it on her lap. Hearing footsteps, she turned and saw a short square-set man with dark curly hair and long sideburns. He had a friendly-looking face. The three men at the counter had their backs to her and were talking to one another. The curly-haired man said something in French. She replied, "One coffee, overmilk." He pondered this a moment; then, with a nod, he turned and went to the counter. A minute later he was back with a mug of coffee and a small creamer filled to the top. He set them down on the table, along with a spoon on a paper napkin, and gave her a friendly smile. "You tell me you won sumting else," he said.

"Thenk you very mutts."

As she watched him walk away, she wondered what he must be thinking. Two of the men at the counter swivelled to have another look. She turned toward the window. Who did they imagine she was? What kind of woman would come to a place like this by herself? She rehearsed what she would say if one of them approached her: *No parleh franseh, no parleh angleh.* She picked up the creamer and poured in as much cream as the mug allowed. She picked up the fluted sugar jar and poured out lots of sugar. She stirred and tasted. The liquid was tepid and bitter. She added more sugar and gazed out the window.

She had a clear view of the stone triplex the woman had entered, and she kept her eye on the pair of doors at the top. She hadn't seen which one she had gone through. She took another sip of coffee, hearing the men's voices around her. She listened but she couldn't understand. They were speaking French. They were probably speaking about her. Now and then they laughed. Outside, a man walking by looked through the window at her. She turned away. One of the men at the counter was staring at her though he pretended to be gazing out the window. She glanced at the floor. It was filthy. She raised her cup to her lips. The coffee was both too sweet and too strong. She glanced down at her handbag and remembered that she hadn't eaten lunch. Inside her handbag was a jar of stewed artichokes and potatoes. She knew she couldn't eat that here. But she was too frightened to order. She glanced at her watch. It wasn't too late to go back to work. She would eat during the afternoon break. She couldn't stay here any longer. She was making a spectacle of herself, exposing herself to all kinds of risk. As she got up, she remembered that she hadn't paid. How was that done? She couldn't go up to the counter. Perhaps she could leave some money on the table. How much could it be? Surely fifty cents would cover it. She sat back down and stole a glance at the counter. The curly-haired man was nowhere to be seen. The others had their backs to her. She looked at her watch again. The door opened and a thin bald man in a short-sleeved shirt stepped in. She thought it might be the man who had stared at her through the window a moment ago. She kept her head down as he went past, and monitored his footsteps. He sat at the table behind her.

She couldn't bear it any longer. She would leave three quarters on the table and walk out. As she reached for her bag, a bright red car flashed in the sunlight. Her fingers froze on the buckle of her bag as it went by, and she watched it turn down Clark. It slowed, stopped, and then backed into a parking space.

A few seconds later, my father stepped out and crossed the street to the stone triplex. At the top of the stairs, he paused, dug into his pocket, searched though his keys, and unlocked the door.

"Every ting okay, madame?"

She turned with a start. "I pay please," she said to the curly-haired man.

"Turdify sen."

She opened her handbag with trembling hands and gave the man two quarters. He reached into a pocket and put a dime and a nickel on the table. When he left, she sat back down and stared at the two coins. But all she could see was my father opening that door with his own key. It was extraordinary how much horror could be contained in such a simple action. She tried to take in all its implications.

Gazing out the window, she noticed that the door remained open. After a minute or two, the waitress stepped out with a child next to her, a boy, maybe four or five. Holding his hand, she accompanied him down the stairs. My father followed behind them and shut the door. At the bottom of the stairs, the woman crouched to tuck in the boy's shirt. My father strutted down the stairs and continued past them to the car. The woman took the boy by the hand again, and the two crossed to the car as well and got inside. A few seconds later, it pulled away.

She sat frozen. She felt faint and didn't trust that she would be able to walk. She would not have been able to say how long she'd remained seated there. Finally, leaving the coins on the table, she rose robotically and staggered out of the restaurant.

She knew her brother and Christina would be at work, but she went down St. Urbain Street anyway. Where else could she go? Maybe the girls would be home. But what could the girls do for her? What could she tell them? She needed to speak to her brother. She stood at the bottom of his stairs and gazed up at the closed door and windows. It didn't look like anyone was home, but she climbed the stairs and rang the doorbell. She peered through the window, hands cupped at her eyes, but she couldn't see past the lace curtain. She rang the bell several times and rapped the window with her palm, her wedding band clanging loudly against the glass. She didn't care if the neighbours heard.

She went back down the stairs and headed toward St. Lawrence Boulevard. Her brother knew. She was certain of it. That was what it had all been about. But he couldn't tell her. Because he was the same? Was he also whoring around with his waitresses? They were all the same. It was time for a full disclosure. But she knew what he would answer. They all stuck up for each other. *How am I supposed to know what Andreas does in his own time?* "Don't lie to me," she said out loud, heedless of the surrounding eyes on the crowded sidewalk. "How many have there been?" she snarled and she saw a woman look at her.

She remembered the face in the photograph. Even then she knew it spelled trouble. With the slicked-back hair, the pencil moustache, the smug good looks, it was the picture of roguishness. And her brother had said nothing. Even after she'd expressed her misgivings. Andreas? Oh no, he was a decent man, hard-working, wholesome as rain. Yet in her bones she knew better. She saw into people's character better than anyone, even when she had nothing more to go on than a photograph. But she had been desperate. And this was her brother, after all. If she couldn't trust him, who could she trust? So she'd ignored her instincts. And she told herself that, even if he were bad, she would set him straight, she would make him good. With love and patience, you could set anyone straight. She firmly believed that. The love of a good wife could reform even the most wayward of men. With such thoughts as these, she let herself be carted off to a cold white land to marry a perfect stranger. And now Tasso was sure to deny it all. *I didn't know! I knew nothing about any of this!* "Liar!" she snapped. Nothing but falsity and deception, her whole life. "To turn me into one of his whores, my own brother!" She saw the eyes peering at her. Let them look. She didn't care. All her life she'd been betrayed by the people closest to her, the people whose duty it was to protect her. Shouldn't *someone* have to pay? Wasn't it only just?

But this was her brother. This was the only person she had left now in this frigid exile. Maybe he did know nothing. He wasn't like Andreas. He was a good family man, hard-working, honest. Had he known anything, he would surely have told her. He was himself misled, like everyone, like everyone who came into contact with that deceiver.

She would wait. She needed to calm down and think things through. She had to be careful, watch what she said. She mustn't say things she would regret later. Tasso was a victim in all this too.

At Mount Royal she turned toward Esplanade. Passing the tennis courts, she kept her head down. She could feel the men in the park watching her. The gossip would start. What was she doing here at this hour? She thought she heard someone call her name but she didn't look up. Seeing some children, she looked around for me. A couple of old men on a bench were staring at her and she dropped her gaze again. As she reached the house, she glanced up and saw Yanni Economides gazing down at her from his balcony.

She climbed the stairs and found her keys. Inside the apartment, she called out my name. There was no answer. She looked in my room, checked the bathroom. In the bedroom, she let herself go at last. She cried and keened and pulled at her hair and clothes like a biblical figure. Her blouse ripped at the seams. She didn't care if the neighbours heard. Let the world know. She fell back on the bed.

When she looked at the clock, she couldn't believe how late it was. She raised herself from the bed and removed the tatters from her. She went to the bathroom and washed her face. She put on a fresh blouse and went to the front balcony. Surveying the street and park, she called out my name. Some girls were skipping rope, and she asked whether they had seen me. They hadn't. Through the trees, she could make out boys in the football field. Again she called out my name.

"If you see Alex," she said to the girls, "please tell him to come home right away."

She went back inside and dialled the Galaxy. My uncle answered. She asked him when he planned to be home. He said not till after seven. She enquired when Christina would be home. He asked her what the trouble was.

"I'm leaving him."

She heard a murmur of voices in the background, the clattering of dishes.

"What happened?" my uncle asked. "Are you all right?"

"What time will Christina be home?"

"Eleni, what happened?"

She wished she could say all she had to say, but she needed him now. "What time will Christina be home?"

"What is this about?"

"I'm leaving him!" she shrieked. "I'm leaving the whoremaster you married me to!"

"Don't shout."

"He has a child! He has a bastard child with one of his whores."

"How do you know this?"

"Don't question me! I've seen with my own eyes!"

"Stop screaming at me."

"The boy and I need somewhere to stay. Can you understand? I have to leave this house *now*! *Right now*! I cannot stay here another minute. Do you understand me? I cannot face that man again. I don't know what I'll do."

My uncle said he would come right over.

She hung up and returned to the balcony. The girls were gone. She peered through the trees and called out my name. She waited briefly. Then she went back inside and started packing.

5

My uncle's place was a few blocks away, but it felt as though we'd crossed continents. Raw, run-down, grimy, St. Urbain Street had always seemed hostile and dangerous, the people coarse and aggressive, like the people down by the wall. It was all grey and brown. There was constant traffic and the noise was always in your ears. You couldn't get away from it even indoors. At my uncle's place, you could hear the street in the living room and kitchen. At night I had to learn to sleep to the sound of traffic and the arrhythmic knell of a loose manhole cover. During the rush hours, the street was a raceway, the cars speeding along as fast as they did on Park Avenue. My cousins claimed that a couple of kids got hit each summer. Our first week, there was a screech of tires and everyone rushed to the balcony to find all the neighbours also out on their balconies and stoops, gazing down at the street praying it wasn't one of their own. That afternoon there were only the splattered remains of a flattened squirrel.

My mother and I were put up in the *salóni*, which was at the front of the apartment, opposite my cousins' bedroom. My mother slept on the sofa-bed and a cot was brought in for me. The day after our arrival, my aunt led me to the tiny room in the back, where she kept her sewing machine, and spoke to me of the vicissitudes of adult life and marriage and explained that *mamáthes* and *babáthes* sometimes had problems children could not understand and that I was never to forget that, whatever happened between my parents, they both loved me and were only interested in doing what was best for me. What I wanted to know was when we'd be returning home, but I could get no clear answer. I saw little of my mother those first few days, as she was usually locked away with my aunt, and I kept my distance, as I couldn't bear the sounds of her wailing and sobbing. I had no contact at all with my father for two weeks. When we finally spoke on the phone, he intimated that things would soon get back to normal and I shouldn't worry. He called again a couple of days later and told me to come by the restaurant whenever I wanted. I explained I wasn't allowed to. He said he and my mother had reached an agreement and I could now see him whenever I wished. I asked my mother about this, and she sighed. "He's your father. You can change your friends and you can change your spouse, but you can't change your parents."

I went by the restaurant a couple of days later. He was in the back booth with his cronies, but seeing me he leapt to his feet and stretched out his arms. He'd never greeted me this way before and it felt awkward. He even hugged and kissed me.

"Are you hungry?" he asked. I shook my head, trying not to cry. "Let me make you a submarine. Or would you rather have a pizza?"

"I don't want anything."

"How about an ice cream?" he said, guiding me into an empty booth. He looked different, diminished, not just thinner but *smaller*. But how was that possible? It occurred to me that he'd never been absent from me this long. I wondered whether the separation had given me a fresh perspective, whether I was seeing him more clearly. He seemed like a stranger. "Why are you crying?" he said, and I turned toward the jukebox and scanned the titles. I remember "Crocodile Rock," "Delta Dawn," "Midnight Train to Georgia." I felt my father's hand on the back of my head. "I'm going to make you a sundae. What do you want? The usual?"

I didn't answer and he went to the kitchen. I flipped the metal leaves of the jukebox. By now I knew every title, though not all of the songs. Most you never heard. The most popular were "Seasons in the Sun" and "Bad Bad Leroy Brown." My father returned with a chocolate sundae in a tall fluted glass. He put it down before me and laid down a long spoon on a paper napkin. "Why are you crying?" he said, sitting across from me.

I pressed the buttons on the jukebox.

"Don't do that," he said, pulling my hand away.

I stared down at the Arborite.

"Listen, my boy, you have to learn not to take things so seriously. These are the follies of adulthood. You'll soon learn yourself, life is full of reversals and disappointments. And you have to learn to take them in stride. You're a big boy now. You know what I went through at your age? So your parents had a spat. Big deal. Think how old I was when I lost my father. One day he's there and the next he's gone. What do you think that was like for me? I was even younger than you are. And what about my sister? First my father, then her. But I'm still here. I haven't gone away. You still have both your parents. Both healthy and strong. Right?" He struck his chest with a fist, like Tarzan. "We had a little spat. This stuff happens with married couples. It's nothing. It's normal. Come on. Look at me. See? You still have both of us. Nothing's changed."

"How can you say that?"

He handed me some napkins from the dispenser. "Go on," he said as I wiped my cheeks, "eat your ice cream. It's all a misunderstanding. Your mother will calm down and we'll get back to normal. I promise you. This will all blow over." He reached out to pat my cheek but I pulled away.

"Then why was I put in another school? If things are going back to normal, why did they change me to another school?"

"Because..." Some customers walked in and he straightened up and flashed a smile. "Because you're starting high school." He rose to his feet.

"But I was already in a school, and they changed me to a different one."

"Because it's closer to your uncle's place. We don't know how long this is going to be, and for now—"

"But my friends are at the other school. I don't know anyone at this one."

"So you'll make new friends."

"I don't want new friends."

He gripped the back of my neck and joggled me reassuringly. "Look, when everything returns to normal, we'll transfer you back. Okay? Come on, your ice cream is melting."

"I told you, I'm not hungry," I said, but he already had his back to me and was heading over to the customers who'd just arrived.

In the coming days, I could see no evidence things would be getting back to normal. At the end of September, my mother, against my aunt's and uncle's protests, began paying a monthly rent. By then we'd become as a single household, our lives and routines melded with those of our hosts. My mother had taken up her share of the cooking, cleaning, laundry, and other chores, and we did everything together with the Anagnostopouloses—eating, watching TV, visiting other families. Sundays, we went to church, my uncle included. I couldn't get a grip on my uncle's stance on religion. He could be as censorious of the Church as my father, yet he freed up most Sundays on his schedule to attend mass with us. Otherwise, I saw hardly more of him than I had my father. Both of them were always at their restaurants. At home, my aunt managed almost everything, with help from my cousins. I did my part, but being a boy, I had far fewer domestic duties. I would do the occasional light cleaning, go to the store to buy bread and milk, and now and then help my uncle with small repairs. But this was nothing compared to my cousins' duties, which included helping with the laundry, cleaning, cooking, sewing, ironing, and much else. Most afternoons, when they arrived home from school, they had to do chores. When they weren't doing housework or homework, they watched TV. The TV was always on, even when no one was in the room watching it. Mimi talked on the phone with friends, or she would lie on the couch, flipping through teen and gossip magazines.

I was never close with my cousins. Eleftheria was two years younger than I, Dimitra three years older. And they were girls, so we had nothing in common. When we were small, my aunt would bring them to Esplanade so they could play in the park, and now and then we'd visit St. Urbain Street. But since the rift, only my mother kept up these visits, and with the passing years, she would make them on her own as I refused to go with her. On the rare occasions my aunt still dropped by, she would be without the girls, as they had no more interest in my company than I had in theirs. So when we landed as refugees on my uncle's doorstep that August afternoon, I hadn't seen my cousins in two years. My aunt, having been warned that we were coming, was waiting for us at the door and disbursed consolations and hugs while Terry stood behind her in the corridor, watching with doleful eyes. Further back stood another, older girl, who I assumed to be a friend of Mimi's. Tall and fleshy, she wore a tight pink smocked tube top, white denim cutoffs, and white exercise sandals. Mimi was nowhere in sight. The presence of this stranger infuriated me and I waited for her to leave, but she just stood there gawking at us. My anger was focused on my aunt for not having booted this girl out. The situation was humiliating enough without our being served up as entertainment and gossip fodder for Mimi's nosy friends. Only when my aunt turned and admonished the girl to help carry in our things did I realize she was Mimi herself.

I couldn't believe my eyes. I wouldn't have imagined such a transformation possible. It was something out of a science fiction or horror movie. Not only was Mimi taller and stouter than when I'd last seen her, she looked like a completely different person. Her facial features were finer, her hips wider, her legs plumper and proportionally longer, and she had the most magnificent, bounteous, womanly pair of breasts I had ever seen on a girl her age. The way they swelled and swayed beneath her top as she bent to lift a tote bag, it was all I could do to restrain my eyes against their tidal pull. *This is your cousin*, I kept telling myself, *this is your cousin*.

The entire drive over, I had been in a quiet panic. My mother had told me only that we would be staying with my uncle for a while. This alone filled me with horror. I couldn't imagine being constantly in the company of my cousins. Would we be sleeping in the same room? Would I ever have a moment alone? When would I see my friends? To prepare myself for the worst, I tried to imagine all the frustrations and indignities I might be in store for, but *this* never crossed my mind. How could it? There had been no signs or warnings. My aunt looked nothing like this. Was Terry going to mutate too? You wouldn't predict it looking at her. But you wouldn't have predicted it looking at Mimi. Yet here she was transformed, in the blink of an eye, into this unearthly fleshpot, this hourglass-shaped daemon, this pornographic nightmare, which I would have to learn to live with day after day for who knew how long. How was I going to manage?

I'd been raised with the understanding that cousins, even those at some remove, were subject to the same taboos that ruled relations between siblings. How this had been transmitted to me I can't recall, but it was so firmly instilled that to find myself suddenly unable to be in the presence of my older cousin without getting a raging boner put me in a metaphysical panic. This was one of the things for which one burned in eternal hell fire. Nor did it make any difference that, whatever her outward changes, Mimi would quickly reveal herself to be as dull as ever. Moreover, she had acquired along with her new looks a cheeky brazenness and self-regard, so that she was now as obnoxious as she was arousing. At home, she would bounce about in skimpy tops and hot pants. My aunt, straitlaced and tradition-bound as any Greek mother, seemed unbothered by such behaviour. This puzzled and scandalized my mother. And though she said nothing to my aunt directly, she could not hide her approval when my uncle, the only other person in the house who seemed to deplore Mimi's immodesty, would admonish his daughter to have some self-respect and go to her room and put on something decent. In later years, and after I'd gotten to know Mimi better, I would wonder whether my mother was ever moved by my cousin's antics to recall her life under the colonel and her own seditious efforts at autonomy.

As for myself, Mimi was in those days a constant torment. I dreaded her company as much as I craved it. I couldn't keep my eyes off her and could barely make it through dinner or sit through an entire TV show without yet another desperate trip to the bathroom. How long would it be before someone noted the frequency of these visits, or the length of my showers? And, in the end, what was it all for? At home and school it had been drummed into me that the sin lay not just in the deed but in the thought. I was going to hell.

But matters were to get even worse when I began school. Having been set to attend Holy Cross High School, I transferred to St. Thomas Aquinas. I would have preferred Holy Cross even with the longer commute, as I dreaded going to a school where I knew no one. But St. Thomas did have one significant advantage: it had recently become co-ed. The consequences of having girls in my classes, however, were not what I had imagined. The girls at St. Thomas had undergone the same accelerated ontogeny as Mimi. Most were older than me and towered over me. The girls in my year also made a point of expressing their preference for what they called the "mature boys," by which they meant the boys in the upper grades. As St. Thomas had only begun admitting girls the year before, the school had a preponderance, not just of males, but of older males who, having no girls in their own years, necessarily had to come fishing after those in ours, and against whose height, brawn, chest hair, spending money, and driver's licenses even the coolest of the guys in the lower grades could hardly compete. What hope did a runt like me have? I knew not even to bother trying. Thus, surrounded by these Amazonian beauties who barely knew I existed, I would spend every school day in a near-permanent state of tumescent delirium waiting for the bell to ring so I could rush home and apply myself to such rites and lustrations as alone could extinguish, however briefly, the infernal fires that consumed me.

Despite my concerns about not knowing anyone at St. Thomas, once I got there I wished to keep it that way. Wretchedly isolated as I may have felt, I was terrified of meeting new people. In those days, divorced and separated couples were virtually unknown, and the rare occasion you heard mention of such, it was in the tones reserved for the most shameful of topics. Not wishing to become the object of such talk, I kept to myself and hoped, like the exiled Dante, that no one would notice the wound of fortune I believed lay visibly upon me and for which I was sure I would be held accountable. At school, I avoided contact, and when I saw fellow Thomasites on the street, I maintained my distance and kept my head down. Not that anyone noticed. The only kids interested in me were the Frenchies, in whom I aroused a malign curiosity. Small and unaffiliated, I looked to them like a piece of raw meat. One particularly evil-looking trio could never pass me without directing a collective minatory scowl my way, and whenever I saw them coming, I would drop my gaze and give them a wide berth. One morning, however, one of them cut away from the pack and slammed up hard against me. Shaken but unhurt, I kept going while listening for a possible follow-up strike from behind. Mercifully, I heard only mocking laughter, followed, a few seconds later, by jeers of *"Modzi wup."* This came as both a relief and an annoyance, as I hated being called a *wop*. Even worse was when they called us *pea soup*. Why would they throw our slurs back at us? It didn't make any sense and only made them look stupid. I wished I could sit them down and explain, *"You're* the pea soups, not us. You, and only you. *You're* the pea soups, frogs, Pepsis, peppers, May Wests. The Italians are the wops. The *Italians*. Not the Greeks or Portuguese or Ukrainians. *Just* the Italians. Figure it out."

After this incident, I altered my route between home and school. One afternoon, however, as I rounded a corner, I spotted the nefarious band in conclave. They were standing at the bottom of a staircase, cackling and smoking cigarettes, and the instant I saw them, I turned and beat it. I heard a flurry of footfalls at my back, and seconds later I was pushed from behind and, hurtling forward, landed on the sidewalk. To the sounds of malevolent mirth, I picked myself up shakily and examined the scrapes on my hands. Both knees and my right elbow throbbed. Turning, I came face to face with the kid who had bodychecked me a few days earlier. He had a pug nose, big brown freckles, reddish-blonde greasy hair, and a chipped tooth. "*Quest-ce-que tu veux?*" I whimpered as he swaggered toward me like a juvenile John Wayne. "*Quest-ce-que j'ai fait a toi?*"

He crowded me up against a low wrought-iron fence so that its blunt finials dug into my back. I scanned the windows and balconies on the other side of the street but could see no one. Not a single pedestrian was in sight, or even a passing car. The Frenchie said something in French and his friends chortled. There was a smell of tobacco on his breath. Raising a hand, he began slowly loosening my scarf. I didn't understand what he was doing. I had once heard of a boy who, on his way to school, had been pinned to the sidewalk by a group of older boys, stripped of his pants and underwear, and left to run back home naked from the waist down. It was one of the most horrific things I had heard in my life. I couldn't imagine anything more humiliating, and now it might happen to me. Removing my scarf, the Frenchie stepped back and stretched it out as if to admire it while his friends snickered again. Then, as he ostentatiously wound it around his neck, there was the sound of a door opening behind me. The three ruffians froze, turned toward the sound, stared for an instant like startled deer, and took off. A few houses over, a rumpled middle-aged man came out on his stoop, coughed several times, and lit a cigarette. He was dressed in a windbreaker and striped pyjama pants and took no notice of me. I gazed down at the fleeing Frenchies, and when they turned the corner, I headed in the opposite direction. The guy on the stoop gave me an indifferent glance as he chewed on a cuticle.

In the coming days, I made further changes to my commuting habits. Mornings, I would leave the house fifteen or twenty minutes earlier than usual, and after school I would spend an hour in the library before making my way home. I stuck to back alleys. These posed their own hazards, but I preferred to take my chances with the bums, junkies, and dogs. Summertime, the alleys were filled with children playing or scavenging, but this time of year they were desolate and spooky. The alleys gave you an unguarded view of the neighbourhood. Out front the houses presented their mannerly public faces—the windows hung with lace curtains, the staircases swept, the porches and balconies clean and orderly—but here you saw them in their underwear and ratty slippers. Here were the rabbit pens and pigeon coops, the trash cans, junk piles, compost heaps, the furnace rooms (or sheds, as we called them). Everywhere, there was rotting timber and rusted tin; the porches and balconies sagged, the plank fences leaned drunkenly, everything held together with string and spit. The front gardens were planted with herbs and flowers, while here you saw tomatoes, zucchinis, peppers, onions, cabbages, and riotous vine trellises. In the afternoons you could smell the stews, soups, ragus, and meats cooking in kitchens; you could hear people quarrelling, laughing, talking on phones, mothers screaming, children crying. In wine season in the fall, you smelled the fermenting grapes. Without posted addresses, it was hard to know where you were exactly, which house was which. People would gaze at you suspiciously from their yards, wondering who you were and why you were skulking about in their alley. Out front, the yards and balconies were public space: people understood they were on display. But the hindquarters had a privacy and intimacy about them and you could feel like an intruder. On the clotheslines you would see corsets, panties, boxer shorts; you'd see shirts you recognized and realize it was the house of a kid in one of your classes. Next to them you might see his underwear or his mother's bras.

One afternoon, as I was making my way though St. Urbain's west-side alley, a flyer stapled to a wooden lamppost caught my attention. I'd been seeing lots of fliers like this, and they gave me the creeps. This one featured a black-and-white photo of three men seated behind a table. It looked crude and amateurish, and the photo was dark and grainy so you couldn't see the men clearly. All the same, you could see the anger on their faces. One of the men was familiar from other flyers and TV. In a couple of years, he would be premier of the province, but at the time I didn't know much about him except that he hated immigrants and wanted to kick the English out and make Quebec a separate country. There was some print beneath the photo, but it was in French and I couldn't piece the words together. Even so, I got the message. It was evident in the flyer's crudeness. The malice was manifest in its mere intrustion of the alley. I felt it as a personal threat and tried to imagine who had put it up. The fucking little queers. I knew this was a joke, but I didn't know what the initials really stood for. Something in French. They were bad people who did bad things, like planting bombs and kidnapping and killing people. A few years earlier, they'd made it so that it was dangerous to leave the house. We were ordered never to walk the streets alone or go downtown. Outside the fire station on Laurier and the Armoury on Esplanade, soldiers stood ready with machine guns.

As I studied the flyer, I was startled by a sound behind me and, before I could react, felt a stinging pain on my right calf. Spinning around as I let out a cry, I saw the redheaded Frenchie. In his hand was a long thin branch. I looked about but didn't see his Myrmidons. He was alone. Wagging his switch, he grinned at me as if to say, *You think you could hide, but I will track you down wherever you go.* He'd spotted me from Fairmount, or maybe he'd been walking along Groll. This was what happened when I let my guard down even for a few seconds. It was a lesson I must never forget.

The Frenchie was wearing my scarf, and, in case I hadn't noticed, he showily adjusted it around his neck. But I was preoccupied with how I might make an escape. My best hope was to get to St. Urbain via Groll, but I couldn't outrun this guy. Before I could make any move, however, he swiped again, this time striking me across the shins. "*Laisse-moi,*" I whimpered as I backed up against the lamppost. He smirked sinisterly, clearly fixing to swat me again. I kicked him and made a break for it, but I felt a tug on the back of my collar, and the next thing I knew I was on the ground. I rolled over to my side and covered my face with my arms as the blows fell fast and indiscriminately, slicing my hands, my neck, my legs. I screamed and begged but he kept flogging. Then there came a cry from somewhere, a cry not my own, and the lashes ceased. Still balled up on my side, I heard a scuffling of feet and opened my eyes. My assailant was standing with his back to me, facing another figure standing further away. Rolling over onto my knees, I wiped my face and neck and checked my hands for blood.

"Let's see you with someone your own size," a voice said in English.

I wiped my eyes, and when I looked up again, I recognized Carlos Medeiros. He stooped to pick something off the ground, and when he straightened up, I saw it was the Frenchie's switch. Thrusting a foot forward, he stood with legs apart like a fencer and twirled the end of the switch before the Frenchie's face; then, drawing his arm back, he wheeled the switch forward in a swift wide arc and swatted the kid across the face.

"Jesus!" I cried as the kid screamed and reeled.

"Not so tough now, eh?" Carlos said as I scrambled to my feet and retrieved my schoolbag. The Frenchie pawed at his face and stared at the blood on his fingers.

"Not so tough with someone your own size."

I'd heard about Carlos Medeiros even down on Esplanade. He was known throughout the neighbourhood. People said he was a mental case, like his older brother Ernesto. He was wild and dangerous. He was also one of the top players in Sun Youth's Little League, and I'd seen him play a few times. Once, he almost hit the ball over the fence.

"Here, look," he said, tossing away the switch. The French kid was bent over, wiping his face. "Hey, look!" Carlos shouted and held up his hands. The kid glanced up. "You and me. No weapons." The kid sputtered something in French. Serenely, Carlos stepped toward him and, with boggling speed and ferocity, landed a fist flush in the kid's face. I'd never seen anything like it. I had seen fights, but guys pulled their punches, made a show of swinging. Occasionally you'd see a smack to the side of the head but mostly it was body blows. I'd never seen anyone connect to the face, or not with such force. I recoiled as if I'd been struck myself.

The kid fell to his knees, screeching and sputtering unintelligibly.

"No! Please!" I shouted as Carlos grabbed his hair. "What are you doing? Stop!"

But I might as well have been ringside at a wrestling match. Carlos gripped the kid's hair close against the scalp and forced his head back. The kid stared up with gimpy eyes, his mouth covered with blood and snot. There were bloodstains on my scarf. The kid breathed heavily and made a low gurgling sound. "Let him go!" I pleaded as Carlos clamped his right hand around the kid's jaw. He squeezed hard, as if to pry the kid's mouth open, but the kid pressed his lips tighter. Carlos let go the kid's hair and pinched his nostrils shut. "Stop, please," I whimpered as he got a firmer grip around the kid's slick jaw and squeezed harder. The kid groaned and kept his lips pressed tight. But then, after a few seconds, he had to open up for air, and the same instant, Carlos horked back and let fly a fat green gob straight into the kid's mouth.

He stepped back and the kid fell to his hands, spitting and gasping. I thought he might retch. Carlos lunged at him again. "No!" I shouted. I felt I should intervene, but I was too frightened. Grabbing a clump of the kid's hair again, he clutched it and, in a slow, smooth, almost balletic motion, pulled him to his feet. The kid hung like a marionette, his gleaming eyeballs tilted at Carlos as though in search of clues to what fresh horror awaited him. "No!" I shouted as Carlos raised a fist. "Please! No!"

For several seconds, Carlos remained poised with his fist raised; but then he let the kid go, wiping his hands, front and back, on the kid's jacket. "If I ever see you around here again, or..." He pointed at me. "...if you ever go near that guy...I promise you'll end up in the hospital. *Tu comprends?*" The kid was barely conscious. His face was glazed with blood and goo. "*Va t'en!*" Carlos said and kicked him in the ass. Staring straight ahead zombie-like, the kid staggered away.

I didn't know what to do. Was I safe? Should I take off? For several seconds, Carlos watched the kid head up toward St. Viateur. Then he turned to me and said, "You're lucky I was in the yard and heard you."

I was still shaking, though I didn't know whether it was from the beating I'd received or the one I'd witnessed. "Thanks," I said.

"You're Mimi and Terry's cousin, right?"

"Yeah."

He observed me silently. "Are you living with them?"

"For now."

"And that lady is your mother?"

"Yeah."

I was sure I knew what was coming next.

"So what are you doing now?"

Unsure how to take the question, I didn't reply.

"Wanna play pitch and catch?" Carlos asked.

This took me aback. It wasn't what I'd expected, and I thought it pretty decent of him, especially given all I'd heard about him.

"Sure," I said.

"Java mitt?"

Again I hesitated.

"Java baseball mitt?"

Since we'd left Esplanade, my mother had made several trips back to the house to retrieve clothing and other items, but my mitt hadn't been among these. She'd invited me to accompany her on a couple of these expeditions, but I declined for fear we might bump into my friends. It hadn't occurred to me to ask her for my mitt. I never imagined I'd have any use for it.

"I have one," I said, "but I don't... I mean, I have it at home, but..."

"Sawright, I got an extra. Why don't you go home and leave your schoolbag, and then meet me back here."

I needed a moment to take this in. For several seconds, I stood motionless, watching Carlos go into his yard; then I turned down Groll and ran as fast as I could to my uncle's place. I couldn't believe this was real. I was hanging out with Carlos Medeiros. Was such a thing even possible? The news would get to my friends on Esplanade eventually and I tried to imagine the rumours that would spread. I wondered whether they would be as exaggerated as those about Carlos Medeiros, who, as it turned out, was nothing like his reputation. Yes, he was tough and scrappy and fearless, and occasionally he was even volatile and aggressive, but he was no mental case. He was one of the smartest guys I'd ever met, though not in a bookish or academic way. He was also warm and funny and extremely generous. Though he was a year older than me, he was still in elementary school because his parents had put him back two years when they'd arrived in Canada from the Azores. He'd had no English, so they had decided he should start school all over again. They did the same with his brother Ernesto, who, a year older than Carlos, was put back *three* grades. They themselves had no schooling at all and couldn't even write their own names. They signed cheques with an X.

Carlos and I would grow very close. For some reason, he developed a peculiar fondness for me. It was clear why I was so attached to him. He helped me navigate this new world I had entered. On his side, it was less obvious. Having saved me from the Frenchie, maybe he felt responsible for me. I got to know his friends, most of whom were Portuguese, Italian, and Greek. Many I'd seen around before, though we'd never spoken. A couple were in my classes. All of them were fanatical about sports, even the guys who weren't particularly good. That was how they spent most of their time outside school. Fall and winter, they would play touch football and hockey, while in the summer it was non-stop baseball. Once school let out, we played baseball every day. Sometimes we played kids from other parts of the neighbourhood. As these matches put your street's honour on the line, they could get ugly. Fights would break out. I learned to avoid these contests or sit them out, usually by volunteering to act as umpire. I had developed a reputation as an impartial and honest broker.

Perhaps because of his experience in Little League, Carlos liked to maintain a strict order and method around our sporting activities. He kept record books in which were documented not just wins and losses but also detailed individual statistics, such as goals scored, assists, touchdowns, home runs, batting averages, RBIs, ERAs, bases stolen, penalties, and so on. Frequently, participants would also include post-game personal reflections and prose commentaries. Each sport had its own spiral notebook, each a different colour, and every now and then Carlos pulled them out and we would browse the pages together and reminisce about past games, recalling highlights and lowlights and drawing important lessons.

When we weren't playing sports, we would play board games, card games, table hockey (which had its own record book), and street games like Simon Says and Babies. Now and then, we'd gather at the De Melos's place and make crank calls. Everyone collected trading cards and we'd play topsies, nearsies, flips, knock-downs, and other such games. Sometimes we'd just hang out on someone's stairs and shoot the shit or wrestle on the sidewalk. There was one group of guys, consisting primarily of Doug Rowley, Manny Oliveira, and the De Melo brothers, who were dedicated shoplifters. Doug Rowley was one of the few Anglos in the gang, and one of the few among us who didn't live on St. Urbain Street. Doug and Jose had met in elementary school, and bonding over their shared affinity for petty larceny, they'd become fast friends. Doug and both De Melo brothers were banned from most of the variety stores in the neighbourhood, so they did their shoplifting downtown. It was amazing what they could bag. They had ingenious techniques and strategies, and besides the usual kid's stuff, like candy bars, chips, gum, and comic books, they would cop porn magazines, record albums, clothing, sporting equipment, tools, and even more unlikely spoils. Some things they stole for themselves, others they sold to kids at school. For a fee they'd take special orders.

A few months after I arrived on the scene, Manny Oliveira made an extraordinary discovery. Something of a mechanical prodigy, Manny was the guy everyone took their bikes to when they needed serious repairs. A compulsive fixer and tinkerer, he discovered that spring that if you hammered down a penny to roughly the size of a quarter, the resulting slug could fool a wide range of vending and arcade machines. Even better, its unavoidable imperfections would often cause it to catch inside the coin slot and induce the machine to cough out extra credits. Manny disclosed his discovery to a trusted few of us (among whom I was included because of Carlos's imprimatur), but none of us believed him. So we all went down to a St. Catherine Street arcade for a demonstration. He might as well have trotted out the hen that laid golden eggs. We went nuts. We were restless to begin minting these things.

The problem was, producing these counterfeits was arduous and time-consuming. Perhaps Manny only revealed his secret because he needed helpers. Essential to the process was a grindstone, and as Manny was the only one who had not only access to such a tool (his father's) but also any proficiency with it, we would meet in his backyard when his parents were at work. Manny would station himself in the shed, and while three or four of us applied ourselves to the callus-forming labour of hammering down pennies in the lane, he would do the finishing work of smoothing and rounding out their edges on the grindstone. Those of us in on the enterprise had been sworn to secrecy. We'd also vowed never to use the forgeries in neighbourhood joints, as the owners kept a close eye on us, and it wouldn't have been difficult to figure out where they came from even if we weren't caught red-handed. We reserved them for the downtown arcades, where we had anonymity and, given the lack of personnel and oversight, little risk of getting caught.

Until that spring, I had hardly ever been downtown. Twice a year, my parents took me to Eaton's or Morgan's, but otherwise I rarely ventured south of Pine Avenue. Downtown Montreal was the most glittering, glamorous, exciting place I'd ever seen. I loved the crowds and traffic, the noise, the skyscrapers. I loved the way the people looked and spoke, the men in suits and ties, the thin, beautiful, stylish women, the sound of their exotic unaccented English. Some of them probably lived and worked in the surrounding buildings and skyscrapers, natives of that numinous white-collar world I knew only from TV. I pictured them in high sunlit offices with big windows and spectacular views, the men speaking into intercoms and dictating letters, cross-legged women scribbling on notepads or tapping on typewriters at their desks. And everyone constantly attending meetings. I wasn't sure what meetings were for. None of the adults I knew went to meetings. But on TV they made up an important part of people's jobs.

At first, I would go downtown strictly for the arcades, but soon I tagged along for other reasons. I even tried my hand at shoplifting, confining myself to books and magazines. But it didn't last long. One day, as a group of us prowled the aisles of Eaton's toy department, I watched in horror as Doug Rowley got collared by a store dick a few feet away from me. I was sure I was next, even though I had nothing on me. But no one noticed me or realized that Doug and I were together. Still, merely to see him nabbed and frogmarched away was enough to scare the thieving itch out of me forever. All they found on him was a pack of magician's cards, but as it was his third offense at Eaton's, they sent him to Station Ten and had his father come down to collect him. We heard about it the next day, Doug showing us the welts and bruises on his arms and back. Some, he said, were put there by the cops, others by his father. He sounded almost proud. I found it hard to believe the cops would beat up a fifteen-year-old over a pack of cards, but the others said this was typical of Station Ten. They were known for brutality. Whatever the truth, the incident had not the slightest effect on Doug, who was back at the shopping centres the next day.

I tried to picture my parents getting a phone call from the police and picking me up at the station. I wouldn't get a beating, but I wouldn't need one: the shame and humiliation would be enough, their horror and disappointment leaving far deeper wounds than the abrasions Doug Rowley showed us. I decided I wasn't prepared to take such a chance.

Since being rescued by Carlos, I had never again been harassed by the Frenchies. They backed off. His reputation extended even into their circles.

I continued to rove the back alleys, usually on garbage days. It was amazing what marvellous loot you could find there, what people considered garbage. Since moving to St. Urbain, I had found a yo-yo, a wooden top, a tennis racket in its press, tennis balls, a baseball bat, a working transistor radio, and a couple of *Playboy* magazines. One afternoon, while roaming our own lane, I saw in the distance a guy I recognized. He was seated cross-legged on the ground and rummaging through a large box. Though I knew who he was, we'd never spoken. Most of Carlos's gang lived south of Groll and this guy lived up near St. Viateur. He also didn't go to St. Thomas.

As I got closer, I saw that the box was full of books. "You claiming all of those?" I asked.

He gave me a quick glance. "You can take some if you want," he said. "Except those." He pointed to a stack of paperbacks beside the box.

I crouched beside him and began fingering through the books. They were divided between paperbacks and hardcovers. Some of the hardcovers were missing their jackets, and a few of the paperbacks were soiled and waterlogged, but all appeared to be intact and legible.

From the corner of my eye, I could see my neighbour scrutinizing me. "You read books?" he asked.

I looked at him. I was mad about books, but it wasn't something I ever talked about. "Yes," I said, feeling a strange relief in finally being able to tell someone.

"Me too."

I resumed my search through the box with a sudden sense of elation. I knew this stranger and I would be friends.

"You're Mimi's cousin."

"Yeah."

"I go to the same school as her."

"I know. You're Perry Kanaris."

"And your name's Alex, right?"

I nodded.

"But I don't know your last name."

"Doukas," I replied, pulling out a green paperback.

Perry glanced at it. "That's shit." The cover illustration showed what was either a robot or some kind of space alien. "Trust me. I've read it."

I put the book back in the box. There was an odd mix of titles and authors, though I wouldn't have known it then. There was Michael Crichton, Charles A. Reich, Susan Sontag, Philip Rieff, James Baldwin, Kahlil Gibran, L.P. Hartley, Samuel Beckett, Sylvia Plath. There were paperbacks by James Michener the size of dictionaries and thin chapbooks of poetry. Thomas Harris was jammed between Alvin Toffler and T.S. Eliot; Leon Uris lay atop Germaine Greer. The names meant nothing to me.

"Hey, I just realized," Perry said. "With you here, we can carry this thing together. My place is just up here," he said, pointing. "Make you a deal. You help me carry these and we'll be co-owners. Fair?"

"Sure."

"Dyn-oh-mite!" He leapt to his feet and brushed the back of his jeans. We put all the books in the box and, crouching opposite each other, lifted.

"You okay?" he asked.

"I'm fine."

We started up the lane, Perry at the front, walking backward. A cat paused mid-stride atop a wooden fence and watched us.

"Let me know if you need to stop," Perry said.

"You too."

He slowed to adjust his grip and the cat bolted. We continued past bulging garbage bags, a pile of grey weathered lumber, a rusted fridge. Somewhere a dog barked. Another answered.

"You okay?" Perry asked.

"I'm fine."

We passed through a smell of piss and rotting fruit. The dogs got louder and stepped up their barking. Inside Perry's yard, we put the box down on a wooden bench, and he opened the shed. As we carried the box inside, we could hear his mother shouting. The shed had the usual dank chemical smells, but there also came from the kitchen a smell of fried onions, garlic, cloves, and cinnamon. As Perry looked around for a place to put the box, there was an angry scrape of slippers against linoleum in the corridor and the sound of Perry's mother shouting again. The instant she saw me, she fell silent.

"This is Alex," Perry said nonchalantly.

The way she smiled at me, I could tell she knew who I was. She was up on the gossip. "How are you, Alex?" she said genially, but her discomfort was obvious.

"I'm fine. How are you?"

"Let's put it here," Perry said, and we set the box down by some paint-stained paint cans stacked in a pyramid. Next to them was a tall metal shelf unit loaded with tools and hardware. More tools and equipment hung on the raw wooden walls. In one corner stood the oil furnace. On the berth above us lay the oil barrel.

"What have I told you about bringing garbage into the house?" Perry's mother shouted.

"It's books."

"I don't care what it is. I don't want cockroaches in the house."

"There's no cockroaches. It's books! We looked through them. They're clean."

"Perikli!"

"But it's not garbage. They're clean. Look at them yourself."

"I don't care what they are, you're not bringing them into the house. Take that box out right now."

Perry stamped a foot.

"Perikli! Now! I don't even want them in the shed. Now, now! Alex, are you hungry?"

"No, thank you."

"Do you want something to drink? Orange juice, Coca-Cola?"

"No, thank you. Nothing."

"You have to have something."

As Perry and I lifted the box again, she disappeared back into the house. We returned the box to the bench in the yard. "I'll bring them in a few at a time," Perry said. "She won't know. I'll put a plastic sheet over it and put it under the veranda. That's actually better. You can come by whenever you want. The gate's never locked."

"No, I'm not just going to break into your backyard."

"It's not breaking in. You want to choose some now? As long as you don't take the ones...Wait, I'll just take them out again." He tipped the box over slightly and straddled the bench.

"It's okay, I know which ones they are."

Behind him appeared his mother, shuffling into the yard in her slippers and holding a couple of glasses of orange juice.

"I don't want orange juice," Perry said. "Did I tell you I wanted orange juice?"

"Take it," she commanded, thrusting a glass at him. Perry set it down on the ground, beside his stack of books. "You're going to break it there!" his mother shouted.

"Where do you want me to put it?"

"Alex," she said, handing me my glass. "Just hold it for a minute." She went back inside, returning a few seconds later with a small foldout table. "Pick up your glass," she said to Perry and set up the table. "Alex, I take it you'll be eating with us tonight. I'll have the table set in half an hour."

"Oh no."

"What no? There's no no here."

"They expect me at home. I can't. Thank you."

"Go inside and phone them. Tell them you're eating with us tonight. I'm making okra."

Perry made a sound.

"You shut up!"

"I understand if you don't stay," Perry said to me in English.

"Do you like okra?" his mother asked. "Or are you like this one?"

"No, I like them," I lied. "But I have to go. Thank you."

"Are you sure? We're just waiting for his brother. Where's Spiros?"

"How am I supposed to know?" Perry said, digging through the books.

"That's disgusting! Don't put your hands in there! You're going to eat soon!"

"So?"

"Alex, tell me if you change your mind. You're welcome to stay."

"Thank you. But I really do have to go."

"I'm not going to pressure you." She turned to Perry. "And *you*! You better wash your hands before you come to the table. Wait till I tell your father."

"Tell him what?"

"I told you to get rid of that. I don't even want it in the yard. Do you do this too, Alex, drag garbage into the house?"

"Of course he does!" Perry shouted. "Everybody does! It's not garbage!"

"What do you call it? What's it doing in the lane waiting for the garbage collector if it's not garbage?"

"Leave us alone!"

When his mother was gone, Perry lifted his glass for a swig. I straddled the end of the bench opposite him and searched through the box. Most of the titles and authors were unknown to me, yet every book beckoned me. With some it was the jacket or cover design, with others, the title or the blurbs; or, as with H.P. Lovecraft and Gore Vidal, the name of the author. Uninitiated as yet into the taxonomies of taste, I picked through the box without design or bias, drawn as much by F. Scott Fitzgerald as by Frederick Forsyth. *The Day of the Locust* seemed to me as intriguing as *The Day of the Jackal*, *Tai-Pan* as exotic as *Typee*. For a long time, I stared at the spine of a red hardcover missing its jacket. Once again it was the author's name that had caught my attention, though the title was also strange. I sounded out both in my head.

"I started that," Perry said. "I thought it was boring."

Intrigued by the title, I placed the book on the ground.

"Have you read this one?" Perry said excitedly, lifting out a blue paperback. I shook my head. "Okay, this you *gotta* read."

I studied the cover. It showed a flying saucer hovering massively above a cluster of skyscrapers.

"You like science fiction," he said, more as an assertion than an enquiry.

"Yeah."

"Okay, you definitely gotta read that."

I placed it on top of the red hardcover. The truth was I wasn't sure how I felt about science fiction. The little I'd read I'd found confusing. But, then, what *didn't* I find confusing? Just about every book confounded me one way or another. Yet I persisted. I still don't fully understand what drove me. I couldn't believe it when Perry said he hadn't finished the red hardcover. I had never not finished a book. I doubted I had ever found one boring. Even when I didn't understand a book, which was most of the time, I wouldn't give up. I would sit with it like a monk brooding on a koan. I would read and reread sentences, paragraphs, entire chapters. I remained spellbound even when befuddled. There was something in the struggle, in grappling with words, in the need to understand, to break through their opacity. Books pointed to a larger world, one remote from mine, a world I didn't understand but sensed I ought to. My own world was narrow and incomplete, false somehow, not the real thing. I knew the real world was out there. Indeed it was all around me; yet, at the same time, it was elusive, invisible. TV offered occasional glimpses of it, but TV, I knew even then, was mostly lies and fantasies; it was counterfeit, deceptive, a shabby simulacrum. Perhaps this was the reason for my impatience with science fiction. It was just more fantasy. I craved the real. And books—or certain books—seemed to offer the best access to it.

"Holy shit," I heard Perry exclaim. I glanced up and he thrust a yellow paperback at me. "Do you know this one?" I read the title and shook my head. "*This* you gotta read."

"Is it science fiction?"

"No, but you won't believe it."

I accepted the book and examined its plain yellow exterior, front and back. "What won't I believe?"

"Just trust me. You won't believe it."

I gathered up all three books and rose to my feet.

"Where you going?" Perry said.

"I gotta go home."

"That's all you're taking?"

"It's enough for now. I'll come back when I finish them."

That evening after dinner, I cut out early and went to my cot. I picked up the yellow paperback and, turning to a random page, saw the word *rabbi*. A few lines below it, I saw the word *Jewish*. I felt a slight tingle. Was it possible? Was this what Perry was referring to? Did he share my confusion? My mother came into the room and went over to her bed. Still in her day clothes, she lay on top of the covers. Through the closed door, I could hear the TV and my cousins' voices. Continuing to leaf through the paperback, I now snagged on a chapter title. It consisted of two words: *Cunt Crazy*. I assumed the first had another meaning from the one I knew. I picked up my dictionary (which I kept on the floor by my cot), but I couldn't find the word in it. I knew what this usually meant—but it couldn't be. I picked up the novel again and began the chapter.

Perry was right: I couldn't believe it. I couldn't believe what I was reading, the actuality of the words themselves. It didn't seem possible.

My mother left to change into her nightgown, and I put down the book, my heart racing. I wasn't worried about being discovered. Even if she had bothered to examine what I was reading, which she never did, she wouldn't understand it. But it still felt uncomfortable reading such a book with my mother a few feet away.

She came over and kissed me goodnight. "I'm going to turn off the light," she said, and as she reached for the wall switch, I turned on the mogul lamp behind me. As she got under the covers of her bed, I settled back and turned to the first chapter. From the first sentence, I had a hard time making sense of what I was reading. I had difficulty understanding simply what was going on. It was all so abstract, almost surreal. Every page was full of words I didn't know—*delusions, incarnations, sallow, suppository, ubiquity, insignia, bonditt, goy, shkotzim*—and some weren't even in the dictionary. Still, it was spellbinding. The book touched upon one of the great mysteries of the world.

Turning over in bed, my mother opened her eyes and asked what I was doing.

"I'm just reading."

"What time is it?" She propped herself up on an elbow and squinted at the clock on the coffee table. "It's after midnight," she said. "You have school in the morning."

"Just a few more minutes."

"No, now. Go to sleep."

I turned off the lamp. But my whole body was vibrating. I had no idea such things could exist in print. I wouldn't have believed such things existed outside my own diseased mind. The novel's narrator described things even worse than anything I'd ever dreamed up. Equally fascinating, though, was the way he described them. The language of the novel struck me as jarringly at odds with the subject matter. I'd never heard the vulgar and obscene sound so decorous and high toned. I was as much captivated by the prose as by the plot and characters, by the shimmer and strangeness of the words, the shape and texture and energy of the sentences, by what, in short, I would in later years learn to call the *style*.

Only when I read *Portnoy's Complaint* again as an adult would I realize how funny it was. That first time there was no laughter. The novel seemed deadly serious. It also seemed scandalous, deviant, immoral. Titillating as it was, it frightened and alarmed me as well, partly because it hit so close to home. The similarities and resonances were uncanny. This was in large measure what made it so fascinating. Despite how alien and often incomprehensible the story and characters were, much was familiar. Aspects of the narrator's family and his domestic situation were mysteriously and sometimes disturbingly recognizable. We even had the same name. Then there was the more private and degenerate stuff, which I found reassuring, even liberating. It gave me reason to hope, to believe that I might not be as bent as I thought. It turned out there were others like me—even worse than me! Perhaps such fantasies and impulses were more widespread than I had realized. Perhaps they weren't so deviant after all. There was also something comforting, as well as admirable, about the narrator's candour, in the matter-of-fact way he discussed his worst depravities.

I ripped through the book in a week. Then I spent another week rereading parts of it, perhaps most of it. By the time I was ready for my next book, I wasn't in the mood for aliens and monsters, so I chose the red hardcover. One Saturday afternoon, I grabbed it and rode my bike to a small park I often went to in the warmer months to read. It was one unfrequented by my friends, so I could usually count on remaining undisturbed. The park was quiet and I snagged my favourite bench, which faced the high stone church on the east side of the park. Stacked like a wedding cake, the church had a pinnacle turret up the middle and a profusion of columns, colonettes, niches, balustrades, friezes, cornices, medallions, and other forms of dizzyingly ornate stonework. I removed the book from my sissy bar, where it was fastened with a couple of rubber bands, opened to the first page, and began reading. I got as far as the second sentence. It read: "He trudged along St. Dominique Street to within sight of the school." I read the sentence several times. It was like *Portnoy* all over again: I found myself doubting my eyes. I looked up for a street sign. I confirmed the name: St. Dominique. I glanced back down at the book. Okay, so there was another St. Dominique Street somewhere. I knew it was not uncommon for streets in different cities to have the same name. New York had a Park Avenue, and Paris a Boulevard Saint Michel. There were hundreds of Main and Elm and Oak Streets. Still, it seemed an amazing coincidence that I should be reading a novel containing a St. Dominique Street while I was seated on another St. Dominique Street. What were the odds?

I kept reading, and in the next paragraph I paused over another familiar name: Fletcher's Field High School. This second coincidence sent a jolt through me. Then I saw the word *Outremont*. There was no question about it: I was reading about Montreal. I was reading a novel set in Montreal—and not just in Montreal, but in my very own neighbourhood. I discovered further that the main character even lived on St. Urbain Street—and not just on St. Urbain Street, but on my very own block.

I refastened the book to my sissy bar, jumped on my bike, and rode as fast as I could to Perry's house. Perry's mother answered the door and led me to his room. Perry was lying prone on his bed, reading a comic book. Before he could even get up, I was waving the hardcover at him, panting, "This is *here*. This novel's about *here*. About this neighbourhood!"

He scowled at the book and said, "Yeah, I know. That's the one they made the movie of."

"What movie?"

"The one they made here a couple of years ago, remember? When they closed down the streets? And there were those old cars all over the place?"

Of course I remembered. Two years earlier, a film had been shot in the neighbourhood and it was all anyone could talk about. I hadn't seen any Canadian movies other than the drab black-and-white documentaries forced on us at school. I didn't know Canada made any other kind. But this one had appeared to be the real thing, with actors, costumes, vintage cars. Some of the actors were Americans. The shooting lasted for weeks, and every day people would try to find out where it was taking place so they could watch from the sidelines. Some went hoping they would get picked from the crowd to act as extras. Lambros Arvanitis's uncle and cousin had managed to get themselves in a couple of scenes.

"That was based on this book?" I said.

"Yeah." Perry grabbed it from me and looked at the spine. "*The Apprenticeship of Duddy Kravitz*. Stupid title."

"You know what it means?"

"I didn't finish it."

Having looked up the word *apprenticeship*, I had thought the book might be a historical novel about somebody learning to be a carpenter or blacksmith. I agreed it wasn't a very good title.

"I thought it was boring," Perry said, tossing the book back at me.

"But it takes place on this block. He lives right on this fucken block."

"So?"

I couldn't understand Perry's nonchalance. A novel set in Montreal seemed to me monumental. I didn't know it could be done. Everything I had ever read was set in places like New York or London or Paris, or outer space. And there was little difference among these, New York, London, and Paris having no more reality for me than Mars. To read a novel set in my own drab insignificant corner of the world felt seismic.

But there was something else, almost equally momentous. By coincidence, both *Portnoy's Complaint* and *The Apprenticeship of Duddy Kravitz* dealt with what, after sex, was for me one of the most consuming and impenetrable of life's mysteries—namely "the Jews." I didn't know it then, but my neighbourhood had once been a Jewish ghetto. It was no longer such, but quite a few Jews remained, mostly Hasids. We knew them simply as "the Jews." Thus, throughout my childhood, in my mind a Jew was a bearded man with side curls and complicated headgear or a woman in a long boxy dress pushing a multi-seat stroller. I still remember my confusion when I'd learned that the pharmacist on Park Avenue and the elderly couple who owned the grocery store on Marie-Anne were Jews. I heard the rumours about Captain Kirk and Mr. Spock. They too were Jews. As were Jerry Lewis, the Three Stooges, the Meathead on *All in the Family*, and Sammy Davis Junior. But what possible connection could these stars have to the grim figures who stalked our neighbourhood? If Captain Kirk and the Three Stooges belonged to the same group as these stygian isolates, then who were "the Jews"?

There was no shortage of information on this subject. But it was confusing and contradictory. For instance, it was well known that the Jews were rich. But to look at the ones in our neighbourhood, you had to wonder what they did with all their money. You also had to wonder what in the world these woolly men in black satin coats, white hose, and hats like birds' nests could possibly do that was so profitable. Many of them owned or worked in butcher shops and groceries and clothing stores, most of which weren't doing so well. True, every now and then you'd see one driving a Cadillac or Lincoln Continental, but most didn't even own a car. And if you peeked through the open windows and doorways of their houses in the summer, their apartments looked no different from our own. A common explanation was that they were involved in illegal activities like loansharking and selling drugs or stolen goods. But one day Tina, Lambros's sister, asked, "If they're are all so rich, why do they live here? Why aren't they in Westmount?" I had wondered about this myself. Mike the Knife said it was because they were cheap. That was why they wore the same clothes and drove jalopies. Mike said they saved up their money and kept it in suitcases under their beds. He was also the one who told us that when a Jewish woman married, she had to shave her head. "That's why they wear wigs," he said. I'd never noticed this. But when I looked more closely, it appeared he was right. From Tony Cabral we learned the Jews had sexual intercourse through a hole in a bedsheet, and on Saturdays they couldn't touch electrical switches or appliances, drive a car, or ride an elevator. Dennis Leacock and Nick Tsoukalas said they couldn't eat pork, drink alcohol, or watch television. But Nick Papatheodoridis said the Jews were liars and hypocrites. He had a cousin on Jeanne Mance who was sometimes invited into his Jewish neighbours' homes to turn lights and appliances on and off, and he'd had glimpses of TVs and stereos inside cabinets and closets, stashed bottles of wine and liquor, and packages of hot dogs and bacon in the fridges. He had even seen the suitcases of money under the bed. And, once, through the chink in a doorway, he'd caught sight of a woman bald as Kojak.

It was Nick Papatheodoridis as well who told us about the kids in the synagogues. He said the basements of synagogues were full of kidnapped children in cages, whose blood the Jews would drink during their religious ceremonies. Louis Cabral said this was a lie, that it was cat's blood they drank. Victor Kowalchuk said they ate a special bread made from people's flesh. Some kids enquired why, if these things were true, we never heard of any of us going missing, and why, if *we* knew about these things, the police didn't? Mike said the police were paid off. They were in the pocket of the Jews, like the government. I wondered why, if the Jews were murderous bloodthirsty maniacs, we weren't more afraid of them. Given all these rumours, how was it we dared to taunt and ridicule them as we did? There were guys who would go up to a group of Jews walking by and roll pennies at their feet. I knew this was terribly insulting, but I didn't understand why. Just as I didn't understand the associated jokes: How do you get a Jew into a church? Throw a penny in it. How do you get twenty Jews into a Volkswagen? Throw a penny in it. How do you start a Jewish parade? Throw a penny down the street. What was it about pennies? Why were the Jews so enamoured of them? Was it the colour, the copper, the engravings? Even as an adult, I assumed the penny-tossing had been some piece of nonsense of our own invention. It wasn't until my thirties that I learned the practice had a long and international history. In Brooklyn it had a name: "Bend the Jew." As far as I know, we had no name for it. It also had no effect. I never saw any of the Jews take the slightest notice of the pennies or the boys throwing them. And if they did, none of it ruffled them. Maybe the Jews had no better understanding of the acts than I did.

That was certainly not the case with another prank, which though equally mystifying to me, never failed to get the Jews' attention. This one entailed raising an arm in a Nazi salute and shouting "Hi Hitler." It was also strictly for the most intrepid and fleet of foot as it invariably sent the Jews into paroxysms of outrage, and breaking into clamorous pursuit, they would dodge traffic and barking dogs, climb over fences and walls, and tramp through snow and ice and mud to apprehend the offenders. Draped as they were in their sepulchral vestments, however, they never did succeed. What would they have done with those boys if they'd caught them, beaten them up? Caged them up in the basement of their synagogue? Called the police? Actually, that's what they sometimes threatened. Abandoning the chase, they would return to chew the rest of us out. But what did *we* do? *We* didn't say anything. But this didn't cut it with these guys. We were *all* to blame, it seemed, and they would shake their fists at us and threaten to call the police. The police! What were the police going to do? Arrest us? For what? A stupid salute? I couldn't understand why it got them so worked up. Their reaction seemed grotesquely out of proportion to the provocation. We all hated Hitler, but we didn't fly into a murderous rage because someone flashed the *Hi Hitler* at us. We knew the gesture from bad movies and sitcoms, so for us there was something cartoonish and absurd about it. It contained also a kind of witchcraft, which I imagine now accounted for much of its compulsive allure. This is not to say there wasn't plenty of malice and scorn in it as well. But, looking back, I can't help thinking that the kick for those boys was in the gesture's inexplicable wizardry, in the mysterious and exhilarating power it gave them to transform, with the wave of a hand, these most reserved and mild-mannered of men into raging berserkers. Would they have done what they did had they understood what they were doing? I have to believe not. Perhaps I underrate the malice and cruelty of children; but there's also no rating the cruelty inflicted by mere ignorance.

I thought of asking my parents about it, but I knew better than to reveal to the adults what we were up to. Also, when I'd once asked my father about the kidnapped children and the blood, he'd slapped the back of my head and told me not to talk nonsense. As with the Russians and communists, my father was a hard one to figure out on the subject of the Jews. Often he and his friends would talk about them the same way the kids did. They would talk about how rich the Jews were and how they looked out only for themselves and how they ran the banks, the media, the government. I'd heard my father describe them as crafty and dangerous. But he would praise them too, often for reasons not so different from those for which he'd denounced them. "One thing about the Jews," he would say, "is they know how to raise their children. They value learning and culture, and they know how to preserve their wisdom and traditions and pass them on to future generations. We used to be like that, but no more. There's much we can learn from the Jews. Do you think they dominate the world simply because they're smart and resourceful? Other people are smart and resourceful, too. It's because they stick together. That's the main thing. They look out for one another. We've never had that, even in our heyday. If we could come together like that, there's no telling what we could accomplish. But we're constantly at each other's throats, tearing our house down from the inside. Take it from me, friends: if we Greeks are ever going to amount to anything again, we need to be more like the sons of Abraham."

Such, in short, were the dark shores on which those two novels had washed up like messages in a bottle. Hearing such talk afterward, I wanted to press these books on the person speaking, thinking perhaps they would do for him what they'd done for me, that they might hold up a mirror to his own ignorance and shine a light that would enable him not only to see farther and deeper but to see with new eyes what was right in front of him. But I knew, even then, that this was only childish naïveté.

If I retained any hopes of a reconciliation between my parents, they were put to rest that April. My father moved from Esplanade into a small rental on Park Avenue.

A few weeks later, my uncle announced that he'd bought a house in Park Extension. The Anagnostopouloses would be moving as well. It was understood my mother and I would not be going with them. My mother was livid. She'd had no idea my uncle was looking for another house. Why had he kept it a secret? She blamed my aunt. *She* had put him up to this, simply to be rid of us. For a while, my mother stopped talking to both of them. My uncle kept explaining to her that he had no plan to sell the St. Urbain property and we could remain in the apartment as long as we liked. She could even set her own rent, pay whatever she thought she could afford. But my mother would not be mollified and she kept up her sulking and scolding to the end, even as the movers were carrying out the last of the boxes. It appeared she'd been under the impression we would be living with her brother's family forever. If indeed my aunt wished to be unburdened of us, who could blame her?

But my aunt had always wanted to leave St. Urbain Street, from the outset. She'd made no secret of it. The neighbourhood was a slum. She envied friends who lived in Park Extension, which Greeks deemed more respectable. I never understood it. Park Ex was dreary and charmless. It was full of ugly highrises, the houses were drab, with tiny front yards or no yard at all, and the few places I'd been into struck me as pokey and jerry-built. But it was newer than Mile End, and this made all the difference. For most Greeks, Mile End retained a whiff of the boarding house. It had all kinds of associations from which they wished to distance themselves. Park Ex had been built after the war; it was new and fresh, and this alone gave it in immigrant eyes a sheen of bourgeois gentility. How could anyone have known then how quickly the sheen would fade, how in a few short years Park Ex would itself become a landing point for a new wave of immigrants, these ones of still darker origins and complexions, and prompt yet another Greek exodus to regions even further north?

Since coming to St. Urbain, I couldn't stop worrying about when and where we'd be moving next, and lived in dread of having to adjust yet again to a new environment and make yet another new set of friends. So when it turned out the Anagnostopouloses would be leaving and we'd be staying, I was ecstatic. As soon as they cleared out, I felt an ease and lightness I hadn't felt since we'd left Esplanade. A sense of stability and rootedness returned to our lives. At my aunt's insistence, most of the furniture and appliances had been left behind, including even her doodads and *bikhlibíthia*. The move to Park Ex represented a major step up, and she was determined her new home would be filled with new things. This benefited us significantly, as we wouldn't have had the money to furnish the place from scratch. My mother would have had to go begging to my father, which she loathed doing.

We settled in as soon as the Anagnostopouloses were gone. My mother took over the master bedroom while I got my cousins' room, along with the salóni, which I converted into a study. Apart from the emptied closet, the master bedroom was virtually unchanged. Even the items on my aunt's vanity were still there, including her combs and brushes, the little boxes of hairpins, her two-sided chrome swivel mirror, cracked on one side, the row of near-empty spray cans and bottles of perfumes and lotions, and her lacquered black music box with the ballerina with the broken leg. My mother kept them all. Nor did she seem to have any qualms about sleeping in her brother's matrimonial bed. Among the few pieces of furniture the Anagnostopouloses had taken was the dining room set, so we transferred much of the salóni's furniture there and turned it into a living room. The implication seemed to be that we would not be having any future dinner guests, and, if we did, they would have to content themselves with the kitchen.

Of the items we inherited from the Anagnostopouloses, the most significant for me was my uncle's subscription to the Saturday *Star*. It was at my request that he transferred the account to my mother's name. I had never understood why he had the subscription in the first place. Apart from the TV schedule and comics, which my cousins would seize and fight over the moment the paper arrived, the hulking remainder would be discarded like a gutted sturgeon. Seeing it languish with the preceding weeks' editions until they were all bundled up and thrown out, I took to appropriating it. At first, I only read the sports and entertainment, but soon I was browsing the other sections too, occasionally taking a stab at one of the articles, especially if I saw a headline connected to one of the confusing topics I had heard the adults talking about. These articles were usually dense and hard to understand, yet this spurred me on, and with the help of the dictionary and my encyclopaedias and globe, I would puzzle my way through their tangles of verbiage and try to make sense of them.

My favourite part of the paper by far was the arts and entertainment section, its pages mapping an obscure world of glamour and sophistication far removed from the world I inhabited. What captivated me were the sombre, high-minded pieces—profiles of writers and artists I had never heard of, tributes to local luminaries unknown to me, commentaries and think pieces I didn't even half understand, and reviews of movies, plays, concerts, and exhibits I knew I would never see. Reading these pages, I felt like a vagrant peering through a mullioned window at some high-society ball. I especially loved the movie ads, with their evocative imagery and their portentous taglines: "Shocking." "Riveting." "A masterpiece." "What cinema was meant to be." "The movie everyone's talking about." I wondered whether any of the movies at the Regency were masterpieces. I had an inkling they didn't even come close to what cinema was meant to be. But what *was* it meant to be? I desperately wanted to know. And who was doing all this talking? Not anyone I knew. I wanted in on this. I wanted to know what they were saying. I wanted to be shocked and riveted. The arts section conveyed that there were big, important things going on out there and confirmed my suspicions that my own amusements and pastimes were crude and second-rate and outdated. At the same time, it revealed that even the blandly familiar, the things I knew and that seemed mundane and trivial, had a depth and urgency I hadn't picked up on, that a sitcom like *The Jeffersons* or *Maude* or the latest album by Elton John or Donna Summer could contain political, social, and moral profundities worthy of reflection and serious debate.

Walking past the theatres downtown, I would see lineups and wonder what could possibly inspire such determination and patience. Thanks to the *Star*, I often recognized the movie advertised on the marquee and knew what people were saying about it. *Provocative. Scintillating. A passionate tale of obsession and longing.* By the time I was thirteen, I could name almost every movie playing in the city and tell you how long it had been showing. In the late winter, I could tell you how many Academy Award nominations it had, and in the spring, how many it had won. But I had yet to see a single one of these films.

I faced a couple of impediments. One was money, the price of a movie ticket then being over three dollars. The other was my age. The movies I most longed to see tended to be rated fourteen-and-over. I knew guys who'd seen such movies (Carlos and Perry among them) but either they were (like Carlos) actually fourteen or (like Perry) they looked older than their age. When I had tried to get into one, going with a couple of friends to see *Dog Day Afternoon*, I had been asked for an ID, and so as not to spoil things for the others, I had returned home on my own. But the experience had been so embarrassing, I was unwilling to try it again.

I couldn't wait till I turned fourteen. Weeks before my birthday, I decided what movie I would see the day after and arranged for Perry to come with me. Among my friends, he'd be the most amenable to the sort of thing I was interested in. He knew of the film, having caught some of the controversy around it, and was also curious to see it. I was flush with birthday cash and paid for his ticket. The theatre itself was a huge disappointment. Generally, the downtown movie houses didn't look like much outside, but inside I'd imagined them to have huge lavish hallways with grand winding staircases, gleaming arcades, voluminous crystal chandeliers, and vast velvet screening halls with colossal screens. This place, which was inside a shopping centre, was small and featureless. It made the Regency look like an opera house.

The movie we saw was *Taxi Driver*. It had been much in the news, praised and attacked with equal fervour, and I was eager to see what the fuss was about. Afterward, it was clear that neither Perry nor I had understood it, an awkward fact we skirted by focusing on the character of Travis Bickle and Robert De Niro's performance. The film had seemed meandering and shapeless. It had the rawness of a documentary. Even the dialogue, with its halting and jagged rhythms and fumbling syntax, sounded clumsy and impromptu, more like the talk of real people than the scripted lines of actors. Yet these qualities gave the film a gritty immediacy that was novel and daring and exciting. This was the first time I'd heard swearing in a movie, and it shocked me. I couldn't believe Hollywood actors knew such words. Even more confusing than the movie was the main character. I couldn't figure out what we were to make of him. He was clearly disturbed, and maybe a little stupid. Yet I found him sympathetic, even inspiring. I worried there was something wrong with me. But I couldn't deny it: I saw Travis Bickle as a noble and heroic figure. I understood his anger and alienation. I understood what it meant to be God's lonely man, to long for a real rain to come and wash away the scum off the streets. Here was a man who stood up against the scum, the filth, the shit, etcetera. I could appreciate that. I admired it. I didn't tell this to Perry.

I read everything about the movie I could get my hands on. I had devised a foolproof technique for stealing magazines (which involved one person slipping a copy inside a newspaper that an accomplice, coming in a few minutes later, would pick up upon entering the store and take to the counter for purchase), and soon I had amassed a pile of purloined issues of

Time, Rolling Stone, Film Comment, Sight & Sound, The Village Voice, and other periodicals featuring articles about the movie. One day at the New Miss Bernard, I was startled to hear Lazaros Katsouranis and Leftheris Asikis talking about the film. They were at the counter, and I tried to listen in on what they were saying. From what I could make out, they hadn't seen the movie and were discussing what they'd read about it in the Greek papers. When I left a half hour later, I paused at the counter and said to them, "You know, that movie about the taxi driver may be one of the best movies ever made. And Robert De Niro is the best American actor since Marlon Brando." I had seen two Brando movies my whole life.

"You saw that movie?" said Lazaros, the surprise on his face verging on scandalized incredulity.

"Yes. And you shouldn't believe everything you read. That movie shows how things really are in the world and some people don't like that."

"I hear it's very powerful," said Leftheris.

"Exactly. And some people can't deal with that."

When I dropped by the restaurant again a few days later, my father immediately signalled to me to wait for him in the back booth. I wondered if I was in trouble.

"What's this I hear?" he said when he joined me a minute later.

I tried to think of what I'd been up to recently that he might have gotten wind of. There were a number of possibilities.

"I was told you saw that movie about the taxi driver. Is this true?"

This I hadn't seen coming. "Yeah," I said, relieved.

"With who? When?"

"With Perry. A few weeks ago."

"Perry made you see this movie?"

"Nobody made me. In fact it was my idea."

"Really? *Your* idea?" My father nodded with mock approbation. "Bravo."

"What's the big deal?"

"You listen to me. Yiorgakis saw that movie and I couldn't believe what he described. Don't make a face. I can't believe they let a boy your age in. What kind of country is this? It made me shudder to hear Yiorgaki talk about it. He described some of the scenes, and the language. I thought he was joking."

"Yiorgakis barely knows English."

"I have a customer who saw it, an Anglo, and he told me he had to walk out, he was so disgusted. This is a movie for degenerates. It's pornography."

"It is not pornography!"

"I don't need you to tell me what it is. You know what that customer said to me? Do you know what he said?"

I waited.

"This is an educated man. An Anglo. He has a degree from McGill. And you know what he said to me? He said that if my thirteen-year-old son is seeing movies like that, I should be worried."

"I'm fourteen."

"I should be worried, he said. And I *am* worried. I don't know what's going on with you."

"I'm not thirteen."

"I don't care what you are. You are not to see such movies. Do you understand? I forbid it. These are not movies fit for a child your age."

"I am not a child!"

"They're not fit for adults. I can't believe the government allows movies like this to be made. What's wrong with this country? If my English were better, I would sit down and write a letter. Don't make that face at me. I'm telling you, if I ever get wind of—you listening? If I ever get wind of you going to a film like that again...I'll tell you this right now...I'm not even going to say anything. I'm just going to strap you down in a chair, pull your eyeballs out, fry them in olive oil, and feed them to you. Do you hear me?"

"A film like what? What kind of film are we talking about? How will I know whether I can see it or not?"

He raised a hand as if to smack me and I twisted back just in case.

"Don't play dumb. You know what I'm saying."

I could see Leftheris sneaking glances at us from the bar.

"Do you hear me?" my father said.

"Yeah, I hear you."

"Don't you talk to me like that. I'm serious."

"Yeah, okay! What do you want me to say?"

I didn't take this confrontation lightly. It had shaken me. And I drew an important lesson from it: never again would I say a word to any adult about my personal affairs. My parents' generation inhabited a different world, all of them, and anything I said or did was sure to be misinterpreted and distorted. I had no intention of abiding by my father's injunction. I would have gone to the movies every weekend, but having overcome the age barrier, I still faced the problem of money. By the time I was fifteen, it was the central problem of my life (apart from girls, which was not unrelated.) My interests were expanding and becoming more expensive, my love of music exceeding even that of film. But at four and five dollars a pop, albums were even further from my reach than movie tickets, never mind concerts. The situation was unsustainable.

I knew from TV that North American children got something called an "allowance," but my parents were unfamiliar with the concept. If I wanted something, whether a movie ticket, a pair of jeans, or a bag of chips, I had to ask them for money, which they usually refused. What to me was an urgent need was for them an extravagance. There was only one solution: I had to get a job. Already many of my friends worked. Tulio had a summer job at the Dairy Queen, Nino had a paper route, and Perry was already working for his uncle. Carlos had been working since the age of nine, delivering bread for a Portuguese bakery. As he did his rounds weekday mornings between 5:00 and 7:30 and collected payment on Saturdays, he was able to work even while going to school. I started looking for a job of my own, scanning the classifieds and scouring the neighbourhood for help wanted signs. I also put the word out with friends.

One afternoon, my father said to me, "What's this I hear you're looking for a job?"

I was sitting in my usual booth, reading the orange paperback edition of *1984* I'd found in our book box. "Who told you that?" I said, feeling a little like Winston Smith.

"Leftheris heard from the Armenian that you were in his store the other day asking for work."

"Which Armenian?"

"The grocer." He pointed vaguely. "Next to Kosta." He sat down opposite me. "Why didn't you tell me you're looking for work?"

"Why would I tell you?"

He leaned across the table as if to slap me. "You tell me *everything*. I'm your father."

"Do you tell me everything?"

"*I'm* the father. You're the child."

"I'm not a child."

"Let me explain something to you. No matter how old you get, you're the child in this relationship. That never changes. Why didn't you tell me you were looking for a job?"

I shrugged.

"If you're ever in need of anything, you come to me first, you understand? If it's work you want..." He leaned back and threw his arms out. "There's plenty I can find for you to do here."

"I want a *paying* job."

"I'll pay you."

"Oh yeah. What?"

"What I'd pay anyone."

"And what's that?"

"What the law says." In English: "Minimum wades."

I had considered this. I'd even come close to asking him. But I wasn't sure how I felt about working for my father.

"It would be good for me too," he said. "Having someone around I can trust. It would free me up a little. But, make no mistake: you'd be an employee like any other. Don't expect any special treatment."

"I never expect any special treatment from you."

"I see. That's the thanks I get."

I didn't know how my mother would react to the news. I thought she might get angry, maybe forbid it. I couldn't see her face when I told her. She was at the kitchen sink, peeling carrots, the back of her arms jiggling. Lentils were boiling on the stove. It was a Wednesday, so we were having a meatless dinner. In the last couple of years, she'd instituted a strict fasting policy: besides the standard abstentions on major holidays, we didn't eat meat, fish, eggs, or dairy on Wednesdays and Fridays.

"How much is he paying you?"

"Three dollars an hour."

"That's not very much," she said, adding a carrot to the celery stalks and onions in the upturned pot lid on the dishrack. I had expected greater resistance. I wondered whether this was a sign of how strapped we were.

"He says it's what he'd pay anyone."

"But you're not anyone."

Given how smoothly this had gone, I tried the next hurdle. "I was thinking I might keep thirty dollars a week." The figure was not arbitrary. My working friends handed over the bulk of their earnings to their parents, and I had asked them how much they kept. My figure was slightly above the average.

"Thirty dollars? What will a boy your age do with that kind of money?"

"It's not so much."

She picked up the brimming pot lid and carried it to the kitchen table. "What will you spend thirty dollars a week on?" she asked as she sat down.

"Who says I'll spend it? I'll save some. I'll open a bank account."

"We already have a bank account."

"I'll open my own."

"What for?" She cupped an onion in her hand and began dicing it, the knife blade slicing thumb-ward. "We'll say twenty."

"Twenty? That's nothing these days."

"That's plenty for a boy your age."

"How about twenty-five?"

"Twenty. And I want to know where you spend it. You're going to keep a written account. I want to know where every drachma goes."

I started at the restaurant a few days later. By now I had a good idea how it operated, but my father went over everything in minute detail. When Marie-Thérèse saw me in the kitchen in a white shirt and apron, she let out a cry. "*Ben voyons!* You work ear now?" Marie-Thérèse was a career waitress in her late forties. She had been at the restaurant since before my father took it over and was a crucial support and counsellor during the transition. Tall, thin, brassy, super-efficient, she applied heavy doses of sky-blue eyeshadow beneath pencilled eyebrows and piled her hair up in a high blonde bouffant like cotton candy. Coming over to me, she gave my cheek a hard pinch, a habit I knew from Greek women. "*Tsi choux*," she murmured, squeezing till I squealed. "Ey," she said, turning to my father, "your son da boss now?" He was at the grill with Demosthenes and he gave her a stern frown. "My son no have restorun. No stupid like father." He tapped his temple. "My son going work with brain."

For the first few weeks, I was confined to the kitchen—washing dishes, stocking, cleaning, helping the cooks. Later I was given busing duties and trained on the cash register. The work was monotonous and hard and I was on my feet all day. At the end of a shift I was bone tired. My whole body ached. The most taxing part of the job, however, was being around my father and his cronies—or "the droogs," as Perry dubbed them—for such extended lengths of time. The droogs were, among my father's innumerable friends and acquaintances, that core cohort who would drop by the restaurant on a regular basis. There must have been fifteen or twenty of them, some of whom would come in every day, or even several times a day, and others who'd pop by once or twice a week or every couple of months. Some would hang out for hours and order no more than a cup of coffee, if that. Over the course of the day, there was usually a contingent of the droogs, its size and members shifting from hour to hour. Some weren't happy about my working at the restaurant. I cramped their style. They'd been put under strict orders to watch themselves in my presence, though most didn't do a terribly good job of it.

Usually they would congregate in the back booth or at the bar. They would often be there even when my father wasn't around. As some were shop owners or independent contractors, they often discussed business and money, blabbering endlessly about taxes, interest rates, wages, revenues, etcetera. There was incessant talk of prices, what this cost against that, what you paid here versus there, where the best deals were, what you were likely to pay for the same thing tomorrow or in ten years. If they had the presence of mind, they would drop their voices when the talk turned to horses and gambling. And if they saw me coming, they would abruptly change the topic. They liked to gossip about businesses and businessmen around the city, particularly the successful ones, and they would trade stories and rumours about them, about the methods by which they'd made their fortune, the people they knew, the people they'd screwed, the palms they'd greased, and they would debate the lessons to be learned from their example. To me such talk was the howl of the void, a reminder not only of how boring and bleak the grownup world was but, more depressingly still, how ill-equipped I was for it.

Occasionally, I would hear the droogs talk about my father. This was how I finally learned how he had come into possession of the restaurant I wasn't even sure that I'd heard correctly. It was too preposterous to be believed, just another of the outlandish rumours these guys trafficked in.

But I couldn't get it out of my head, and when I mentioned it to Carlos and Jose, I noted their silence and the freighted glances they exchanged.

"Wait," I said, "you know something about this?"

There was more silence and then some hemming and hawing, but I got it out of them. My father had won the Miss Bernard Restaurant in a poker game. The tale was legendary. I may have been the only person in the neighbourhood who didn't know. No wonder my mother had reacted as she had. She'd probably guessed at the truth, or something close to it. Her behaviour now didn't seem to me so extreme. Carlos and Jose said they had always assumed I knew. They told me other stories as well, some even more outlandish than those about the restaurant. It turned out my father was something of a local Nick the Greek.

"Come on, man," Carlos said, "no one takes this stuff seriously. Everyone knows it's bullshit."

"How do you know? How do you know it's bullshit? You don't know."

"Come on."

"You gonna tell me you don't believe any of it?"

"We shouldn't have said anything," said Jose.

"Of course you should have. You should have told me a long time ago."

"Why? Look at how you're reacting," said Carlos.

"He's right," said Jose. "No one takes this stuff seriously. We know your father, we know what he's really like."

"No, you don't. You have no idea what he's like. *I* don't even know him."

"Come on, man," Carlos said. "Like your dad really sells drugs?"

"I don't know."

I would hear many more such stories, some from the droogs themselves. Things slipped out. As the years passed and they grew more comfortable around me or forgot I was there, they became careless, less guarded. One evening, while I was working the cash register, Sotiris Tagalos eyed a young waitress we'd just hired and, leering at her wolfishly as she went by, turned to me when she disappeared into the kitchen and said, "How long you think before Andreas is banging that little girl?" The remark hit me like a fist to the solar plexus. But Sotiris gave me a knowing smirk and a wink, as though he'd offered me a personal compliment.

I was beginning to see my father as he really was. I noticed things about him that had stared me in the face yet I'd somehow failed to see. Even as a child, I was aware how his manner would change around women, how he would become all suave and silky and joke and banter with them in what seemed to me a disingenuous and smarmy way, but I had attributed such habits to his Old World breeding and old-fashioned notions of etiquette. Only now did I see that he was *flirting*. How was I so blind and naïve? Watching him now with our female clients and waitresses was painful. With his pencil moustache and greased-back hair, his natty but outdated suits, his preening, simpering, sham courtliness, and his oleaginous and ungrammatical English, he seemed a grotesque caricature of the swarthy European playboy. Had he not been my father, I might have found him comical. But I felt embarrassed. I felt embarrassed for him and for myself. He was like a cartoon Casanova. It was hard to believe any woman could fall for his shtick, yet to hear the droogs talk, he was a Balkan Valentino. He couldn't keep the gómenehs away. Sometimes he would juggle several at once. He'd had affairs, or tried to, with most of the waitresses who had passed through our door. No wonder there was a constant turnover.

One afternoon, as he put the moves on a couple of French girls not much older than me, it dawned on me my father belonged to a certain type. This was a type of guy I knew well from St. Thomas Aquinas, the type who wore designer jeans and roach killers and permed his hair and listened to the Bee Gees and Giorgio Moroder and on weekends hung out at the Limelight and Club 1234. We had loads of these guys at St. Thomas and they struck me as little more than well-accessorized ruffians. Yet they were the cool guys, the guys who got the girls, even the nice girls and the smarter ones. These were the guys who got laid. And this, I realized that afternoon, was my father. He was one of these guys in middle age. My father was what these guys turned into.

"There's so many. We all know *deemocracy* and *pheelosophy* and *theolodzy*, but there are some you can't even tell. For example, do you know *khaïdzeen*?"

"Say it again."

"*Khaïdzeen*."

It was a Sunday evening, and apart from the droogs at the counter, there were few people in the place. I was seated by the cash register trying to read, but I was having trouble focusing.

"Ask our young scholar."

I groaned inwardly.

"Aleko! Reh, Aleko!"

Grudgingly, I glanced up.

"Do you know *khaïdzeen?*" asked Stavros Marangopoulos.

"What?"

"*Khaïdzeen, khaïdzeen.* Do you know this word?"

"I don't know what you're saying."

"Do you mean *khaïdzak?*" said Lazaros.

"No, no," said Stavros. "That's when you take over an airplane. I'm talking about *khaïdzeen.*" He turned back to me. "Do you know this word, where it comes from? It means cleanliness, being clean."

Light broke. "Hygiene."

"*Khaïdzeen,*" he repeated, as if correcting my pronunciation.

"What about it?"

"Do you know where it comes from?"

"No," I said and went back to my book.

Having opened the restaurant in the morning, my father had left as soon as I'd arrived at 1:30. Now, nearing seven o'clock, the convention of droogs had been at the counter in one configuration or another all afternoon and I'd grown profoundly weary of them. I longed for peace.

"You don't know where it comes from?"

I couldn't suppress a sigh of exasperation.

"You're the educated one, with all your books. You don't know?"

"No," I said without looking up.

"*Iyía,*" he declared confusingly.

Was he toasting himself in triumph? I glanced up to determine what was going on.

"It's from the Greek," Stavros said. "Iyía. Except in English it means clean or cleanliness rather than health."

It took me a moment to put the pieces together. I didn't show it, but I was impressed. I was also miffed I hadn't known this. Stavros couldn't always be trusted on such matters, but this one seemed credible.

"It's amazing what they've taken from us," said Stelios.

"I thought the word for clean was *clean,*" said Panayotis Toumbas.

"And not just us," Stavros said. "Latin too."

"English is not a real language," said Stelios.

"Can I tell you something?" interjected Kostakis Orologas. Kostakis was once a sailor and sported an honest-to-goodness tattoo of a ship's anchor on one arm, on the other a mermaid. These days he worked as a night cleaner.

"It's a parasite," said Stelios.

"It's a language cobbled together from other languages," said Stavros.

"Can I tell you something?" repeated Kostakis.

"It's like the English themselves, filling their museums with the loot of other countries."

"There's more of the Parthenon in London than at the Acropolis."

"I've seen photos. Have you seen photos of the British Museum?"

"Can I say something?" Kostakis said, raising his voice.

The others fell silent and turned to him.

"The English lifted themselves up on our books and wisdom. Enslaved for four hundred years, oppressed by ignorance and illiteracy, we had thrown out our books and learning, not knowing what we were doing." Kostakis spoke with the grave and measured manner of a preacher. "We didn't know these books even existed anymore. We wouldn't have known what they were if you had shoved them in our faces. We didn't know how to read anymore. Under the yoke of the oppressor, we had become ignorant and unlettered. So when the English came, they saw these books, they found them lying around, neglected, and they picked them up and read them. And they couldn't believe what they saw. They understood immediately what was in them. They recognized the wisdom and value in them. And they took them. They took these books away with them. *Our* books. It was not only our marbles they took, but also our knowledge and wisdom. And the Turks let them. Why? Because they *wanted* us ignorant. They *wanted* us unlettered. While the English built themselves up on our stolen heritage. It's on our foundation stones they've built their civilization, on our writers and philosophers and artists."

"When Shakespeare was inventing the English language," Stelios interjected, "he had to steal most of his words from Greek."

"You all know, of course, that in English the twelve planets are named after the gods of Olympus," said Panayotis.

"Greek is the language of medicine everywhere in the world," said

Stavros. "Whatever the local language, the doctors of every nation in the world know Greek."

"It's the language of science."

"Do you know the original American constitution was written in Greek?"

"Can I say something?"

"This is why Greeks make such good doctors."

"The first doctor was a Greek."

"Hippocrates."

"But it's not just medicine."

"Can I tell you something?"

"That's why studying medicine is easy for Greeks."

"Doctors everywhere have to take the Hippocratic oath."

"Even in foreign universities they already know the terminology."

"All the first scientists were Greek, physics, geometry, astronomy."

"If you're German or French, it's like learning a new language, but for a Greek, they're all familiar terms. Do you realize most of us here already know more medicine than your average Canadian medical student?"

"Biology, chemistry, geometry—"

"We already said geometry."

"A Greek doesn't have to sit there and spend hours memorizing everything."

"Pythagoras and Euclid."

"This is why the Germans and French don't make good doctors."

"Can I say something?"

"They say the Italians are the worst."

"What about the Chinese?"

"Let me say something!" Kostakis rapped the counter with the palm of his hand, his wedding band clacking on the Formica. Everyone fell silent. "Why do you suppose the New Testament was written in Greek?" Everyone nodded solemnly. "Was it because Christ liked Greeks? It's because Greek is the language suited to the mind of God. It's the language closest to truth, to the divine. There was no other language the New Testament could have been written in. Alex. Alex, am I right?"

I glanced up. "I don't know, *Kýrieh* Kosta, you know more about these things than I do."

"I only recount what I've heard. Tell me if I'm wrong."

The door sounded and my father sloped in. Without greeting anyone, he went to the kitchen. It appeared the afternoon had not gone well. The droogs continued their deliberations, and I returned to my book.

Ten minutes later, my father reappeared and stationed himself at the end of the counter. Ever since, the year before, my mother had had to go into the hospital, the two of us hardly spoke. Actually, it was I who would not speak to him, and he'd had no choice but to follow suit. Even a year later, I was still furious at him for how he'd behaved. The talk at the counter now was on the Middle East, and my father stood and listened while the others debated a recent announcement by Anwar Sadat. Sadat was another of those ambiguous, shape-shifting figures. There were so many—Yasser Arafat, Menachem Begin, Konstantinos Karamanlis, Josip Tito, Fidel Castro, even Pierre Trudeau. At one time I'd thought we approved of Trudeau; my father had a grudging admiration for him. But in recent months he'd shifted. Now he regarded Trudeau as another capitalist stooge. Meanwhile Sadat had undergone rehabilitation, transforming from a grubby third-world despot to an astute and high-minded statesman. The year before he'd won the Nobel Peace Prize. Among the droogs, opinion remained divided. Some saw him as a canny and courageous diplomat and praised him for his enlightened reforms while others described him as a traitor and a patsy.

Such debates made me think of my aunt Christina and the story she liked to tell of the doctor in Kypseli and his brothers. After the war, my aunt had worked for this doctor as a domestic servant. He came from a wealthy family and had two brothers, one a professor and the other a notary. The three men were close and saw one another regularly, but they disagreed about politics and would argue bitterly. Overhearing these debates, my aunt had drawn a crucial life lesson. "I was sixteen, seventeen years old," she would say, "and I knew nothing about the world. These were educated men, well-travelled, well-read. Yet when it came to politics, they couldn't agree on anything. Here they were from the same background, the same parents, the same upbringing, but one was a royalist, the other a Venizelist, the third a communist. No matter what the issue, they fought. And listening to them, I realized this: there was no end to such matters. I told myself, if these three can't agree on anything, what hope is there for the rest of us? It became clear to me that no one knew anything about anything, no matter how educated they were. It was all opinion, prejudice, and self-interest. No one knew what was up or down. So I said to myself, forget about it. There's no exit from this labyrinth. Don't enter it in the first place. That's been my attitude to politics ever since. Don't go through that door."

My father was still on the sidelines. He did this sometimes: he would stand back and let those around him debate and argue while he observed without comment. A faint sardonic smirk would pass over his mouth, or an eyebrow would arch skeptically, but he would remain silent, letting the others have their say, until, when all voices and opinions had been heard, all objections, refutations, and qualifications tendered, he would at last speak, presenting his view with a tone of authority and finality that suggested this was the definitive word on the subject.

He now sidled in closer and placed a hand on the counter. The time had come. He tapped the countertop. The others fell silent.

"Sadat," he intoned, "is a malákas."

It was like Marlow's voice rising out of the darkness aboard the *Nellie*. The remark didn't seem at all surprising and it was accepted in total silence. "These negotiations," he continued, "are nothing but theatre, a pantomime of diplomacy." Unfortunately, several customers approached the counter to pay. "The Jew," my father said as I dropped my book and sprang up, "will never relent or compromise." Having a sense of what was coming, I put on my best customer service smile and rang up the bills as quickly as I could. "These negotiations are no more than a cover for Israel's continuing expansionist program, a program that will not cease until every last barren inch of that god-given god-forsaken desert is fully occupied by the children of Abraham. All, of course, done with the approval and support of the Americans."

My father, in these diatribes, employed a high-flown rhetoric I found hard to follow, so my translation can only be an impressionistic approximation. When he got going like this, I was lucky if I understood half of what he said. At this moment, however, I was more concerned about what the customers might be picking up. *Evréï, Americáni, theós, théatro, Avrám, Ízraël*: you didn't have to be Greek to know what these words meant. And these days everyone knew maláka.

"Sadat is a chump," my father said while I maintained my beneficent retail smile. "Another Faisal. He's being strung along." Happily the customers were speaking among themselves, paying no attention to the other end of the counter. "The Jews are never going to compromise. The Palestinians will never have their own country. Nobody wants that, not even the Arabs. Especially not the Arabs. And I sympathize. I understand the Jews' point of view. I understand their fears. I would even be willing to defend their policies. Except for one thing. The hypocrisy. The Jews say they're entitled to their own nation and are prepared to destroy the world to attain it. But when others ask for the same thing, what do they do? When we, also an enslaved people, beaten, despoiled, enfeebled under four hundred years of Turkish subjugation, when we rose up to reclaim our land and territory, our rightful legacy, our own ancient sacred birthright, what did the Jew do? He sided with the foreigner and oppressor. He sided with the Turk. And then again in the First World War, what did he do? He sided with the Bulgarians in stealing our northern provinces. And what about today in South Africa? Shameless hypocrisy." Having rung out the last of the customers, I returned to my stool. "All the years in our country, did the Jews learn our language, adapt to our ways?"

Even as he uttered these words, my eye fell on the stack of newspapers by the register. Grabbing a section of *La Presse*, I walked to the other end of the counter and slapped the newspaper down. My father looked at me. I pointed at a headline. "Do you know what that says?" I asked.

He gazed at the paper a few seconds, then he narrowed his eyes at me.

"Can you read these words?" I said. "Do you know what they say?"

He refused to look back down.

"It's a simple question."

"Who invited you to the dance?" he said.

"I'm just curious if you can read this."

"Don't you have work to do?"

"Why won't you answer me?"

The look on his face suggested that, had no one been around, he might have socked me one.

I turned to the others. "Can any of you read this?"

"Let me see," Lazaros said. "I know some French."

My father snatched the paper away and began to crush it. Lazaros glanced back and forth between the two of us with a befuddled look on his face. It appeared my father was the only one who understood the point I was making.

"Go make yourself useful," he said to me.

I ignored him. "By the way," I said, addressing the others, "have you all made up your minds how you'll be voting in the referendum?"

There was an instant eruption of howls and invective. In a few days, Quebecers were going to be voting in a provincial referendum on whether the province should pursue sovereignty, and I knew perfectly well how these guys would be voting. They were rabid anti-separatists and were terrified of a French nationalist takeover of the province. Some were threatening to leave if the yes side won. Most knew hardly a word of French.

"What's the matter with you all?" my father shouted. "Don't pay attention to him! He's being a smartass!" To me he said, "I know you think you're being clever, but you're only revealing your own ignorance. Don't think I don't know what you're doing. But there's no equivalence."

The others stared, antennae wriggling.

"You can't compare Greece to Canada," he said. "Greece is a nation. Canada is a *state*. So don't make ignorant comparisons." This was dry gumwad. I'd been hearing it all my life. The Greeks were an *ethnos*, Canada was a *krátos*, a *khóra*. Anyone from anywhere could become a Canadian, but one could not become a Greek; one could only be born a Greek. When my father asked someone their nationality, he never accepted "Canadian" as an answer. "No, no, what country you come from?" he would ask. "From where your people?"

"Greece is an ancient civilization," he continued. "We've been around three thousand years. Everyone here is an immigrant, even the French and English. They've just been here a few years longer. If this country belongs to anyone, it's the Indians." The others made assenting noises. This appeared to be one thing all Greeks agreed on, that Canada belonged to the Indians. "Everyone else comes from somewhere else," my father said. "Everyone's a foreigner, including the French."

"What are the two of you fighting about?" asked Stelios.

"No one's fighting," said my father. "My son's an ill-mannered donkey, so don't pay attention to him." To me he said, "You're not needed here. Go help in the kitchen."

That's how it was with us. We could barely tolerate each other. I couldn't stand being in the restaurant. Over the previous year, my father had been increasingly absent, and I'd had to take on more managerial duties—scheduling, tracking inventory, placing orders, and training and supervising staff. This had given me insight into how he ran the business and I was appalled. He habitually denigrated Greeks for their *koutopon-iryá*, the word denoting something like low cunning, and describing what, according to my father, defined the mindset or modus operandi of the peasant and the grasping, illiterate immigrant. Somehow he didn't see his own "hollow cleverness," particularly in the way he conducted his business affairs. My father operated on the premise that everyone was out to take advantage of him, so better that he take advantage of them first. He also bullied everyone. He hectored and browbeat his friends, and he ordered his employees around like a Dickensian factory boss. He was especially horrid with the waitresses. When he wasn't flirting with them, he was scolding them like children, which was no doubt the other reason the help wanted sign was taped permanently to our window. Apart from the thick-skinned Marie-Thérèse, who could give as good as she got, our waitresses rarely hung around for more than a few weeks. I had urged him to moderate his behaviour and suggested he might even be legally liable for some of the things he said and did, but I always got the same response: "When you have your own restaurant, you can run it your way."

One day, after he'd reduced a new hire to tears, I said, "You're the biggest hypocrite in the world. You scream about the capitalists and the exploitation of the masses, but what are you? You run a business. That's what this is. And you treat your workers like shit and pay them almost nothing. If you could, you'd pay them even less, except the law doesn't allow you. So what does that make you?"

"You tell him!" shouted Euripides from the back of the kitchen, where he was assembling pizza boxes.

"How are you any different from Shell or Alcan or any of the other capitalist parasites you're constantly screaming about?"

My father gave me a wan smile. "You think you're clever."

"You're worse than them. They probably pay their employees better."

"You tell him!" shouted Euripides.

"Go read Karl Marx," my father said and walked away.

Things came to a head that summer. One day while I was scouring pots, I heard my name and, hurrying to the dining hall, found my father standing with a delivery man I'd never seen. He was a small guy, no taller than five-foot-two, with South American features. He wore denim overalls and a blue trucker's cap. He was holding a clipboard and had a pen tucked behind one ear. Next to him was an upright dolly, and beside that, near the counter, some sealed cardboard boxes

"Tell this idiot here," my father said, "that I have an agreement with his boss not to pay until the next delivery. He doesn't speak any English."

My guts knotted. I glanced around. Mercifully, there were few customers. A couple of droogs were arguing in the back booth. In my limited French, I conveyed my father's message. The man barked back at me in a French worse than mine. I turned to my father. "He says his boss told him not to leave without full payment. He says you haven't paid in five months and that if you don't pay now, he is ordered to take it all back."

"Five months? That's a lie." My father turned to the man and laid a chummy hand on his shoulder. "My friend," he said in English, "ease okay. No wary. I am friend with Meester Sammy. He know. Next time I pay, he tell me that. Next time." Smiling sociably, he patted the man's shoulder. Still on edge, the delivery man pointed at the phone by the register, and my father's smile faded. "What does he want now, the wanker?"

"Ey, no! Me no maláka! No maláka!"

"Look at him," said my father. "He understands."

The few customers in the place were watching us now. The two droogs in the back were still caught up in their own quarrel.

"No, no. No you," my father said, patting the man's shoulder again. "I say heem, my son, maláka. No you."

The man turned to me and said in French, "I have to phone my boss."

My father reached across the bar and retrieved the phone. "Call your boss," he said in English. "I speak to heem." He activated a line and thrust out the receiver. "Call your boss. And give to me."

The man placed his clipboard on the bar, pushed back his cap and dialled. He muttered into the phone and passed the receiver back. Picking up his clipboard again, he glared at my father. I was relieved to see that the diners were no longer paying attention.

"Meester Sammy? Is Andreas. What your guy say to me?"

My father listened awhile in silence.

"But I no *heff* now," he said. "What I say to you?" Seeing the delivery man staring, he turned his back to him. "But Sammy, I tell you. How long we do business together?"

There was another pause.

"For soor next time. Okay...Okay, Sammy. Thenk you."

"Don't hang up," shouted the delivery man in French as he lunged for the phone. He pulled the handset from its cradle and raised it to his ear.

"Is okay," my father said. "I pay next time. Mister Sammy say okay."

The delivery man slammed down the phone and glowered.

"He say is okay. Give me sign." My father reached for the clipboard but the delivery man pulled away. He picked up the handset again and started dialling. At this point, even the droogs were watching.

"What you doing?" My father snatched the handset. "He say okay." He returned the phone to its place while the man shouted in his broken French.

"I know my instructions," he said, and stepped toward the boxes. My father blocked his way.

"Alex, take these to the kitchen."

"You let me go," the delivery man screamed in French.

"Now," commanded my father.

"I'll call the police," shouted the delivery man.

"You calm down, calm down," my father said in English.

I went into the kitchen.

"Where are you going? Alex! Where the devil are you going?"

"What's happening?" said Demosthenes as I stormed past. I pushed open the back door and stepped into the alley. Pigeons scattered upward. I shut the door and stood in the pounding sun. Before me lay a disorderly heap of empty cardboard boxes and there was a smell of rotting fruit and cooking oil. I heard the hum of an exhaust fan, distant traffic, children's voices. To my right stood a pair of battered metal garbage bins and some empty plastic buckets. The sun beat down oppressively but there wasn't a spot of shade. Just as I began to consider going back in and quitting, the door burst open and my father stood glaring at me.

"What the devil was that? Why did you abandon me? What's wrong with you?" An air conditioner groaned to life. Pigeons warbled overhead.

Something rattled. "When I ask you to do something, you do it," he said. "You know that wanker has gone off with the whole order? He took it all, thanks to you. Do you hear me? I'm talking to you."

"What did you want me to do? Sit on him? Tie him up?"

"I wanted you to put the boxes in the kitchen. I would take care of him."

"What do you think I am?"

"What do I think you are? You're my son is what you are."

"And so? That means you have to involve me in all your dirty work? I have to do whatever you ask me, no matter what?"

"Dirty work? I asked you to take those boxes into the kitchen."

"The man was just doing his job."

"You worry about *your* job. Which is to do what I tell you."

"Why? Why do I have to do what you tell me? Because I'm your son? I'm sick of being your son. I'm ashamed to be your son. You're a liar and..." I couldn't think of the appropriate Greek word. "You're a thief. It was disgraceful how you acted in there. And I'm tired of being mixed up in your..." Again I couldn't think of the appropriate terms and repeated "dirty work."

My father was bobbling his head. "Do you even know what happened? Do you have any understanding of the facts?"

"I could hear Sammy shouting when you hung up. So could the delivery guy. You think everybody's stupid. You think you can...you can just *play* everybody. Because you're so smart and they're so stupid. But it's you who's the *vlákhos*."

My father gave a faint smile. "I see. And you, you're the modern educated Canadian. Is that it? A man of learning and culture, a grandee. The Pasha. But, tell me," he said as he backed me into the wall. "Who put you on this high throne where you sit in judgement of peasants like me? Where you can sniff at how we run our lives? How is it you've come by your elevated position?" I watched a squirrel racing along an electric cable. "What do you know of the world? Or of anything at all? With your TV and comic books and rock and roll? Born into comfort, never having known want or pain or hunger, you think you can shit on those who've sweated and sacrificed to give you what you have. You're ashamed of me, are you?" He made a movement and I flinched, but he only crowded me in tighter. "You don't like the way I run my business? You don't approve of how I conduct my life? Well, how do you think you got to where you are, you little turd? Who do you think put you on your stilts? Do you know what lies behind all your privilege and education and contempt? Do you hear me?" He grabbed my chin and forced me to look at him. "Just remember this you little piece of shit: However small and despicable you think your parents are, however stupid and uneducated and embarrassing we seem, until you've seen with their eyes, until you've lived what they've lived, and until you've sacrificed for someone what they've sacrificed for you...you're not worth the paper they wipe their asses with." He let me go but I remained worried he might strike me. "*Skató*," he said and spat on the ground. He wrenched open the door and went inside.

There was a sound of cooing and flapping wings. I remained in the blinding sun, considering my options. "Fuck you!" I imagined saying to him. "I quit!" How deeply satisfying that would be. I imagined the scene over and over again. But I knew I mustn't let my emotions get the better of me. I had to be practical, think of the future. It was still only June and I didn't want to find myself jobless the rest of the summer. I would have to hold my tongue. But I would start looking for another job. Immediately, tomorrow. This time I would really do it. But what kind of job could I get? I would have to go back to waiting tables, maybe even busing and dishwashing. I wouldn't make as much money, or have as much flexibility. And I would certainly not be able to read. I would never have it this good again. If I could just last through the summer. Or maybe another year.

But all my agonizing was for nought. Within a month, the New Miss Bernard would be out of business.

My father knew not to schedule me for Sunday mornings. My mother wouldn't stand for it. Even after I stopped believing, I always accompanied her to church. I now can't remember when or how I lapsed, so I assume it was a slow process. Then again, what was it I ever believed? Even with all my church-going, my faith had no real anchorage. My religious training consisted of folklore and superstition, a hodgepodge of edicts, injunctions, taboos, threats, and tall tales. Unlike my Catholic friends, I never studied catechism or attended Sunday school, and I had little knowledge of even the most basic tenets of the Greek Orthodox Church. In Greek school we received cursory religious instruction, but it was shallow and trivial. If you had asked me what distinguished our church from others, I doubt I could have pointed to anything beyond the length of our services and our clerics' beards. In church I could barely follow the liturgy. The chanted New Testament Greek was largely unintelligible to me, while the surrounding icons, symbols, and devices may as well have been those of a Hindu temple. Yet I considered myself a believer, a Greek-Orthodox Christian, even if I couldn't have told you what I believed or what a Greek-Orthodox Christian was. But I was not an atheist. Atheism was incomprehensible to me. I also found it disturbing and frightening. I couldn't understand how any decent, sensible, thinking person could *not* believe in God. Yes, I would regularly hear my father rail against the Church and clerisy, but even as a child I understood he was attacking the institution, not the Deity or the beliefs the Church represented. Because a book was soiled didn't mean its contents were untrue.

One day, however, during one of his anticlerical tirades, I heard my father denounce the church for its treatment of Nikos Kazantzakis in a manner that sounded like an endorsement of the writer's atheism. For the first time, I asked him whether he believed in God. His answer shook me to the core. He said, "God is for the gutless, my boy. The gutless and feeble-minded. They say man was created by God, but it's the other way round. Read Karl Marx."

I was eleven. As we were sitting with the men in the park, I didn't say anything more. I had asked the question for reassurance, expecting a very different response. I never imagined my father could be an atheist. I had heard of atheists. I knew they existed, but in the same way I knew cannibals and lepers existed. I was sure I'd never met one. That my father was one seemed unfathomable, and put me into a panic. If it could happen to him, it might happen to me, and in my nightly prayers I implored God to preserve me from such a fate. As a child, I had a notion of adults as existing in a benighted condition. Though they might possess worldly knowledge because of their greater years and experience, they seemed to lack basic common sense, to be blind to certain truths that to me—and, from what I could tell, to most children—appeared self-evident and irrefutable. It was my notion that children were endowed with a special, though perhaps fleeting, knowledge or insight, a kind of lucidity or grace, which abandoned them as they got older. Adulthood was a lapse into darkness. And there was no stronger proof of this than atheism. All atheists were adults. No child could embrace such a perverse and nonsensical view. So I prayed to God for protection, fearing I too might be liable to devolution.

My entreaties fell on deaf ears, for by the time I graduated high school, I was, if not an atheist, then well along the path of agnosticism. In the meantime, my mother had grown more fanatical. In the spring of 1977, she fell under the sway of a preacher she heard on one of her Greek radio programs and she began to attend his monthly gatherings. She learned of an outfit in Park Extension that trafficked in religious books, audiotapes, and other spiritual paraphernalia. She shopped there once or twice. Then, as with most of our household errands, the task was fobbed on to me, and every couple of weeks I would be dispatched for books, pamphlets, and tapes. The place was in the basement of a duplex rowhouse on a residential street. The first time I stepped into the wide, low-ceilinged room, I felt as though I were entering an illicit den of some sort. It was dimly lit, with scattered floor lamps emitting a warm honey glow, and from the PA came a murmur of Byzantine chanting. On all sides, the walls were lined with floor-to-ceiling bookcases. Further back, there was a second, smaller room where the walls were densely hung with icons, crucifixes, and *támata*, and two long tables bore an assortment of censers, oil lamps, jar candles, charcoal discs, and other accoutrements.

My first time there, I found the place bizarre and creepy, but I warmed to it. Its tranquility and sense of monastic remove were very congenial. In all my visits I rarely encountered another customer, which made me wonder how the place stayed afloat. It was run by some kind of charitable organization and staffed entirely by men. The personnel would rotate from month to month according to no discernible pattern, except for one skinny old guy who was usually stationed at the desk. At first, my mother would give me a list of titles or authors, but eventually she left even that up to me, though she would sometimes specify themes or topics. Often I relied on the recommendations of the staff, who were unfailingly helpful and affable and never once preached or proselytized.

The books and tapes piled up. We had to install a bookcase in the living room for them. One day I sat down and made a full accounting. The sum was staggering. It didn't seem to me this was an expense we could afford.

My mother had also become inordinately munificent at church, regularly dropping two-dollar and even five-dollar bills into the collection basket. Her piousness was turning into a kind of pathology.

I decided to speak with my father. I was still unclear about my parents' financial arrangements, but I knew he still provided meagre support, so I figured he would be interested to know about these expenses.

"Do you lack for anything?" he said to me.

This was not what I'd expected. "No, not at the moment, but—"

"So...as long as she keeps you fed and sheltered, how she spends her money is her own business."

I told him about the hours she spent in bed reading her religious books and pamphlets and listening to her tapes.

"She's always done that."

"No, she hasn't. She just started buying this stuff a couple of years ago."

"You don't know your mother."

"Well, yes I do. I live with her, remember?"

"You don't know her as I do. Your mother has always been a weak-minded, priest-ridden woman. She was like that from even before we got married."

"Right, but she only found out about this place a couple of years ago. She didn't used to lie in bed all night reading religious books and listening to tapes."

"She's always been like this. You just didn't realize. You were young. And I was a moderating influence on her."

I chose not to comment on this. "No, you don't understand. This is new. She's not acting normal."

"Sounds perfectly normal to me."

"No!" I said, growing angry at his refusal to listen to me. "She's acting different. Stranger than usual. It's gotten worse."

"What's different is you're getting older and seeing her more clearly."

It was plain he wasn't going to budge, so I let the matter drop.

But things worsened, my mother's behaviour becoming more erratic and disquieting. She experienced strange ailments, regularly coming home from work complaining of dizziness and nausea. When I suggested she see a doctor, she answered angrily that no doctor could address what afflicted her. One evening she couldn't even get out of bed to prepare dinner.

When I again implored her to let me take her to the hospital, she flew into a rage. This was when I learned of her recent troubles with Zazák.

I hadn't heard this name in years. I'd always known of my mother's longstanding difficulties with Zazák (whose name, it had dawned on me, was Jean-Jacques). These dated back to the days when I would go to the factory for lunch, but for the last couple of years I hadn't heard him mentioned and I'd forgotten about him. As I discovered, however, tensions between him and my mother had grown worse and had recently culminated in a bizarre flareup. I couldn't grasp all the details, but I gathered Zazák had been summoned by the bosses to answer for some stolen company property. Some tools or instruments had gone missing, and, for whatever reason, suspicion had fallen on him. In the end nothing was proven and nothing came of it, but Zazák was convinced it was my mother who had smeared him. In reprisal, he'd installed some kind of hose or pipe beneath their adjoining machines through which he would intermittently spray her with foul and nauseating odours over the course of the day. She'd decided to forbear quietly, not wishing to escalate things between them and thinking he would stop after a few days, especially if she showed no reaction. But he did not stop, and now, a couple of weeks later, she was beginning to feel ill and was worried the spray might be poisonous.

There was much in my mother's account I didn't understand, but I had no reason not to believe her. I asked her why she didn't just remove the hose or tell the bosses about it, which only irritated her. She *had* tried to remove it, but she couldn't find it, so ingeniously had it been installed. When I asked her whether other people smelled the odours, she became livid. "What do you think?" she snapped.

I spoke to my father again.

"Why doesn't she tell the bosses?"

"I asked her that, too."

"And what did she say?"

"She gets angry when I ask. She thinks the other workers are in on it and that if she goes to the bosses she'll get in trouble."

"She's out of her mind."

"Yes! That's what I've been trying to tell you."

"And what do you want *me* to do? She's had incidents like this with Zazák before. It'll pass."

But it didn't pass, and my mother's behaviour only grew more bizarre and disturbing. Every evening, she would go about the apartment from room to room with a hand censer of burning incense and trace figures of the cross with it in the air while muttering prayers under her breath. At dinner she would hardly eat and sometimes not eat at all, claiming her food tasted of poison. One evening she spat a mouthful out on her plate. I would wake up in the middle of the night and hear her pacing in her room and talking to herself.

"She's praying," my father said. "She always did that."

"No. No she didn't."

"Your mother's always praying."

"But not at three and four o'clock in the morning."

"She'd pray round the clock if she could."

"She has to go to work in the morning. She never did this before. Get up and pray in the middle of the night? I'm sorry, this is new."

"She has insomnia."

"No," I said, close to tears. "Something's *wrong* with her. In her head."

"There's always been something wrong with her head."

"Will you listen to me? There's something *wrong*. She's imagining things. She has suspicions for everyone. I think she suspects even me now. I've become afraid of her. The way she looks at me sometimes. Do you understand me? I've become afraid of my own mother."

"You *should* be afraid."

"No! Fuck! Why don't you listen?"

A few nights after this exchange, I was watching TV on the living room couch. My mother had installed the couch opposite her bedroom so she could see me from bed when I sat there, and she always kept the door open, even late at night. On this particular evening, the lights were off and she was prone under the covers, and I had the volume on the TV turned down as low as possible. Now I saw her rise in the darkness and come to the bedroom door.

"What is it?" I asked as she stood at the doorway, glowering at me

"I suppose you're going to tell me you don't smell anything."

I straightened up on the couch. "What?"

"How long do you intend to keep this up?"

"What are you talking about?"

Rushing toward me, she grabbed my arm and dragged me through the kitchen to the shed. She flung open the door and lurched back and covered her face.

"You don't smell that?" she growled through the crook of her arm.

I turned on the light and leaned in. "It smells like the shed."

"That smells normal to you?"

"It smells like it always smells."

Turning, she stormed back to her room. I pulled the light cord and shut the door. When I got to her bedroom, she was back under the covers.

"What are you telling me?" I said from the doorway. "Zazák is smelling up the house? Or is it me? You think Zazák and I are working together?"

There was no response.

"Is that what you think?"

Still no response.

"You know what, I've had it! I can't stand this anymore! Tomorrow I'm going to *babá's*!"

As I turned off the TV, I could hear the springs of the bed.

"So that's the plan, is it?" she said. She was barely visible, my eyes still adjusting.

"Plan? There's no plan. Just as there's no smells. You've lost your mind. And if I stay here, I'm going to lose mine too."

"Go then. Go live with the whoremonger and his whoreson brood. Why not? He's taken everything else. My life, my home, my dignity. Let him take my child too. It was only a matter of time. Go ahead and kill me." She retreated to the bedroom and slammed the door shut.

I stood there in the dark a long time, the contours of the living room slowly re-emerging. I didn't know what to do. I had no wish to live with my father. There was no guarantee he would even take me in. But I was desperate and frightened.

I got into bed and managed to fall asleep. But in the middle of the night I was awakened by sounds in my room. My mother stood by the window, peering out past the edge of the curtain.

"What are you doing?"

She didn't reply. I looked at the clock. It was just before five.

"Stay where you are," she hissed as I approached the window. "No!" She grabbed my arm but I pulled free. "Alex, please," she said in a whisper.

As I drew back the curtain, she fled the room. I could see nothing unusual outside. The street was deathly still. Not even the branches of the trees moved. I heard my mother in the living room. She was dialling the phone. The lights were on.

"What are you doing?" I shouted, racing over in my bare feet. For some reason, it was unnerving to see the apartment lit up at this hour. "What are you doing? Who are you calling?"

She didn't answer, so I seized the phone and sank the plungers.

"Give it here!" she shrieked, clinging to the handset. I wrenched it away. "You don't know what you're doing. You're endangering both of us."

"Who were you calling?"

"Alex, you're too young."

"Who were you calling?"

"Listen to your mother," she said, her voice abruptly altered to a pleading, childlike tone.

"What were you looking at through the window?"

"They don't want what's good for you, Alex. Trust me. Trust your mother. I'm the only one who loves you. I'm the only one who will protect you. Don't listen to what your father tells you. They want to hurt us."

"Who? Who are you talking about?"

She made a lunge for the phone.

"Alex, I beg you. Listen to me." She dropped to her knees. "I beg you!" Tears were streaming down her face. "Please." She pressed her palms together in supplication. "Please listen to your mother."

"Who were you calling?"

She started bowing repeatedly, head dropping to the floor, while she crossed herself over and over and murmured under her breath. It felt like a scene from *The Exorcist*. I hurled the phone to the floor and returned to my room. I changed out of my pyjamas and went out to the hallway. My mother was still on the floor, prostrating and praying, but when she saw me putting on my shoes, she leapt to her feet.

"Where are you going?"

I thrust out a hand. "You come near me, I will hurt you."

"Alex, listen to me," she said as I put on my coat. "My darling, please listen. I'm trying to protect you. You don't know what you're involved in." I crouched to tie my shoes. "I love you, my soul. Nobody loves you as I do. I'm only looking out for you. Don't let them take you away from me. That's what they want."

She made a move in my direction. I leapt back, holding out my arm again. "I'm not joking," I said. "Don't come near."

"Alex, my darling, don't leave this house. You don't know what you're doing. Don't go out. There are things in the world you don't understand."

I grabbed my bag and made for the door, slamming it shut behind me. I got as far as the bottom of the stairs before the nocturnal calm was shattered by my mother's cries. I raced up St. Urbain, her howls convulsing the night.

It was six when I got to the restaurant. I locked the door and sat in the front booth as dawn broke over the rooftops. Now and then, a solitary pedestrian would go by, rushing to work, maybe coming from work. No one noticed me in the unlit restaurant.

My father arrived shortly before seven. Seeing me through the glass as he unlocked the door, he frowned with concern. "What are you doing here?" He sat opposite me without turning any lights on. I was in tears. He listened quietly. He didn't argue, didn't contradict me. He asked a few questions. He told me not to worry. He told me to go to school, carry on my day as usual. He would take care of everything. I went over the same details again and again. I feared he still didn't appreciate the gravity of the situation. I told him I would not, under any circumstances, go back home. I said I would sleep on the street if I had to. He assured me I would not have to sleep on the street. I must go to school, get through the day. After school, I was to come to the restaurant. If he wasn't here, I was to wait for him until he returned.

I did as he said and spent the day in a haze of anxiety. When the bell rang, I gathered my things and got out as quickly as I could. Crossing the schoolyard, I saw my uncle on the other side of the street. He was leaning against his car. He smiled and straightened up as I approached. My father was nowhere in sight. My uncle clutched the back of my neck and shook it fondly. He asked how I was, his tone unconvincingly upbeat.

"What are you doing here?" I said.

He opened the door on the driver's side. "How was school?" he asked.

"What's going on?"

"Get inside. Everything's fine."

"I'm supposed to meet babá at the restaurant."

"You're staying with us. Get inside and I'll explain."

I didn't move. My uncle got into the car and shut the door. He lowered the window and glanced up at me. "Come on," he said, "get in."

"Where's mamá?"

"Get in the car. I'll explain on the way."

We drove for a long time in silence. Finally, he said, "Your mother's fine. Everything's going to be fine." He turned slightly to look at me. "She's with one of the best doctors in the city. Do you know Xenopoulo?"

"Who?"

He turned his eyes to the road. "He's a professor at McGill. One of the best psychiatrists in the country."

A Greek psychiatrist? Was there even such a thing? And when did my uncle become an expert on psychiatrists and professors?

"Where is she?" I asked.

"At the Victoria. She may be there for a while."

"What's a while?"

"A few weeks. I don't know. Just so the doctors can keep an eye on her. Make sure she's better before she returns home. In the meantime you'll stay with us." He glanced at me. "We'll go by the house first so you can pick up what you need. Just the basics. We can go back later for more."

"I was supposed to meet babá. He said I'd be staying with him."

"We decided it's better you stay with us."

"Who's *we*?"

"All of us."

"How's it's better."

"It's easier. You'll be with your cousins, you'll have your aunt to cook for you, do your laundry. For your father, it's not so easy."

"Why?"

"He's got the store. He's got his own problems."

"What problems?"

"It'll be better this way, trust me. It'll be easier for everyone. Especially for you." He tousled my hair. "Believe me."

"Does he live with someone?" My uncle turned a questioning scowl on me. "Does he have a woman with him? Is that why?"

"A woman?" he said, gazing forward again. "Who told you that?"

"Because I don't care. It doesn't bother me. It doesn't have to be a secret anymore."

"Who told you there's a woman?"

"I don't care if there is."

"But there isn't. Who told you that? There's no woman."

"How do you know?"

He was silent for a while. "I know. Don't worry. I know what goes on with your father."

Apparently, everyone knew what went on with my father except me. "The two of you don't even talk," I said. "How do you know what he does, how he lives?"

"I know," he said, sounding like my mother. Where did all this certainty come from with these people?

"I don't care anyway," I said. "It doesn't matter. I'll sleep on the floor."

"You're staying with us. It'll be easier for everyone."

"But, no, that's not true. It won't be easier for *me*. For me it'll be shit. I need to be near school and the restaurant. How am I going to get to school?"

"Calm yourself. You'll take the bus. You'll get up a few minutes earlier and take the bus. We're not far. When I can, I'll drive you. But the 80 stops a few blocks from us. What is it, a ten-minute drive to St. Joseph?"

"It's longer than that."

"No it's not."

We sat in silence awhile, the traffic creeping along on St. Laurent.

"What did they do to her?" I asked.

My uncle took his time answering. "The doctors gave her something to calm her down. She's fine. When I left her, she was sleeping. Xenopoulos is one of the best doctors in the city. He's world-renowned. He's written a book. A customer of mine went to him and can't praise the man enough. He says Xenopoulos saved his life. And this guy had worse problems than your mother. Far worse, believe me. And you should see him now. She's in good hands. There's no one better. We're lucky to have him."

I gazed out at the kids on St. Urbain Street on their way home. On the railing of a balcony was draped a huge fleur-de-lys. In a window two houses over was a much smaller Canadian flag.

"She's going to be fine," my uncle said again as he came to a stop in front of the house. I remained seated, gazing out the windshield. The other side of the street, an orange school bus idled in front of the synagogue.

"What does she have?" I asked.

My uncle sighed. "Alex, your mother has always been a nervous and melancholy person."

"But what's wrong with her?"

"I don't know. But it'll pass. She's in good hands. She'll be fine, I promise." He stroked the back of my neck. "Do you want me to come up?"

"No."

I kept my face down as I exited the car. I tried to envision what the neighbours would have seen earlier that day. I pictured men in white coats, my mother...in a stretcher? A straitjacket? My blood ran cold. They would have probably had to sedate her. I wondered what people had heard, what they were saying. Climbing the stairs, I imagined the eyes watching me.

The grey manor house stood on the crest of a hill. Even in sunshine, it looked the archetypal haunted house. I pictured bats and ravens circling the tower at night, bolts of lightning. Actually, places like this were scarier than haunted houses. Haunted houses didn't exist. But these places did, they were real. To me, the scariest movies were not about ghosts and vampires and zombies; they were movies like *One Flew Over the Cuckoo's Nest* and *Psycho*. I didn't believe in ghosts and goblins; I'd never encountered a vampire or zombie. But I had seen plenty of psychos. Our neighbourhood was full of them, gaunt odorous men in ratty coats muttering to themselves and screaming at passersby, or witless childlike simpletons, like Monsieur Phillipe, who for a few pennies would pop out his dentures like a cash register, or Marty (so named because of his resemblance to Ernest Borgnine), who, for no charge at all, would open his fly and, to the gleeful howls of teenage boys, pound himself in goggle-eyed transport until the spume spurted and the queasy hilarity curdled into jeers and curses, and poor muddled Marty would have to put his pecker away in a hurry and, under a torrent of stones and rubbish, run for his life. These men filled me with horror. How did they get this way? At one time Marty and Monsieur Phillip would have been children. I tried to visualize it. They would have been like all the other children. And then something happened. Wasn't it possible the same could happen to me? Oddly, it had never occurred to me that it might happen to my parents. Why was that?

Reaching the top of the winding driveway, we turned into a parking area. My nausea returned. I'd been sick with a fever and diarrhoea. I'd missed school and there had been talk of taking me to the hospital. I refused, insisting it was nothing and would pass. Stepping out of the car, I walked on wobbly legs. The air was damp and smelled of trees and earth. The manor house was surrounded by woodland. Until now I'd never paid attention to this place, even though we'd passed it many times in the car. I had assumed it was part of the Royal Victoria Hospital and didn't know of its having any special function. I had heard of a place called the Douglas, which was in Verdun. The kids would make cracks about how so-and-so should be taken to the Douglas, or, watch out because they'll send you to the Douglas. I had never seen the Douglas or been to Verdun. I pictured a squat sprawling building surrounded by barbed-wire fence and empty fields. I had no idea there was such a place in our own neighbourhood. This one was surrounded by manicured lawns and tall trees, and to the south was a panoramic view of the city sloping down to the river.

We walked to the entrance, my uncle leading the way. As he opened the heavy wooden door, I felt another wave of nausea. I let my aunt go in ahead of me and we stepped into a wide, high-ceilinged lobby. To my relief, it was empty but for a uniformed guard in a glass office at the opposite end. Around us, grim, whiskered men glowered from paintings on the walls. We walked down a long corridor, my uncle still leading the way. We passed open doorways and I glanced in compulsively, terrified of what I might see. Mercifully, there were only empty rooms and offices, a closed cafeteria. Up ahead, a man and woman approached, walking side by side. The man was in striped pyjamas and slippers, and something coiled in me at the sight of him. I dropped my gaze, not wanting to seem rude, but glanced up again as they passed. The man stared ahead emptily.

We went into an elevator and the doors closed with a sense of finality. In a few seconds, they would open and I would have to deal with whatever confronted us on the other side. I imagined the possibilities. I thought of Jack Nicholson in *Cuckoo's Nest*, his pantomime of a lobotomized patient. I wondered what my mother would look like. Even more, I worried about how she would react to me. I feared she held me responsible. I'd never thought through the consequences of my actions. I'd just wanted to get out of a confusing and terrifying situation. I'd had no idea the series of events I would set in motion. Had I known, would I still have acted as I did? What other choice did I have? But there was no explaining any of this to her.

The elevator doors opened, and my aunt and I followed my uncle down another long corridor. We went by a nurses station and he waved at the two white-frocked women behind the glass. I kept my eyes forward, and we went into a small room. The lights were off and a heavy beige curtain hung over the window. There were two beds, one unoccupied and bare. To my horror, it was rigged with restraining straps at each corner. I felt faint. In the other bed lay my mother. She appeared to be sleeping. I looked for straps on her bed and was relieved not to see any.

She opened her eyes and glanced about anxiously. Seeing me, she gasped and sat up.

"Oh my soul!" she cried. "My heart."

"Your son," my uncle said, helping her out of bed.

Dressed in a blue-and-white striped hospital gown and grey socks, she held out her hands. As we hugged, I started bawling like the child I was. I seemed to tower over her. She felt tiny in my arms, as if I had grown or she had shrunk in the week we'd been apart.

"What has your mother done to you?" she whimpered. "Dishonourable, unjust world. To punish the helpless and innocent." She kissed my neck and face. "Oh my poor boy. My precious, innocent boy. Forgive me." We kissed each other's tear-streaked cheeks. "Forgive me, my angel," she said. "Forgive your poor stupid mother."

6

WE HAD AGREED TO MEET at a restaurant on Park Avenue my father frequented since he'd started driving a cab. Arriving twenty minutes late, he walked past me with barely a nod. He knew the owner, of course, as well as the cook, and he had to make his obligatory stop in the kitchen. When he returned, he took a seat across from me and asked for a Molson Export, letting the waiter know he'd already placed an order for a hamburger steak with the cook. He asked if I wanted anything and I told him I'd eaten at home. I already had a beer in front of me. He settled back with a groan and lit a cigarette. He had on an old brown wool sports jacket and clashing blue shirt, no tie, and had lost weight. Lately, all his clothes were ill-fitting. He hadn't bought anything new in ages and was uncharacteristically rumpled, though his hair (greased and swept back, and now, by the look of it, bolstered with Grecian Formula) was back in style.

When his beer arrived, he poured it with his usual care to avoid a head and asked why I wanted to meet. For several months, he'd been hounding me about my plans for university. Like most immigrants, my parents regarded the physician as the summit of intellectual and social achievement, and since grade one, my father had made it clear I would be going to med school. By high school I knew this wouldn't be happening, though I hadn't told my parents. But neither had I made up my mind about what I would do instead, and with the deadline for undergraduate applications looming, I'd had to make a decision. Left to myself, I might have gone in for English literature or philosophy, but even I understood that these were subjects better suited to trust-fund babies and people with family connections who didn't have to worry about landing a job after graduation. They were unlikely to win my father's support. So I hit upon what I thought was a brilliant subterfuge.

I didn't get the reaction I'd expected.

"*Klassikés spouthés?*" my father said, looking at me as though he'd just bitten on a lemon.

"Do you know what that is?"

I'd had to look up the term and liked the ring of it in Greek. It sounded more distinguished than mere classics. But my father looked unimpressed. I outlined the program, emphasizing that I would focus on Greek language and literature. This, I thought, was my ace in the hole. But the way he reacted, I might as well have said I planned to study early Mandarin.

"What are you going to do with ancient Greek?" he said.

"That's just a part of it. You have to know the language to read the original writings. But you study everything, the language, culture, history." I mentioned Homer, Plato, Aeschylus, Sophocles. I figured invocation of these sacred names would dispel all merely sublunary concerns.

My father hauled on his cigarette and stubbed it out.

"And then what?" he said, pushing the ashtray to one side. "What are you going to do? Walk around St. Catherine Street barefoot lecturing people on virtue?" He smirked at his witticism. "How are you going to put food on the table?"

I had considered he might not be thrilled with my choice, but I'd never imagined such disdain. I thought racial pride would subvert pragmatic concerns, even perhaps that he would feel a sense of personal triumph.

The waiter having arrived with my father's order, I remained silent till he was gone. "I'll never understand you," I said as my father studied the food on his plate. "All my life, I've listened to you go on about the ancient Greeks, and now..."

I couldn't tell if he was even listening. Still focused on his hamburger steak, he picked up his fork and carved out a hunk.

"I don't know," I said. "I don't understand you."

He looked up at me. "Worm lib engine Athens. This endanger particles."

"What?"

He finished chewing and downed some beer. "We're not living in ancient Athens," he said. "And this isn't the age of Pericles."

I shook my head. "You're such a hypocrite."

He scowled and licked his teeth. "Hypocrite?" he said, reaching for the saltshaker. "How am I a hypocrite?" He poured salt over everything on his plate. "It's true that I don't see how a person claiming to be educated can not know Homer and Plato, like so many of your compatriots. But you also need to keep a roof over your head. Life is hard, my boy." He stabbed his fork into some fries and dragged them through the gravy.

"I know it's hard."

"No you don't," he said, stuffing his mouth.

"Yes I do."

He shook his head and mumbled something. I waited. "You have no idea," he said after he'd swallowed. "You have no idea how hard life can be. And I hope it stays that way. May you be one of the lucky few who never find out. That's what any parent wishes for his child. Of course I want you to get an education, I want you to be a man of culture. But I don't want you to be one of those well-read fools who knows a lot of big words but can't wipe his own ass. Better you become a grocer."

"What about your father, the great poet and artist? How with all my opportunities, I could be all the things he never was?"

"Exactly! My father was a good-for-nothing."

"*What*?"

"My father was a talented, brilliant, self-educated good-for-nothing. If not for my mother, we would have been out on the street."

"I've never heard this. All you've ever told me is what a great man he was."

"He *was*. He was brilliant, gifted. But he couldn't hold down a job. It was my mother who fed and clothed us. My father was an accomplished wastrel."

"I can't believe this."

"I thought you wanted to be a doctor. What happened to that?"

"No, that was you. *You* wanted me to be a doctor." He pulled a face. "I never wanted to be doctor. I just played along. I would be a terrible doctor."

"What do you want to be then? An erudite waiter?"

"I'm not thinking about that right now."

"Well, that's your prerogative. But I don't have that luxury. I *have* to think about it."

"Why? What does it matter to you? As long as I'm in school, I'm educating myself. Why can't you just let me do what I want?"

He pinched some napkins from the dispenser and wiped his mouth. "It matters to me, first...because you're my son...and I care about your future. Even if you don't. But, second, I can't afford to throw my money away." He took a swig of beer. "I believe you desire some financial assistance from me, correct? It's true..." He tucked in his chin and let out a burp. "It's true that what you do with your life is your own business. But what you do with my money... You want to study classical studies, or whatever it is, go ahead. You're a grown man. But don't expect me to pay for you to sit around and feed the chickens. You want me to help you out. Fine. I'm your father, so I'll do everything I can to help. But you have to show there's a likely return on my investment."

It so happened that in 1981 a full year's tuition in Quebec was around six hundred dollars, an expense I could almost afford. But it would mean having to work part-time. I was worried about how I would do in university and wanted to have as much time as possible for my studies. Since the New Miss Bernard had shut down five months earlier, I had been unemployed, and there was no question of my mother going back to work. Our only sources of income were her small welfare payments and whatever erratic support my father provided. Unless he kicked in a little more money and did it more reliably, I would have to get a job. Applying for a student loan or bursary never crossed my mind. I knew nothing about such things or how they worked. In any case, I would have been terrified of going into debt. If that were my only alternative, I would have opted for a job.

But there was also a principle involved. Six years since their split-up, my parents had still not divorced (and never would). I expect my mother was deterred by the sheer scandal and shame, plus she was cowed by all forms of institutional authority. She probably wished to spare herself the strain and exposure. For my father there were significant benefits in maintaining the status quo. No divorce meant no alimony and allowed him to control the meagre and intermittent payments he made to us. By my calculations, even with the money I hoped he would contribute for tuition and expenses, he would be less out of pocket than he would have been if my mother had demanded a divorce. I was sorely tempted to point this out to him.

But I tried a different tack.

"What if, after the Bachelor degree, I did law? How do you call it in Greek? Law studies."

"You mean to become a lawyer?"

"Yes. What if I did that?"

He sat back in his seat. "Why can't you just do that right now?"

"That's not how it works." Fudging things, I explained that one had to do a Bachelor's degree before one could go to law school. I said that the degrees most esteemed by law schools were philosophy and classics.

My father regarded me silently, his tongue scrubbing a molar. "And how long is that, the Bachelor's?"

"Three years."

"And how long is law school?"

"Maybe another three or four. It's less than medical school."

His face relaxed and he almost smiled. "A lawyer," he murmured. He gazed back down at his plate, inordinately pleased by what he saw. He cut a piece of meat and lifted it to his mouth. "I thig you'd may grey lore."

Having had the ancient Greeks shoved down my throat all my life, I'd hardly read any. Perhaps it was a silent protest. I also didn't believe most of what I heard. I assumed it was the usual hyperbole. But as I ploughed through my course readings that fall, I began to understand the adulation. In some respects, the early Greeks exceeded their reputation. Nonetheless, I wasn't crazy about the courses themselves or the professors who taught them. I had particular difficulty with ancient Greek, which was dry and tedious. It also struck me as absurd that I was fretting over the semi-deponents and aorist formations of a dead language when I could barely speak the language of my birthplace. I was much more excited by my electives, where we read Schopenhauer, Nietzsche, Wittgenstein, Camus, and Barthes. It occurred to me that there was no reason I had to stick with classics. Neither of my parents was paying attention to what I was doing in school, and whatever I may have told my father, I didn't require this major for law school. So, without telling anyone, at the end of my first year I switched to philosophy.

My life became increasingly constricted and monotonous, revolving around school, work, and home. I saw less and less of my friends, very few of whom went on to university. Many had moved to the suburbs, and even those who remained in the city had left St. Urbain Street. All of us still lived with our parents, except for the few who had married. Carlos was the first to get hitched, at twenty-one. Initially moving in with his in-laws on Drolet, he and Goretti were able, with her parents' help, to buy a bungalow in Chomedey. The De Melos also moved to Chomedey, one street over. Like Carlos and Ernesto, both De Melo brothers were pulled out of school at sixteen and sent to work. Filomena, the younger of their two sisters, made it to CEGEP and was even offered a scholarship at McGill, but her parents didn't want her to go to university. She got a job as a bank teller. Carlos found work in a butcher shop but after a couple of years had the sense to enrol in a government program for high school dropouts. The program provided clerical and administrative training and enabled him to complete his diploma, and found him a position with a small importing company, where by his native shrewdness, doggedness, and idiosyncratic personal charms, he rapidly worked his way up to sales director.

I hardly ever saw Carlos or the other guys anymore. Even Perry and I rarely managed to meet. One reason was that, unless I was going to work or school or running an errand, I couldn't leave the house without putting my mother into a flap.

"You're going out with your friends again? You just saw them."

"I haven't seen anyone in weeks."

"And what about me? I never see you. You're always out with your friends."

"What are you talking about? I don't have any friends anymore. I don't have a *life*."

"And what about me? What life do I have? Who are *my* friends? When do I go anywhere?"

"And whose fault is that?"

"You think I want to be alone?"

"I'm just going out for a few hours. I'll be back by midnight."

"*Midnight*?"

These scenes ended in tears. When I managed to get out, it was a waste of time anyway. Wherever I might go, a movie, a concert, a restaurant, I was a wreck. All I could think about was my mother lying in bed alone in the dark, and I'd feel a gnawing anxiety to get back home.

Ever since she'd come under Dr. Xenopoulos's care, she had become something of a mystery to me. Much of the time I had no idea what she was thinking or feeling, and I didn't ask for fear she might tell me. My only concern was to maintain peace and order and live my life. Nonetheless, I wondered about her state of mind. Was she still obsessing about Zazák and nursing conspiracy theories? Was she still smelling odours? She must have been to some degree, as she was constantly sucking on candies, presumably to mask them. But maybe the candies served another purpose. I wasn't going to ask. I was especially curious about how she looked back on her own behaviour and the hospitalization. Did she recognize her craziness? Did she now see her delusions for what they were? What must that have been like? I thought of the Maenads in the *Bacchae*, of Agave at the end of the play gazing at her son's head in her hand. Surely an analogous insight or awakening must be an integral part of the therapeutic process, a requirement of recovery. But how did one live with such knowledge? What did one do with it? How did one go on with oneself? I could imagine her sense of humiliation, the scorching shame in knowing she'd lost her mind, and that everyone knew it too. Greeks did not take a particularly enlightened view of these matters. Most would have rather had a family member carted off to prison than put in a mental asylum. When she was in the hospital, my aunt and uncle advised that we tell people she was having heart problems. But such things could not be hidden, especially as my father couldn't pass up the chance for public vindication. Here was scientific proof confirming everything he had ever said about his estranged wife, and he would make damn sure everyone knew of it.

During her hospital stay, I never spoke to a doctor or nurse. All information was relayed to me through my uncle. Then, one day several weeks after my mother's release, my uncle informed me that Dr. Xenopoulos wished to meet. I called and made an appointment. Arriving at the hospital, I was shown to a tiny windowless room with a bare wooden desk, a single foldout chair, and a narrow metal bookcase. I didn't know what to expect of Dr. Xenopoulos. I couldn't even imagine what he might look like. I'd never met a Greek professional, and the idea of an educated middle-class Greek was a bewildering abstraction. A Greek, almost by definition, was either a labourer or a merchant.

When Dr. Xenopoulos arrived, what struck me first was his height. I must have been anticipating someone tall and imposing, but he was unusually short and thin, with a bald pate and black thick-rimmed glasses. He asked me in English how I thought my mother was progressing, his deep resonant baritone at odds with his compact frame, and his accent making me wonder when he'd come to Canada.

"She seems better," I said, "but I don't know what's going on in her head."

"I think see is *mutts* better," Dr. Xenopoulos said. "And if see continues to take hair medication, see will continue to get better. Wheats ease why I need you to keep an eye on hair. And to let me know if you ever see anytheeng...unusual."

I nodded, waiting. "Okay," I said.

He stared stolidly, slumped in his chair.

"Is that what you wanted to talk to me about?" I said finally.

He shrugged. "Ease there anything you would like to talk about?"

There were a number of things I wanted to ask, but I wasn't sure I had the stomach for it.

"My uncle says she has schizophrenia," I said. "Is that right?"

His eyebrows lifted. "Who toll heem that?"

"I assumed you did."

He leaned forward and drew a pen from his pocket protector. "I dawn like those labels," he said, clicking the pen repeatedly. I wondered what a psychiatrist would make of this. "People hev these labels and theenk you can tsooz between one or the ahther. But ease not so easy in reality." He paused to reflect. "Simply put," he said, "your mahther is deeprest."

For some reason, this seemed to me worse than schizophrenia, more heartbreaking. I found myself fighting back tears. It was impossible Dr. Xenopoulos didn't notice.

"But what about the hallucinations?" I said. "I thought hallucinations indicated...I thought—"

"Depression is a complicated thing," he said, putting down his pen.

"Dzess because you hev hallucinations dawn mean you hev skeesophrenia. Your mahther hez what ease sometimes called psychotic depression. Though see may present with schisotypal symptoms, the patient is not necessarily skeesophrenic. With some patients, like your mahther...ease not so easy to make a diagnosis. See hez hed a difficult life." He fell into another meditative silence. "Your mahther ease of a tradzeek dzenerayshon," he said.

I had more questions, but they remained inchoate. I wasn't sure how to phrase them or whether they were even appropriate. I worried they might be insulting. I had recently looked up *paranoid schizophrenia*: "A psychosis characterized by systematized delusions of persecution or grandeur and notions of hostile conspiracy. Associated features include excessive or irrational suspiciousness and distrustfulness of others, hostile projection, anxiety, anger, argumentativeness, excessive ratiocination, and an inability to bear criticism." This description applied to most Greeks I knew, and had Dr. Xenopoulos and I met up again some years later, I might have asked him how psychiatric science was able to distinguish between what he called *schizotypal symptoms* and what someone of a more philosophical disposition might call *weltanschauung* or *lebenswelt*. I would have enquired into how he distinguished between biological and cultural pathologies and what effect the pills he prescribed had on the latter. But I was barely eighteen; and even if I had been able to put my dim and embryonic thoughts into words, I would not have had the gumption to voice them.

Returning from the hospital, my mother had resumed her old routines and for a while we'd managed. To my immense surprise, she even went back to work at her old factory, though not her old machine. Then, one February afternoon, fours years after her treatment, without warning or prompting from anyone, she calmly and with no explanation asked that I take her back to the hospital. This shook me, partly because I hadn't noticed anything unusual about her behaviour, but also because the request was so out of character. This alone was proof of the urgency of the situation, and I wasted no time getting in touch with Dr. Xenopoulos. By this point, I was twenty-one and remained at home on my own. My mother was in the hospital three weeks and was put on a different drug regimen, one that, while softening her edges, made her lethargic and dopey. Over the years, she would also develop symptoms of dyskinesia, most noticeably a tremor in her hands, which would require still more drugs to mitigate. She would never be able to work again.

It eventually dawned on me that I was no more beholden to go to law school than I had been to stick with klassikés spouthés. What would my father do? Demand his money back? Actually, he might. For a while, I thought I would do a Master's in philosophy, or even English. But in the end I didn't have the guts. I couldn't go back on my word, and so, in the summer of 1984, I returned to McGill as a law student.

I knew my first day that I'd made a horrible mistake. A week before classes, I attended an orientation session where I felt painfully out of place. All my prospective classmates were there, and I could practically smell the testosterone in the room, much of it emanating from the women. Nor did the speakers do anything to allay my apprehensions. Each was bent on impressing upon us how brilliant, talented, and deserving we were simply by virtue of being in that room. The people around me seemed to believe it, which only confirmed that I had no business here.

The coming days would provide further confirmation. Philosophy students had proven to be even more nerdish and socially awkward than I was. Most had a genuine interest in the subject and valued ideas for something other than the prestige and power that might accrue from them. The program could breed its own kind of competitiveness and status-seeking, but it was nothing like the venal and aggressive striving and manoeuvring I encountered in law school. I was surrounded by sharks and barracudas, by every manner of go-getter, blowhard, hustler, and sharpie. Everyone was brimming with ambition and confidence. Many of the students were older, some in their thirties and forties, but even the younger ones had funds of experience and knowledge I could only envy. I overheard talk of foreign exchange stints, travels through Europe and Asia, internships in companies and NGOs, volunteer work in Africa, and of family members and friends in prestigious law firms and government ministries. It was in law school that I first heard the word *networking*. If even half of what I heard was true, I was cooked.

The reality was probably different, but I would only see this in retrospect. I expect there were plenty of others like me, students who were just as frightened and intimidated. But if there were, they didn't introduce themselves. I was alone and isolated. I had never in my life felt so out of place, outclassed, doomed. I could not compete with these people. And even if I could, I had no desire to make a career of it. Who would choose to live like this? Better to be a waiter, erudite or otherwise.

Yet I persisted, which was how I met Soula Pagonis. Soula and I were in the same class, but we didn't meet until second year when we ended up in a study group together. Big, brassy, plushly contoured, she combined the dusky features and dark coiled mane of a Middle Eastern pop singer with the curves and bounce of a Robert Crumb pinup. And she dressed to accentuate her high relief, favouring form-hugging pencil skirts, tight blouses with plunging necklines, stiletto heels, her face gessoed and under-painted with a palette knife, to vivid effect. She was a woman you couldn't help noticing, and one you would never have expected to notice the likes of me. And yet she claimed to have spotted me that first day in orienta-tion. She also said I was the only person in our group who didn't know she had what she called "the hots" for me.

And she may have been right. I'd always been stupid about such things. On the other hand, Soula was not the easiest person to read. To me she was a paradox. I was surprised to discover that she considered herself a feminist and had been valedictorian of her high school graduating class. In law school she would make the Dean's list every year. Yet she also attended church every Sunday. Yes, I attended church every Sunday too, but Soula meant it. She believed. She bought into the whole program— the big bearded god, the son's divinity, the flood, the snake, the apple. This woman who dolled herself up like some high-end call girl or TV anchor-woman believed in the one holy universal apostolic Church.

But the biggest surprise of all came one Saturday evening during a pit-stop on the Mount Royal lookout. Like me, Soula still lived at home (her parents owned a triplex in Park Extension), so we had few opportunities for physical intimacy; she had her own car, however, a gift from her father for getting into law school, and whenever possible we would drive up to the lookout and go at each other like a couple of teenagers. But a full month after we'd started seeing each other, we had yet to pass the prelim-inaries. Exploring hands encountered fierce defence. I was growing restless and, while having taken my mother's admonitions to heart, that evening, rather impulsively and in the heat of the moment, I made a play for Soula's breasts. I felt a sharp poke in my ribs and found myself shoved to the other end the seat.

"I'm taking communion tomorrow," she said, wasting no time doing up the two measly buttons I had managed to get to.

"So?"

"I've been fasting."

"I wasn't trying to feed you."

"I know what you were trying to do."

Through the windshield, the city spread out below us like an electric brocade. My eye bent toward my old house on Esplanade. It was hard to discern through the trees, but I thought I could make out our balcony. Toward the horizon, the stadium's tower leaned in silhouette against the sparkling lights.

"I just wanted to see," I said foolishly. I knew the moment it came out of my mouth it was a childish, uncouth thing to say. Still, Soula's reaction struck me as a little extreme.

"What?" she howled. "What did you say?"

"Calm down. What did I say?" You would have thought I'd asked her to let me pee on her or something. "I'm sorry," I said. "I just thought...I don't know...we've been going out now for—"

"I thought you respected me."

This took me aback. "Don't tell me you're going to pull that on me."

"Pull what on you? What am I pulling?"

"What are you saying, that because I like you, because—yes, I admit, I find you attractive, I find you arousing—"

"Please don't talk like that." She put her hands over her ears. "I thought we had something serious. I thought you were serious about us."

I waited for her to drop her hands. From a neighbouring car came the muffled dance beat of a stereo.

"So what are you telling me?" I said. "That if I'm sexually attracted to you—"

"Will you please stop saying that. I hate that sort of talk. I hate it when you reduce it to *that*."

"Reduce what? Reduce what to what? What are we talking about?"

"I don't want it to be just about *that*?"

I threw my head back and moaned.

"I'm sorry, but I don't," Soula said.

I looked at her. "What is this *that* that we're supposed to be so fucking terrified of? What is it, *that*?"

"Don't play stupid."

"And why does it have to be just about *that*? Why *just*? Why can't it be about *that,* along with a whole lot of other things?"

"I thought you were serious. I thought you were serious about us."

"You keep using that word. What do you mean by *serious*?"

"You know what I mean. You're just playing stupid, being a man. I thought you were better than that."

That evening I learned that Soula Pagonis, Soula of the lip liner and spider lashes, of the stiletto pumps and the tight skirts and blouses and the unabashed cleavage, was a virgin. Moreover, she was "saving" herself. That was the expression she used. She was saving herself, she said, for the right person, this being, I assumed, her husband. She further hinted this person could be me, but that would partly depend on my not making any more unseemly demands on her. There had been numerous contenders before me, and all had been sent packing for "pushing their luck." She was not one to be disrespected, she said.

What were the odds? What were the odds, first, that a woman with Soula's looks and bearing would turn out to be a virgin; and, second, that such would be the woman to offer me my first prospect of physical intimacy? It was a cruel and grotesque joke. Did Tantalus have it worse?

I didn't mention that I was a virgin too. I feared Soula might lose respect for me. Somehow she had formed an impression of me as a worldly sophisticate, and I wasn't sure how she would react if she learned the truth. She had never asked about my previous relationships, and perhaps she'd read my own silence on the subject as indicative of racy dalliances and manly exploits best left unspoken. Nor had she realized, that night a month earlier when she'd pushed me up against a tree and painted my mouth fuchsia, that I had never kissed a woman.

We sat in the car for two hours. Soula did most of the talking. With little prompting, she laid out all her plans and dreams. It was astonishing. She had her whole life mapped out in the most minute and hair-raising detail. Already she knew what kind of law she would practice, where she would article, the kind of firm where she'd like to work. She knew what salary she'd be making by the age of thirty. She even knew what her husband would be making. She knew where they would live (Outremont), how many children they would have (two), and where they would vacation (Greece, Italy, and the south of France in the summer; Mexico and the Caribbean in the winter). I felt like a prized candidate being given a tour of the company facilities. But how could Soula think I was even remotely qualified for the position?

Then again, what did she know about me? Even if not by design, in the little time we'd been together my conduct would have reinforced her image of me as the good Greek boy. But what did she know of the rancour and resentment that seethed inside me, of the cynicism and self-loathing, the disdain I had for all the things she prized so dearly? At the time, I had little insight into these things myself. And to the extent that I did, I knew not to reveal them to the likes of Soula. No doubt I struck her as offbeat, perhaps a little moody, but to judge by what I heard that evening, I was "husband material."

That talk on the lookout represented for Soula a turning point. She felt it had brought us closer and suggested it was time we take our relationship to the next level. This entailed, among other things, meeting each other's parents. I was opposed. Such a meeting was tantamount to a publication of the banns. I didn't tell Soula this, remarking only that it was still too early to bring our parents onto the scene. But she disagreed and we quarrelled. And she wouldn't let the matter drop. She brought it up every time we got together. We appeared to have reached a crossroads.

How far was I prepared to go to gain admission to Soula's carnal mysteries? Was I prepared to marry her? I will admit I thought about it. What were the chances providence would ever again drop in my lap a woman as physically stupendous? I envisioned our life together, the home in Outremont, the two children, the sun-drenched holidays, Soula in a bikini, Soula *out* of a bikini—god help me! I imagined what my parents would make of her. It wasn't hard to predict my father's reaction: he would be shocked and delighted his son could snag such a *mounára*. It might even put to rest the suspicions I feared he harboured that I was gay. But my mother? I would have to get Soula to tone down the drag or she was sure to be pronounced a tramp. She would have to emphasize her homey dreams and churchy ways. With the right preparation, she might just go over, especially given how my mother had lately become obsessed with my marriage prospects.

Around the time I met Soula, my mother had begun prying into my social life in a way she never had before, asking whether I had any girl-friends (plural) or whether I was serious about anyone. All of a sudden, I was presumed to have a love life.

"I don't get you," I said to her one day. "My whole life you tell me to stay away from girls, and now, just like that, you want me to get married. Tomorrow! I thought I wasn't even supposed to think about girls until I finished school."

"I didn't know it would take *this* long. At your age, most men are married. You should be starting a family."

"I'm twenty-three!"

"At twenty-three, most people are married."

"No, they're not! You weren't."

"You don't want to follow my example." She asked whether she should speak to the ladies at church. *Kyra* Stavroula had a nice-looking niece who worked at a bank. Should she try to set something up?

"No! This is none of your business. Don't you dare talk to anyone."

"You can't leave it too long. I don't know how long I am for this world myself, and I don't want to leave you on your own."

"You're fifty-four!"

"What will happen to you if I go?"

"What will happen? You think I can't take care of myself? I can't manage without you?"

"I can't bear the thought of stranding you alone stin xenityá."

"This is not xenityá for me! I was born here, remember? This is my home."

"A man needs a wife and family. Children are life's greatest blessing. Why are we here if not to bring life into the world?"

"That's ridiculous. You make it sound as though people without children have worthless lives. Not everybody thinks like you do. Not everybody wants the things you want. This is something you've never understood."

But she wasn't listening: she had slipped into one of her reveries. Palms pressed to her chest, eyes to the ceiling, she was panting with emotion as she said, "Oh, to see you with children! Four. That's the ideal number. I wanted four for myself. That was my dream. The boy can have a boy for company, and the girl can have a girl. It would be so easy for you. You and your wife could live downstairs and have your jobs while I take care of the children."

My mother had been talking about grandchildren for years. They were now her fondest wish in life, what kept her going. A baby would do more for her than all the Haldol and Risperdal in the world, a fact that had no small part in my cost-benefit analysis of whether I should marry Soula.

In the meantime, Soula stepped up her own pressure campaign. One day she confessed that she had told her mother about us. She had yet to tell her father because if he found out about me, he would demand an immediate meeting. Her mother too, now that she knew, had begun asking when I would come by the house.

"I don't know what to tell her," Soula said. "She wants you to come over for dinner. What do I say? He refuses to meet you? And she doesn't like to keep secrets from my father. We're not that kind of family."

"Then why did you go and tell her?"

"Because I'm tired of lying. I'm not like you with my parents."

"We've been through this. I don't want to bring the parents into this."

"Why not?"

"We've been barely going out two months."

Soula stiffened. "Alex," she said, "do you love me?"

I knew where this was going. "Why do you ask me this?"

"Just answer me. Do you love me?"

"Of course."

"Of course what?"

"Yes!"

"Jesus! Why can't you just say it? Alex, I love you. Sometimes I don't know why, but I do. I...love...you." She paused. "Do you love me?"

"Yes, of course."

"Of course what? Say the fucking words!" she shouted. "Why is it the only time you say I love you is when you're trying to feel me up?"

"That's not true."

"Will you just say it!"

"I love you."

"Jesus!"

Clearly, this could not go on much longer. Either I relented and met Soula's parents or the relationship would be over before the holidays. The problem was I dreaded both options.

To complicate matters, I was also in the midst of a parallel crisis, one that had been intensifying even as Soula pressured me to meet her parents. I had grown more anxious and discouraged than ever about law school. I'd spoken to Soula about my unhappiness, but she didn't grasp how dire the situation was. At the end of November, I announced I was quitting. We were having lunch at a restaurant near campus, and at first she didn't seem to understand. She thought it was my usual griping, and I had to interrupt her customary reassurances to clarify that, no, I was *literally* quitting: I was not going back to classes and would not be writing exams. She looked at me as though I had just enlisted in the army or joined the Church of Scientology.

"Have you lost your mind?" she said. "It would be insane to quit now. It would be the biggest mistake of your life." She suggested I was reacting to the stress everyone felt at the end of the semester. All law students were struggling. At the very least, she said, I should finish the term. She was sure the results would put my worries to rest.

I tried again to explain my aversion to law school, how my anxieties weren't like those of other students. "I'm more worried about what comes *after* law school," I told her. "I can't see myself as a lawyer. It would kill me."

"Kill you? Why?"

"I'm not cut out for it. It's not what I want to do."

"Then why the hell did you go into law school?"

"For god's sake, you know why. We've talked about it a million times. Why is it such a big deal? Why does so much hinge on it? Why is it such a tragedy if I quit?"

"Are you kidding me? And what would you do? Wait tables the rest of your life?"

"What would be so wrong with that? I'd rather be waiting tables than be a lawyer."

She narrowed her eyes at me. "Do I know you?"

"What's so fucking great about being a lawyer? Why is it so important to you?"

She gave me a long searching look. "You know, I have to say...I didn't think you were so weak."

"Weak? I thought I was being strong. Going to law school is what's weak. Living your life to please other people is what's weak."

The next day, I was informed over the phone that the relationship was over. I felt crushed. I tried to talk Soula out of it, but she wouldn't budge. She was cold and hard in a way I'd never experienced before. We were on the phone no more than ten minutes. I hung up, and then, before my strength ebbed away entirely, I went down to the university to let them know I was withdrawing.

For weeks afterwards, I felt bereft and disoriented. I couldn't stop thinking about Soula. I even spoke to Perry about what had happened, though I wasn't sure why. Perry had an extremely restricted, if not distorted, picture of my relationship with Soula. I'd been reluctant to introduce them and they'd only met once, when Soula and I bumped into him one afternoon on St. Catherine Street. Everything Perry knew about Soula was based on that five-minute encounter and what I'd told him about her, which wasn't much and wasn't entirely honest. He knew nothing about Soula's religiosity and old-fashioned notions of propriety. So I didn't go into all the details of the breakup. I spoke about Soula's material ambitions and her objections to my quitting law school. Much of Perry's advice was largely beside the point. He had no real understanding of the situation. He told me I'd made the biggest mistake of my life letting such a *tartána* go and that if I had any sense I would do everything in my power to win her back, even if it meant returning to law school. These conversations were not terribly helpful.

My parents' reaction to the news that I had quit law school could not have contrasted more sharply. My mother hardly batted an eye. She may have even been secretly pleased. My father, on the other hand, was aghast. He was bewildered and scandalized. If not the first, then the second thing he said to me was, "What am I going to tell everyone?"

"That's what worries you?"

"I'm going to look like an ass. I've told everyone you're going to be a lawyer."

I was prepared for a lecture on honour and duty and the sanctity of one's word. I feared he might even demand his money back. He only asked what I planned to do next. I had a ready answer.

A couple of months earlier, my father had come into a new business, a pool hall on Park Avenue that he'd acquired from an old friend. The circumstances around the deal remained hazy and steeped in rumour, but I knew that my father was running the place alone, working round the clock seven days a week. He needed help. Since the closure of the New Miss Bernard, I had been working on and off at the Galaxy, but the hours were sporadic. I also hated the job. It was hard, hot, dull, physical work. I hadn't forgotten what it was like working for my father, but I was older now, more mature and seasoned, and I figured I'd be able to handle him better.

Initially he seemed not just surprised but disappointed by my proposal. "This is what you want to do the rest of your life?"

"Who said anything about the rest of my life?"

"What else are you going to do if you quit school now?"

"Maybe I'll go back one day."

"To study what?"

"I don't know. But not law, I can tell you that."

He shook his head ruefully. "I always thought you were destined for better things."

"At the moment, I just need to make some money. And you need help. Right? Think about it."

He shrugged. "If this is what you want."

I'd never been inside the Symposium. The place was an institution, as much a social club as a pool hall. Its owner, Vassilis Tsoulos, had opened it in the mid-sixties and done very well. He had a second commercial property in Park Extension and a house in Outremont. In 1983, however, his wife had passed away, and with his two sons running a restaurant in Ottawa and his daughter and her family living in Greece, he began to talk about selling the business and returning to Greece himself. The main person he talked to about this was my father, whom he'd known since the two had worked together in a restaurant in NDG in the late fifties. I only found out about all this after my father took over. I knew Vassilis only by name and reputation and had had no idea that he and my father were such close friends.

My father had been driving a cab since he lost the New Miss Bernard.

To get a taxi permit, you had to write an exam, but having acquired a copy ahead of time from one of his cabbie friends, he aced it. He drove six, more often seven days a week. But he'd never lost sight of his main goal, which was to open or acquire another restaurant. When Vassilis began talking about getting rid of the pool hall, he saw an opportunity. I didn't know the particulars, but the way my father told the story, Vassilis felt a great debt of gratitude for some favours or services my father had rendered him in the past, and Vassilis himself saw an opportunity to repay that debt. What these favours or services were, my father of course wouldn't specify, but to hear him tell it, you would have thought he'd pulled Vassilis from a burning building or taken a bullet for him. Whatever the truth, Vassilis was prepared to offer my father such terms that he could purchase the pool hall at a time when, only five years after almost declaring bankruptcy, he could not have had much savings or collateral.

I had no trouble guessing how my mother would react. Pool halls were dens of iniquity, the haunt of crooks, hustlers, pimps, pushers, drunkards, and junkies. Under her influence, I'd thought the same as a boy. The Symposium had seemed even shadier than most, which was why, even after I started frequenting pool halls in my teens, I would not go there. Apart from its reputation, there was the problem of the venetian blinds in the window, which made it impossible to scope out the place from the street. You never knew who was inside, and I couldn't take the chance of being spotted by someone who recognized me. If it ever got back to my mother that I'd been seen in a pool hall, let alone the Symposium, I couldn't imagine the trouble I'd be in. By law you had to be eighteen to go into the Symposium, but my friends would hang out there occasionally. The place was always full of teenage boys. Every now and again a cop would clear the place of minors and make a show of giving management a stern warning, but the teenagers would be back the next day. Clearly, Vassilis, and then my father, had an arrangement with the police, but I was never let in on the details.

When I broke the news about my new job to my mother, she gave me one of her fierce angled stares. She'd heard that my father had become owner of some pool hall on Park Avenue, which in her mind seemed perfectly apt. But my working there was another matter.

"So that's the plan," she said.

"What plan?"

"Your father's a bum, and now he wants to make you into a bum too."

"It was my idea," I was quick to reply. "I asked for the job."

She sneered. "Is that what he told you to tell me?"

"What do you think we do? What do you take me for?"

"I know what goes on. He's been working on you for years, shaping you in his image. But it's my own fault. I've known all along and I let it happen."

Ironically, the situation was the reverse of what she imagined. What she should have worried about were my marriage prospects. In losing Soula, what I really feared was not so much that I would never meet another woman like her, as that I would never meet another woman, period. And now that I'd dropped out of school, my odds were even slimmer. At the Symposium I was surrounded by men all day, and much of the rest of my time I spent at home with my mother. How was I ever going to meet a woman?

Expressing these concerns to Perry, I discovered he had similar woes. Indeed, he seemed to be even worse off than I was. We didn't talk much about such things, or at least not honestly, and I hadn't realized how lonely and desperate he was. I assumed Perry had never been in a serious relationship or I would have heard about it. He would make vague references to "dates," but I suspected he was lying. I now suggested that he and I needed to make changes in our lives. We needed to get out more, try to meet new people.

That winter we started going to bars and clubs. We didn't do it often, maybe once every couple of weeks. And for the most part we did no more than stand around clutching our sweaty bottles and appraising what Perry called "the meat." Usually we would end the night at a diner or deli, just the two of us, and drown our discontent in grease and nitrates before heading home to our solitary consolations. Though these outings were my idea, I soon wondered why we bothered. Most nights I ended up feeling worse than when we'd started. I was better off staying home and watching TV with my mother. It was less depressing.

One night, in a bar on Bishop Street, Perry turned to me during one of our protracted lulls. "What the hell are we doing here?" He'd been drinking whisky and seemed drunker than usual. "I hate these fucking places."

"Me too."

"So why the fuck we keep coming?"

"I don't know."

"It's not like I'm going to meet my wife in one of these fucken dives." He took the place in with a slow rotation of his head, stopping at a group of women at a nearby table.

"Look at them," he said.

"Please don't."

"Would you marry one of those *karyóles*?"

"Perry, please."

He turned away before any of the women noticed. "Tell me something," he said, fixing me with a steady gaze. "You ever go to hookers?"

I snorted and shook my head.

"What? Why you react that way? You telling me you never paid for it?"

"No. Have you?"

"Sure. Lotsa times. Why, you think there's something wrong with it? You think it's immoral or something?"

"I didn't say that."

"It's better than these fucken places. With a pro at least it's out in the open. You know? It's honest. Everyone knows what it's all about. No fucken games, no wasting time. And let me tell you, there's some fucken hot women out there now. It's not like in the old days. There's some real fucking babes. When was the last time you were in a strip joint?"

I had to give this some thought. "I don't know. Probably the last time I went with you."

"When?"

"That time with Jose. We went to that place upstairs. It had just opened."

"No way! You mean with that chick with the teddy bear?"

"I'm pretty sure that was the last time," I said, lowering my voice so that he might lower his.

"That was years ago! Man, you have no idea. Things have changed." He drained his glass and leaned in closer. He explained there were now clubs where, for a small surcharge on a lap dance, you could feel up the dancers. In some joints, you could even rent a private booth and do almost anything short of fucking. There were dancers who would see you on their own time and provide a full range of services. "You don't have to deal with fucken streetwalkers anymore," he said. "You get to see the merchandise beforehand, see what you're paying for. And let me tell you, some of the meat in these places, we're talking USDA prime grade tenderloin. I'll take you sometime."

I nodded, hoping he would calm down and change the topic.

"Seriously, we gotta go."

"Awright, awright," I said, his offer as enticing to me as if he'd invited me to take a bath with him.

Still, he'd struck a nerve, and one night a week or two later, as I was going home after closing up the pool hall, I hopped on the 80 and headed downtown. As it was a Monday, I expected St. Catherine would be quiet, but perhaps because it was such a warm and humid night, the street was crowded with cars and pedestrians. At St. Laurent, I could see the lights of the 55 and I considered going straight back home. But, having come this far, I kept going and pushed deeper into the surging crowd.

The faces around me glowed pink and orange in the neon light, and I felt as though everyone could tell what I was there for. From the curb and door stoops, hookers stared at me aggressively and occasionally called out. They were bedecked in garish makeup and trumpery and addressed me in English, which I found unnerving. How did they know? I felt as though everyone I passed could see right through me. "Looking for company, cutie?" one of the hookers purred nasally. Another urged me to "Come to mommy." A tall bony woman in torn fishnets and a preposterous red wig promised me the blowjob of my life. I had stepped into *Taxi Driver*.

At a strip joint I paused to study the photos in the display. A bruiser with a shaved head and dressed in black materialized and exhorted me in French to go inside. I fled, plunging down a side street at the next corner. I continued to Dorchester and returned west. Walking up St. Laurent, I came upon another strip joint and again stopped near the entrance. Through the open doorway came indeterminate odours and the dull rhythmic thump of dance music. At the far end of the vestibule hung a black curtain. I came a little closer, hoping I might be able to peek in. But the moment I put a foot on the stoop, there was a sound of male voices and I beat a hasty retreat.

I was done. It had been a stupid idea from the outset, a testament to how far gone I was, and I continued up St. Laurent, my sole gratification that night the steamies and fries I wolfed down at the Montreal Pool Room before taking the 55 home.

It was three years since my mother's second hospitalization, and during this period she'd been largely free of the worst of her delusions and hallucinations. This was not to say she was what one might call normal. Her mistrust and paranoia couldn't be extirpated by mere pills. With her ever-growing lethargy, I bore an increasing share of our domestic duties, and while she still prepared meals, I helped with the cleaning and did most of the shopping. Eventually she would be sending me out to purchase even her shoes, underpants, and brassieres.

But shopping had always been a complicated and cathected affair in our household, going back to Esplanade. My parents would quarrel about it, my father viewing my mother's habits as irrational and neurotic. My mother held to a firm belief that every twenty years the world was fated to suffer a catastrophic conflict or economic collapse. She also believed she'd survived the last only because of her own mother's frugality and foresight. My grandmother had kept them well-stocked with olive oil, grains, legumes, and other non-perishables, so that while everyone around them was dropping from hunger during the occupation, they held body and soul together. It was a lesson she would never forget. And while the years passed and began to exceed, even by decades, the twenty-year interregnum of her theory, the delay meant that when the next, inevitable smash-up came it would be all the more devastating. Only when we lived with the Anagnostopouloses was she able to moderate her behaviour. Under my aunt's rule, she had no choice. But as soon as they'd moved out, she reverted to her old ways, her suppressed hoarding habits resurging with a vengeance. Within months, she'd converted my aunt's sewing room into a storage space, filling the tall metal shelf units she had me install with jarred and canned goods, canisters of olive oil, boxes of detergents, soaps, and cleaners, and a range of other supplies. What's more, our stock expanded over time, as when something ran low, it was replenished at a surplus. While most people invested in term deposits, bonds, and equities, my mother put our savings in household goods and non-perishables.

Meanwhile, she grew ever more listless. She hardly left the house except for medical appointments and church. Often I would come home from work in the early evening to find her lying in bed, the house pitch black. "Why do you have all the lights off?" I might say, turning on a lamp. "It's not even six."

"What's there to look at?" she might reply. Or she might complain the light hurt her eyes, or gave her a headache. Some days she would fall into long bouts of sighing and moaning for no apparent reason. "Do you really have to do that?" I would sometimes snap. "I can't take it anymore." We might be in the kitchen having dinner, or I'd be lying next to her, reading.

"What am I doing?" she would say.

"All that sighing and moaning. Is it necessary?"

"You don't know my pain."

"But do you have to make all those noises?"

"They come on their own."

"No they don't. You don't make them in church. Does your pain miraculously go away then? If you can control yourself in church, why can't you do it here?"

"I don't know what you're talking about. I can't control my pain."

"What is this pain? What's hurting you?"

"Everything. If you only knew."

Did she groan and sigh like this when she was alone, or only for the benefit of those around her? One day I went to an electronics shop downtown and bought a mini cassette recorder. I splurged for an expensive model, as it purported to be both highly sensitive and silent. The next day, before leaving to do some shopping, I hid the recorder under my mother's bed while she was out of the room. When I returned, I retrieved the recorder at the first opportunity and hustled it to my study. Waiting until she was back in bed (as she would often come to see what I was up to and either sit with me or try to talk me into joining her in her bedroom), I plugged in the headphones and rewound the tape. For several minutes, I heard nothing but hiss and dim intermittent background noises—a dog barking, distant hammering, birds, a truck in the alley. I advanced the tape. There was more hiss; but then I heard what sounded like footsteps. They grew louder and stopped. A pause. Then the creak and whine of the bed. Then nothing. I turned up the volume. I thought I heard pigeons. I pressed the headphones tighter against my head. Nothing. I kept the tape playing. And then it came: a sound low and forlorn, muffled but unmistakably human. And then it sounded again, louder and more distinct. There it was: the tree in the forest. Why did I feel a terrible sinking feeling? What did that say about me?

Like our stockpile in the back room, my mother's repertoire of aches and ailments kept expanding. And they would change from week to week, from day to day. Yet both Dr. Xenopoulos and Dr. Giannakis, my mother's GP, took her complaints seriously. As a result, I was constantly taking her for tests and to specialists. I lost track of the doctors we'd seen.

"So what is it you're feeling, Mrs. Doukas?"

"Pain."

"Where do you feel this pain?"

"All body."

Here the doctor might turn to look at me.

"She means everywhere, her whole body."

"Tell him I feel weak and dizzy," my mother might say in Greek. Then to the doctor: "I deezy!"

"You're dizzy," the doctor echoes sympathetically. I admire and envy his forbearance. "When do you feel this dizziness? When does it come? Are you standing, are you walking, are you lying down?"

"Very mutts."

Again the doctor looks at me. "When does she feel dizzy?"

"She's constantly dizzy." She's crazy, I want to say. Look at her history.

"Pain!" my mother shouts. To me: "Tell him I feel pain all over."

"You told him already."

"Tell him!"

I sit silently.

"Too mutts pain! Oh mine gahd!"

"Okay, Mrs. Doukas," the doctor says with genuine concern. "We'll make the pain go away." He prescribes something, sends her for more tests.

A few days later, we're in another dreary crowded waiting room under cold fluorescent lights. Everyone clutches hospital cards and pink numbered slips. Sighs long and frequent are exhaled, mostly by my mother. Across from us, a brittle old matron in a wheelchair is scolding a Filipina attendant. At the far end of the room, two women in lab coats take turns stepping through a doorway and calling out numbers. One is a young woman with a shaved head. Plump and featureless, she has the look of a giant baby. Despite my prayers, she's the one who calls out our number.

I gird myself and help my mother up. Anticipating trouble, I walk ahead to present a pleasant face. As I pass the woman our documents and cards, I notice she has a tattoo on her hand. But she's friendly and warm, unlike much hospital staff I deal with. My mother enters the narrow room and sits.

"Mrs. Doukas," the woman says, sitting opposite her. "How are you?"

My mother turns to me. "Is it a man or a woman?"

Through my clenched smile, I say, "How do you know she doesn't understand Greek?"

"Does she look Greek to you? What's that on her hand?"

The woman swabs my mother's arm and inserts a needle to draw blood. "Pain!"

"It's okay, Mrs. Doukas. It's okay now. No more pain."

"*Yes* pain! Oh mine gahd!"

A few weeks later, we are back with the specialist. He's gazing at the computer monitor on his desk.

"Well, your mother's tests are all normal. Liver and kidneys are good. Heart excellent. Mrs. Doukas, you're in very good health."

My mother stares viperously. Unsure how to read her expression, the doctor repeats, with more pep in his voice, that she's in very good health.

"No good!" barks my mother. "Bad!"

The doctor gestures at the clipboard on his desk. "You're in very good shape for a woman your age. Tell her she's in very good shape, all things considered."

"The tests show you're in good health," I say in Greek.

"What does he take me for?"

The doctor glances in my direction, waiting for my translation.

"The tests show your insides are healthy," I say. "You're in good health. This is good news. You should be happy."

But my mother doesn't come to the hospital for good news. She comes for confirmation of her misery.

"No!" she shouts at the doctor.

Visibly confused, he looks at me. "Is she upset about something?"

"She says she doesn't feel well."

"None of the tests show anything."

"I understand."

He leafs through the sheets on his clipboard. "I see Dr. Kwan pre-scribed iron supplements," he says, glancing up at my mother. "Are you taking the pills Dr. Kwan prescribed, Mrs. Doukas?"

My mother looks at me.

"He wants to know whether you're taking the pills that Chinese doctor gave you." I turn to the current doctor. "I think she's taking all her pills."

"Peels make more bad," my mother interjects. "No more better. Say make better, but make more bad."

The doctor looks at me.

"She says the pills make her worse, not better."

The doctor shakes his head. "That's not true."

Of course it's not true! She's crazy! Have you looked at her records?

"*Yes* true!" my mother shouts. "*Very* bad!"

The doctor goes to the trouble of explaining how iron pills work and why they should be making her feel better. My mother glares at him with naked contempt. "*I* know, *I* know," she says, thumping her chest. By this, she means something like, *I know the pain I feel, and none of your fancy talk and scientific hocus-pocus will make it go away*. But the doctor thinks she's agreeing with him and he smiles.

"Okay," he says, putting his clipboard away. "Let's examine you."

I help my mother climb onto the bench. The doctor begins to take her blood pressure. She casts a suspicious eye on the swelling cuff. Raising her eyes to the ceiling, she begins:

"Pain! Stop!"

"Please, Mrs. Doukas. You don't have to scream."

"Scream because pain! Alex!"

But I'm already gone.

"Alex! Alex!"

"Please, Mrs. Doukas."

"KEEL ME! KEEL ME!"

The only friend I now saw with any regularity was Perry, though we con-tinued to drift apart. Our interests and views were diverging. We hardly read the same books anymore. I felt bored and irritable in his company, and I sensed he felt the same about me. But it was hard to know what was in his head. He'd grown sullen and non-communicative, and I sometimes thought he might be suffering from depression. As a teenager he'd shown a talent for drawing and painting and talked about becoming an artist. After high school he'd enrolled in one of those private colleges that advertised on late-night TV, but upon receiving some kind of diploma in graphic design, he'd kept working for his uncle. As far as I could tell he hadn't made the slightest effort to find a design job. I didn't understand it and never asked him about it. I sensed it was a sensitive and embarrassing topic. Maybe the only reason Perry and I remained friends was that we were among the last of our group still living on St. Urbain Street and we led similar dead-end lives.

One evening I said to him, "What are we doing, man? Why are we still here? We're thirty years old and still living with our parents. Doesn't that ever bother you?"

We were sitting in his front yard drinking beer and he turned to me with a scowl of incomprehension. "Why would it bother me?" he said. "We're not like the blokes. We don't abandon our parents as soon as we turn eighteen."

"We're not eighteen."

"Why would I give up free room and board to go sleep on a futon in some rat-infested hole with a bunch of hippies?"

"Why would you have to do that?"

"Are you aware of rents these days? You see that house across the street? They just rented the middle apartment for six hundred dollars. For a five-and-a-half. I told my parents, we gotta do something. We gotta get rid of those fucking deadbeats upstairs and jack up the rents. Are you still paying that ridiculous rent at your place?"

We were.

"Yeah, well you're lucky. Try finding another place and see what it costs."

Was it any wonder Perry and I had drifted apart? What had happened to him? Was he always like this, so complacent and conventional? Or was it me? Having just turned thirty, I was in crisis. That summer I'd developed an unhealthy obsession with figures like Napoleon and Julius Caesar. Already I had read two biographies of Alexander the Great, and by the fall I would have gone through the entire Mary Renault trilogy. I'd become obsessed as well with figures like Einstein, Hume, A.J. Ayer, Pascal, and other thinkers and writers who had achieved early greatness. I'd read that most Nobel Laureates produced their most important work before the age of thirty. By thirty, Einstein had already had his *annus mirabilis*; Hume had written *A Treatise of Human Nature*, Ayer, his *Language, Truth, and Logic*. By thirty, Shelley and Keats were dead, the Beatles had split up. I brooded like a medieval flagellant.

By the end of the fall, I'd decided to go back to university. What else was there? I wasn't about to conquer Persia or overturn the prevailing model of the universe. Having some money now, I could return on my own terms, and I settled on a Master's in philosophy. I didn't want to return to McGill, however, and in any case Concordia was more accommodating to working and part-time students. When I informed my parents of my plan, what mainly concerned them was how they would be affected. My father was relieved I wouldn't be quitting the pool hall but annoyed that I might need to reduce my hours and require a more flexible schedule. My mother was worried that she would see less of me.

What I didn't tell either of them was that I also planned to get my own apartment. This was crucial. If I were going to change my life, if I were going to start living like an adult, I had to start living on my own. But I wouldn't say anything until I'd signed a lease. With my name on a binding contract I would be better able to withstand the emotional assault I was sure to endure.

Perry was right: I couldn't believe the high rents. My mother and I had become insulated living in my uncle's place. Luckily, I was able to find a bachelor apartment at a decent price. Though somewhat decrepit and dingy, it was well located, in an old stone building downtown, just north of Sherbrooke; and with its original cockled plaster walls, wood mouldings, and double-hung wood-frame windows, it had a certain charm. I ended up keeping quiet about the place. I didn't even tell Perry. I furnished the apartment slowly through the summer and by the end of August it was ready. I'd even installed a telephone line (number unlisted). All it lacked was an occupant, as I had yet to move in. And I had still not told anyone about it.

Once school began, I visited the apartment almost daily, dropping by between classes or at the end of the day to study or just to listen to music or read. But I never slept there. And the squat ancient fridge moaned emptily. Still, the place was furnished and presentable should the need arise.

That wouldn't happen till the next semester.

Though Heather Freeland may not have been exactly my type, there was no denying her allure. Tall and slinky, with long blonde hair and pale green eyes, she had an abstract porcelain beauty. She also had the straightest, most resplendent teeth I had ever seen. In law school I had realized that you could tell a lot about someone's background by their teeth. Heather's were implausible, and I would stare at them the way I'd stared at Soula's cleavage. Heather was clearly much younger than I, yet I found her intimidating. Most of our class did. Besides being (or at least sounding) extremely smart, she had an air of mystery. She spoke in a hushed, breathy murmur and peppered her comments with arcane references and gnomic pronouncements that obliged you to lean in and focus on what she was saying.

We were in a course called *Epistemology and Ethics*. There were a dozen students, and Heather sat across the conference table from me. One day as we were leaving class, she came up from behind me in the corridor and, in her blurred undertone, complimented me on the seminar I had just given on Bernard Williams. I confessed I wasn't so happy with it and felt I'd been jittery and mealy-mouthed. She said I had no cause for apology and then proceeded to challenge all my main points. As usual, I only half-understood her, and I offered no rebuttal.

Out on the street, she slipped on a pair of oversized fun-fur earmuffs and green cable-knit wool mittens and asked which way I was headed. I'd been planning to go home, but I pointed toward my pied-à-terre. She said she was going the same way, and we walked up to Sherbrooke together. She said she lived in the Plateau, somewhere near Duluth. For a long time, we walked in silence, the freshly fallen snow squeaking beneath the soles of our boots like Styrofoam. She seemed ill-clothed against the cold. She had on a lime-green tulle coat with big white buttons, thin cotton brown pants tucked inside black riding boots, and a brown-and-red wool scarf. From her shoulder hung the green canvas military bag she always carried. As a rule, Heather's wardrobe was of the thrift store variety, and she dressed with an air of studied dishabille. Her clothes were always thrown together in a carefully slapdash manner and without apparent regard for whether they matched one another or flattered her figure.

As we neared Sherbrooke, she asked what I thought of Professor Doyle.

"I don't know," I said. "He's unbelievably knowledgeable. It's super-human how much he's read."

Her silence made me think this was the wrong answer. Nor was I reassured when she followed up with another question.

"What do you think of the assigned readings?"

I hadn't given the matter any thought, but I sensed that to express approval or even indifference would be a mistake. I wasn't sure what to say. It seemed to me the readings were what they were and my job was simply to make sense of them. Heather Freeland, however, was not so naïve. She knew not to take the readings assigned in a graduate seminar at face value. She knew how to weigh and assess them on her own terms.

"What do *you* think of them?" I asked.

She said she had no objections to the readings "per se," but she thought the way they were organized and contextualized betrayed dubious ideo-logical underpinnings. She went on at length on the topic, but it was alto-gether too abstruse and subtle for me, and I mostly looked pensive and posed the occasional question to create the impression I followed. At my corner, I came to a stop. Heather kept on talking, fully caught up in her subject. Waiting for a suitable pause, I pointed out that I was just up the street.

"Oh," she said and fell silent.

I wondered whether I should invite her up. But we hardly knew each other, and I worried that such an invitation would seem too forward. Moreover, I had nothing in the apartment to offer her, which might seem odd. I had abandoned the habit of keeping food and snacks there, as they always went to waste, and my fridge and cupboards were empty.

"Well, I guess I'll see you next class," Heather said.

I made a mental note to do some grocery shopping as soon as possible.

At the next class, Heather sat beside me, and we spoke for a few min-utes before Professor Doyle arrived. She told me of a Fassbinder film she'd seen over the weekend and asked if I liked him.

"I don't really know him."

"You haven't seen any of his films?"

I'd seen a couple, but I'd found them ugly and amateurish and was sure I hadn't understood them. "I don't think so," I said.

"Oh," she said excitedly, as if remembering something. "Do you like Peter Greenaway?"

"I've only seen *A Zed and Two Noughts*."

"This Friday at the conservatory they're showing *Drowning by Numbers*. You interested?"

I would have been interested whatever the film, and we made arrangements to meet Friday evening.

The next morning I went to the Webster library and tracked down several scholarly articles and a book on Peter Greenaway. I skimmed through the articles and signed out the book, taking it with me to work. Even with all this preparation, I found the film boring and annoying. Heather loved it and, during dinner at a Mexican restaurant afterward, expatiated on its philosophical themes and implications. I mostly listened, now and again offering a choice, unattributed aperçu.

As the evening wore on, I learned a bit about her background. She was twenty-four and hailed from a small town in Ontario. She'd been in Montreal less than a year and loved living in the Plateau.

After dinner, we walked east along St. Catherine, and I invited her to my place for a drink. I had stocked the fridge and cupboards and had even opened and partly emptied some of the jars and packages. As we entered the apartment, I noticed a quizzical expression on Heather's face.

"Is something wrong?" I looked around for cracks in the Potemkin veneer.

"Spartan," was all she said.

"Ah...yes." All of a sudden, I noticed how stark the place was, how bare the surfaces. Why hadn't this struck me before? I made a mental note to get some posters and knickknacks.

"How do you keep it so tidy?" she said. "You should see my place. And it's a lot bigger."

"My mother's place isn't far," I said as I hung up our coats, "and I still keep a lot of my stuff there."

"You see your mother often?" she asked as she headed to the couch.

"Well...I'm an only child, and...she's alone...so..."

I went over to the tape deck and slipped in a cassette.

"Keith Jarrett?" Heather said.

"Is that all right?"

"Sure," she replied, but her tone was ambiguous. She'd mentioned over dinner that she liked Pavement, P.J. Harvey, the Breeders, as well as various bands I'd never heard of, but I didn't think that sort of thing suited the circumstances. It was also late and I didn't want to disturb my neighbours. But now Keith Jarrett sounded fey and new-agey.

"I could put something else on," I said.

"No, this is fine. I like Keith Jarrett."

I put a platter of nuts and cheese on the coffee table and opened a bottle of red wine. I sat on the other end of the couch and we clinked glasses. Heather asked how long I'd had the apartment. I lied. She asked about my parents and childhood, and, providing cursory details, I directed the conversation to other subjects. Over the next hour or so, we emptied the bottle and I went to the kitchenette to get another. When I returned, Heather had moved to the middle of the couch and was leafing through one of the books on the coffee table. I sat beside her and poured the wine. She took a sip, put her glass down, and moved in closer. I gave her a pinched smile and put my own glass down. She leaned in and kissed me.

It was electric. I hadn't kissed a woman in eight years. As all I'd known was Soula's amplitude, Heather felt slight and delicate in my arms. But it was a thrill to hold her.

After a few minutes, she unbuttoned my shirt. When she began to pull it off, I drew away. She stared glassily.

"I don't think we should," I said.

She frowned.

"It's late, and I work tomorrow. I have to be at the pool hall at seven."

"Oh, okay." She sounded unconvinced. Could she tell I was lying?

"Yeah, I'm pretty tired," I said. "I mean..."

"Whatever."

I felt ridiculous. But I had told my mother I was going to a party in Laval and would be home around midnight. I also had no confidence I could carry on my imposture, that I could continue to pretend I knew what I was doing beyond this point. Heather wasn't Soula and I doubted I could fake my way with her. But I wasn't prepared to come clean either.

To relieve the strain and give myself space to think, I excused myself and went to the bathroom. When I returned, Heather was at the door pulling on her boots.

"What are you doing?"

"You said you have to work tomorrow."

"Yeah, but...I didn't mean...you don't have to leave right away."

"Well, you have to be up at seven," she said, putting on her coat. I couldn't tell whether she was being sarcastic.

"Sorry," I said, "I feel like..."

"It's okay, I'm tired too."

"I hope you understand."

"Of course," she replied genially, though she wouldn't look at me.

"Should I call you a taxi?"

"Oh, no," she said, eyes still diverted. "I'll be fine."

As I opened the door, I wondered whether I should stop her and give her a kiss. But she was gone before I could make up my mind.

I lay back on the couch. I was ashamed, anxious, confused. After several minutes, I got to my feet and tidied up. I washed the glasses and dishes and phoned for a cab.

When I got home, I could hear my mother snoring. This was a good sign. If she knew I hadn't returned as promised, she wouldn't be sleeping. I went directly to bed. But thoughts of Heather assailed me. Yet again I had failed to foresee the most obvious contingencies. How obtuse could a person be? But how could I have predicted things would move so quickly? I'd had no idea whether Heather Freeland was even attracted to me. Even as we were sitting in my apartment, I assumed her interest must be platonic. What was she thinking now? She had appeared angry. Was it over? Might we still be able to develop something? But how would that work? I would have to be candid with her. But what would she make of a thirty-one-year-old virgin? Would she understand? I imagined she would see me as some stunted retrograde Mediterranean mamma's boy. And what if she told others, spread the news around the department? Was Heather Freeland to be trusted? I barely knew her.

She wasn't at our next class. I suspected it was because of me. I hoped she'd dropped the course, but the next week she showed up, coming in late and sitting some distance from me. She didn't look at me the whole time.

We would speak again, but we would never again see each other outside class. Toward the end of the term, I found out she had taken up with a tall, good-looking neo-Kantian in the PhD program. I occasionally saw them together and wondered what she'd told him about me.

The title I proposed for my thesis was *Epistemology and Politics in the Life of Henri Bergson*. Professor Glaus, my supervisor, rejected it out of hand. "What does that even mean?" he huffed in his blustery Brooklyn accent, undiminished after more than twenty years in Montreal. "I might understand epistemology in the *thought* of Henri Bergson, or just *epistemology* in Henri Bergson. But epistemology in the *life* of Henri Bergson? What's that?" I came back with *The Epistemology and Politics of Henri Bergson*. He liked that better, but when I submitted a draft, he became ornery again. "This is speculative pseudobiographical psychologism. You're supposed to be doing philosophy. This doesn't even read like a history thesis. It's more like literary theory. There's no rigour. You need to make up your mind what you're doing. If it's history and biography you're interested in, you're in the wrong program."

By now I could barely remember why I had chosen to write on Bergson. The historical and biographical scaffolding of my thesis seemed to me the sturdiest part of the thing. I wasn't sure I even understood Bergson, but I had become fascinated with his life and times. The thesis I finally submitted was entitled *Knowledge, Memory, and Politics in the Life and Works of Henri Bergson*, and there's no denying now that it was a dog's breakfast. But it was approved and passed, and that was all that mattered.

Already before I'd finished it, I'd made up my mind that I was done with philosophy. Whatever Professor Glaus's opinion of it, my research had given me a new respect for the historian's trade. It seemed more grounded than philosophy. One reason I had veered into biography and history was that they'd offered relief from the esoteric abstractions I was mired in. I envied the way historians yoked the general and the particular, how, by the careful accumulation of data and evidence, they could reveal complex patterns and connections in random, scattered facts, how they could make lucid and intelligible what seemed at first sight a boundless chaos. I formed a conception of the historian as a humanist cousin of the scientist, an intellectual journeyman who, by stringently empirical means, worked to establish a set of concrete truths about the world that, however slight or banal they might appear on the surface, were ultimately of greater value to the world than yet another meditation on the nature of subjectivity or the ontology of the sign. Marx famously denigrated philosophers for doing no more than interpreting the world, but they weren't even terribly good at that; if it was interpretation of the world you wanted, poets and novelists did it far better. And, anyway, who read philosophy anymore? Beside the best historians, most philosophers of the day looked like nattering cranks, churning out unintelligible journal articles not even other philosophers read. Where truth was concerned, a few homely, solid facts properly discerned and arranged were worth more than an empyrean of cloudy abstractions. I needed to turn my efforts to something more practical. I wished to contribute something of measurable value to the world.

I was now thirty-four and what had I done? I had lived my whole life in abject fear. And of what? Of being a bad son? Of letting my parents down? And what was the result? Pain and misery for everyone. Disappointment all round. If only I'd left home and pursued my own goals. Everyone would have been better off, including my mother—especially my mother. She would have learned to cope. Our relationship might be on an adult footing. Instead, I remained in a state of arrested development, raging and moping and blaming my parents for ruining my life. And all in the interest of fulfilling my filial duty. What a grim irony.

I had to learn to treat my mother as an autonomous being. I had to stop thinking of her as my mother. I had to stop being her child. I had to detach. I had to see her as an ailing, aging, suffering fellow creature who was in need of my help. But if I was going to put my relationship with both my parents on a proper footing, I would have to make a clean break. I had to leave the city. There was no other way, though the thought of it made me woozy. It seemed impossible. But I must simply begin. I would set the plan in motion by taking the first steps, put one foot in front of the other in a mechanical fashion. That first step was always the hardest. Beginnings. Which, of course, are always also endings.

I started submitting applications to graduate programs right across the country, identifying my main research area as the history of Greek immigrants in Canada. Though I had no intention of following through on this, I thought it might gain me my father's support and possibly even pry open his wallet a little. It was also the sort of topic that admissions committees and funding bodies went in for, and given my unremarkable academic record, I figured I should make the most of my name and background and leverage whatever cultural capital I had. I soon started receiving acceptance letters. One was from the University of Toronto, which I had already decided was my best option, as it was ideally located—far enough, but not *too* far. I would still be able to make regular visits home and reassure my mother that I was close at hand. Toronto required qualifying courses in history and historiography, completed at my current GPA. On the positive side, I could do them at Concordia. This meant I would be able to delay the most difficult part of my plan: I could put off informing my parents for another year.

Some days after receiving the letter from U of T, however, I got one from McGill, which plunged me into a frenzy of indecision. I considered throwing the package out, but in the end I opened it and found inside another conditional acceptance. I felt nauseous. I remembered how, even as I was completing the application, I had questioned the wisdom of applying to McGill. But I had overridden my instincts and sent it as a safety measure, in case no one else accepted me, though keenly aware of the potential difficulties I was creating for myself.

And now I was seeing them realized. My resolve wavered. Why was I so overwhelmed by choice? Here I was chronically lamenting that my life was ruled by contingency and constrained by external and arbitrary impediments, yet as soon as I was presented with alternatives and possible remedies, I seized up. It was easier to be ruled by circumstances and necessity: you did what you had to do and that was all there was to it. No regrets, no second guessing. Now, again, faced with a choice between what was right and what was easy, I became immobilized. I knew what I needed to do yet couldn't bring myself to do it. One reason I had decided on a PhD in the first place was to give myself an invincible pretext for leaving the city. But how much easier my life would be if I stayed in Montreal and went to McGill. The financial savings alone were incentive enough. But the whole point, I kept reminding myself, was to get out of Montreal.

I agonized for days, unable to make a decision. One afternoon while I was brooding at my desk, my mother shouted from her room that Oprah was on. She didn't watch much TV these days, confining herself to the

Greek programs on cable, old variety shows in reruns, and figure skating. News programs and talk shows were beyond her competence, and she had no interest in them anyway, the exception being *The Oprah Winfrey Show*. Something about its host and atmospherics seemed to soothe and even cheer her, and apart from those episodes dealing with battered women, child abuse, drug addiction, and that sort of thing, she followed the show religiously. When I was around she would try to get me to sit with her and translate. Doing nothing productive that afternoon, I went to her room, where I found her lying on top of the bed covers dressed in her day clothes. I assumed she was having one of her bouts of hot flashes but I said nothing. Kicking off my slippers, I lay beside her on the bed.

Oprah's guest was a young Hollywood star much in the limelight. Just back from shooting a film in Africa, he was talking about what a thrilling and humbling experience it had been to work with its legendary director. He then told a rambling story about a safari trip he and his famous girl-friend had taken in Kenya that had Oprah and the audience in stitches. After a commercial break, Oprah shifted to a graver register, asking about the star's philanthropic work and social activism. Humbly paying tribute to her own greater accomplishments, he spoke about his involvement in the fight against AIDS, and about a meeting with Nelson Mandela, where the two, he said, discussed numerous issues of global importance.

Hard as it was not to cringe at such spectacles, much of the disgust I felt that afternoon was directed at myself. Sneer as I might at the star's self-importance, here he was in his mid-twenties holding summit meetings with Nelson Mandela and contributing to the fight against AIDS. What was I doing at his age? As I recalled, my main pursuits were getting Soula to bare her breasts and surviving law school.

Lost in these reveries, I felt a grip on my wrist. My mother raised my hand to her mouth and started kissing it repeatedly while gasping and murmuring to herself. Turning toward the TV, I understood. Nothing thrilled my mother like the sight of a baby, and at that moment there were nine or ten of them on screen, all dressed in diapers and frolicking about in a bare white room in some kind of surreal commercial. Whenever a baby appeared on TV, no matter the context, my mother would go into raptures, and now, while kissing my hand again and again, she babbled breathlessly about her own golden child, her joy and light, her angel, her treasure, her paradise on earth. Usually at these outbursts, I would storm from the room full of rage and revulsion, but this time something odd happened. The rage and revulsion were still there, but they were vitalizing and sobering. An extraordinary calm descended upon me. The fog and paralysis suddenly lifting, I knew what I needed to do. I knew where I was going. I was ready to act.

7

As usual, *Kyr* Spyros arrived with the end of the morning rush, after the last of the teenagers had cleared out in a hurry to make the bell. Kyr Spyros owned a total of two suits, both of them corduroy. This morning he was wearing the brown one along with the matching vest he wore in the cold months, a blue flannel shirt, and a green tie with diagonal yellow stripes. Though the snow had melted, he had on his black rubber boots. In his early eighties, he walked with the aid of a wooden cane, its handle the shape of a tilde and the shaft etched with tiny wine bottles, stem glasses, and clumps of pale pinkish grapes. On his head was a brown wool toque, which, as he approached the counter, he removed to reveal a full head of cottony white hair that matched his bushy moustache. Shoving the toque in a side pocket of his jacket, he hooked the crook of his cane on the countertop and, with a quiet grunt, eased himself onto the closest stool. Consistent with his Laconian origins, he uttered a gruff "Kaliméra" and then gazed up at the TV. In his chattier moods, he might comment on the weather, but not this morning. He stared up at the screen silently. When his coffee arrived, he carefully lifted his *flitsanaki* and, uttering a low "*Issiya*," took a long sibilant sip, followed by a sip of water.

The TV was tuned to CBC *Newsworld*, and when the hourly newscast began, Kyr Spyros reached over for the remote and turned up the volume. On the screen flashed white missile streaks against a blue-black sky, dim silhouettes of burning buildings, orange fireballs, pale-grey smoke clouds, and other bleared intimations of carnage. Though he knew hardly a word of English, Kyr Spyros cocked an ear with his hand as a tinny male voice explained that, because of improved weather conditions, NATO had completed its most intensive air attack of the campaign. NATO forces had landed bombs and missiles on roads, bridges, fuel depots, and military command centres. In an effort to cut the Yugoslav army's lines, targets included the main road from Belgrade to Pristina, an army headquarters in the eastern city of Nis, and a military barracks near Prizren in Kosovo. According to a US spokesperson, the bombing campaign would continue without remission until Yugoslav President Slobodan Milosevic ended his ethnic assault. Kyr Spyros understood little of this, but he kept listening as the images on the screen suddenly brightened, the shuddering infrared blur of predawn attacks giving way to crisp daylight shots of bombed-out highrises, bandaged casualties laid out on hospital beds, and roaming crowds of refugees. Kyr Spyros shook his head. The voiceover cited Serbian television reports claiming numerous civilian casualties as a result of NATO missile strikes on homes and apartment blocks in Aleksinac and on a medical clinic near Belgrade. The voice warned these claims could not be independently confirmed.

Kyr Spyros had many questions (you could tell by the look on his face), but, as always, he would hold off until the end of the report. His hand still cupped around his ear, he continued to stare at the screen, which now showed a gathering of men in suits. A close-up of one caused Kyr Spyros to thrust out his chin and spit out a "*Ptoosoo.*" At the same moment, the door behind him sounded, and, turning around, he saw Dzonaras entering. Before the latter could get out a greeting, Kyr Spyros raised a finger to his mouth to shush him. Dzonaras glanced up at the screen and, seeing what was on it, crept to the counter. Taking a seat two stools down, he motioned for coffee. On the TV screen, crowds of protesters marched and shouted in the streets of Athens. They carried banners, giant crosses, and American flags painted over with swastikas. A voiceover explained that the Clinton administration was demanding the Greek government maintain NATO access to crucial ports and roads. The only viable route for ground troops and armoured vehicles was through the port of Thessaloniki and the north end of Macedonia, and so far the support was not there.

The Greek government had long been seeking an end to the bombing and was calling for a pause during Orthodox Easter. With protests and anti-war sentiment growing, there was fear the government would bow to public pressure to withdraw support for NATO.

Again the door sounded, and turning around this time, Kyr Spyros saw Dzonakis coming in. Dzonaras kept staring at the TV. Approaching the counter silently, Dzonakis perched himself to the right of Dzonaras and, unzipping his windbreaker, signalled wordlessly for his coffee. Like the other two, he stared up at the screen, which showed masses of refugees trudging across fields and grasslands. A voiceover explained that NATO military strategists were confident a relatively small and well-armed ground force could establish safe havens, though these plans were contingent on the support of the Greek government. At the moment, 500,000 refugees were estimated to have fled the Yugoslav province, with 300,000 having arrived in Albania and another 130,000 in Macedonia. A further 150,000 were massed at the Macedonian border. According to reports by aid workers, people were dying at the rate of two an hour.

"You hear that?" barked Dzonaras.

"What's happening, what did they say?" asked Kyr Spyros, the newscast having moved on to the next story.

"Did you catch that, *Kathiyité*?"

"What's happening?" Kyr Spyros enquired again.

"Five hundred thousand!" Dzonaras shouted. "So tell me: Who are the war criminals? Who's responsible for all those refugees? Milosevic? Kathiyité!"

Greek for *Professor*, *Kathiyité* was a high honorific among Greeks, having a weight and status even greater than its English equivalent, but Dzonaras, who had been calling me this since I was a Master's student, did not intend it that way. I silently poured two glasses of water, placed them on the counter, and returned to the *bríki* on the electric burner.

"Why don't you answer me?" Dzonaras said.

I waited for the coffee to start bubbling and lifted the bríki. Dividing its contents between two flitsanákia, I turned slowly with one in each hand and placed them on the counter. Dzonaras was staring at me.

"What's wrong with you? I'm talking to you. Did you hear what they just said on the TV?"

"I heard."

"And?"

"And what? What do you want me to say?"

"I thought maybe, with all your learning and degrees, you might be able to shed some light on the situation. I just want to know, is this all Milosevic's doing? Is he the one who's driven those people out of their homes?"

"I don't know," I said, which was the truth. After all these years and with all my schooling and degrees, I had no better understanding of the world than when I was a boy. Maybe the next degree would do the trick.

"Did you hear those numbers?" said Dzonaras. "Five hundred thousand. How many did Milosevic go after?"

"I don't know." The figures were cited in news reports endlessly, but they were inconsistent and I never knew which to believe.

"A hundred?"

I made a face.

"No?" Dzonaras said, pulling out a handkerchief. "All right, how many then? Five hundred? A thousand?" He raised the handkerchief and blew three quick blasts. Shoving a thumb up a nostril, he rotated it vigorously, wiped the catch on the handkerchief, and stuffed the handkerchief back in his pocket. "How many did Milosevic get? Say it was two thousand. Make it even five thousand. That's still a far cry from five *hundred* thousand! And don't forget Milosevic was going after drug dealers and terrorists. Just as I can assure you Misters Clinton and Blair would have done in his shoes. But when Milosevic does it, it's *dzenoside*. When it's Albanian bandits you're chasing down, it's *ethneek klenzeeng*." Dzonaras was proud of his knowledge of English. "But bombing Serbian hospitals and civilians. That's humanitarian. And driving five hundred thousand people out of their homes...which is another thing: if Milosevic was doing all that *ethneek klenzeeng*, then explain to me where all these Albanians came from. Given the reports in the media, shouldn't they have been exterminated by now? But it turns out there's a half a million of them with nowhere to go. Who's going to take them in? Who's going to take care of all those people?"

"I didn't know you cared so much for Albanians."

"You *know* what I think of Albanians. They should all rot to death, the shit-dogs. But they're like vermin, you can't get rid of them. Did you see them up there? They're like cockroaches. They get in through the smallest cracks until they're inside your walls and cupboards and have taken over your house. And who's going to stop them? Clinton and Blair? Are they going to fly them to the US and Britain? *Na!*" He gestured toward his crotch. "They'll pour into the bordering countries and demand sovereignty there too so that Greece will be surrounded by Muslims. Which is what the Americans want."

"This is what the Americans want?" I said.

"They want Greece isolated," Dzonakis said.

"They don't just want us isolated," Dzonaras said. "They won't stop till they've destroyed us."

Dzonakis nodded gravely.

Who would have ever imagined? O Dzonaras and O Dzonakis, Big John and Little John, standing in solidarity. A few years ago, they would have been at each other's throat. Both named Yannis, everyone called them by the English equivalent, which from Greek mouths came out as *Dzon*. The respective suffixes had been added to distinguish between them and derived not so much from their obvious physical differences' as their personalities and reputation. At six-foot-two, O Dzonaras stood well above the other men at the Symposium, but the mock-heroic augmentative was a tribute less to his physical stature than to his penchant for bluster and self-aggrandizement. Having spent time in the merchant marines, Big John loved to spin yarns of his sailing adventures and derring-do. His listeners never tired of hearing them and would egg him on. Like the Venetian children who would chase after Marco Polo, chanting "Tell us another lie, Master Polo," they would say, "Come on, Dzonara, tell us again about that time you were surrounded by pirates off the Philippines"; or "Reh, Dzonara, Kostakis here says he's never heard your story about the Arab and the tiger. Tell that story again." And, either deaf to the mockery or unable to turn down an opportunity for self-display, or both, Dzonaras was happy to comply.

Little John could not have been more different. Apart from standing five-foot-four, Dzonakis was modest, soft-spoken, polite, self-effacing. He didn't drink or gamble, didn't care for sports, and had no interest in billiards. He had probably never even *held* a cue. He was unlike just about everyone at the Symposium. He was simply not the pool hall type.

He'd begun hanging out after his wife died, and he came strictly for the company.

At one time, Dzonakis and Dzonaras would not have been able to be in the same room together. But something odd (and to me still obscure) had happened in recent years. The Greek political landscape had changed in ways I didn't fully understand, and the old distinctions had blurred. There had been a slow ideological shift, such that once remote and contrary positions were converging. Dzonaras was still proud to call himself a royalist and made no apologies for his support of the Junta in its early years. Dzonakis remained, in some form, a man of the left, managing not to succumb to the cynicism and nihilism that had taken hold of so many in his camp. Like my father, Dzonakis had been an avid supporter of Andreas Papandreou and was jubilant when PASOK came to power in 1981. At the time, my father called the victory "the rebirth of democracy in Greece." The new administration quickly enacted bold and, for Greece, radical reforms. This included official recognition of the resistance, amnesty for communists who had fled to the eastern bloc, enshrinement of civil marriage, legalization of divorce, decriminalization of adultery, abolition of the dowry system, and the creation of a national health program. But just as quickly Papandreou began breaking key promises and, in the ensuing years of his protracted reign, would descend to a level of squalor and corruption that would drive party stalwarts like Dzonaras and my father to despair.

When Greeks talked politics, it was rare there wasn't reference to something they called the *kathestós*. I was never sure what this term referred to, but it seemed to denote "the regime" or "the ruling order," though with distinct and culturally specific connotations. The word was fraught with evil and menace. For people like my father and Dzonakis, the kathestós was what PASOK had been elected to do away with. But once in power, the party seemed only to expand and solidify it, extending the graft, cronyism, featherbedding, *baksísi*, and *rousféti* of the spoils system that had characterized Greek politics since the Ottomans while giving it a populist veneer. Created expressly for the purpose of liberating Greece from its imperial overlords, PASOK had called for Greece's withdrawal from the EC and NATO and the closure of its American military bases, but once in power, Papandreou had reversed himself. As Prime Minister, he argued

that such measures were not in the country's economic or strategic interests while at the same time continuing, and indeed even ramping up, his
anti-imperialist, anti-American, and anti-Western rhetoric. My father
decided that the man was a mountebank. By the late eighties, he was calling Papandreou the most corrupt and corrosive political leader in the
country's history, worse even than Metaxas and the colonels. With them
at least you knew what you were getting. They were honest and forthright
about who and what they were. In opposition, PASOK had held out a
promise of renewal, but following the party's betrayals and abuses, there
remained only the bleak conviction that the kathestós was immovable and
ineradicable. With the collapse of the Soviet Union, however, and the rise
of an increasingly unipolar world, there was a reversal among many Greeks
in their attitudes toward Europe. This included many leftists, who came
to believe that only by formally linking itself to Europe did Greece stand
a chance of saving itself from itself. If Greeks couldn't get their house in
order themselves, maybe others could do it for them.

My father, however, surrendered. He gave up completely, turning not
only against Papandreou and PASOK but against all reformist parties and
movements—effectively, against politics in toto. It was a big scam, he said,
a vicious joke. All politicians were liars and hucksters. As rabid an enemy
of the kathestós as ever, he now had even more contempt for anyone who
promised an alternative. He regarded revolutionary and reformist schemes
as not just preposterous but wicked. Where, in the past, the political
arena had comprised conservatives, royalists, socialists, communists, and
so on, now there were only *tomárya*, *kathíkya*, *lopothítes*, and *kathármata*
(roughly, scoundrels, piss buckets, thieves, and scumbags). Any talk of
right and left, of this-ism and that-ism, was but a ruse and a delusion.
There was only money and power and the struggle for these. The rest was
talk and propaganda. Even those with genuinely noble motives, my father
believed, were doomed to corruption once in power. It was simply how
the world worked, a law of nature, and there was nothing you could do
about it.

The notion of false consciousness had been turned inside out: the scales
having fallen from my father's eyes, he believed he now stood above all
ideology. He saw things as they really were and disdained anyone who
couldn't do likewise. Democracy was a fable, at best a historical aberration,

a dazzling short-lived miracle that, having died with the ancient Athenians, persisted only as a useful myth or illusion to contain and control the
restless and ignorant masses. He had once been such a chump, but never
again. When I told him he sounded like Bobby Trifonopoulos, he became
indignant. Bobby was a fool and a reactionary, and he was neither of those
things. Much as he had turned against the left, he denied with all his
might that he had any sympathy for the right.

It was all rather confusing. But Greek politics and political categories always had been. Terms like left, right, socialist, capitalist, liberal, and
others had elusive meanings in the Greek context. My father, for instance,
though calling himself a socialist, had always railed against Canada's welfare system, which he saw as taking money from hard-working people
(immigrants) and giving it to lazy spongers (the French). In a country like
Canada, he claimed, the only people with an excuse for being jobless were
the sick and disabled. Anyone who wanted work could find it. He railed
as well against the country's liberties. A champion of freedom and democracy, he believed Canada was *too* free, the proof being the degeneracy of its
culture and society, its wantonness and frivolity, its crime, drugs, dissolute-
ness. To me, it seemed that, whatever their political leanings, all Greeks
had two things in common. One was they were Hobbesian. Wherever
they might fall on the political spectrum, Greeks had a streak of authoritarianism, and shared the conviction that a peaceful and orderly civil society, whether socialist, capitalist, monarchist, or whatever, required a strong
central authority. The other (not unrelated) was nationalism. By the time
I was working at the Symposium, I had met Greeks of every political per-
suasion, from the extreme right to the extreme left, and I had not encountered a single one who was not a nationalist. The centrality of *ethnos* cut
across party lines. Perhaps there was a moment in the thirties and forties
when this category had receded amid the rhetoric of class solidarity and
internationalism, but in the last few years even communists had found
their patriotic footing. While the anti-imperialist and anti-American left
shed its internationalist pretensions, the nationalist right grew more comfortable expressing a kind of repressed anti-Americanism. It had become
increasingly difficult to tell the two sides apart. Thus, on such issues as
Macedonia and the wars in Yugoslavia, Greek opinion was virtually unani-
mous. Current polls showed 97 per cent of Greeks around the world

opposed NATO's intervention in Kosovo. This was an astonishing figure. On what issue since Mussolini's invasion had Greeks been so united? After decades of discord and polarization, here we were at last standing as one in our determination to preserve the Greek race and nation. In the streets of Athens, Communist party members marched shoulder to shoulder with corporate executives, secular democrats linked arms with cassocked longbeards, and middle-aged suburban housewives shouted death chants alongside mohawked anarchists.

And at the lunch counter of the Symposium Pool Hall, Big John and Little John stood together in defense of the Greek nation against the West.

"Why would the Americans, or anyone else, give a shit about Greece?" I said to them both. "You think this is what occupies the West, how they can destroy this puny insignificant country?"

"Greece is not insignificant," said Dzonakis.

"And it's not just about Greece," interjected his comrade. "They want to eliminate the entire Orthodox world."

I laughed. "You think the West gives a damn about the Orthodox world?"

"Then why are the Americans supporting the Muslims? Why are they creating a Muslim noose around us?"

"Since when have American been supporting Muslims?"

"The Americans want what's good for America," said Dzonakis. "They'll support anyone who helps them maintain their power, even Muslims. Because Milosevic is one of the last holdouts in the Eastern bloc who refuses to submit to America's plans for global domination."

"What do *you* think this is about?" Dzonaras asked me. "Why is NATO raining bombs on Serbian civilians and hospitals? Why has it driven five hundred thousand Albanians out of their homes? What do *you* think its motives are?"

Moments like this, I thought of my aunt Christina and her story of the brothers. I had no answer for Dzonaras. I knew the official line, and while wanting to believe it, I smelled something fishy. Given early reports, Milosevic had to be stopped, but once the bombs started falling, I grew confused. While it was hard to credit the paranoid theories circulating at the pool hall, the Western media seemed hardly more plausible. What was one to think when the US ambassador to the UN commended the press for its "exemplary coverage?" How would we react if Milosevic made similar comments about Serbian media? If our press and politicians were to be believed, the world had entered a new era, in which the progressive nations of the West would unite whenever necessary to advance democracy and defend the rights of the oppressed. The war in Serbia was a new kind of war, an "enlightened" and "liberal" war, a war based on "humanitarian principles and values." Could this be true? I wanted to believe it. If the war violated the UN and NATO charters and the American constitution, weren't these, under the circumstances, negligible technicalities?

But when and how had this extraordinary new world order come about? It had snuck into existence without anyone's noticing. What had altered so radically as to make such a war possible? Wars of the past, even the recent past, had been more straightforward and intelligible. It was easier to deduce causes and motivations, to decipher tactics and objectives. It was also easier to discern the propaganda. With Vietnam or El Salvador, or even the Gulf War, it had been easier to see through the diversions, distortions, and lies, to infer ulterior goals and hidden agendas. But Kosovo was a destitute Muslim backwater in an obscure region of the world with no oil or valuable minerals, no communist insurgents, no anti-American terrorist cells—so why all this fuss? To protect ethnic Albanians? Since when did the US give a shit about *Albanians*? Undoubtedly, the circumstances demanded attention, perhaps even intervention, but so did those in Iraq and the Congo and Gaza, and the West didn't seem too troubled by the suffering of people there. Why weren't charters and constitutions being violated to stop the massacres in Rwanda and Chechnya? Why wasn't there a "humanitarian intervention" to protect the Kurds or Abkhaz Georgians? Why was the word genocide never used by the US President in relation to Tsutsis? What made Milosevic so different from Tudjman or Suharto or Netanyahu? Why was it Milosevic alone who was hauled before an international tribunal? Such were the questions rained on me constantly at the Symposium, and I didn't have any good answers. With all my schooling, I still couldn't hold my own against these guys; I couldn't persuade even myself.

Dzonaras stared at me, waiting for my response. The phone rang and I excused myself.

It was my father. "How's everything?" he asked.

"The usual."

"Is Kaldaras there?"

"Not yet."

"He said he'd be in at ten."

I glanced at the Pepsi Cola clock. "It's not even nine thirty."

"He usually gets in early."

I'd made sure to be scheduled to work the late shift, but my father had called at six that morning to request that I open for him. He didn't provide an explanation, but I had a pretty good idea what was up. Hearing my annoyance, he had reminded me of Kaldaras. "So why didn't you open the fucking store yourself," I wanted to say. Mikos Kaldaras was a big deal. Once or twice a month he booked the thomatiáki for his exclusive use and he paid handsomely for it. Why he chose the thomatiáki of all places was beyond me. His were notoriously high-stakes meets that typically went on till the small hours. Kaldaras was a shady figure, though all I knew about him was based on hearsay. A jeweller by trade, he was supposed to be involved in all kinds of dubious activities, more feared and talked of than seen. With his dark demeanour, thick jowly face, hairy paws, and long tapered pinky nail, he looked like someone you wanted to avoid crossing. He was one of the few people my father seemed to be intimidated by.

"Everything's ready," I said. He asked about the room and I told him I'd cleaned and tidied it up and filled the fridge with booze and mezéthes.

"All right. Good. I'll see you later."

"Do you know when you'll be here," I said quickly, before he hung up. He didn't answer and for a moment I thought I was too late. But then I could make out a faint twittering and buzzing in the background. "Hello?" I said.

"I don't know. I have to go."

"But I'm still closing tonight, right?"

"I don't know. We'll see."

"No! You promised," I said, my voice rising. "I already told mamá."

"So then what's the problem?"

"I don't like lying to her."

"You're *already* lying to her."

He had me there. As in past years, I had demanded my father schedule me for the late shift during the early days of Holy Week so as to give me an excuse to miss the first four nights of vespers. I still attended the Good Friday and Easter services, as my mother would not permit me to miss these under any circumstances.

"I'm closing tonight," I said.

But the line was dead. My father had hung up.

Relations between us were more strained than ever. Two weeks earlier I'd received a follow-up letter from the University of Toronto outlining the doctoral enrolment process, and for several days, I carried it in my knapsack, waiting for the right moment to show it to him. Why this need for material evidence? It was as if without it I would lack credibility and moral suasion. But the right moment never presented itself. My father had been in a prolonged and especially rancid funk, and it wouldn't let up. So one evening, after we'd closed, I sat him down and handed him the letter. He eyed it suspiciously as he slipped on his reading glasses. He lit a cigarette. I gave him a minute.

"Do you understand it?" He examined the letter as though assessing it as an artifact rather than reading it. "I've been accepted to do a PhD at the University of Toronto. In history. I start in September."

He gazed over his glasses at me. Unsure how to read his expression, I launched into my prepared explanation. I told him that U of T's program was the best in the country, that it had the best scholars in my area of research, and other half-truths. I didn't mention the small scholarship I had received. I was still hoping I might wheedle some money out of him.

"What does your mother say about this?" he asked, removing his glasses.

"I haven't told her yet."

"Are you taking her with you?" he said, putting out his cigarette.

"She'll be fine. She can look after herself. You've been saying yourself how I only encourage her by treating her the way I do. I'm thirty-six years old. How long am I supposed to take care of my mother? How old were you when you left Greece?"

"I was responsible only to myself. I had no family."

"I'm going to Toronto to do a Doctorate. I don't think that's so unreasonable."

"Why can't you go to McGill? It's the best university in the country."

"Not for what I want to do."

"Which is what? I still don't know what that is."

Time for my coup de grâce. "I'm going to research the history of Greek immigrants in Canada," I said. "Maybe write a book. There isn't much on the subject."

He peered at me under furrowed brow. "Greek immigrants? What do *you* know about that?"

Why was I surprised? How did I not recall that the same tactic had failed eighteen years earlier?

"Are you joking?" I said.

"You were born in Canada. What do you know about immigrants? You can't write a book on something you know nothing about, something you haven't lived yourself."

"If that were true, we'd have no history books at all. No one would have any knowledge of the past, of other people, of anything in the world except themselves."

"That's right," my father said. He handed me back the letter. "You can't do this," he said. "You can't leave your mother here alone."

"Is *that* the issue?"

"There are many issues. What it comes down to is you can't do this. It's impossible."

I took a moment to compose myself. "Let me explain something. I didn't come to you for permission. I'm just informing you. I'm going to Toronto. It's settled. I've given my answer. This is a huge opportunity for me, and an honour. And, stupidly, I thought, as my father, you would be proud of me and support me. I'm thirty-six. I've sacrificed enough of my life for other people. It's time I started thinking of my own future."

"I've supported you plenty over the years, and where has it gotten us? I've gone well beyond what either the law or duty require in supporting both you *and* your mother. Who paid for your law school? Who's given you work and an income all these years? Eh? And what's come of it? You've had all the advantages and opportunities a person could ask for, and what have you done with them? You've done one degree after another, and where are you today? Working in a pool hall. For your father. And now you want to go back to school. At thirty-six." He shook his head and lit another cigarette. "You want to do a Doctorate," he said, wisps of smoke curling around his lips and nostrils, "that's your business." He puckered sideways and blew. "But you also have your responsibilities. I don't see why you can't go to McGill."

"I just explained it to you. Toronto's better for this."

"McGill is one of the most renowned universities in the world."

"They don't specialize in what I want to do."

"Which is what again? Greek immigrants?"

"Yes. Canadian history."

"Who are these people?"

"What people?"

"These specialists in Greek immigrants. What are their names?"

Did such specialists even exist at the University of Toronto? If they did, I didn't know of them. It was still my intention to declare another area of specialization as soon as I possibly could. "What does it matter?" I said. "It's not like you've heard of them."

"Why? Because I'm an illiterate hick? I can't know about such things?"

I pushed back my chair and got up. "I'm not asking for permission. I'm telling you what's happening. I'm leaving in August."

My father gazed up at me glumly. "Obviously I can't stop you, you're a grown man," he said, prematurely stubbing out his cigarette. "But understand one thing." He rose to his feet. "Don't expect me to step in for you with your mother."

"Is that what you're worried about?"

"No matter *what* happens."

We stared at each other through the cinerous haze.

"You want to go to Toronto?" he said. "Do it. But it's on *your* head."

"What's on my head?"

"Whatever. All the consequences. Whatever happens."

"Yes, of course."

"I just want to be clear."

"It's clear."

"And one more thing," he said.

I waited.

"Don't come running back to me when you make a mess of everything again."

I held his gaze, labouring to maintain my self-control.

"Don't worry," I said. "I won't be bothering you again."

I couldn't tell how he interpreted the remark, but I meant it literally. I had made a decision: after I left Montreal, I would never have anything to do with my father again.

"They've already taken over Park Extension and now they're spreading here."

"They're taking over the whole city."

"They're even moving into Outremont."

"The other day I saw a whole tribe of them over on Waverly. You can smell them from across the street."

Lazaros, Dzonaras, and Karolos the Armenian roosted side by side at the counter, with Kostakis standing between the latter two, one foot propped on the riser. At one of the billiard tables, Stelios Maniatis and some guy I didn't recognize were playing poker pool, and a group of French kids was huddled around the Mortal Kombat machine. Three young guys sat at a table near the counter drinking coffee and chatting in English. I kept trying to hear what they were saying, but they were drowned out by the group at the counter.

"I'm telling you, they're taking over the whole city," said Lazaros.

"It's already happened in Europe," said Kostakis.

"It's happening in Greece," said Karolos. Though born in Armenia, Karolos (whose real name was Garo) spoke fluent Greek. Having fled with his parents to Greece when he was a child, he spoke with only the hint of an accent. "Have you seen Omonia Square?"

"It's a sewer," said Dzonaras.

I kept glancing at the young guys behind them. We didn't get many of their sort. These three had shown up a few months earlier and had been coming in once or twice a week ever since. I guessed them to be in their early twenties, probably students. You could tell they were well-educated. They also sounded as though they were from outside the province, maybe the US. Anglos and out-of-towners were moving into the neighbourhood. Studiously unkempt, they favoured loose baggy pants and oversized T-shirts with cryptic logos and prints. They never played pool or the machines and often ordered Greek coffee, requesting it *métrio*. All three had been to Greece and liked talking about their travels with my father. "Beautiful country, Andreas," they would say as he grinned proudly. Though they liked to toss out what little Greek they knew whenever they could, they always addressed him in the nominative—*Kaliméra, Andreas! Ti kánis, Andreas?*—which undermined the casual insider status they strove to project. Nor did my father mind their use of the singular. He appreciated the effort. Even with their ear studs and tattoos, he seemed to like them. But I suspected they were having us on, laughing at us.

Watching them now, I was trying to discern whether they were picking up anything from the conversation at the counter. But they were immersed in a heated debate about Hugo Chavez and the situation in Venezuela. I wondered what they made of the Sun of Vergina draped on the wall behind me. I wondered where they stood on that issue.

"You can't walk around Omonia at night anymore," Dzonaras said. "You'll get mugged."

"It's all Albanians now," said Kostakis.

"Not just Albanians," said Dzonaras. "There's even worse."

The door opened and my father moped in. He was freshly shaven but pale and haggard.

"*Ti néa*, Andrea?" Lazaros hazarded.

My father nodded distractedly and examined the contents of the cash register. He shut the drawer and, gripping my arm, led me to the far end of the counter. He looked even worse up close, his eyes glazed and drawn, as if he'd just woken up. He asked about Kaldaras. I told him he'd arrived just before ten and I hadn't heard from him since.

"How many are there?"

"Seven. Including Kaldara."

He gazed glassily past my shoulder. "I better check on them. You can go."

"What?"

"Do the cash and go."

"No way," I said in English.

"I don't need you."

"You promised."

"You can stay if you want, but as of this moment you're off the clock." He headed toward the back.

I walked to the register, ignoring the eyes at the counter, and removed the drawer. I went through the slips and cash. When my father returned, I handed him the zippered pouch and, without a word to anyone, collected my things and left. I kept thinking of his call that morning: *You're already lying to her.* He was right. I lied to my mother all the time. So why, in select instances, did I feel compelled to maintain a sense of probity? Why, in this one, should she know that I'd left work early? If I didn't tell her, how would she ever find out? Approaching St. Urbain, I came to a stop. I could make good use of the unexpected free evening. I'd been putting off some urgent things far too long.

Doubling back, I went into a phone booth on Park Avenue. I still hadn't told Silvana about the latest letter from U of T. I'd avoided seeing her since its arrival. She had recently bought a clandestine cell phone, specifically for the two of us, but I knew she would still be at work so I dialled her office. I tried to sound cool and upbeat. I didn't often call her with off-the-cuff invitations and didn't want to raise suspicions. I explained I was off work early and asked if she'd like to have dinner. I suggested an Indian restaurant she liked.

Silvana and I had met a year and a half earlier. She was in front of me in line at the Concordia University bookstore. It was the start of the fall semester and the line was long, and growing impatient, she turned around and, seeing the books in my hands, unabashedly tilted her head and examined the spines. She herself was lugging a stack of fat textbooks with titles like *Principles of Corporate Finance* and *Leadership Theory and Practice.*

"Foucault," she said. "Have you read *Madness and Civilization*?"

"No," I said. "Have you?"

"Oh, yeah. I thought it was amazing," she said, her accent confirming my guess that she was Italian.

"Really?" I said.

She flinched. "Really what? That I thought it was amazing? Or that I read it?"

I felt my cheeks burning. "No...I didn't mean...I mean—"

"You think because the way I'm dressed and the books I'm holding, all I care about is money."

"No, of course not, I—"

"Tsawright, I'm used to it," she said, facing forward.

"No...please...you misunderstood."

"Oh yeah, I misunderstood." Turning her head toward me slightly, she said, "You think people like me only read authors like Stephen Covey and Anthony Robbins." *You tink people like me only read authors like Stephen Covey an Ant Knee Robbins.*

"No, honestly, I didn't—"

She faced me fully. "Thing is, I may not be the person you think I look like. You shouldn't prejudge."

"I'm sorry. I misspoke."

"Tsawright," she said, showing me her back again.

Her turn came at the counter. When I stepped up to the next register, she finished paying for her purchase and stood by the entrance. As I approached her, she said, "I'm sorry for jumping on you. I'm not really insulted. I just feel self-conscious in these clothes. It's cause I came straight from work. This is not who I am. If it were up to me, believe me, I would never dress this way."

"There's nothing wrong with the way you're dressed." I just stopped myself from telling her she looked gorgeous. She had on a tight navy-blue skirt suit that she filled out splendidly.

"Don't lie to me."

"I'm not lying."

"It's all right, we can drop it."

I figured I should take my leave, but as I was about to say goodbye and accelerate ahead, she asked if I'd like to have a drink.

"Sure," I said. "And it's on me. I owe you one."

"Stop with that."

The pub she suggested was crowded with students, but we found a high table in a corner. She ordered a glass of wine and I had beer. On the walk over, she'd enquired into my background. Now, sipping her drink, she said, "You don't look Greek. I would never have guessed." Given her accent, I had thought she might have come to Canada as a child, but I learned she was born in Montreal. She had gone to one of those bilingual schools in St. Léonard, which may have accounted for her English pronunciation. Unlike me, however, she was fluent in both English and French. She was twenty-seven and still lived at home with her parents and brother. Her mother had worked in a garment factory, but it had closed down and she'd taken an early retirement. Her father worked in construction. Both her parents were from Calabria, and Silvana was the first in her family to go to university. Indeed, she was the first to finish high school. Her brother, three years her senior, had dropped out after grade ten. He, too, worked in construction. Silvana was in the midst of an MBA, which she was doing part-time. In high school, she had thought she might study journalism or psychology, but her parents disapproved of both, so she majored in Commerce.

"This is not me," she said again, gesturing at her outfit. "This is a costume."

Unable to contain myself any longer, I said, "You look fantastic. You really shouldn't be apologizing."

I could see from her face this wasn't what she wanted to hear. "But this is not the real me," she said, sounding almost dejected, deflated. "I never dress this way except for work."

"No, I know what you mean," I said, belatedly.

She explained that she worked as a low-level accountant for an insurance firm and hated her job. But with her current credentials, she had little chance of finding something better—hence the MBA, which she hated even more. "You wouldn't believe the things the profs say in class, straight-face. It's all about money. Money, success, status. It's not just the students. It's what they teach in the program. It's how they train you to think. And if you don't go along, you're made to feel like a loser. I can't stand it."

"So why are you doing it?"

"I just told you." *Adjust toll you.*

"But you're twenty-seven. You have a full-time job, paying your own way. Why not do journalism or psychology, or whatever else you want?"

"Right. That's easy for you to say. You're a guy. You can study philosophy or history or whatever you want.".

"But my circumstances aren't so different. I know where you're coming from."

"You have no idea."

"I have some idea."

"No, you don't. It's like my brother. If he wasn't such a *stroonz*, he could have gone and studied whatever he wanted. No one would have said anything. But with me, you know what would happen if I said I'm gonna get a degree in psychology? My father would beat me."

"Are you serious?"

"My father didn't even want me to go to university. I had to fight him."

In the coming weeks, I would learn a great deal more about Silvana and her family. Though not as religious as Soula's parents, Silvana's were far more controlling. Even her brother policed her comings and goings. In high school and CEGEP, she had been forbidden to speak with boys, and she was still forbidden to see men they didn't know and hadn't approved of beforehand. She'd been in two serious relationships, both clandestine and not very long-lived. She had not been on her first date until she was twenty-one. It was understood that she would marry an Italian, and her father and other relatives kept trying to set her up, but she refused. She loathed Italian men. They were all mama's boys and cheats.

"What makes you think Greek men are any different?" I said.

"I don't know what Greek men are," she said. "I hope *you're* different. Are you?"

I knew Silvana and I could have no long-term future, but I liked her. She was warm, sensitive, generous, kind, and I enjoyed her company. We were simpatico in many ways. I could be myself with her. I was even candid about my sexual past—which is to say, about the absence of one—as well as about my covert apartment. None of it fazed her. It didn't even seem to surprise her. She'd thought of getting an apartment herself. We had much in common. We understood each other. It was sometimes tricky to get together, but we both had long experience leading double lives and evading domestic surveillance. We managed to see each other once or twice a week, and I gave her a set of keys to the apartment. She would go there on her own to study or read. Sometimes she went to get away from her family. She offered to pay half the rent, which of course I refused.

Barely two months after we'd met, Silvana told me she loved me. This took me unprepared and I told her I loved her too. Yet I assumed she understood there was no future for us, that this was temporary. I had been clear about my plans. She knew of U of T's conditional acceptance. Sometimes I wondered whether she saw me as one of those windbags and fantasists we talked about, guys like Perry and her brother, who boasted constantly about all the big things they were going to accomplish even while they continued to live at home with their parents and had their mothers making their beds. And I feared I may have reinforced the impression, when at the end of the fall term, overwhelmed by my workload and worried about maintaining the requisite GPA, I requested a year's deferral from U of T. It was granted and I was able to spread my courses over a longer period of time.

But now all requirements had been met and I'd received approval to begin in September. That was what the latest letter was about. The mature thing would have been to meet Silvana at the apartment, but I chose a restaurant, reckoning that a public setting might curb the emotional outbursts. It would also allow for a quick escape should one prove necessary. The place I suggested was a dark subterranean bunker with narrow hopper windows that let in little outside light. Even in the daytime, much of the illumination was provided by the few electric wall sconces that flickered feebly between the sequin patchwork tapestries and paintings of dancing gopis, and the tealights on the tables. I arrived early and was happy to find the restaurant almost empty. Even so, I chose an isolated table in the back, next to a wall niche with a wooden statue of Ganesha. Silvana arrived in good spirits. She'd had a rare good day at work, and she ate heartily.

We were about halfway through the meal before I finally said, "So, it's official. I got a letter from U of T. I start in September."

Silvana lit up. "Congratulations!" she said, reaching for my hand. She sounded genuinely pleased. "Not that there was ever any doubt," she said in a tone free of regret or resentment. "Have you told your parents?"

I related my conversation with my father and admitted that I had yet to speak with my mother.

"Don't let them guilt you. Cause that's what they'll do. Your father's a prick, but you knew he would be, so...You have to be strong now and do what you have to do. You have to live your life, fucking shit."

She continued eating with apparent enjoyment while I maundered on about all I had to do, hoping that in the outflow of words those that needed saying would emerge spontaneously and perfectly composed.

"You'll be fine, you'll be fine," Silvana said. "And your mother will be fine. It'll be tough at first, but she'll adjust." She stabbed into a cheese curd with her fork. "You have to be strong. This is something you need to do and you're being brave to do it. Don't ever forget that."

I found it hard not to cringe at this sort of new-age cheerleading even though I knew Silvana meant it. In some ways, her sincerity made it worse.

"And what about you?" I said.

"What about me?"

"How do you feel about things, me going to Toronto?"

She picked up her napkin, wiped her mouth. "I think it's great. Why? We knew this was coming. I'm totally behind you. Do you question that?"

The waiter arrived to clear the table, and Silvana ordered a gulab jamun and a chai. I ordered a regular coffee.

"You had these plans before we even met," she continued. "I knew what I was getting into, and I'm the last person who would get in your way. Am I happy that we're going to be apart? Of course not. But we'll figure it out."

"Toronto's over three hundred miles away."

"I know how far Toronto is."

"And I don't know how long I'll be there, right? Or if I'll ever come back."

"What do you mean?"

"I doubt I'll find an academic position in Montreal. It's not like looking for an accounting job. Who knows where I'll end up."

"Why are you worrying about these things? We'll take it day by day. And who says I want to stay in Montreal? After I finish this stupid degree, you think I want to stay here? With an MBA, I can get a job anywhere. It's not like we're the first couple in this kind of situation. There's lots of people in long-distance relationships." She leaned in, the tealight giving her face an amber glow. "Alex, I love you," she said, grasping my hand. I knew what was coming. "Do you love *me*?"

I tried to hold her gaze.

"Of course," I said as the dessert and coffees arrived.

Friday we had an early supper of oil-free *fasolátha*, raw onions, and bread. Good Friday and Holy Saturday were the two days of the year when everyone—sinner, apostate, heretic—went to church, and my mother insisted on going early to secure a seat. These two nights, the congregation spilled out to the sidewalk, where the liturgy blasted over loudspeakers. On Friday, the high point was the procession of the *epitáphios*, a flower-bedecked palanquin symbolizing Christ's tomb. Late in the service, it was taken out and carried through the streets, making a slow quadrilateral orbit of the church. I would have been content to remain inside with the elderly and infirm, but my mother wouldn't hear of it; leaving some items of clothing on our pew to reserve our place, we always joined the procession.

We made our way out early and waited while everyone assembled. At the head of the procession was the choir, followed by the priest and a detachment of altar boys equipped with lanterns, banners, and totemic shields and staves. Then came the epitáphios and, behind it, the congregants, chanting and holding tall candles with white or red plastic protective cups giving them an appearance of lambent tulips. As a teenager, I had found these tribal displays mortifying. It was one thing to perform our primitive rites behind closed doors, but why flaunt them before an unsuspecting, uncomprehending, and hostile public? And why be so ostentatious and pushy? Streets had to be cordoned off, traffic blocked and diverted. Police were put on duty. And though they were cordial and professional, I worried about what they thought of us and how they felt about the assignment. On the sidelines, crowds gawked. People peered down from balconies and windows. Drivers gazed out from stranded cars with looks of annoyance. I was amazed we were given official permission for such an ado, let alone material support. One year, a man on a balcony yelled down, "Hey, aren't you guys a little late?" Another year, someone shouted, "Who died?" But such reactions were rare. Generally, onlookers regarded us with an indulgent and benign curiosity, even delight. Some people applauded. As a self-conscious teenager, I would nevertheless steer my mother toward the middle of the pack so we would be less visible.

These days I just felt bored and resentful. I was also angered by the spring in my mother's step. Every Good Friday her aches and debilities vanished, as if by miracle. This year, I chose to see her vigour as confirmation that she could take care of herself. She would be all right.

"Kyra Eleni!" came a voice from behind, and we turned to see Kyra Fotoula and Kyra Despina, two women from the neighbourhood my mother was friendly with. Wrapped as always in their widow's weeds and babushkas, they marched arm in arm. We dropped back beside them and there were the obligatory holiday greetings. I asked how they were.

"Eh," said Kyra Fotoula, gently bobbing her head. "We'll say fine."

I nodded in solemn acknowledgement of the wisdom of her response.

"As long as we have our health, we have the riches of the world," said Kyra Despina.

"Health, health," my mother said. "The highest good."

"This is the truth," said Kyra Fotoula.

"We haven't seen you in church this week," Kyra Despina said to me.

"I've had to work."

"His father has him working in the evenings," said my mother sourly.

"What can you do, what can you do? This is life."

"Are you still studying at the university?"

"Yes."

"*Still?*"

I nodded resignedly.

"So many years."

"But you still find time to take mamá to church."

"When I can."

The two beamed at me. What a nice boy. So polite, so dedicated to his mother. Such a shame he's a *yerontopalíkaro*.

Presently, we were back before the church, and the epitáphios was heaved up the stairs, rising and dipping amid the crowd like a boat tossed on the waves. At the entrance, it was held aloft by numerous arms and the congregants stooped under it one by one on their way inside. My mother and I reclaimed our pew, and some minutes later the epitáphios was returned to its place on the solea.

Toward the end of the service, an altar boy came through a side door of the iconostasis with a microphone stand. Stepping around the solea, he set the stand down a few feet in front of the epitáphios. With the lamentations ended, there followed a brief silence, and the priest advanced. For a long time, he surveyed the congregation with a grim expression. He tapped the microphone and cleared his throat.

"My beloved Christians," he said. "Before we leave tonight...to return to the warmth and safety of our homes...I must say a few words." He spoke in a slow, rhythmic manner, regularly pausing and shifting tone and volume for dramatic effect. "As you all know, tonight we are gathered here to commemorate dark events. We are here to recall an infamous act...a heinous act...an act of barbarism and savagery...occurring two thousand years ago upon a place we call...the place of the skull. For those of our faith, this is a monumental event, an event fraught with symbolism and meaning. And this year, it has taken on an added significance.

"On this night every year, we remember when a young man was brutally murdered. A man who preached charity, forgiveness, love, and who was condemned by the authorities of his day to die like a criminal... like an animal...on the cross. To some of us, living so many centuries later, that cruel and terrible drama may seem remote. But it is a drama that has reverberated throughout the history of our faith...and that plays out even as I speak to you.

"We cannot turn on the television news without seeing pictures of the Middle East. How often are we shown the anguish and sorrow there? How often do we see images of Jews supplicating at the Wailing Wall? How vividly are the sorrow and yearning of this people portrayed...a sorrow and a yearning rooted in such ancient wrongs as the destruction of the Temple in Jerusalem, and the loss of the Tablets of Moses? Similarly, how often are we shown images of the Muslims of the world, prostrating or protesting? How often have we seen the masses circling around the Kaaba? And how often are we shown, at Christmas, and during Catholic Easter, the hordes of pilgrims outside St. Peter's?

"We see these scenes day after day, year after year. And what, my fellow Christians...what lessons are we to take from such images? Is it not the lesson that these places are not like other places, that they are distinct, special, unique? That they are, in a word, *sacred*? Sacred to the millions who live there, pray there, worship there, and journey there from around the world. And yet, how often, when we glance at the newspapers, and turn on the television news, do we see images of our own glorious and desecrated Constantinople? Of the sorrows and yearnings of the beleaguered, friendless Christian community that endures there? Of the shocking defilement of the Hagia Sophia? Who understands, among the general Canadian population, among those reading these newspapers and watching the television news...who understands the significance of *this* ancient holy city? Who understands its sacredness and its place in the hearts of the world's Orthodox?

"We are told in the media that Israel belongs to the Jewish people, that it is the land bestowed to them by God. And so it is. Israel is the holy land of the Jews. Jerusalem is their capital. Just as Mecca is the capital of the Muslim world. And as Rome is the capital of the Catholics. But what of *our* Holy Land? What of *our* capital? Of this we never hear a word.

"Likewise, you will never hear a word from the media about the true meaning of this place called Kosovo. Who here knows what this place means to its original inhabitants? Let us remember, especially on this night, that as the Jews have their Jerusalem, as the Mohammedans have their Mecca, as the Catholics have their Rome, and as we Greeks, in our hearts, and in our dreams, have the ancient and holy capital of Constantinople, so our brethren in Serbia have Kosovo.

"The media tells us eighty percent of the population of that ancient land is Muslim. They tell us about the repression of the Albanian population. About its poverty, its disaffection, its grievances. But there are things they don't tell us. They don't tell us that Kosovo is one of the historic and sacred sites of Orthodox Christianity. That it is the cradle of the Serb nation. And that it stands to this day as the capital of Serbian Orthodoxy, and at the heart of Serbian culture and Serbian identity.

"Perhaps some of you are aware that Kosovo is called the Land of Churches. The medieval Serbs were not only devout Christians, they were also tireless builders. And what they built most of all were churches and monasteries, by the hundred. Hundreds upon hundreds, which still cover the region today, and which are now being bombed without mercy or shame by NATO forces. Ask yourselves: Would NATO dream of destroying the sacred places of other nations? Can you imagine NATO forces bombing the Dome of the Rock? Or the Western Wall? Or the Grand Mosque at Mecca? Yet they do not hesitate to destroy the holy sites of Orthodoxy.

"Last December, the President of the United States suspended military action against Iraq during the Muslim holy days of Ramadan. Yet today, despite the protests and pleas of political and religious leaders around the world, including some Protestants in the United States, NATO rains its bombs upon Kosovo's holiest sites unrelentingly, and will continue to do so even during the holiest days of the Orthodox calendar.

"But this is not the first time we have seen such profanation. Most of us here remember how the Germans marched into Athens on this, the holiest week of the year. But we should also remember how, that same week, they bombed Belgrade on Easter Sunday, killing over twenty thousand Serbs. Yes, my brothers and sisters in Jesus Christ: Easter Sunday. And how three years later, in 1944, the Americans had their turn killing thousands more, when they bombed Belgrade on Easter Sunday a second time. And today, fifty-five years later, NATO is doing it again.

"But why such determination? Why such hatred and hostility for this particular faith? In the past, other religions have come under attack by the prevailing powers. In ancient Rome it was the early Christians. During World War Two, the Jews were the targets of European hatred and aggression. And in between, other faiths have come under violent attack by one ruler or another. Today, on the threshold of the millennium, it is world Orthodoxy. We must ask ourselves, why?

"In Greek memory, the year 1453 burns like a scar. For the Serbians, the scar is 1389. In that year, Tsar Lazar, or Saint Lazar, as he is known today, the leader of the Serbian nation, had to make a difficult choice. He had to choose between, on one side, the glory and wealth of the world, and, on the other, the heavenly kingdom of God. And choosing eternity and salvation, he prepared to fight the invading armies of the Muslim Turk.

"Before the battle, he and all seventy-seven thousand of his Serbian soldiers received Holy Communion, the body and blood of Christ sacrificed on this very day for the salvation of mankind. How many of NATO's soldiers received communion before they commenced their bombing of innocent civilians and the decimation of a small, poor, helpless country? That earlier battle ended with all seventy-seven thousand brave Christian soldiers dead on the battlefield. That day was the Serbs' Good Friday. That battlefield, their cross. In that year, a terrible darkness spread over Serbian Orthodoxy. A darkness that would soon extend even further. For the Serbs, this darkness lasted six hundred years, first under the Turk, and then the atheist communists. These were their years in the wilderness.

"But here is a profound mystery. Who can say whether by losing that battle, the Serbs did not gain their soul? In 1989, on the six hundredth anniversary of the Battle of Kosovo, the Serbian president gave an extraordinary speech, one that, belying the shameless propaganda directed against its author, was notable for its humanity, its humility, its generosity. A speech that pleaded for tolerance, cooperation, and peaceful coexistence among all the citizens of Serbia. Regardless of race or creed. In that speech, President Milosevic said, and I quote, 'It is difficult to say today whether the Battle of Kosovo was a defeat or a victory for the Serbian people. Whether thanks to it we fell into slavery or we survived in this slavery.'

"And, in this light, I myself ask...can it really be a coincidence that the great Serbian leader in the Battle of Kosovo should bear the name of the man whose feast we celebrated one week ago? The man from the village of Bethany, whom Christ, foreshadowing His own and mankind's fate, brought back from the dead? Can it really be a coincidence that the great Serb leader was named Lazarus? Such correspondences between worldly events and scripture are never coincidental. They are signs, my good Christians, signs we must understand and heed.

"In that speech ten years ago, the Serbian president pointed out that what defeated the Serbs six hundred years earlier was not the military superiority of the Ottomans, but their own, the Serbian people's, disunity. It is *disunity*, he declared, that has been at the root of Serbia's difficulties throughout its history. And yet, ten years ago, this poor embattled nation managed, at last, to regain its national and spiritual integrity. For the first time in six hundred years, Serbia stood united. And unity, President Milosevic wisely observed, brings dignity.

"These are words all Orthodox peoples of the world must obey. Because the brutal events today are an attack not just against Serbia, but against *all* Orthodoxy. We have seen this before. We have seen it throughout history. Such has been the very character and essence of our faith since its inception. For ours is a faith founded upon affliction and forged in the fires of oppression. But it is also precisely by such trials, and by its ability to confront, to endure, and to overcome whatever impediments and evils the devil, in his tireless dedication, has contrived to set against it, that our church has demonstrated, and will assuredly do again, its strength, constancy, and worthiness before the eyes of God. By these same trials the Lord has shown us that faith itself must, in times of unrest and tribulation, serve as our shield, and our sword. From the beginning, the devil, through his proxies, has subjected our church to every persecution and indignity his fiendish mind can devise. First there were the Romans. Then came the Franks and Ottomans. But, however superior they may have been in numbers and in power...we prevailed. More recently there were the communists. We prevailed over them too. And now we have the neoliberal secularists, who, no less than our previous enemies, are bent upon stamping out the light of truth, wherever it may shine. And where they see it shining brightest, my brothers and sisters in Christ, is in the Orthodox nations.

"Do not be fooled. What we are witnessing is a global campaign, not just against the Serbs but against all Orthodox nations. It is a campaign whose objective is the eradication of every last particle of Orthodoxy from every corner of Europe. Once again, the devil has ranged the most powerful forces in the world against us. Today it's the Serbs. Tomorrow it will be the Greeks. Do not doubt it. This is why, now more than ever, the Orthodox of the world, from wherever they may hail, and wherever they may reside, must remain united. For only through unity will we regain our dignity."

Here, priest and congregation crossed themselves.

"Oh God of Justice, who has saved us from destruction throughout the eons, hear our voices. Guide all nations and their leaders. With your mighty hand, protect us from the evils of injustice, prejudice, enmity, and war. And bring salvation from this day. May the Holy Trinity protect us always. Amen."

To judge by my father's notebooks, the weeks leading up to the Easter holidays were unusually stressful. Having, for close to a year, imposed some self-discipline and put his life back in order, he'd begun to backslide. At first it didn't appear that way, as he was on a winning streak; but that ended and he felt himself spiralling out of control again, to the point that, for the first time in his life, he considered getting professional help.

Then came the dream. Its timing alone seemed portentous. It came the morning of Good Friday, and he could think of nothing else the rest of the day. He spent Saturday at the pool hall and by nightfall was restless beyond endurance. Mopping up a spill, he thought he heard chanting and turned down the volume of the TV. He couldn't tell where it was coming from. There was no church nearby. Opening the door, he thrust his head into the cold night air and the sound vanished amid the hum of traffic. A car went by with a pair of passengers in the back holding unlit candles. He shut the door and stood motionless. The chanting was gone. Another hallucination? They'd been coming in profusion lately. Was he becoming like his wife? He glanced at his watch again. It was still only 8:30. He surveyed the pool hall. The group of Vietnamese was still at the carambole table, and two boys were playing Mortal Kombat. He couldn't bear it anymore.

"Tonight Greek Easter," he called out. "I close airly."

The boys left after five minutes, and the Vietnamese soon followed. He was upstairs before nine. He had a quick bite, showered and shaved, put on a suit and tie. By eleven o'clock he was in his car. Passing a small crowd outside the old-calendar church, he caught himself making the sign of the cross and laughed silently. What was happening to him?

As he crossed the bridge, he gazed at the white spindly building on the opposite shore and felt himself vibrate with excitement. It glowed brightly over the dark waters, the spiral exoskeleton of some giant space creature. He remembered his first visit to the place thirty years earlier, the futuristic aura it had had for him then. He wouldn't visit it again until a quarter century later, when it was resurrected as a casino. Today its spell was stronger than ever. He couldn't step inside without a sense of excitement and imminent adventure. Whatever might be going on outside, in the world at large, in here there was always hope, a sense of possibility. If only they had a stricter code of conduct and dress. His conception of casinos derived from old movies, and the patrons at this one bore little resemblance to those at Rick's Café or the gaming houses in James Bond movies. Most were loutish and loud and dressed as though for a hockey game or backyard barbecue. He still associated casinos with high society. They retained for him an aura of glamour and sophistication, and he always put on a jacket and tie for his visits, even in the summer.

His game was blackjack. He had tried his hand other games, and he never did as well or enjoyed it as much. He loathed the slots and their flocks of old ladies and simpletons. A game ought to call on your judgement and skill. This not only improved your odds but also allowed you to take some credit for your gains. Sociable by nature, he usually went to the casino alone. He enjoyed the solitude and peace it afforded, the stillness amid the clamour. He found it a welcome break from the clubby atmosphere of the pool hall, which sometimes became suffocating. On rare occasions he would go with a friend, or he might bring a gómena to impress her with his classy and worldly ways. He did bump into friends on the premises—the place was full of people he knew—but though he might stop and chat or even have a drink at the bar, he played alone. He needed the solitude to concentrate. He loved the single-mindedness and absorption of the tables, the way everything dropped away and time and space dissolved. It may have been the closest he came to serenity.

The previous year, he had stopped going to the casino. Following a protracted smash-up, he'd sworn off wagering. He even avoided the thomatiáki. But at the beginning of January he decided, being so long virtuous, to allow himself a brief indulgence and sound out the new year. He wished as well to try a new system, or, rather, a modification of a previous one. He was curious whether some small (though, as he saw them, ingenious) adjustments he'd devised over his hiatus would make a difference. The system involved playing two hands at once and was designed not so much to enhance his winnings as to curb his losses and extend his time at the table.

His first test went well, and he did even better on his next few visits. But then, toward the end of the month, fortune turned her wheel. Seated at one of his favourite tables one afternoon, he was making slow but steady gains when she brought him an inauspicious visitor. Having just doubled down on a pair of fives, he thought he detected, from the corner of his eye, a menacing sight, and glancing up with a sense of foreboding, he confirmed his hunch. Coming his way was a woman in a tight canary-yellow blouse and pink track pants. He didn't know this woman, but he saw her regularly. She was hard to miss. She spent most of her time downstairs among the slots, but now and then she could be seen, and heard, here on the upper levels. Probably in her mid-forties, she was slovenly and dressed in cheap, tawdry, ill-fitting clothes. Though he had never exchanged a word with her, she induced in him a powerful revulsion and loathing.

Glancing to his left, he groaned at the sight of the empty stool at the end of the table. He tried to concentrate on the cards as the *patsavoura* passed behind him. Just as she parked herself on the stool, he was dealt a three of clubs and jack of hearts, busting him out. A second later, he heard her shout something in French, and he was horrified to realize she was talking to *him*. He turned away for fear he might sock her one in the mouth. The Chinese guy to his right was giggling. She started babbling at the dealer, a tall distinguished-looking man in his fifties, who found her amusing, as did the *Kinézos*, who kept snickering. He couldn't believe the lack of courtesy and professionalism. Why was an *ápliti* like this even allowed here? If the management had any sense of propriety, she would have been barred from the premises. She continued blathering even after play resumed, and no one did anything about it. He tried to concentrate on his cards, but after losing five hands in a row, he huffily cashed out and searched the other tables. Fearing he would lose his momentum, he grabbed the first vacant stool he could find. The table had a higher minimum than he would have liked, but at least he was out of sight and earshot of his slovenly nemesis.

Even at a distance, however, her sway was undiminished, and following a series of pulverizing losses, he cashed out and went home. A self-proclaimed rationalist, he was nonetheless a great believer in luck—in spells, curses, jinxes, charms. Though he may not have been able to provide a scientific explanation of how such things worked, he regarded as a fool anyone who discounted fortune as a force in the universe and in men's lives. One had to pay her the proper obeisance. One had to be sensitive to her moods and know how to respond to them. For the next two weeks, he refrained from all wagering, including even lottery tickets. That seemed like sufficient time.

On his return to the casino, however, the situation was unchanged. He lost hand after hand, and, blowing through his allotted roll in a mere forty minutes, he broke away from the table and went to the smoking lounge. He needed to collect his thoughts. Taking out his pocket notebook, he leafed through its pages. Studying the neat columns of dates and figures, he appraised the previous year's losses with disgust. How could he have let himself sink so low? Yet here he was apparently prepared to do it all over again. Did he need help?

After a second cigarette, he exited the lounge and strolled through the casino's less familiar regions. He did this when he needed to clear his head or disrupt a bad run. He stopped at a craps table and watched a pretty blonde woman dicing. She was pleasant to look at. But he didn't fully understand the game and he soon got bored and moved on. Pausing at a roulette table, he watched a few rounds from a distance. He didn't have a feel for roulette either, but the game fascinated him. It seemed to him the quintessential casino game, the most glamorous and aristocratic. Some of the guys at the pool hall sneered at it, said it was rigged. But they thought everything was rigged: slot machines were programmed, card decks were gaffed, croupiers dealt seconds or received signals. Roulette wheels could be rigged with magnets or spring pins, and croupiers could steer their way by means of subtle and undetectable throwing and spinning techniques.

Such practices were taken for granted and to question them was to expose yourself as a dupe. Whenever he found himself at a roulette table, he would look for signs of trickery, keeping a close eye on the croupier's feet and hands, his face and eyes, the way he snapped the ball and handled the wheel. But he had never seen anything remotely suspicious.

He rarely played the game himself. Lacking sufficient understanding of it, he had no clear strategy and felt self-conscious. He worried he was making a fool of himself. Yet the game held an irresistible appeal. He found it mesmerizing. Watching the wheel's slow revolutions and the ball's jumpy gymnastics, he felt an exquisite tension, a kind of focused suspense that was hard to distinguish as pleasure or pain. And wasn't it here where the juice lay? Didn't the spell of hazardry lie, not in the winning and losing, but in the not knowing, in the relinquishment of control, the surrender to chance and providence, in the delicious agony of those terminal seconds before the final card fell, the die settled, the ball dropped, and your fate was revealed? There was something almost mystical in it, as if one were stealing a glimpse into the clockworks of the cosmos.

Approaching the uncrowded table, he positioned himself where he could have a clear view of both the wheel and the dealer. The players were on their feet but for a heavyset bald man slumped over his chips on the opposite side. Next to him was a trio of raucous middle-aged French women. He did not approve of women gamblers, and these three were trashy and probably drunk, talking and cackling loudly. The croupier, a young handsome man with straight shoulder-length black hair, dark eyes, and vaguely Spanish looks, handled them with admirable composure. Now and then, he would respond with a well-timed witticism of his own, which would elicit peals of drunken laughter. He performed his tasks with panache and politesse, his movements and gestures, from spinning the wheel to snapping the ball to gathering and disbursing the chips, executed with an elegance and precision that was almost balletic. Tall and straight-backed, he had an aloof, aristocratic air. At times he seemed distracted or lost in thought, and he performed his tasks as if unconsciously.

Observing this, my father had a thought: What if he'd been looking at the situation from the wrong end? What if the reality were the opposite of what everyone said? What if, rather than controlling the action, the croupier was paying no attention at all? What if, like a worker on an assembly line, he was in a kind of oblivion or mental fog? My father gazed at the wheel. In the past he had focused on the numbers and colours, but now he took in its topography, dividing it mentally into quarter sections. He watched the croupier's hands, the way he handled the wheel and the ball, and kept track of the results from one spin to the next, noting not so much on which number the ball landed as on which quarter of the wheel. It wasn't long before he detected something interesting: the ball had a tendency to drift five to ten pockets clockwise from one spin to the next. The pattern wasn't perfectly consistent, but it appeared reliable enough that one might be able to do something with it.

But could this be? It seemed implausible.

He kept watching and the pattern persisted, with occasional deviations. He studied the wheel and the layout, trying to determine whether there was a betting scheme that could exploit his discovery. The task seemed dauntingly complicated, but after some reflection, he saw how, if he could identify a section of the wheel the ball was likely to land on, he could lay out his bets so as to cover four or five contiguous pockets within it. But would that be enough? And was he prepared to take the plunge?

With the French women having cashed out and the table now less crowded, he purchased some chips. But for several rounds, he placed no bets. When he finally started laying down chips, he had to think and act quickly. He was working things out when the wagering was called off. He glanced back and forth between the wheel and the layout to verify he had distributed his chips appropriately. His intention had been to cover a five-pocket sector with 8 as the fulcrum. He could have widened his coverage and weighted his bets more effectively (a matter for further study), but he was pleased with his work and turned his attention to the wheel.

The ball was a ghostly streak along the upper track. Slowing and dropping, it pinged off a bumper and hit the rotor. Hopping about frenetically, it landed perfectly in the 22 pocket, only to pop out again the next instant and, riding the number band, hover torturously between the 23 and 10. Veering toward the 5, it slithered past the edge of his sector and seemed about to drop into the 24 when, taking an unexpected bounce, it leapt over the 24, and over the 5, to land snugly inside the 10.

He stared at the ball in stunned disbelief, as if expecting it to make another leap. But the brass weight had been dropped, and with trembling hands he gathered his winnings. He sat out the next round, needing to collect himself, but he played the subsequent nine and came out a winner in six. He would have continued, but the Spanish-looking croupier was called away and relieved by another. On the drive home, he reviewed what had happened and cautioned himself not to leap to conclusions. It was a fluke, a freak of fortune. It was ridiculous and dangerous to believe otherwise. In any case, different croupiers would produce different results; and even the same croupier would likely perform differently on a different day. Still, he savoured an Archimedean exultation and resolved to give the matter further study. He took some flyers from the casino to bed that night and pondered their illustrations of the layout and the wheel.

The next afternoon, he was not surprised to find the Spaniard nowhere in sight. He watched another dealer for fifteen minutes, but failing to discern a pattern, he moved on. It was not until the third table that he thought he saw something. He purchased chips, and for the first half hour or so saw steady gains. But then, all at once, the pattern dissolved, and losing big several rounds in a row, he cashed out. His total winnings were negligible, but, driving home, he felt more convinced than ever that he was onto something. He felt an overpowering urge to tell everyone of his discovery. But he knew what people would say. They would tell him it was an aberration or it was all in his head. They would tell him that, given the physical forces and variables involved, the patterns and regularities he thought he was seeing were all but impossible. They would say he was deluding himself. And he didn't want to hear it. He knew what he knew.

On his next visit, he was delighted to see the Spaniard, and stationed himself at his table. To his amazement, the same pattern emerged. He bought a quantity of chips, but a few rounds after he started placing bets, it dissolved. The ball became erratic and after twenty minutes he was down to his last chips. He sat out a few rounds and waited for something to emerge, but it never did. He cashed out and moved to another table, where, spotting a pattern, he lost another couple of hundred dollars.

He left the casino that night feeling dismal. Had he duped himself again? He recalled his vow. But, no, he was not prepared to give up. He simply needed to be more disciplined, more patient, perhaps more cautious, sit out more frequently. He needed to trust to his instincts more.

He did better on his next few visits, winning several thousand dollars, but then lost it all on the subsequent few. And so it went: the appearance of a pattern with the attendant winning streak, and then, suddenly, incoherence and entropy. He began to suspect something underhanded was going on. Was he being strung along? The casinos had cameras on him. There were cameras everywhere. He wouldn't have been surprised if they had them in the bathrooms. Could it be they knew what he was up to? He scrutinized the pit bosses, the way they traded signals with the dealers. Were they signalling about him? Was he crazy in seeing correlations between these interactions and the results on the wheel? Was he imagining it? Was he turning into his wife? But, no, he knew how the world worked. He understood how such establishments operated. He'd heard the stories. These were profit factories, their operations worked out with scientific precision. There were armies behind the scenes monitoring every player and every move at every table. They could tell what players were thinking, what they were up to. There was a science behind such things. It was not crazy to suppose that it was they who had lured him on, who from the beginning had induced him to act as he had. With today's technology, they had any number of ways of manipulating you and making you do as they wished. But what to do? Already he had begun drawing on his credit card, which he had vowed never to do again.

He would give himself one last shot. He made a pact with providence. He would make one last withdrawal, and if he lost, he would swear off hazardry forever. All of it—cards, casinos, horses, lotteries...*everything*! And this time he meant it. He was on the brink again of losing all he had, ending up on the street. If he had to, he would even join one of those support groups. He returned to blackjack. The guys were right. You couldn't trust roulette. Blackjack was his game. It was safest. And no more systems. He would go with his gut.

He played conservatively and made small gains. But then he lost them. Then won them back. Then lost them again. After four hours, he was just below even. Groggy and dizzy, he took a break. He hadn't eaten since lunch. Perhaps he should call it a night. He played another twenty minutes, and, losing repeatedly, he headed down to the deli.

Again, he considered calling it quits. He felt burnt out. But a burger and a couple of coffees restored him. He'd also had a premonition, one of those inexplicable but powerful twinges that told him something good was about to happen. One never knew where these portents came from, but he knew not to ignore them.

On his return upstairs, the ten-dollar tables were full, so he put himself on a wait list. By now the crowd had thinned out and he didn't have to wait long. Seating himself at the head of the table, he won several hands in a row, but that was followed by a slow downward trend, fitful but steady, and his chips shrunk to a couple of stubs. Then, just as he was about to quit, something shifted. He could feel it. Something invisibly turned: the stars realigned, some force in the cosmos changed direction, and slowly the columns began to rise again. He continued playing cautiously, but with the wind at his back now. Where a couple of hours earlier he'd felt exhausted and ready for bed, he now felt alert and lucid. He was almost clairvoyant in his ability to predict what cards were coming.

And then he remembered Kaldaras. He cursed. Checking his watch, he was astonished at the time. He had not intended to stay this long. But now that he was riding this wave, what was he to do? There was still so much force in it. He could feel it. He played several more hands and added to his winnings. He glanced at his watch again. He had no choice. Turning in his chips, he hurried to the nearest phone.

He was back at the same table in under ten minutes. He was even able to get the same seat. But as he'd feared, the momentum was broken, the animus lost. And yet he kept playing. Why? The thing had abandoned him, so why keep chasing after it? It was over, it was gone. The signs were unmistakable. But he kept going, with some notion of luring it back. What was wrong with him? Why did he never learn?

That was what he kept asking himself afterward. Driving home in the blinding sunlight, he felt wrung out and sick, as though he'd stuffed himself to the gills and then vomited himself empty. The next day, he was ragged and desolate. At night he tossed in bed, sleeping in snatches and dreaming of kings and queens, of green baize and spinning wheels and mounds of chips.

Only on the third night, exhausted and on the brink madness, did he fall at last into a deep slumber. Again he dreamt, this time of his childhood home in the village. He couldn't remember the last time he'd dreamt of his childhood. In the dream, his house looked nothing like his real house. It was bigger, more lavish. He was seated at the end of a long table in a large modern kitchen with a fridge, stove, counter, and wooden cabinets. The table was crowded with sumptuous dishes, and on one side sat his mother. At the head of the table, opposite him and seemingly far, far away, stood his father. He was dressed in what in the dream he understood to be an *andártiko* uniform, but which, upon awakening, he recognized as resembling more an army officer's uniform. The jacket was green with gold buttons and braided epaulets and covered with medals. On his father's head was a fez. In his hand, he held a bread knife. It was New Year's Day and he was cutting the *vassilópita*. Despite the military uniform, the dreamer knew that it was after the war and that his father was living at home again. There were many other people at the table, none of whom he could remember later, and they were smiling and talking and laughing. With the tip of the breadknife, his father traced the sign of the cross three times on the bottom of the vassilópita. He then placed it on a large plate and began slicing it. He announced that the first piece was for *Christouli* and placed it on a smaller plate. Then he cut a second piece for *Panayítsa* and set it beside the first. The third piece was for the house, and this too was placed with the others. His father looked at him across the table, which now didn't seem so long, and, smiling at him, announced that the next piece was for Andreas. He cut the biggest piece yet, and as he placed it on a plate, everyone could see the glinting edge of the florin wedged in the pith and began to applaud. There now seemed to be even more people around the table, and everyone was standing and clapping, and as he took the plate from his father and removed the florin from the cake, his mother clasped his head with both hands and kissed him.

He could not recall the last time he'd had a dream so vivid and stirring. Sitting on the edge of the bed when he awoke, he played this one over again and again in his head, wishing to embed it in memory. He generally didn't remember his dreams anymore. He usually awoke barely aware if he'd even had any. He continued to think about this one even after he'd finished his lunch. He couldn't remember the last time he'd dreamt of his father. It was not unusual for people in his dreams not to look like themselves, but this was especially true of his father, who took on a different guise in each dream. In this one, however, he felt as though he had been presented with a perfect likeness of him, one dredged up from the depths of his memory, and he kept trying to revive the image so that it might endure. If he'd had the ability, he would have drawn or painted it. Though he felt like a village widow, he plumbed the dream for meaning. It overflowed with signs and omens. Some, like the military uniform and the fez, he couldn't make any sense of. Others couldn't have been more transparent. Among these were the long table surrounded by people, the New Year occasion, the round vassilópita sliced into sections, and the florin. One would have been a fool not to see the meaning and implications of these, or to fail to act on them. One other point the dream seemed clear about, however, was that of timing, so he knew he would have to wait until *anástasi*.

Good Friday passed slowly and uneventfully, and that night he had trouble sleeping again. Saturday was interminable. Business was slow and the minutes crawled. Driving to the casino, he turned on the radio and caught a newscast on one of the English stations. From what he could make out, the bombs continued to rain down in Serbia. At the casino, he was surprised by the crowd, but then he remembered it wasn't Easter for most people. Many of the people there weren't even Christian anyway. Having some minutes to kill, he considered getting a drink at the bar but decided he should remain as lucid as possible. He loitered on the lower levels, wandering aimlessly through the buzz and clatter of the candy-coloured slot machines. He kept checking his watch, and a couple of minutes before midnight, he made his way upstairs. Riding the escalators, he thought of how everyone would be lighting their candles and chanting *Christós anésti*. Soon they would be home with family and friends, cracking eggs and eating their *mayirítsa*. He found a congenial spot at a roulette table and purchased his chips. He sat out several rounds, waiting for his mind to settle. He had no scheme or system. He did not pay attention to the dealer or the numbers. He did not look for patterns or calculate odds. He would not think or analyze. He would only watch for the signs and follow where they led.

All at once, he felt a profound calm descend upon him. Picking up some chips, he noticed his palms were sweaty. The ball tottered down the wheel and the dealer dropped the brass weight and cleared the table. When the betting for the next round began, he distributed his chips on the layout, his hand moving about autonomously, as if it had been resting on the planchette of a Ouija board.

The dealer gave the wheel a nudge and snapped the ball. The betting was called off. The wheel turned. The ball spun furiously. For the first time in ages, he said a prayer.

8

Welcome to Toronto
Keep Your Distance

The signs on the 401 were a couple of hundred metres apart, the second obviously a warning to tailgaters. Perry had to put a different spin on it. "You see that?" he hollered. I was at the wheel, trying to focus on the road. "Welcome to Toronto! Keep your distance!"

"Yeah, I get it," I said.

"That says it all. It's perfect."

I could see him staring in my direction.

"I get it, I get it."

I was still on edge. I kept picturing my mother as I'd left her, lying in bed with her back to me, whimpering. Perry had begun his raillery the moment we'd set off, oblivious to my mood. Trashing Toronto was a favourite pastime among my friends, though almost none had been there.

"Look at this place," he said. "It's a fucking wasteland."

"We're in the suburbs! Have you been to the suburbs in Montreal?"

"It's not like this."

"How's it different?"

"It's different."

I had made my first trip to Toronto two months earlier to search for an apartment. At the time, I had yet to reveal my plans to my mother; I told her Perry and I were spending a week at Spiro's cottage in St. Agathe. I would let her know I was moving after I had signed a lease. I had booked a cheap hotel for six nights, figuring this was plenty of time. I would learn very quickly how naïve this was. I knew Toronto rents were higher than Montreal's, but I hadn't realized just how high. I had envisioned getting a one-bedroom or a studio, which proved a fantastical notion. The only such places within my means were subterranean hovels or far from campus, so I started looking for shared accommodations. But this was equally disheartening. Every place I saw was crowded or dirty or occupied by people I could not imagine living with. I recalled Perry and his aversion to hippies. By the fifth day I was in a panic. I began the morning as usual at the university's housing office. Among the new listings, one seemed promising: *Third year female med student looking to share large bright two-storey apartment with one other. Females and vegetarians preferred.* It was nearby and the rent was reasonable. Ignoring the dietary and gender restrictions, I called from the housing office.

"Jesus," said the woman who answered, "I just put the sign up an hour ago." She sounded annoyed.

"I just got here," I said. "The place sounds perfect. I know you asked for a female, but I was hoping you might waive that. I can be right there."

"Uh...that's not possible. I'm going to the cottage for the weekend and won't be back till Monday. At the earliest."

"I can be there in a couple of minutes."

There was silence.

"Please."

"Well, as I said—"

"I'm in from Montreal and have two days left to find a place. I'll admit it: I didn't know what I was doing. I didn't know how hard it would be."

"I sympathize but—"

"I beg you. I'm at the housing office. I can be there in a few minutes."

"But even if you come, I have to see more applicants."

"Listen, I don't think you'll find a better roommate. I'm not a kid. I'm in my thirties. I'm starting a PhD in September. I'm quiet, I'm clean, I'm considerate. You won't need to see other applicants, I promise you."

"You haven't even seen the place. And I wanted to rent it for August."

"My plan is to move at the end of August, so that's perfect."

"But what if you don't like it? It's a small room."

"Well, I need to see it." There was an encouraging silence. "I beg you. Just let me see it. In the time we've been talking, I could already be there."

I heard a long intake of breath. "All right."

"Thank you, thank you. I'll be right there. Oh, my name is Alex."

"I'm Laura."

The house stood on a leafy street lined with the sort of stout Victorians you saw everywhere in Toronto, their gabled roofs casting shadows like sharks' teeth on the pavement. The laminated icons of the Virgin Mary on some of the porches suggested Portuguese or Italian households, which I found comforting. They gave me a feeling of home.

The woman who answered the door was not what I'd expected. She looked about thirty years old and, wearing a loose tie-dye halter top, short denim cutoffs, black sheer ladder-run stockings, and a battered old pair of Birkenstocks, did not match my idea of a med student. Tall and gaunt, she had a long angular face with almost masculine features and spiky asymmetrically cut hair dyed black with streaks of purple. On the helix of her left ear was a row of small hoop earrings, and high on her back, just below her left shoulder, a large dark mole, which on closer view proved to be a tiny tattoo of a spider. On matters of appearance and grooming, I could be as pharisaical as my parents and took a dim view of epidermal etchings and needlework. But I tried to withhold judgement.

The house was larger and airier than it appeared on the outside. As she showed me around, Laura explained that her father had purchased it so she could be near med school. At first she'd had two roommates, but that had proven too much and she'd scaled down to one. Seeing that all the rooms but her own were empty, I asked her where her current roommate was. She said that she'd been living alone for a few months, adding, "It's a long story." These were signs, which even at the time I recognized. But the place was so good and I was so desperate that I ignored them. Indeed, by the time Laura took me into the kitchen for a formal interview (a pen and clipboard in hand), I was ready to beg on my knees for the room.

"But you're the first person I've seen. I can't give it to the first person."

"Why not? If it's the right person?"

"I'm going to be honest with you. I've had all kinds of problems with roommates in the past and I need to be careful."

"I'll be honest too. You won't find a better roommate. What kind of responses do you usually get? I imagine it's mostly undergrads. As you can see, I'm no undergrad. I'm thirty-seven." I looked younger than my age. Laura's expression suggested my disclosure may have been a mistake. I might seem *too* old. What kind of thirty-seven-year-old rents a tiny room in a student house? Moving on quickly, I said, "I'm quiet, responsible, considerate. I'm not interested in partying or entertaining friends. I don't know anyone in Toronto. And from everything you've told me about yourself...I think I'd be the perfect roommate."

Laura stared at her clipboard. "I don't know..." She gave me a regretful, puncturing look. I was sure she was going to tell me I would have to wait. But, rising to her feet, she asked if I'd like some herbal tea.

I looked at my watch. "Don't you have to go?"

"I'm in no rush," she said, heading toward the counter. A few minutes earlier, she was telling me the opposite.

I wasn't one for herbal tea, but I wasn't going to decline. As she put the kettle on, she asked me about my life in Montreal. I told her about the pool hall and my parents and also mentioned Silvana, explaining that the relationship was coming to an end. Laura said she was in a similar spot. I waited, but she didn't go on. We talked for another hour, at the end of which she announced without warning or ceremony that the room was mine. She said I seemed nice enough and it would be a relief not to have to interview more applicants.

"You don't know what this means to me," I said. "I don't know what I would have done." I wanted to hug her. "I guarantee you've made the right decision. This is going to work out great, I promise."

A few days later I told Perry about the apartment.

"You're shacking up with a wench?"

"We're not shacking up. I'm renting a room. We're roommates."

"Roommates," he said, nodding. "I guarantee by the end of September you'll be grinding genitals."

"Let me explain something to you: I have no desire, whatsoever, to grind genitals with this person."

"Is she ugly or something?"

"That's not the point. I just don't find her attractive."

"Why not?"

"I don't know why not! She's not my type. Why am I even having this conversation?"

"It is written: when man and woman live under the same roof, there must be grinding."

"You're like my mother."

"It's a law of nature."

"Yeah, that's what she thinks."

"Well, she's right."

It was times like this I wondered how Perry and I were still friends.

When we pulled up in front of the house, Laura was out on the porch and I introduced her to Perry. She apologized for not sticking around to help us. She was meeting friends for dinner. She led us down to the basement to show us where we could store things. I wondered what Perry made of her. Dressed in a loose apple-green floral blouse, the battered Birkenstocks, and a short red-and-black plaid skirt that she wore over faded denim bell-bottoms, she was even more weirdly put together than at our first meeting, deliberately and ostentatiously unsexy. Was this some Toronto thing?

As Perry and I made our way to the van, I waited for his response. He said nothing. While he began unloading, I borrowed his cellphone and called my mother. She was crying when she picked up. "I can't believe you've done this. I can't believe you're in Toronto. Tell me this is not happening." She spoke as though she'd been expecting the whole thing to be a joke, as though, after Perry and I had loaded the van, I would show up at home and announce that I'd been kidding all along.

"I can't talk now," I said. "Pericles has started moving things."

I hadn't told my mother I was sharing a house with a woman. I'd said I was renting a room in a residence. I had fudged some other details too. I'd told her McGill had turned me down and that, among the universities that accepted me, the one closest to Montreal was U of T. None of this registered. I was abandoning her. Amid her howls and tears, I had shown her on a map how close Toronto was to Montreal and promised to make frequent visits and spend every summer with her. Nothing made a difference. "Please," I kept saying, "I can't change things now. Everything has been arranged. I have to do this. Try to understand. I have to think of my future."

"And what about my future? How will I manage on my own?"

"How do other women manage?"

"They have husbands and families, children, grandchildren."

"No they don't! Not all of them! You think everyone in the world has children and grandchildren. And that all families live happily together in the same place. You live in a dream. You think you're the only single woman in the world. There's plenty of women in worse situations than you. There are people out there with no one at all. You have your brother and Aunt Christina, and others."

"But I'm sick. My legs won't carry me. Who will do my shopping?"

"You have no problem going to church, you can go to the grocery store. And they can even deliver, if you need."

"I can't believe you're doing this to me, my own son. What crueller fate is there than this, to be alone?"

And so it went, day after day, till the very end. The morning of my departure, she followed me around the apartment like a dog, whimpering, "Please don't go. Don't do this to me, Aleko. *Aleko mou*, please don't go. Don't do this." She pawed at me, clutched me, wept on my chest, begged on her knees, literally. There were moments I questioned whether I could go through with it.

"How could you do this to me?" she now wailed on the phone. "Abandoned by my only child! What else do I have in the whole world?"

"I have to go. We'll talk when I have more time." I waited, listening. She seemed to be hyperventilating. "Okay?" I could hear banging and scraping behind me. "I'm hanging up now. We'll talk tomorrow. Goodbye."

"Everything all right?" Perry asked as I pressed my head against the steering wheel.

"Yeah, I'm fine. I'll be with you in a minute." I lifted my head and turned around. "Sorry, I need to make one more call."

"Take your time. Is your mother all right?"

"No."

"What's wrong?"

"Nothing. The usual."

I flipped open the phone and dialled. At least Silvana wasn't in tears. "I can't talk long. Perry's unloading the van."

"How was the drive?"

"Fine. I can tell you more later."

"When?"

I took a moment to breathe. "I don't know. As soon as I can."

"Tonight you mean?"

"Probably not tonight. Tomorrow...hopefully."

"Why hopefully?"

"Silvana, please, I don't know. I just got here. I'm going to be pretty busy the next few days."

"Too busy to call? You're going to be unpacking boxes. You can take a break for a phone call."

"Okay. Yes. I'll call you."

"I miss you already."

"Yes," I said. I felt exhausted. "Me too."

It didn't take long to unload the van. When we were done, we walked to a restaurant Laura had recommended. The way Perry looked around, you would have thought we were in Beijing or Marrakesh.

"You have to admit it's a pretty nice neighbourhood," I said. "It reminds me a little of Outremont."

"It's *nothing* like Outremont."

"A little bit."

"It's *nothing* like Outremont."

It was a warm night, so we sat on the patio. After we'd ordered, Perry said out of the blue, "So what's wrong with her?"

"The usual. She's worried about how she's going to manage alone."

"I'm talking about Laura. Your roommate. I think she's kinda hot."

"You gotta be kidding me."

"She's a little quirky, but."

"Quirky? Did you see what she was wearing?"

"She's a bohemian."

"That's not bohemian. It's just fucking weird."

"She seems smart."

"Based on what? You hardly spoke to her."

"She seems nice. She's quirky."

"Since when do you like quirky?"

"I don't know, she's got something. There's something there."

"*That* I agree with. There's something there. And it makes me nervous."

"You *should* be nervous."

I frowned. "Just drop it."
"By the end of the month."
"Please."
"I'm telling you. By the end of the month."

In the coming days, my guilt and anxiety worsened. At night I had trouble sleeping. I told myself I'd feel better when classes started; I would have something to occupy me, confirmation that it was all worth it. I phoned my mother and Silvana every night. My mother always broke into tears.

But when classes started I was overwhelmed. The amount of reading was inhuman, and already there were deadlines for papers and seminars, along with administrative requirements like putting together exam committees and submitting a new thesis proposal to supplant my dubious Greek-immigrant placeholder. I couldn't understand how one kept up. How would I get back to Montreal before Christmas? I was also again feeling alienated from everyone at school. Even though I was one of the oldest in the program, I found my classmates intimidating and felt out of my depth. I spent the better part of every day in my library carrel, weekends included. What little free time I could make for myself, I would go to the movies or explore the city. I couldn't help recalling famous exiles and émigrés, artists like Henry James, Ernest Hemingway, Paul Bowles. How gutless and lame my own flight was by comparison. I thought of Auden, Joyce, Wittgenstein, of Morley Callaghan, Mordecai Richler, Leonard Cohen. These men had fled their parochial and confining origins for destinations like London, Paris, Berlin, New York, China, Morocco. And they'd left in youth, in their teens and early twenties. I had managed to leave home at the age of thirty-seven in order to resettle five hundred kilometres away in one of the blandest and most unromantic cities in the world. I still retained my old prejudices about Toronto, which I associated with puritanical liquor laws, censorship, thuggish police, bad restaurants, and bad TV. It was a city of bankers and hosers. And now that I was here, it struck me as homely. It was a nice place to live, but I couldn't imagine anyone wanting to visit it. Walking the streets, I would recall those lines of Pascal's and think to myself, *What are you doing here? How the hell did you ever end up here?* Here was Toronto, and here was I, but by what logic were the two joined?

But there was nothing new in any of this. I had been asking myself these questions my whole life. They had merely taken on a new colouration. When I was seventeen or eighteen, I had read an article about Pierre Trudeau that described how, as a student at Harvard, the future Canadian prime minister had hung a sign on the door of his dorm that read "Pierre Trudeau: Citizen of the World." I'd thought this was one of the wisest, most radical things I had ever come across and adopted the credo as my own. Only days later I had found occasion to use it on my father.

"Look here," he'd said, "the boy's been reading Socrates!"

I groaned. Not again. "What are you talking about?"

"That's Socrates you're quoting."

"No it's not. It's Pierre Trudeau."

"Trudeau?" We were at the counter at the New Miss Bernard, and my father turned to the droogs nearby. "I am not an Athenian, I am not a Greek, I am a citizen of the world. Does anyone know that line?"

"I've heard it," someone said.

"That's Socrates."

Christ! Why did everything have to go back to the Greeks? In any case, why would my father or any of these guys want to claim such a motto as their own? It ran perfectly counter to their own attitudes. Whenever I dared to tell anyone in this group that I identified more as a Canadian than a Greek, they would cry out in protest. "No, no! You are a *Greek*! You are a Greek first and foremost!" That I was born in Canada and had never stepped foot in Greece was immaterial. "There's no such thing as a Canadian," my father would say. "What is Canada? Snow and ice and hot dogs. It's not a real country. It has no history or culture." A couple of droogs were adamant that the name Canada came from the Spanish *Qui es nada*: "There's nothing here."

"It doesn't matter where you were born or where you live," my father would say to me. "You spring from the civilization of the Hellenes. It's in your blood and bones and memory, even if you don't know it. And there's nothing you can do about it."

"It's Pierre Trudeau who said that," I insisted. "He had it taped on his door when he was in university. I read it in a magazine article."

"He could have had it taped to his head," my father said. "It was Socrates who first spoke those words."

In the end, it didn't matter to me who had said it first. I clung to the motto. I could think of no wiser stance to take toward the world. In those days, following Terence, I conceived of a citizen of the world as someone for whom no person or place was alien, someone who was at home every-where on the planet. Now, however, a citizen of Toronto, I wondered what you might call the obverse, someone who felt at home nowhere, who everywhere felt out of place. Was there a name for *that*?

Soon after submitting my revised thesis proposal, I was summoned to my supervisor's office. Sounding personally affronted, Professor Babić wished to know why I had departed so radically from my initial proposal, which in his opinion was not only more interesting but also offered "greater opportunity for original and path-breaking research." My new proposal, he said, was "unfocused and namby-pamby" and he couldn't approve it. This was a blow I had not anticipated.

Those first few weeks I hardly ever saw Laura. Most mornings she was gone before I rose and usually didn't return home till after I'd gone to bed. One evening, however, she came home early and caught me in the kitchen while I was cleaning up after dinner.

"Oh my god! Look who's here!"

Behind her followed a woman and two guys, one carrying a twelve-pack of Moosehead. "You exist!" said the woman.

"Why do you have the door closed?" said Laura. "There's no one here." Before I could answer, she turned to her friends and said, "This is Alex, my new roommate." There was an exchange of nods and greetings. Their names were Nicola, Jeff, and Lucas. "You mind if we put on some music?"

"No, of course not."

While Laura put a CD on, Lucas got down on one knee and installed the bottles of beer one by one in the fridge. As I grabbed a towel to wipe my hands, Lucas thrust a bottle of beer at me.

"Oh, no thanks. I have to get back to studying."

"Oh, come on," Laura said, joining the others at the kitchen table.

Lucas unscrewed the cap and placed the bottle on the counter. "You can have one beer."

"Sit down," said Laura. "Let's get to know you."

She was in an buoyant mood. At this stage I hardly knew her, but she didn't strike me as an upbeat person, and something in her manner seemed strained and artificial. I wondered whether she was on something, though none of the others looked stoned or drunk. I could tell she had been at the hospital, as she had on one of her professional ensembles—charcoal blazer, pleated white blouse, and grey trousers. To me, the outfit clashed with her punk hair and ear hoops. Jeff and Nicola wore jeans and plain cotton shirts. Lucas, on the other hand, was even more semiotically complicated than Laura. He had on black horn-rimmed glasses, a grey wool toque, a black cowboy shirt with silver piping, and baggy faded jeans. Between the right pocket and a belt loop drooped a silver key chain. His fingers were covered with rings of either silver or pewter, and around his left wrist he wore a multicoloured braided hemp bracelet. Beneath his lower lip was a tuft of beard that I would learn was called a "soul patch." I assumed there was some kind of ironic intent in Lucas's getup that eluded me.

"He's been here almost a month," Laura said, "and we've hardly spoken."

Lucas twisted around and dragged over an empty chair. "Have a seat."

I picked up the bottle and sat down, leaving the chair where it was, at some distance from the table.

"I think he only comes out of his room when I'm not around," Laura said. "Maybe he's afraid of me. Are you afraid of me, Alex?"

"I'm afraid of everyone," I said, which got a mild general chuckle. "So, are you all in medicine?" I asked, to shift the focus away from me.

This elicited a collective squawk. "God no," Laura said. "Only Jeff. He's just about the only med student I have anything to do with."

I learned that Lucas was a freelance web designer, and Nicola was doing a Master's in museum studies. Laura knew them from art school, where she had spent a year. Before that, she had done a Bachelor's in psychology and worked at a shelter. But finding it monotonous and emotionally draining, she had decided to pursue what she called her "first love" and registered at the Ontario College of Art and Design. (The fun-fur fruit and sequin vegetable still-lifes in the kitchen and the watercolour abstracts in the corridor were hers.) But she'd suffered "a crisis of values," and, dropping out of the program, she'd travelled through India, Nepal, and Tibet in order to figure out who she was and what she wished to do with her life. On her return to Toronto, she applied to medical school.

"Why won't you have anything to do with med students?" I asked.

"Don't get me started," she said. There were polite snickers around the table. "Med school," Laura continued, "is a fucking old boys' network. Yeah, I know, things have gotten better, more humane, blah-blah-blah... but the reality is, it's still run by arrogant, misogynistic, Type-A assholes."

"Sounds like law school," I said.

"No, no. It's nothing like law school. Trust me. Bad as lawyers may be, and I know how bad they can be—my father and brother are lawyers— but doctors are worse. They've just got better PR. Med school is a factory. It's a hegemonic heteronormative institution designed to stifle creativity, independent thought, and human sympathy. Most med students, present company excluded, are passive little ass-kissing, status-seeking conform- ists. They're so...*normal*. And they're the biggest fucking money-grubbers in the world. Worse than lawyers. And most aren't even all that smart. It's true! They're memorization machines. They're like cows. They can regur- gitate copiously. And they have stamina, I'll grant you that. Which is what you mainly need. These are people who can go days without sleep and cram like bulldozers and take all kinds of abuse, physical and emotional. But what kind of doctors will they make? Of course there are exceptions. I'll be the first to admit there are some brilliant people at U of T, among the staff *and* the students. But they're the exceptions."

This brought on a long silence. The others had clearly heard all this before, and I sensed a mild discomfort.

"But once you get that MD," Laura resumed, largely, it seemed, to alleviate the tension, "you can do amazing things. I'm in it for the long haul. As a doctor you can have a real impact on the world. But med school itself is a fucking nightmare." She glanced over at Jeff, who was nodding in weary affirmation. "We just need to get through the next couple of years."

After another lull, Nicola pointed out the time and asked what the plans were for the rest of the evening. I finished my beer and stood.

"Where are you going?" Laura said.

"I have to get back to work," I said as I rinsed out my bottle at the sink.

"Classes have barely started."

"I know, it's unbelievable. I'm already swamped. I've got tons of read- ing. And I have to work on my thesis proposal."

"Oh come on. It's a Friday night."

I walked to the fridge. "I'm not exaggerating. I really have to work."

I put the bottle in the empty case and went upstairs. I was at my desk no more than ten minutes when there was a knock on the door. I swivelled around to discover, to my dismay, that Laura had already opened it and poked her head in. "Sorry to bother you," she said as I rose. "We decided to see *Eyes Wide Shut*. Have you seen it?"

"No," I said. She opened the door wider and stepped into the room.

"Great, then you should come."

"I've got—"

"Don't start that again." She grabbed my wrist. "Come on," she said, shaking it gently. "Afterwards we'll go for a drink. It'll be fun. You need to get out. And we need to get to know you a little."

She let go my wrist and I stood silent, thinking.

"We'll be waiting for you," Laura said and turned around. "But hurry," she said as she went down the stairs.

I glanced at the time. I had already called my mother, but I had yet to speak with Silvana. I called and told her I couldn't talk long. I explained that I felt obliged to socialize with my roommate and her friends. Silvana was curious: she wanted to know who these people were. I said again I didn't have time to talk and promised I'd call tomorrow.

After the movie, we went to a bar called the Blue Door. Located in an alley, it had no exterior sign or other token of its identity (save the eponymous postern, which was more turquoise than blue). Inside, it was a sprawling low-ceilinged warehouse of a place with brick walls and exposed pipes and ducts with plastic creepers and multicoloured minilights wound about them. Clusters of mismatched sofas and armchairs were haphazardly arranged to form discrete sitting areas, and along the walls were rows of wooden tables with straight-back tavern chairs. The music was loud and the patrons young. My party knew a group of people there, and extra chairs were scraped together for us to join them. Someone mentioned where we'd been, and talk turned to the movie. Nicola called the film pornography for the culturati, to which Laura added, "It's not just pornographic, it's necrophilic. The whole film is naked women strewn about the place like corpses. And I got sick and tired of having Nicole Kidman's ass shoved in my face." A woman who had seen the film earlier called it "Orientalist." Lucas and another guy made a half-hearted attempt to defend it, though mostly on technical grounds such as Kubrick's use of lenses and film stock. Someone remarked on the campy acting and dialogue and wondered whether the whole thing wasn't meant as some kind of joke.

"What did you think?" Laura asked, turning to me. "You haven't said anything all night."

I didn't know what I thought. I needed to see the film a second time. I was not inclined to dispute the accusations against it; many of Kubrick's previous films could be arraigned on similar charges. But they were still worth seeing. As always, I liked this one for its look and feel, but I was intrigued as well by what it implied about the impossibility, or perhaps the inadvisability, of perfect candour in a marriage, about how some things, even between the closest of intimates, might be better left unsaid.

My remarks infuriated Laura. "Spoken like a true academic," she said. "That sort of phallic intellectualism only serves to dignify and legitimize the sexist fantasies and castration anxieties of an emotionally stunted man-child. I don't buy it. Sorry. I actually find it offensive."

I had not previously encountered "phallic intellectualism," which struck me as an oxymoron. And Laura's wording left open who precisely the "man-child" in question was. But I didn't say anything. It seemed to me best not to comment any further. On our way home later, Laura would apologize for "jumping" on me, and I would brush the matter aside, pretending I wasn't even sure what she was referring to. But I had learned my lesson: you had to be careful what you said around these people.

This would prove trying as, over the coming weeks, these people would come to constitute my main social circle. This was odd company for someone my age, but I knew no one else in Toronto. At thirty, Laura was the oldest, with most of the others in their early- to mid-twenties. To me they all seemed of another generation. They'd grown up with different TV shows, movies, music; they sentimentalized different things. Several of the males were avid film buffs and impressively knowledgeable, though they reserved their greatest zeal for directors like Sam Raimi and John Woo, whose work they would "unpack" and "deconstruct" with the same fervour they did the films of a Tarkovsky or Kurosawa. Some of these same guys were also interested in "new media" and would enthuse tiresomely about "emergent technologies" and how these were going to "democratize the public sphere" and "subvert centralized power structures." They also engaged in endless debate about the potential calamities of Y2K.

As far as I could tell, everyone in Laura's set came from well-to-do backgrounds and English-speaking homes. They were the children of lawyers, doctors, academics, and prosperous business people. Some were grad students, other were trying to launch careers. These were people full of optimism and self-assurance. They seemed at home in the world. They spoke the language. Where I saw cuneiform, they saw Dick and Jane. They *were* Dick and Jane, all grown up. At times I felt I'd infiltrated a secret society. To Laura and her friends, the doctor, judge, and journalist were not mysterious authority figures representing obscure powers and interests; they were their fathers and mothers, their aunts, uncles, neighbours. Here, it seemed to me, was the great advantage of a middle-class upbringing, even greater perhaps than the money and material comforts. It furnished you with a kind of road map or user's manual. These kids had an insider's knowledge of the world. They knew how to make their way in it. For example, even with their backgrounds, most had financed their studies with grants and loans because their parents knew the secrets of asset off-shoring and wealth concealment. I hadn't even known loans existed.

They espoused predictable political causes, speaking on behalf of the "voiceless" and "marginalized" and railing against social injustice. Some even talked of revolution. But this was less politics than the sanctimonious campus moralism of the comfortable. To be fair, there were also the likes of Brian and Nicola, the first with a degree in political science and currently working as a journalist, the other with extensive experience in grassroots activism, who understood more about government and the inner workings of political institutions than anyone I'd ever met, and beside whom my own screeds and pronouncements were, whatever my proletarian bona fides, mere bombast and book-learning. Most of the others, however, took a Manichean view of the world, seeing politics as a battle of good against evil, of women against men, queer against straight, the righteous poor against the venal rich, the pure and decent against the lying and corrupt. From their point of view, suffering was of itself ennobling and the ills of the world were understood as the product not of impersonal material and historical forces but of the evil doings of transnational corporations, greedy tycoons and bankers, corrupt politicians, and sexist, racist, and homophobic hatemongers. The dialectic was dead. And class had been dismissed—or at least demoted. There was occasional talk of "classism," but this was no more than a stilted neologism for snobbery. Then there were those like Aaliyah and Jeff (and, to a lesser extent, Laura), who spoke of a "higher collective consciousness," "the resacralization of nature," and "the derepression of the feminine."

Hearing such talk, I would think of my father. I wanted to say, "Go read Karl Marx." But for these youngsters, Marx was just another dead white male, and the old distinctions between right and left were obsolete and unsuited to today's digitized, globalized world. Talk like this got my back up. St. Urbain Street rising in me, I would pick fights with people, even when at bottom I might agree with them. I also felt no compunction about defending dead white males. I explained to my pious friends what the works of such figures might mean to people without the privilege of being able to take them for granted, who weren't raised in homes with book-lined walls and taken by their parents to concerts and exhibits and lectures. I pointed out to them the aesthetic and intellectual abundance and edification writers like Richler and Roth, or, for that matter, Eliot and Shakespeare, could afford a child of Greek immigrant parents unschooled in *any* canon. I felt no shame in quoting Matthew Arnold's maxim that one should seek out the best that has been thought and said, regardless of who said it, or when. As a result, I was branded a classist and elitist. This seemed to me rich, as well as galling, and I dug my heels in deeper. I took to playing up my ethnic working-class credentials and copping a more-authentic-than-thou attitude. I'd noticed, moreover, that some of my habits of speech and behaviour were a source of amusement and curiosity to some in Laura's set, and that, whatever their political sensitivities, when it came to Greeks and other south Europeans, they were perfectly comfortable with ethnic stereotypes and caricatures. So, where in the past my impulse had been to mask and mute any social markers that set me apart, I now broadcast and advertised them, happily adopting and even hamming up whatever clichés people wished to project upon me. So Greeks were gruff and loud and tempestuous? Well, I could do those things. Or if it was colourful tales of growing up in a rough-and-tumble working-class immigrant neighbourhood they wanted, I had plenty of those too. I must have come across as a parody of a character in a Scorsese movie or *Welcome Back, Kotter*. I cringe to think now what my well-bred young friends must have made of all this mummery. At the time, though, I thought about it constantly. For all my disdain and condescension, I fretted like a teenager about what Laura and her friends thought of me. I craved their approval and acceptance. I wondered how they perceived me, a man in his late thirties with no money or possessions, living in a tiny rented room in a student house. I must have stood for them as a kind of object lesson or cautionary tale, a reminder of everything they hoped not to be when they were my age. I imagined I was what they would call a "loser."

At the end of September I submitted my new thesis proposal. I tried to address my supervisor's concerns while still accommodating my actual interests. Professor Babić declared it worse than the last one. "This is more philosophy than history," he said, uttering the word *philosophy* with peculiar distaste. He used words like flabby, diffuse, quixotic, metaphysical. It was a replay in reverse of what had happened to me at Concordia.

Laura and I had settled into each other's company. I no longer locked myself in my room when she was around, and occasionally we had dinner or hung out. Laura loved asking about my past and was amazed I was still in touch with friends from childhood. She was in contact with none of her past friends. Her current friendships went back no more than four or five years. Laura wasn't shy about asking probing and personal questions, but she was remarkably forthcoming herself. She would blithely volunteer the most intimate details, details I wouldn't have revealed to my closest friends. A few days after I'd moved in, she informed me that she'd been in therapy since the age of nine. To me this was a shocking disclosure not only in its substance but also in the nonchalant way it was delivered. For Laura, the shock was that I'd never been to a therapist. It was as if she didn't even know such people existed. Therapy was for Laura as routine a part of life as going to the dentist or getting your hair cut. It functioned less as actual therapy than as a creed or religion, an ethical framework by means of which she made sense of the world and other people. The reigning deity of this creed was the "unconscious." Sooner or later, everything came back to it. The unconscious, for Laura, functioned as a kind of *anima mundi*. The whole world was a psychiatric hospital.

Such an approach to human relations struck me in principle as reductive, but Laura's attempts to apply it to me were outright ludicrous. She seemed to assume that all families fit a standard model based on her own, and as a result her suggestions on how I should deal with my parents could be laughably clueless. At the same time, though, she could be shockingly astute, identifying patterns of behaviour and their likely causes with a precision that was almost clairvoyant. She was especially good on my relationship with Silvana, though this was a topic I tried to avoid. Besides finding it embarrassing, I didn't need her advice. I knew very well what I had to do. I'd known for a long time, but I'd convinced myself that Silvana would do it for me, that once I got to Toronto she would see how unworkable our situation was and bring it to an end on her own. But the distance between us made her clingier and more invested in our relationship. We spoke on the phone almost every night, and almost every night she would tell me how much she loved me and missed me, which of course necessitated similar declarations from me. At this stage, these were difficult even to fake, and there were moments when I came close to bringing the curtain down right then and there. But given how dishonest and cowardly I had been throughout our relationship, I had vowed that I would at least end it in a manly and honourable way, which, at a minimum, meant not doing it over the phone.

Before leaving, I had assured both Silvana and my mother that I would be making regular visits to Montreal, but as things worked out, I couldn't arrange my first trip back until Thanksgiving. Silvana made me promise to reserve two nights for her. My plan was to give her the bad news right away, meaning there wouldn't be a second night; but I played along. Arriving in Montreal Thursday evening, I spent Friday with my mother and met Silvana the next night at a restaurant in Outremont. She was there already and greeted me as though I were a doughboy back from the front. The other diners observed us with curiosity and bemusement. Silvana seemed to have put on a little weight and looked beautiful in a clingy black dress she had probably purchased for the occasion. She even had on makeup. She looked so eager and forlorn that I knew I was in for a rough night.

She plunged right in. Relations with her supervisor had worsened, and the day before she had lost her temper and said things she shouldn't have. Her home life had become intolerable. It was always intolerable, but her father was drinking again, and he and her brother had a fistfight that left both of them bloody. She didn't know how much longer she could go on like this. Driving me home, she was so overcome that she had to pull over.

She talked about how much she missed me and how hard she found it being apart and said she was thinking about moving to Toronto. I'd heard such remarks many times before so I didn't give them much credence. After twenty minutes, she was able to compose herself and resume driving, but soon she started crying again, and we had to pull over and talk for another hour.

The following day being Sunday, I spent the morning at church with my mother. I had told her I would be with friends in Chomedey all evening and wouldn't be home till after midnight. In the afternoon Silvana picked me up on Park Avenue. We drove to a motel on the West Island in an atmosphere of gloom and foreboding. Silvana had *The Future* playing on the stereo, and both of us sat quietly much of the way, listening to Leonard Cohen's nicotine grumble. Nor did the tacky décor and piss-yellow lighting of the motel room do much to improve the mood. I was convinced Silvana could sense what I was thinking, and as we fell back on the bed, her kisses felt less like an expression of ardour or affection than an effort to stop my mouth. The sex unfolded in the usual, predictable fashion, except this time there was also something dismal and ashen in it. When it was over, Silvana began to cry. This she had never done before, and when I asked her what was wrong, she talked again about how difficult she found being apart from me and made me promise I would not wait so long until my next visit. We drove to a restaurant in a strip mall for dinner and then returned to the motel, checking out just before midnight.

When I arrived home in Toronto, I hoped I might avoid Laura, but she was in her study with the door open, so I was obliged to stop and say hello.

The first thing she said was, "How did it go? Did you tell her?"

I felt a rage welling up. Why did she take such an interest? I regretted ever mentioning Silvana. And why did I tell her we were breaking up? I felt ashamed to admit the truth to her now. But what choice did I have?

"I couldn't do it," I said.

She looked at me with a mix of puzzlement and reproach. "Why not?"

The rage churned hotter. "I don't know. It wasn't the right time."

"Jesus. When's the right time?"

"She's going through a very difficult period."

"Isn't she always going through a very difficult period? Her whole fucking life has been a very difficult period. From what you've told me."

I wasn't sure how to respond to this. It seemed to me Laura knew neither Silvana nor me well enough to speak this way.

"You're not doing her any favours by continuing to lie to her," she said.

"I'm not lying to her."

"Your whole relationship is a lie."

I felt myself clenching up.

"You told me you were done with Silvana back in June, when we met. Remember?"

I remembered all too well. "It's not so easy," I said. "She's vulnerable."

"Oh please! What a dodge! Don't make it so it's about her."

I felt I was reaching my limit, so, pleading fatigue, I apologized for cutting the conversation short and went to my room. I had to remember to be more circumspect. My roommate was not to be trusted. I had seen her behave this way with friends. I found Laura's honesty and bluntness admirable, but there could also be something venomous and unhinged about it.

For the next few days, I reverted to my former habits, spending evenings at the library and, when at home, confining myself to my room if Laura was around. Focusing on my thesis proposal, I was able to hammer together something Professor Babić could sign off on, but by then my heart wasn't in it. Also, I was already beginning to fear that I was not cut out to be a historian. Yet again I'd been kidding myself.

Laura must have sensed I was avoiding her, because late one evening, as I crept up the stairs, she came out of her room in her pyjamas and said sheepishly, "Listen...I want to apologize for the other night."

I pretended not to know what she was talking about.

"You caught me in a bad state," she said, "and I may have overstepped the line. I do that. And people misunderstand my intentions. I've been under a lot of stress with school, but that's no excuse. I was just trying to be helpful. Honestly. I realize it's none of my business, and that people don't need my interventions, no matter how well-meaning, but sometimes I forget. And they *are* well-meaning. I hope you know that."

I brushed the matter aside, telling her I appreciated her honesty.

"I have boundary issues. And people draw their lines in different places, which I can find confusing. You know what I mean?"

I didn't exactly but said I did.

A few days later, Silvana informed me that she was coming to visit. It was already arranged. She had put in a request at work for some time off. She was arriving in a week and would be staying six days. I reminded her that I was already planning to go to Montreal in a week or two.

"But you always say that and then you don't come," she said. "And you'd only come for the weekend. This is six days. I could see Toronto. I haven't been there since I was nine. Maybe we can go to Niagara Falls. *If* you have time. I know you're busy."

I didn't know what to say. But I knew this couldn't happen. Such a trip would only extend the current mess. I couldn't break up with Silvana while she was in Toronto. That would be cruel and perverse. And after that, Christmas would be right around the corner, and I couldn't do it then either. I would have to put it off until January. Then there was the whole comedy of introducing Silvana to Laura and her friends, which I couldn't even think about without a shudder. What would they make of her? No, this couldn't be allowed to happen. But how to stop it?

Coming home the following evening, I heard Laura in the kitchen. I'd continued to avoid her, but now I decided to say hello. She was in her studying clothes—track pants, plaid flannel shirt, Birkenstocks—at the counter, making herbal tea. She offered me some. I sat at the table while she recounted a run-in she'd had with a professor. I made sympathetic noises and agreed the professor had been wrong and she had been right to stand her ground. Placing a mug on the table, she asked how I was doing. "I feel like we haven't spoken in a while," she said. "Is everything all right?"

"Oh...I don't know," I said.

She studied me a moment. She was standing near the door, as if anxious to get back to her study. But now she sat and asked me what was wrong.

"Nothing's wrong, exactly, but...I guess I should let you know that...it looks like Silvana might be coming. Is that okay?"

"Yes, of course."

"I mean, she'll be staying in my room."

"Yes, of course."

"You sure it's okay?"

"Why wouldn't it be? For Christ's sake, you're entitled to have a guest over now and then. Is that what's been worrying you?"

"No...I wasn't worried. I just...I just thought I should let you know."

We sipped our tea in silence.

"How long will she be staying?"

"Maybe six days."

Laura nodded pensively. "Listen...I know it's none of my business..."

I waited out the pause.

"What's going on between the two of you? Are you still breaking up with her? Or have you patched things up?"

"We haven't patched things up."

"But she's coming here. For six days."

I nodded.

"So you're breaking up with her then?"

"Well, no...obviously not."

"Why obviously?"

"I'm not going to have her come all the way to Toronto so I can break up with her."

"Then why *are* you having her come all the way to Toronto?"

"It wasn't *my* idea."

"I'm just repeating what you said."

"Right...but..."

"I know it's none of my business, but...do you not see how insane this is? You want to break up with this woman—you've wanted to break up with her since last summer, if not before. So why are you letting her come? Just break up with her already."

"Over the phone?"

"Why not over the phone? It's better than having her come all this way when you don't even want her here. Is that being kind to her? I don't get this whole fucking phone thing with you. What makes you think it's better or more noble to string her along for...how many months has it been now? You think that's sensitive or considerate?"

"You don't think it's a little shabby to break up over the phone?"

"It is shabby," Laura said. "It's super shabby. But it's not as shabby as what *you're* doing. Better you break up with Silvana by Morse code than what you've been doing. Isn't it better you tell her the truth on the phone rather than have her visit and silently resent her presence the whole time? You don't think *that's* shabby?"

I suddenly felt as though a weight were lifting off me. "You really believe it would be okay to tell her on the phone?"

"Unless you want to fly to Montreal. You should do it right now. The sooner the better."

I glanced at the clock.

"Is she home?" Laura asked.

"Probably. She has a class tonight, but she should be home by now."

Laura left the kitchen. She was back seconds later, thrusting a cordless handset at me. "You can call her from here. I'll sit with you."

"What?"

"Take it. I'll stay here. I'll help you through it. Honestly, I don't mind."

"No."

"I'm happy to do it."

"Okay, but..." I got up. "I'm going to call her from upstairs."

"When?"

"Now. You're right. I need to do it now. But this is a private matter."

"Whatever you think." She gripped my hand. "But I'm here. If you need me," she said, squeezing. I wished to extricate myself but feared it would appear rude if I did it too soon. "You're doing the right thing."

"Yes," I replied. I gave it another few seconds and withdrew my hand.

"Come and talk to me when you're done," Laura shouted as I climbed the stairs.

I shut my door and lay back on the bed. I had to think about what I was going to say, prepare for all of Silvana's possible reactions. Twenty minutes later, I was still doing that when the phone rang. I knew it was Silvana. Who else could it be?

She sounded stricken. "What's wrong?" I asked. "Where are you?"

She was on a park bench in St. Léonard. She'd had another in a series of quarrels with a troublesome colleague in her office. She'd been having difficulties with this woman for months. She didn't do her work properly and Silvana was tired of covering for her. Silvana had finally complained to her supervisor, but instead of showing some leadership, he had equivocated and stonewalled until Silvana had lost her temper and was herself the one reprimanded and threatened with being fired. After work, she had skipped class and gone straight home, where, making the mistake of discussing her work troubles, she had a fight with her father and brother.

She'd had it. She was sick of her life and of everyone in it. Everyone was against her. Both her workplace and homelife were "dysfunctional" and "toxic." She couldn't take it anymore and was ready to give notice at her office the next morning and leave home. I listened quietly, interposing the occasional consoling platitude. And when she was done, I fell back on my customary response, reminding her why she couldn't quit her job until she'd finished her MBA. She was almost there, two more years. Then she could quit, get her own place, do whatever she wanted. She could even leave Montreal. But not yet. She couldn't allow herself to destroy her future now, after all she'd done and all she'd put up with. She needed to be patient. I said all the same things I'd said countless times before.

But this time, it wasn't taking. Silvana was raving. She had no more patience, she said, she *shouted*. She'd been patient all her life and what had it gotten her except abuse. Everyone around her was a bully and a sadist. She literally wished her father and brother dead. If the two of them died in a car accident tomorrow, she would only feel relief and joy. She would thank God. There were times when she feared she might grab a knife and do the work herself. That's why she had left the house that evening, from fear not of what they would do to her but of what *she* might do to *them*.

I administered more of my bromides. I didn't believe them myself, but what else could I do? We were on the phone for two hours and Silvana was still crying when we hung up. I felt exhausted and my head hurt.

Not ten minutes later, there was a knock on my door. Had Laura been listening? Surely my voice didn't carry all the way down to her study. How did she know I was done? Even before I could rise from the bed, the door opened and an inquisitorial eye peered in.

"Is everything okay?"

I didn't have the strength for this. "Everything's fine," I said, remaining seated on the edge of my bed.

She came inside. "Do you want to talk?"

"No."

She sat next to me. "What's wrong?" She lay a hand on my shoulder.

I shook my head and remained hunched over, elbows on knees.

"Did you tell her?"

I flashed back to Silvana's comment about wanting to stab her father and brother. I shook my head.

"Why not?"

What the fuck? What's it to you?, I wanted to scream. "I couldn't."

"Why not?"

"She had an awful day. It just wasn't the time."

"So...she's coming to Toronto?"

"I don't know," I said, slouching over again. "I don't know what's going on. I'm too tired to think right now."

I felt Laura's fingers on the back of my neck. "Alex, this can't go on."

I nodded limply.

"Alex, you don't want Silvana coming here. I certainly don't," she said.

I turned and looked at her. "What do you mean?"

"I don't want Silvana here."

"I thought you said it was all right," I said, straightening up, which at least caused Laura to withdraw her hand.

"I lied," she said. "It's not all right."

"Why not?"

"Why would I want that bitch in my house?"

Laura and her friends had a habit of copping certain idioms that, besides being jarringly remote from their own, should have been anathema to their doctrinaire and delicate sensibilities. I gathered they used such language ironically, but this didn't make the habit any less annoying.

"Bitch?" I said.

"Oh, I'm sure she's a lovely person. But I don't want her in my house."

"Why not?"

"Oh, come on, Alex. Let's not play that game."

I chewed on this a moment. "What game?"

"You're not trying to tell me you don't know what's going on here."

I was beginning to feel dizzy.

"Don't pretend," Laura said, sliding closer to me. "I don't know about you, but I can't continue this anymore. It's too stupid." I could smell the products in her hair. "This Silvana chick is history. It's over. Whether she knows it or not. I don't know what you plan to do about her..." She slid in even closer. I could feel her breath. "But right now I know one thing." I felt a movement against my chest and glanced down. She was unbuttoning her shirt. "Either you're going to fuck me, or I'm going to fuck *you*."

Before I could make sense of what was happening, Laura was on her knees, undoing my pants. I had slipped through some worm hole into an alternative universe. I didn't know the physics here or how to navigate them. I couldn't believe that was me in Laura's mouth. Laura herself had undergone a metamorphosis. It would be preposterous to say I had never seen her like this; more to the point, I could never have *imagined* her like this. When she removed her clothing, I barely recognized her. She looked a different person. I was startled to see she had a nice figure. Until this moment, she had struck me as not just unattractive but almost sexless. She also seemed so pinched and repressed, she came across as a kind of prude. Nothing about her could have prepared me for the fire-breathing succubus that had suddenly materialized before me—or for what followed. Bewildered, alarmed, enthralled, I surrendered to her entirely. I had no idea what the rules of the game were and followed along in gasping wonder. All of a sudden the mild encounters I'd shared with Silvana over the last two years seemed a facsimile of sex. Compared to Silvana, Laura was feral. Moaning, grunting, and whimpering with ravenous enjoyment, she was a wild creature glutting itself on its kill. She came quickly and explosively, and then again, and then again. And when she was done, and I was done, she collapsed into sleep.

I lay there stupefied, a rag. What the fuck had just hit me? I stared up at the ceiling's stucco swirls, reviewing the night's events. I'd just had what may have been the most astonishing, exhilarating, and unforgettable experience of my life. It was also a horrendous mistake. I had known it was a mistake even while it was happening. Even amid the dank hallucinatory aphrodisial fog I had seen the swamp toward which I was hurtling. And now that I was in it, I needed to figure out fast how to get out.

One thing at least was resolved: Silvana was indeed history. I would have to deliver the news as soon as possible. But what was I to do about Laura? Whatever had just happened between us could not happen again. Laura and I could not be lovers. I could hardly think of two more ill-suited people. But how to undo the ceremony? Could we revert to the former order? Would Laura be willing? Was she even capable? With my workload and deadlines, the last thing I needed was to start looking for new lodgings. I hadn't forgotten how hard it had been to find this place. Perhaps I could explain that she had caught me off guard, that with everything piling up in my life, I was in a confused and vulnerable state. But she already knew this. Hadn't she taken deliberate advantage of it? She was the one who had got us into this situation. I was the innocent party here;

she was the aggressor, the seducer, the predator. Surely she would have to concede that much. But I had seen the rancour and venom that misunderstandings far more trivial than this could provoke in her.

Even as I tried to figure my way out of this mess, the highlight reel kept playing. It wouldn't stop, my mind strobing with images of Laura's naked body and of the wanton, wicked, wondrous things she had done with it. Gazing at her as she slept, I had an impulse to wake her up and let her have another go at me. At one point, she stirred gently and, giving me a one-eyed squint, asked why the lights were still on. As I rose to turn them off, she asked me to set the alarm for seven and then rolled back to sleep.

I hardly slept. When the alarm went off, I lay on my back and watched Laura collect her things from the floor. Bending, she gave me a light kiss on the lips and said she should be home around 6:30.

I didn't get up till noon. After lunch, I went to the library, hoping to do some reading and research, but I couldn't stop thinking about the jam I was in and how to extricate myself. That morning kiss was a bad sign, so different from the torrid kisses of a few hours earlier. Its tenderness and intimacy did not bode well.

I got home around six and went to my room. When Laura came in an hour later, I was still on the phone with Silvana. Hearing her footsteps on the staircase, I prepared for the knock on the door; but, after a pause at the landing, she continued to her bedroom.

I was on the phone until ten. When I hung up, I sagged on my bed. I was in no shape to deal with Laura. But I hadn't eaten since noon and felt woozy. Slowly opening my door, I peered down the corridor and saw Laura's door was closed. I stole down the stairs like a cat burglar and went to the kitchen, where I quickly put together a sandwich. I also put together a plan. I would tell Laura I'd spoken with Silvana and she had not taken the news well (perfectly true). I was pretty shaken up and bereft myself (also true) and would need time alone to recover and to process my loss. I needed to grieve and heal, I would say, using her language. Even Laura would grant me this much. I might be able to steer us back to our prior footing. Hopefully, she herself would come to her senses. If she pushed for something deeper, I could explain that I was not ready for another relationship. It would not be fair to Laura herself. I was grateful for the support she had provided over the last couple of months, and I would never forget the night we had spent together, but we could not go down that route. It wouldn't be fair to *her*. And I valued her friendship too much to jeopardize it. Surely she would see the sense of this. Surely even Laura would not throw a man so broken and woebegone and reasonable onto the street.

Having devised my plan, I resolved to confront her sooner rather than later. As if by providence, Laura's footsteps sounded on the stairs. I ran through what I would tell her, but the instant she stepped into the kitchen I knew something was amiss and I might have to change tack. Without looking at me, she headed to the patio door. She was wearing a ratty old purple bathrobe and walking oddly. When she passed the table and came fully into view, I saw she was wearing black stilettos.

"What's going on?" I asked, a mustard-stained butter knife in my hand.

Laura drew the curtain shut and fixed me with a steely gaze.

"What's going on?" I said again.

She loosened her bathrobe and let it drop to reveal herself kitted out in a complicated rigging of black undergarments, straps, garters, and fishnet hosiery. She looked like some goth dominatrix. I stared in mute disbelief. Even after the previous night, I would not have imagined Laura consenting to put on, let alone being the owner of, such a getup. As if recognizing her own absurdity, she gave me a coy, antic smirk. Then, placing one hand on her hip and the other on the wall, she struck a coquettish pose that, campy and ludicrous as it was, made me drop the butter knife, and the next thing I knew my pants and boxers were on the floor and Laura lay spreadeagled before me on the kitchen table.

After that night, I could barely keep my dick in my pants. Even when Laura wasn't around, I would be choking out what little breath remained in it while recalling what we'd done and dreaming up more. When she was around, I was climbing all over her. I was unquenchable as Zeus. Until now, I had been driving in a school zone, and suddenly I was on the Autobahn. There were no limits or restrictions. Laura in bed was the very opposite of who she was the rest of the time. Nothing ruffled or offended her. Dr. Jekyll, removing his clothes, became Mr. Hyde. And Laura's Hyde was entirely without inhibitions. Everything was possible and permissible. She even had devices and accessories—"toys," she called them—along with books and manuals, including the original unshorn *Joy of Sex* and a full-colour *Kama Sutra*. She kept pushing me to be more daring and inventive. "Come on," she would say, "what's your kinkiest fantasy? What's the sickest thing you want to do?" I wasn't used to this sort of talk and found it confusing and thrilling. At first I wondered whether it might be some kind of trick or trap. Laura insisted there was nothing I could ask that would upset her. If she wasn't comfortable, she would just say no. "And I won't judge you," she said. "I already know what a sicko you are. But..." She grinned. "Do you?" But she never did say no. What she said was, "For shitsake, is that the best you can do? What is it you *really* want? You can tell mommy. What's in that sick little brain of yours? Go ahead. Shock me." But she was impossible to shock. Indeed, the more deviant the request, the more it seemed to tantalize and excite her. In any case, it was Laura who called the shots. I was too timid and conventional for her. I was "vanilla." She issued the orders and instructions: Stand there. Sit here. Kneel down. Go like this. Go like that. Take that off. Put this on. Put that there. Tighter. Slower. Faster. Harder. She liked to tell me about the things she'd done with other men, describing their predilections and fetishes to see if they tickled my own fancy. But these aroused in me more an anthropological than an erotic curiosity. Some were so bizarre as to merit psychiatric investigation. But Laura accepted it all. Nothing threw her. Whatever her dogmatic neo-pietist politics, in bed she was a radical libertarian. Was there anything she had ever refused to do? Not that she could remember. Was there anything she didn't like? Sure, but she was still game for anything. If the guy got off on it, she got off on him getting off on it. Laura revealed possibilities that exceeded even my own fevered imagination.

But was this the basis for a relationship? Laura was the person she'd always been, and I had no illusions about what being in a relationship with her would be like. But, as I discovered one evening at the Blue Door, the prospects were even grimmer than I'd imagined. We'd gone to meet friends, and as we entered, I heard my name and saw Morgan Himel waving to me from a nearby table. Telling Laura to go on ahead, I went over to say hello. Morgan was generally reserved, and we'd only ever exchanged a few words, but that evening she was chummy and garrulous and appeared to have called me over for no other reason than to make small talk. I assumed she'd had a few drinks. After several seconds, I noticed that she kept glancing past my shoulder in some meaningful way, and, turning around, I saw Laura standing behind me.

"Oh...I didn't realize you were there."

"Is this your girlfriend?" Morgan asked.

"This is Laura," I said.

"Hi Laura," Morgan said. "I'm Morgan."

Laura smiled wanly. After more pointless small talk, I explained that we were meeting some people, and Laura and I took our leave.

"Who was that?" asked Laura.

"Morgan Himel."

"Who the fuck's Morgan Himel?"

"She's in one of my classes."

"I've never heard you mention a Morgan Himel."

"What's there to mention? I hardly know her."

As we approached our party, Laura split off and sat at the opposite end of the table. She shunned me the rest of the night.

On our way home, she continued to mope. "Are you okay?" I asked. She didn't answer. "You want to tell me what's bothering you?"

She came to a stop and finally deigned to look at me. "What the fuck was *that*?"

This was a standard opener with Laura, the demonstrative pronoun usually even more ambiguous than it was in this instance. From an excess of caution, and partly to signal that, from my point of view, she was making a big deal out of nothing, I opted to play stupid.

"What are you talking about?"

"Are you ashamed of me? Do you know how humiliating that was?"

This took me aback. Maybe I *didn't* know what she was referring to.

"Are you talking about Morgan Himel?"

"Yes I'm talking about Morgan Himel!"

"What was humiliating?" Behind Laura, some distance away, two figures emerged from a front yard. I kept an eye on them until I was able to determine they were headed in the opposite direction. "I honestly don't know what you're talking about."

"Don't play that game with me. In the first place, you leave me standing there like I'm invisible, like I don't even exist."

"I didn't know you were there."

"Then, when that...that insect tries to cover for your rudeness—"

"I didn't know you were there."

"Bullshit! I was standing right beside you!"

"You were behind me."

"Even if that were true...why, when she asked you if I was your..." She mimed air quotes. "...'girlfriend,' why did you deny it?"

"I didn't deny it."

"Yes you did! You said, Oh no. No, no. This is *Laura*. This is *Laura*, you said. This is *Laura*."

"That's your name. And I didn't say, 'No, no.' You're changing things."

"I'm not changing anything. Why did you deny our relationship?"

"That's not what I did. You're twisting things."

"Then why didn't you answer? Yes, this is my girlfriend. Girlfriend! Who the fuck talks like that anyway? What is she, twelve years old?"

I heard what sounded like a door opening and resumed walking.

"You can't deny it," Laura said, keeping pace beside me. "Even if you don't realize it, or can't admit it. That little feint of yours was a denial of our relationship. Like you're ashamed of admitting we're together."

"You're blowing things out of proportion."

She grabbed my elbow and tried to stop me. "Let's get something straight," she said, but I pulled free and kept going. "If you're so embarrassed to be seen with me," she said, catching up to me, "if you can't bring yourself to introduce me to your high-society friends—"

"I can't believe you're doing this."

"—let me know right now. Cause I'm not one of your little Silvanas, Alex. I'm not one of your little neighbourhood chiquitas, and I won't put up with that kind of bullshit. You picked the wrong person if you think you're going to treat me like your other *girlfriends*."

I picked up my pace and pulled ahead of her. My head was spinning.

By the time we got home, Laura had settled down. I thought I'd give it another go. "Laura, if you can please listen to me and give me a little credit: things didn't happen tonight the way you describe. I am sincerely sorry if I seemed discourteous, but you're misinterpreting. Honestly."

"Whenever you hear someone say sincerely and honestly, you know for sure that what they're saying is neither sincere nor honest."

I shook my head. "Wow. You really make it impossible."

"Go on. Say what you have to say. I want to hear it."

"I think I've said all I have to say. I understand why you think I may have seemed rude—"

"Think? Seemed?"

"...and why you would have been upset. But it was just a mistake, an oversight. It was not intentional."

"Skirting that question was not a mistake. It revealed a truth about you."

"Laura, please. Don't turn this into something it's not. You're blowing things out of proportion."

"I don't think so."

"Are you never wrong?"

"Rarely."

I was not going to convince her. But her mood had changed. "I'm hungry," she said. "You want some popcorn?"

Suddenly, it was as though the incident had never happened, though she would return to it repeatedly in the future. Nor would it be long before the next of our dustups, which erupted with depressing, though unpredictable, regularity. I learned always to be on my guard, that every word and gesture was potentially fraught with latent meanings and hidden agendas. I was amazed by the implications she could find in the most trivial remarks and actions. I had never encountered such zealous adherence to the Freudian tenet on accidents. No slip of the tongue was innocent; no word, glance, or gesture was immune to invidious interpretation. Nothing was ever what it seemed. Nothing was ever just nothing; everything was always something, and usually something other than what it appeared.

Nor was I alone subjected to scrutiny. Having spent so many years digging through her phrenic substrata, Laura felt qualified to do the same with everyone else's—friends, enemies, colleagues, celebrities, even total strangers. And she had complete conviction in her interpretations and diagnoses. She understood everyone around her better than they understood themselves. All her years of "work" had given her an insight others lacked. Most people hadn't done the work. Moreover, not to have dedicated oneself to such labours was to a moral failure. She was appalled that I'd never been in therapy. No wonder I was so screwed up. "You're a stranger to yourself," she kept telling me. "You complain about how you make the same mistakes over and over, but you refuse to get at the root of your reactive patterns. You wallow in self-ignorance. Because you're chicken-shit. You're terrified of what you might discover about yourself."

I wondered why she hadn't become a psychiatrist. She said she lacked the requisite detachment. "I have a low threshold for emotional pain," she said. "Physical pain, no problem. It doesn't matter how bad it is, bring it on. But psychic pain? I don't know how to deal with that." I asked her whether she'd ever considered that there might be limits to reason, aspects of existence inaccessible to understanding, or at least to her methods of acquiring it. She found the question incoherent or insane. She called me a nihilist. Contra Wittgenstein that, whereof one cannot speak, one must remain silent, Laura was convinced there was nothing and no one that, with the right diagnostic manual or personality inventory, could not be fixed and formulated and classified. Thus it was plain that Jeff had unresolved father issues, Rachel had an eating disorder, Nicola had dysthymia, Liz had both avoidant personality disorder and dependent personality disorder, Lucas had ADD and Aaliyah OCD, and that Susan and Stuart were doomed as a couple because she was an INFP to his ESTJ. She was always prepared to revise her appraisal as more data became available, but she could never be without a working hypothesis, without her rubrics, heuristics, and taxonomies. All human and social life conformed to strict and intelligible laws of cause and effect; nothing was inexplicable. Yes, there was still much to be learned and uncovered, but if there were aspects of existence and of human relationships we didn't understand, it was because we lacked the necessary tools and knowledge.

I could see why she had no long-term friendships. It was like living under a totalitarian regime. Being in any kind of relationship with Laura, you had to watch your every move, and were doomed regardless: sooner or later you would fail her somehow, and be judged duplicitous, perfidious, the enemy. In my own case, constant self-monitoring made me more prone to the sort of slips I was struggling to avoid. And Laura didn't forget. She hoarded and catalogued every last slight and offense like a collector of precious objects. Indeed she clung to all personal details you shared, no matter how trivial. At first I found her interest in me endearing and flattering, but I soon realized it was a form of intelligence-gathering. One never knew how such details might be deployed. Intimate relations were war by different means. And Laura needed to appraise those close to her the way a combatant appraises the enemy. Looking back, I don't think it was malicious. Whenever she dredged up and shoved in your face something you'd been foolish enough to confide, she would sooner or later apologize for her callousness and beg forgiveness. But it wouldn't be long before you were strung up on your own rope again. She couldn't help herself. It was a survival strategy. It was the only way she knew how to protect herself.

By late November I knew I had to get out. Remaining in the house was out of the question, so I decided not to say anything until after Christmas. I would need time to find a new place. Laura had known since September that I was spending the holidays in Montreal, yet days before I was set to leave, she floated the idea of going to her parents' cottage for New Year's.

"But I'll be in Montreal," I said. "I have my train ticket. You *know* this."

"I'm not saying don't go to Montreal. I'm just asking to spend New Year's together."

"I have a return ticket."

"So change it. I'll pay the penalty."

"Why are you doing this?"

"I just told you. The cottage is available. My parents aren't going this year. You can still have a whole week with your mother, but we can spend New Year's at the cottage. It's so beautiful in the winter. You'll love it."

"I can't."

"Alex, you can do whatever you want. You're an adult."

"You know my situation."

"Your situation is you have no spine. My god, what will happen to your mother if you leave a couple of days early? Seriously. What will your mother do? What has she been doing the last four months? As you predicted, she's managed fine. You've said yourself she feigns helplessness as a way of controlling you. So stop letting her. You've proven to yourself, *and* to her, that she can get by without you. Which was your mission. Great, you've succeeded! You're a free man! Take advantage of it."

"I'm not free."

"Oh my god! What is *wrong* with you?"

"I promised her."

"You promised her *what*? Look, I'm not telling you not to go. Go! Be with your fucking mother! I'm just asking for a couple of days. Tell her you have to come back for school. Something came up. To be honest, I don't see why you have to tell her anything at all."

"I've told her I'm staying till New Year's. I've *told* her. I promised her."

"So what? You make promises constantly you don't keep."

"What are you referring to?"

"We're talking about a couple of days."

"I can't. You've known my plans for months. So let's just drop it. Please."

She folded her arms and glared at me silently a long time. "What if I come to Montreal?" she said. "I'll stay in a hotel."

"No."

"Why not?"

"I won't have time to spend with you."

"Why not?"

"Laura, I beg you. This is already hard enough as it is, you have no idea. Stop making it harder."

"How am I making it harder? I'm offering a solution. If you can't come here, I'll go there."

"No."

"What the fuck's wrong with you? Why not?"

"Because. That's just how it is."

"No, Alex, it's how you make it. How *you* make it. Do you understand? What are you so afraid of?"

"I'm not afraid of anything. You just don't get it."

"Alex, you are the most fucking afraid person I've met in my life."

The next couple of nights, I had to sleep in my own room. We patched things up somewhat, but there was still tension when I left for Montreal. In a way, I was grateful. It would make things easier on my return.

I arrived in Montreal in the late afternoon. Making my way from the train station to the Metro, I kept an eye out for Silvana, whose office was nearby. I didn't relax until I was on the 80. By the time I was towing my book-crammed suitcase up St. Urbain Street, it was already dark.

My mother stood like a ghoul in the window. Before I was halfway up the stairs, she was out on the landing in her floral cotton nightgown.

"Oh my love!" she cried, striking her chest with her palms. "My soul, my light! Who flew and left me all alone."

"Keep your voice down."

"My darling!" She almost knocked me over throwing her arms around me, covering my face and neck with kisses.

"Let's go inside," I said. "You're going to catch cold."

She had prepared a dinner of stuffed vegetables. She talked about her loneliness and isolation and the difficulties in managing on her own, all the things we talked about on the phone. She complained about my uncle. He would drive her to doctors' appointments and shops, but he never came inside for a coffee or to have dinner. He never visited with Christina and the girls, and they hardly ever invited her over to their place. It was all Christina's doing of course. She didn't want my mother around, though she saw her sisters daily. People were selfish and cruel. If they understood her pain, could experience her loneliness for a day, they would not behave as they did. She was grateful, however, to the French couple upstairs, who had kindly taken on the responsibility of clearing the snow. And to the Portuguese couple downstairs, who checked in with her when they went shopping and occasionally brought her cooked meals and sweets.

For Christmas, we went to my uncle's place. Happily, my aunt's sisters were there with their families. I didn't have any particular affection for these people, but their presence had a dampening effect on my mother, who toned down her rants and vented her sorrows with less vitriol. The next day, Boxing Day, I had to do some shopping in the afternoon. I decided to go by the Symposium. I felt compelled to have a look at it, just from the outside.

When my father and I had last parted, it was no different from any other time. There had been no hugs or speeches, no ceremony. After I'd broken my news to him about Toronto, we hadn't discussed the matter again, and he didn't ask for my address or phone number. Nor did I offer them. I suppose we were testing each other. When I moved, I didn't hear from him. Then, in the middle of September, I started getting silent hangups. I star-six-nined them, and all were either from the Symposium or my father's line. Finally, he left a message one day. His tone was stern and aggrieved: "Have you no shame? Is this how a son behaves toward his father? Is this the conduct of a grown man?" I heard a scratching sound and muffled noises. "What can I say? I hope you're in good health. I hope your studies are going well. I hope you're happy in Toronto." Another silence with more noises off. "If it ever suits you, give your father a call." I kept the message (it was still on my voicemail when I abandoned Toronto) but I never replied. And he never called again.

But in December I received a Greek Christmas card, the only personal inscription my father's signature, scrawled beneath the factory greeting. The card also contained a cheque for five thousand dollars. I felt myself misting up. This I had never expected. It was no small gesture, coming from my father, a show of humility and charity I wouldn't have thought him capable of. It may have been the closest I had ever seen him come to an apology. I knew what it must have cost him emotionally and briefly considered giving him a call. I would have rather written him a letter, but I didn't feel my written Greek was good enough and I wasn't going to write him in English. In the end, I did nothing; I had been quite content having nothing to do with him. Life was more peaceful and free. I didn't miss him and had nothing to say to him. Did he really care how my studies were going? He had no respect for what I was doing. I couldn't see how breaking the silence would gain me anything other than grief.

But what to do with the cheque? I could use the money. But could I cash it when I wasn't even willing to talk to him? That seemed pretty low. On the other hand, he owed me, and far more than five thousand dollars. What he owed me he could never repay. This was but a negligible portion of what I was due. The cheque was more a bribe than a gift, its purpose not so much to help me as to ease his conscience. Fuck him! Why should I help him do that? I wanted his conscience uneasy.

The cheque was in my wallet as I approached the pool hall that afternoon. I envisioned myself confronting my father, crumpling the cheque, and throwing it in his face. It was a wet, overcast day, and the streets were alive again after the Christmas lull. I walked on the opposite side of Park Avenue and could see from a distance that the Symposium's blinds were down and there was no one hanging about. The place looked as it always did, and going past it, I turned my head askance and moved quickly.

And that was that. I didn't know what I'd hoped to see or accomplish, and I wouldn't go by again.

When I got home, I called Laura. I'd spoken with her the night I arrived in Montreal. After that, I'd left her a few messages. I never heard back and figured she was still angry. On Christmas Eve, I had said, "Could you call, so I know you're all right? If I'm not home, leave a message with my mother. But call...please...and merry Christmas." I understood that I was being punished, and knowing Laura, she was fully capable of not calling the rest of my stay. But that was fine. It would make things easier when I returned to Toronto.

I tried her again twice that afternoon. When the phone rang a short while later, I picked it up immediately.

"Is this Alex?" It was a woman's voice.

"Who is this?"

"It's Nicola."

I knew this couldn't be good. Even before she broke the news, a chill went up my spine.

Laura was in the hospital. She had tried to kill herself. Nicola wasn't clear on the details. She and Laura had planned to get together Christmas night, and when Laura hadn't shown up, Nicola had been unable to reach her. Eventually she got in touch with Laura's mother, who gave her the news. Nicola had visited the hospital that morning, but Laura wouldn't tell her much.

"I think you should come back as soon as you can," she said. "Laura told me not to tell you anything, but that seems crazy to me. She's not herself. She's medicated and not that lucid. Anyway, it's up to you. But I thought you should know."

I told my mother there was an emergency in Toronto and I had to return. What? No! Impossible! How could I do this? I had just arrived. I explained that a good friend had been in a terrible accident and was in the hospital. The doctors didn't know whether he was going to make it. Who was this person? I said he was an exchange student from Greece. I was practically the only person he knew in Toronto. I had to go back, I had no choice. It seemed to work. I saw a look of surrender on my mother's face.

"Doesn't he have any family there?"

"No."

"How do you know this person? You told me you didn't know any Greeks in Toronto."

"I told you about him. You just don't remember."

"No, I don't remember."

"But I told you. He's doing his PhD at the university."

The next day she behaved fairly reasonably. As I packed my bags, she sat on my bed snivelling, a clump of tissues in her fist. "When am I going to see you again?"

"I'll try to get back before the end of the month."

"In the fall you said you would come back every two weeks and you came back once."

"I'll do better, I promise. I'm so busy, you have to understand."

"And what about me? Who understands me?"

On the train, I tried to read but couldn't concentrate. I was terrified of what awaited me in Toronto. Why would Laura have tried to kill herself? Because I had refused to spend time at her cottage? That couldn't be. I knew she was having difficulties in school, but nothing worse than usual. Perhaps something had happened with her parents.

The hospital was literally déjà vu. I felt as though I'd just been here. And yet, as well acquainted as I was with wards like this, they still made me queasy. Finding Laura's room, I paused at the entrance and nerved myself. I didn't know what kind of greeting I was going to get. I was also concerned about who else might be there and what account they had been given. Inside the room, I found a single bed, unoccupied. In a chair next to it sat Laura's mother, reading a magazine. I remained poised for a hasty retreat. Mrs. Gale raised her head and regarded me silently.

"Hello, Frances," I said, thinking she might not recognize me.

"Alex," she said in her typically affectless manner. "How are you?"

"Fine. How are you?"

"Oh...fine, I suppose. All things considered." Under the circumstances, Mrs. Gale's impassivity was reassuring.

"Where's Laura?"

"Oh," said Mrs. Gale, glancing at the bed. "A nurse took her for a test. She'll be back soon. Come in. Sit down." She gestured at the empty chair a few feet in front of her. I hung my coat on the back and sat down. Apart from the bed, the two chairs, a couple of steel lockers behind Mrs. Gale, and a small bedside cabinet, the room was bare. On the wall above the bed buzzed a naked fluorescent tube.

"Is Robert here?" I asked.

"No," said Mrs. Gale, having gone back to her magazine. "Robert had to meet with a client in Barrie and he's staying overnight."

Mrs. Gale was a gaunt woman with a short bleached shag and complicated maquillage. She had the same angular features as her daughter but
without the mannish severity. Indeed, she was rather handsome. Laura
was sure she'd had "work" done but couldn't say what. If that were true, it
was an exceptional job, as I couldn't detect any signs, save that she looked
much younger than her sixty-two years. Her fashion sense was hardly better than Laura's, if not so anarchic. Today she had on a long red mohair
sweater cinched at the waist with a wide black leather belt, tight embroid-
ered blue jeans tucked into black knee-high leather boots, and a drooping
double necklace with oversized multicoloured oval pendants.

"Did you have a nice Christmas?" she asked, leafing through her magazine. Of course it was a *Town and Country*.

"It was okay."

"When did you get back?"

"A couple of hours ago. I dropped off my things and came straight here.
I only found out last night. Nicola called me at my mother's place—do
you know Nicola?"

She nodded abstractedly. "We spoke on the phone." She was studying
some detail in a photograph. "How's the weather in Montreal?" she said,
raising her head to look at me. "Is there lots of snow?"

"No. Apparently there hasn't been much this year."

She lay the magazine flat on her lap and launched into an extended,
rambling reminiscence about a trip she'd made to Montreal years ago. The
point appeared to be that the weather was "bone-chilling."

"Montreal winters can be brutal," I said.

"It was *bone*-chilling. And it was only the middle of November."

Laura's parents were ciphers to me, creations of my own preconcep-
tions and projections. I'd only met them a couple of times, and even at
this stage in my life, the middle-class Anglo parent was an exotic creature,
seen through the lens of its popular representations and stereotypes. One
of the more remarkable things about the Gales, however, was how neatly
they fit inside those chalk outlines (or is this circular logic?). Mr. Gale
was a partner in a high-powered Bay Street law firm. Tall, fit, handsome,
silver-haired, he could have played himself in a movie. Mrs. Gale did volunteer work. Before the birth of Laura's older brother, she had worked as
a secretary. These days (according to Laura) she filled her days shopping,

lunching, socializing, spaing, running or attending fund-raisers, and taking prescription drugs.

To me, the Gales were the picture of the upper-middle-class WASP family. I was given to understand, however, that there were Lynchian undercurrents beneath the gleaming surface. So forthright in other respects, Laura was unable to speak plainly about her family. But she had, by hints and murmurs, let it be known that there lurked some shameful secret in her family's past, its enormity only magnified by her refusing to name it. I assumed some kind of sexual abuse or impropriety, and assumed the perpetrator to be her father or brother. Mrs. Gale seemed more ineffectual and negligent than evil. Laura liked to call her mother "Cleopatra, queen of denial," and I could see how Mrs. Gale might be willing to turn a blind eye to whatever violated her sense of decorum or threatened appearances. Laura described her as "the type of woman who should not have daughters." Her mother lacked the most basic nurturing instincts and had been "emotionally unavailable" even during her infancy. How she could remember that far back was a mystery to me, but such were powers that psychotherapy bestowed. In any event, she had come to understand that her mother's inadequacies were at the root of her own emotional impairments, including her obsessive-compulsive tendencies, her low self-esteem and dysphoria, and her lack of resilience and inability to self-console.

Her relationship with her father was murkier and possibly even more complicated. She hardly ever talked about him, or *to* him. She always looked uncomfortable and restless in his company, and when she wasn't ignoring him, she was sniping at him. Everything he said annoyed her, and she seemed unable to address him except in a sneering and petulant tone. Mr. Gale didn't seem to notice. Never did I see him lose his cool or snap back. What was unclear was whether this was owing to his extraordinary patience and self-control, or sheer obliviousness: Mr. Gale, whatever his professional and social success, didn't always seem fully *there*. He was often distracted, fiddling with his phone or humming to himself, and seemed uninterested in what was going on around him. In conversation, I felt as though I were speaking with someone wearing mirrored sunglasses. I also could never look at him without wondering what terrible things he may have done to his daughter. Or was it to his son? Laura had never been clear. Then again, maybe the whole thing was a kind of hoax, another of

Laura's teapot tempests, all the innuendo and unspoken allegations, the evasions and allusions, more of the stagecraft and self-authored melodrama by which Laura presented herself to the world as a tragic victim.

Having related her bone-chilling memories, Mrs. Gale returned to her magazine and we sat in silence. I was reluctant to ask my next question.

"So how's Laura?"

Mrs. Gale looked up. "Laura?" She gazed past me with pensive eyes. "Oh...I don't know."

"Has anyone said how long she might be here?"

"Not long at all, I imagine. They need the beds. These days it's all about the beds. But you need not worry about Laura. She always pulls through." She gave me an odd smile that, under different circumstances, I would have been inclined to read as ironic. She shut the magazine and adjusted herself. "Do you know Lady Lazarus?"

I pictured a woman with a parasol and toy poodle. "I don't think so." I braced for a rambling story about one of the Gales' illustrious friends.

"You must be familiar with Sylvia Plath," she said.

"Yes," I replied, all at once remembering Plath's poem. I hadn't read it since my teens.

Twisting in her chair, Mrs. Gale tossed her magazine on a table behind her that I only now noticed. On it were more magazines in a messy heap. So, the *Town and Country* wasn't hers after all. I felt slightly foolish.

"You know Laura is a huge Sylvia Plath fan," Mrs. Gale said.

I didn't know this, but it didn't surprise me. "No," I replied.

"Huge. *Huge*. Since she was a little girl. She started reading her when she was practically still in the crib. But not the best influence, right? But that gives you an idea, the kind of child she was. Precocious, but not always easy. *Very* sensitive. High-strung. Inward. Very inward. As I'm sure you know. But she always had what you might call...let's say an artistic temperament. You know Laura paints."

"I know she used to."

"Does she not anymore?"

"I don't know. With med school and everything."

"She was a very creative child. At six she was writing poetry. Did you know that?"

"No."

"Oh yes. I still have her poems. She was always creative. But also very *emotional*. The two go together. But sometimes things...*life* could be overwhelming. She's delicate. Perhaps I'm partly to blame. You can't always get everything right. You do your best. But it's not easy. Especially with a girl like Laura. She can be easily overwhelmed. Which is what happened again this semester—no surprise, in some ways. Medical school is stressful. I don't think people realize to what extent. You have to be strong. We warned her. Robert and I have several doctor friends, and they all say the same thing. It calls for stamina, an inner strength. Which neither Robert or I were completely convinced she had. We told Laura, it's like boot camp. And this is not the first time, as I'm sure you know."

She paused and raised her eyebrows high. But I wasn't sure what she was referring to, so I waited.

"In certain ways, of course," she went on, "Laura is strong indeed. I know this sounds contradictory, but she's very tough. She'll come out of this just fine. She never means these things. I hope you're not taking it personally. It's just a cry, that's all. I mean, after all..." She leaned toward me and, lowering her voice, said, "One doesn't take..." But then, changing her mind, she straightened up and, waving a hand, said, "Anyway, she'll be fine. She always bounces back. She just needs rest. Often that's all this is about. She's with a very good doctor now. Someone Robert knows. *Very* good." Again she leaned in and dropped her voice. "Harvard educated. He says that—Oh? Ah!" Gazing over my head, Mrs. Gale broke into one of her broad camera smiles.

I turned. Laura stood in the doorway, dressed in a hospital gown and her Birkenstocks. I got to my feet but didn't know what to do beyond that. Should I kiss her? What should I say?

"Alex and I were just talking about your paintings. Remember those lovely still-lifes you did, the ones hanging in the upstairs hallway?

Laura shuffled over to the bed.

"Here, darling," Mrs. Gale said, standing up. "Sit here. I was leaving anyway. I was just waiting for you to get back so I could say goodbye."

Laura laboriously mounted the bed, her movements slow and unsteady. I hovered behind her pointlessly. Mrs. Gale held out a hand but she was shoved away. As Laura settled in, I pulled the covers over her legs. The bed was sloped, and Laura lay at an incline, staring at the ceiling.

Mrs. Gale looked at her watch. "Goodness. Time for me to hit the road." She pulled open one of the steel lockers. "Alex, are you back in Toronto for good now?"

"Yes."

"You'll be coming tomorrow?" Before I could answer, she said to Laura, "Remember I won't be able to come tomorrow, darling. Your father will be getting back, and I have no idea what—"

"I'm definitely coming," I interjected.

"Alex will be here," Mrs. Gale said, putting on her leather coat. "Do you know what time you'll be here, Alex?"

"Mum, I don't need monitoring," Laura said, still staring ahead.

"I'm not saying you need *monitoring*, darling. I'm just checking with Alex to see—"

"Alex will come whenever he can."

"Of course he'll come by whenever he can. I wasn't suggesting otherwise, was I? I was just enquiring as to when that might be."

"Probably after lunch," I said.

"Perfect," said Mrs. Gale. Then to Laura: "After lunch."

"Yes, I heard."

"And you know you can call me any time. I'll be home most of the day tomorrow. Oh no, I may have to go out in the morning."

"Whatever. Don't worry about it. I won't be calling you."

"You don't need to snap at me, darling. I'm just letting you know, if you call and there's no answer, it means I've stepped out, so call again later."

"Okay! Jesus!"

Mrs. Gale bent over the bed and kissed Laura on the cheek. Laura continued to stare at the ceiling.

"Alex," said Mrs. Gale as we brushed cheeks. "Very nice to see you. I'm glad you're back."

I went and stood by the bed. Laura hadn't moved. She glanced up at me. "What?" she said.

"How are you feeling?"

She looked away. It was a while before she spoke.

"How did you find out?"

"Nicola called me."

"What did she say?"

I pulled over a chair and sat down. "She told me you were in the hospital and why. But nothing more. She said she didn't know any more."

"I suppose you think this is all about you."

"To be honest, I can't imagine why it would have anything to do with me."

"Well, I can assure you it doesn't. I want to be clear. I didn't do this so you would come running back."

"That's not what I thought."

"I'm sorry if I ruined your holiday. What did you tell your mother?"

"I told her a friend was in the hospital."

"A friend," she said, smiling faintly. "What friend?"

"Just a friend. I didn't specify."

Laura kept staring ahead.

"Do you want to talk about it?" I asked.

She shut her eyes and inhaled. "Not really." After a few seconds, she murmured, "I'm tired."

I sat quietly another minute. "Maybe I should be going." Laura didn't respond. I stood and put on my coat. "I guess I'll see you tomorrow."

"If you wish."

I bent down and kissed her unresponsive lips. I remained standing by the bed. She shifted her gaze toward me. "I just want to say that, whatever it is that happened...I am relieved you're okay. At least I hope you're okay."

"I'm fine."

"If you're not, I hope you would tell me."

She faced forward. "I'm fine."

The next day I found Laura in the lounge watching TV. She was in better spirits and asked me about Montreal. When I asked about her own holidays, though, her mood sagged. She wanted to return to her room. "Listen," she said on the way, "if you're hoping I'm going to tell you why I did this, the fact is I'm not sure myself. You may not understand that, it may sound implausible to you, but that's the way it is."

"No, I can understand that."

"Really?"

In her room, we sat in the chairs, facing each other.

"You don't owe me an explanation," I said. "You tell me whatever you want to."

"But I feel the question like the elephant in the room. I see it on your face. You should see yourself, the way you keep looking at me, that terrified look in your eyes."

"There's no look."

"Yes there is. You're like a frightened child."

"I think you're projecting. I don't know what you're seeing."

She seemed to lose patience and fell silent for a long time. "It's complicated," she said and then again fell silent. "It was a combination of factors. And I'm not sure...I'm not sure I can or even want to explain them."

"That's fine."

"Everyone says fourth year feels like a breeze after third, but it hasn't been that way for me. I've been having a hard time."

"I know."

"No, no you don't. You have no idea."

I wasn't about to argue.

"The last month has been brutal. There are things I haven't told you about." This was hard to believe. "I was even thinking of quitting." She had been saying this since October. By then it had become clear to me that Laura didn't belong in med school, but the one time I hinted at this, she turned on me viciously and accused me of trying to undermine her. I'd learned that when Laura discussed her anxieties about school, she was looking for reassurance, not confirmation. Her pursuit of a medical degree had little to do with the high ideals she attached to it. It was not about making a positive contribution or changing the system from the inside. But neither was it about money, or even status in the conventional sense. It was, however, about validation. Laura was drawn to the image of the doctor, to the figure she imagined she would cut as one, to the dignity and authority it would bestow on her and the respect it would elicit. What she hadn't given sufficient thought to was the profession itself, to the work, to the day-to-day experience of making one's living as a physician. She reminded me of myself in law school. Once, I had asked her what she wanted most in life, and she had said, "How does one know?" She often said she felt like a replicant from *Blade Runner*. Every time she acted on what she thought was a deep-seated and heartfelt impulse or conviction, it revealed itself as illusory or alien, as something resembling a mental transplant of someone else's dreams and desires. "I don't feel real to myself. I feel as if there's no one inside me." A medical degree would at least make her feel like someone on the outside, or so I surmised. So the stakes were high. To quit now would have been devastating.

"My mistake was talking to my parents about it," she said. "I don't know what I was thinking. I'll never learn."

When she didn't elaborate, I asked, "Talking about what?"

"I don't know how to do it," she muttered, staring into space. "Physical pain, no problem. There are times I welcome it. It's almost a relief." It was as if she were talking to herself. "But the emotional stuff...I don't know how it's done. How to make it stop. So the only thing that can bring any relief is a different pain." She looked at me. "You know what I mean?"

"I think so," I said. It was only recently I had learned of Laura's history of cutting and burning, and I was afraid to ask if she had done such things over Christmas. It was a subject I didn't understand and that made me queasy. She had told me about this history the night I enquired about some of the marks on her body, including the tattoo. She was oddly forthright about the scars. As for the tattoo, she explained she was deathly afraid of spiders. "In the destructive element immerse," she'd said, quoting Joseph Conrad.

"No you don't," she said now. "I don't think you understand any of it."

She may have been right. But to admit as much would make her angry. I said, "You don't think I experience psychological pain?"

"No, I don't," she answered, almost contemptuously. "Not in the same way. I don't think you experience the kind of pain I'm talking about."

"I don't see how one can possibly gauge such a thing."

"I know you. I've watched you. I know how you operate. You know how to self-analgize. I don't know how you do it. I think it's fucked up sometimes, but you still do it."

We fell into another long silence during which I returned to something that was preoccupying me. But I was reluctant to bring it up.

"Yesterday," I began, "when I was talking with your mother...."

Laura watched me with heightened interest. "What?"

"Well, she was talking about, you know...what happened...."

"Yes?"

"She seemed to suggest it's possible I misunderstood—"

"For Christ's sake!" she said, practically shouting. "Just say it!"

"She seemed to suggest this wasn't the first time. That you had done something like this before."

Her eyes flamed. "What did she say?"

"I don't remember her exact—"

"What did she say?"

"Well...she mentioned how you're a big Sylvia Plath fan."

She tilted her head. "What?"

"She made this reference to Lady Lazarus. Which initially..."

I paused, held up by the maniacal look on Laura's face. She stared at me in a smouldering silence; then, her eyes dilating, she said, "What. A fucking... CUNT!" The last word was blasted at top volume and I glanced behind me at the open door. "Did I not tell you?" she said, lowering her voice. "What a pustulent, chancrous, suppurating cunt!" She was still staring at me goggle-eyed. "Now do you believe me? Do you see what she is?"

"But it's not like I didn't believe you."

"But you see now how she operates?" She fell into a reflective silence, shaking her head. "You know what? I'm glad." Now she started nodding. "I'm glad she let you see for yourself what a fucking rancid bitch she is. I want others to see what I see. I feel better, actually. I'm glad you told me. What a bitch! My god, she has absolutely no empathy, that woman. No empathic imagination. Or basic decency. Or *discretion*...for someone so concerned about what everybody thinks. There's never a moment when it isn't a good time to stick it to you. This is who raised me. Can you believe it? Even when you're down in the gutter, down in the dirt, *especially* then, she'll kick you in the teeth...but with a pair of fluffy bunny slippers on." She continued to stare at me wild-eyed. "Do you see now? Do you see?"

I said I did.

As her mother predicted, the hospital didn't keep Laura long. More surprising, she was back at school by mid-January. This was on the advice of her doctor, who thought it would be best for her to resume her life as normal. Needless to say, I put off looking for a new place. Moreover, something had shifted between us. The old resentments and antipathies had dissipated. Laura was more even-tempered, less combative and suspicious. Pharmaceuticals had a lot to do with it, but I wasn't going to put a gift horse through a blood test. We got along better, hardly bickered, didn't fight. The sex wasn't as frequent or spirited (again the meds, perhaps), but we had a good time together. We went out, saw people, and Laura was more relaxed and congenial than I'd ever seen her. She seemed to do better at school as well. She didn't come home spitting bile. With the help of her therapist, she had worked out a set of strategies for dealing with the pressures and frustrations of school. By a stroke of luck, she had front-loaded her semesters, so she had already been through the more onerous rotations, and the winter semester was turning out to be more manageable and enjoyable.

But it was not to last. In March she was assigned another arrogant and pushy supervising physician, and she became fretful and brittle again. "What is it with these guys? They're like pedophiles. Because they were abused in med school, they have to abuse us in turn. I'm sick of it." I fell back on my own set of strategies, reminding her that she was almost done, that the finish line was within sight, she just needed to hang on a few weeks. My plan was to make it to the end of the semester, after which I would be spending the summer in Montreal, where I would have time and space to consider my next steps. But Laura grew more dejected and frantic. And then she started talking of quitting again. Panicking, I said, "You can't quit now. You're in the crunch. It's normal to feel anxious. Stick it out, do your best and get through the next few weeks. Don't think about the results. Just do what you have to do. It would make no sense to quit now." I sounded like Soula. This was how she would speak to me in law school, and almost as effectively. Laura continued to sink. She even threatened to stop therapy, which she'd never done before and which was especially alarming. "What's the point?" she said during one of her sleepless nights. "It's bullshit. All my psychiatrist cares about is keeping me alive. That's her sole mission. To keep me alive."

"Well...that is her job," I said obtusely. I wasn't at my best at 3:30 in the morning.

"Sorry, that's *not* her job," Laura shot back. "She's a therapist, a healer. It shouldn't be just about survival, how to keep going with your miserable existence. What if you have good reason to kill yourself? I hate that sanctity-of-life crap. The bullshit about how all human beings are precious. It's all lies and they know it. It's like the fundamentalists who'll keep a person in a vegetative state. 'Because who are we to play god.' Psychiatrists are the same. They're psychic ventilators. If they can keep you breathing, they've done their job. Even if your life is shit and consists of nothing but unremitting pain and suffering. Who's the fucking crazy one?"

"But your life's not shit."

"Please don't you start too. You're not good at that sort of bullshit. I know you don't believe in any of it."

Whatever I might think of Laura's psychotherapeutic orthodoxies, without them she descended into a nihilism, an abject determinism half Darwinian half Skinnerian. The chicken was nothing more than the egg's way of producing another chicken, while the chicken's own beliefs about her self-worth and freedom were but a sustaining illusion whose purpose was nothing other than to ensure the production of more eggs. I found this a hard position to deny, but, for whatever reasons, it didn't affect me the way it did Laura. In any case, there was no arguing with her, as the game was rigged: no matter how trenchant my arguments, they were only more of those sustaining illusions. So I kept quiet and listened.

The last few weeks were touch and go, but Laura made it through the program and even graduated with distinction. Her mood turned instantly. The gloom and nihilism were gone. She became almost manic. She started going out again and reconnecting with friends (except for Nicola, with whom she'd had a falling out she refused to talk about). I wanted to get to Montreal, but Laura's convocation was in June and there was no way I was going to leave before it. That would be far too hazardous.

Then one day Laura said out of the blue, "Let's go to Europe."

I felt the usual knot in my stomach. "Europe? When?"

"My internship begins in July, so who knows when I'll get any free time again. I was thinking either France or Italy, maybe both."

Genially as possible, I said, "Laura, you know I can't do that."

"I'm talking just a couple of weeks."

"First of all, I don't have the money."

"I'm paying. I'll pay for everything."

I looked at her askance. "You're not going to pay for *anything*."

"It's not me, stupid. It's my father's money."

"That's even worse."

"It's a gift. For my graduation. My parents are giving me a trip to wherever I want, among other things. Don't worry about the details."

"I'm not taking money from your parents."

"They're not giving it to you. They're giving it to *me*. This is not about you, you egomaniac. Don't put obstacles where there aren't any."

"But there is an obstacle. I have to be in Montreal."

"*Have* to."

"Yes, *have* to. *Have* to. We've been through this a million times. I don't understand why this has to keep happening. I've told my mother, she's expecting me. I've promised her I'm spending the summer with her. It's on that understanding I'm able to be in Toronto."

"On that *understanding*? What are you talking about? You're in Toronto of your own free will, because you want to be."

"I made her a promise. I don't want to talk about it anymore."

"You have July and August. Two whole months. Two months during which we are not going to see each other...*at all*...because I'll be so busy. I'm talking about two weeks in June. All expenses paid. Luxury accommodations, fine dining, whatever you want. I'm thinking a week in Paris, then Provence. We'll rent a car. Oh, Alex, you'll love it. You've never been anywhere. Treat yourself. You'll have a great time, I promise. You need this."

"I can't."

"Oh my god," Laura muttered under her breath.

"I have to work."

She stared at me open-mouthed.

"I need to make money."

"You are unbelievable. I've never seen anything like this in my life."

"I've already committed to my uncle for June, and I can't back out now. He's counting on me to fill in for vacationing employees."

"When did you do that?"

"A long time ago. He's depending on me." This wasn't quite accurate. We had discussed my working at the Galaxy, but my uncle couldn't make any promises. And his employees didn't take their vacations until July.

Laura looked defeated. "A measly two weeks?"

"I promised him. I can't back out now."

"One week. A week in Paris. All expenses paid."

"Will you stop saying all expenses paid? I won't accept any money, from you or your father or anyone else."

"Why not? You just said you need money."

"No. It's out of the question. I'm not discussing this."

I was braced for a blowout, but Laura remained surprisingly composed. Those medications were something. "The truth is," she said calmly, "I was prepared for this. I was hoping you might prove me wrong. But you came through once again, old boy. Congratulations." She gave me a mordant smile. "You are such a child. So predictable. You know I'm going to go anyway, right? To Europe. Whether you come or not."

"As you should. You deserve it. This *is* for you, after all. That's what your parents are paying for."

"And I'll have a fucking good time, I can assure you."

"Good. I hope so. Why else go?"

Soon after, she informed me that she would be spending two weeks in France, flying to Paris from Montreal.

"Montreal?" I said.

"It was the best flight I could get. But, in any case, I wanted to visit you, spend a few days in Montreal. It's on the way, so it made sense. Or do you object to that too? Don't tell me: you're going to be taking your mother to church every day and grocery shopping all afternoon and working at your uncle's all night."

I felt bushwhacked. "I think it's a great idea. It'll be fun."

I left two days after Laura's convocation. There were so many books and papers in my suitcase, I could barely lift it. In Montreal, I studied for exams and resumed my old domestic duties. Now and then I got together with Perry and the other guys. And everywhere I went, I kept an eye out for my father. I dreaded bumping into him. In April I had received a second cheque, this one double the amount of the first, and again I had held on to it. I had both in my wallet, though at this point I was no longer interested in a confrontation and fervently hoped I would make it through the summer without seeing him.

Then, one afternoon, stepping out of a store on St. Laurent, I saw Karolos the Armenian coming up the street. Before I could slink back inside, he spotted me. "Reh, Aleko," he said, breaking into a smile. "Are you in town?" He appeared genuinely happy to see me and shook my hand with brusque affection. He asked about Toronto and my studies. He seemed to have no knowledge of the state of affairs between my father and me.

"How long are you in Montreal?"

"Maybe another week. At most."

"When are you coming by? Your father didn't even say you were back."

"I don't know."

"What do you mean you don't know? Everyone will want to see you. They ask about you constantly."

"I'll try."

"You'll *try*? What's the matter with you?"

"I'm here only a few more days, and I have a lot to do."

"You have time to come by the Symposium."

No doubt this would get back to my father. But what could he do? Come to the house? Phone? And what if he did? Why did I become so anxious about it? Even as I fretted over such contingencies, I began to think that maybe I should go by the pool hall after all. But to what end? Was I ready to patch things up? Did I really want my father back in my life? Or was I looking for a fight? For days afterward I was in a tumult. But then Laura arrived, and suddenly I had bigger worries.

She flew in on a Thursday, three days before her departure for Paris. Since her graduation she'd been spending money with uncharacteristic abandon, and for Montreal she booked a room in a posh hotel. Catching sight of her at the airport, I remembered our first meeting. How different she was now, dressed in a beige lace tunic and jeans. Gone was the sullen granola goth from just a year earlier. Her hair had grown out and she no longer dyed it, and lately she'd begun to shop at designer boutiques. She was starting to look almost bourgeois, as if she were finally growing into what she was meant to be. Watching her among the other arrivals, I thought she looked better than ever, and as we kissed, I felt an odd twinge, a foretaste of what I would miss when it was all over.

After dropping off her things at the hotel, we walked around downtown and ate dinner in Old Montreal. Afterward we strolled through the cobbled laneways but, at Laura's behest, cut our wanderings short to go back to the hotel, where we achieved an incandescence we hadn't experienced in a long time. It made me wonder whether Laura had gone off her meds as she'd threatened some weeks earlier. But I didn't dare ask, as it was sure to spoil the mood. And in any case, what did it matter now?

She spent the next morning shopping and visiting galleries and then met me in the afternoon. On Saturday she was determined to see where I'd grown up, so we arranged to have lunch at a bistro on Hutchison and then walk around the area. I told my mother I had a friend visiting from Toronto and would be spending the day with him. I'd planned out an itinerary ahead of time, and we meandered through Outremont up to Bernard. From there we wound our way south through the smaller and more picturesque streets, ending up at Fletcher's Field. I pointed out my old house and Laura stared at it with bemusement.

"*This* is where you grew up?" she said. She looked up and down the street and at the park. "But this is gorgeous. You talk as though you grew up in a slum. This is beautiful. This is not what I'd imagined."

"Things have changed. This used to be a working-class immigrant neighbourhood. These buildings are condos now. I have no idea who lives in them, but they sure don't work in factories or drive taxis. When I was growing up, these houses were falling apart and filled with rats and roaches. There was a fire every week with some landlord setting his house ablaze for the insurance because he couldn't afford repairs and couldn't get anything for it on the market. The street didn't look like this."

"But the park was here."

"Back then it was full of rubbies and junkies. And down there"—I pointed toward Duluth—"it was a hangout for bikers."

"Do you have to say rubbies and junkies?"

"The point is, at night it was scary. It was a different place."

"But this is where you lived when you were a kid. Where are you now? I mean, where's your mother's place?"

I gestured north.

"I'm confused. You mean we passed it?"

We hadn't, in fact. At the corner of St. Viateur and Esplanade, I'd made the last-second decision to take a right turn and avoid St. Urbain Street altogether. How could I know what would follow from it?

"But I want to see your house," Laura said.

"There's nothing to see. It's a plain old rowhouse."

"But it's your rowhouse."

"So was this," I said, hoping to divert her attention. I pointed above us. "That's where my bedroom used to be. From my bed I could see the cross." I turned and pointed at the mountain.

"But I want to see your current place, where your mother lives."

Even now it wouldn't have been too late to regain the road not taken. What would have happened had we gone back? Where would I be today had I taken Laura to St. Urbain that afternoon? Where my mother? Instead I said, "Well, it's kind of far. Maybe we'll go by later. Since we're here, I thought we'd hike up the mountain. Believe me, you'll enjoy it more than St. Urbain."

Without waiting, I led us across the street and through the park. Laura came along grumpily. At Park Avenue, there was a traffic light where the underpass used to be and we crossed to the monument. As we climbed the broad gravel path to the summit, I could see Laura's spirits lifting. Amid the greenery, she seemed to forget her anger. She started naming things again like Adam. Emerald ash, gingko, trout lily, hickory. I hadn't realized how vast her knowledge of the natural world was. Earlier that afternoon, as we'd roamed the streets, she had stopped often to admire the gardens and expound on the plants and flowers.

"How do you know all this stuff?" It turned out her mother was an avid gardener and had passed on much to her. "So how come you haven't done anything with that patch of dirt in ourbackyard?"

"I'd love to. I would love to grow some herbs and vegetables."

That afternoon I had learned Laura's favourite flowers were irises and peonies. I admitted that I didn't know what irises and peonies looked like.

"You're joking," she said. "How is that possible?" She had started testing me. "What are those?"

"I don't know."

"You're kidding. You really don't know?"

"No idea."

"Hydrangeas," she said. And so hydrangeas came to be. She studied my face, as if waiting for me to break character. "You really didn't know that?"

"I've heard of them. Like I've heard of most of them. I've seen the names in print all my life. But I don't know what they look like."

"That's incredible. That makes no sense. They're everywhere. Didn't you ever notice them?"

"In a way...no."

"You know what those are?"

I looked. "No."

"Good heavens. Those are tiger lilies. What about that?" I shrugged.
"You don't know that's a cherry tree?"

"I didn't know there were cherry trees in Montreal."

"Okay, now you're joking."

"I associate cherry trees with Japan and Chekhov. I think of them as exotic."

She shook her head. "I don't know what you're doing. I don't believe you anymore."

Now, as we wound our way up Mount Royal, she resumed testing me. "Rosehip," she said and so rosehip came to be. Where before there had been trees and grass and flowers of different sizes, shapes, and colours, now there were oaks and elms and sugar maples; there was trillium, jewelweed, milkweed, and black-eyed Susans. She could even identify all the birds. I was in awe. The names were familiar to me, but I had never attached them to anything. I remembered a magazine article on Richard Feynman in which he reminisced about childhood walks with his father through the Catskills. Turning over rocks and earth, his father would tell him about the bugs and worms they found, explaining their physical and biological properties and processes. One day, a boy pointed at a bird and asked Richard what kind it was. When the future Nobel laureate admitted he didn't know, the boy said, "That's a brown-throated thrush. Doesn't your father teach you anything?" In fact, Melville Feynman had taught his son that every bird had many names, that in France it was called one thing, in Italy another, in China something else, but that one could know the name of a bird in every language and still know nothing about the bird. Instead of worrying about what a bird was called, the elder Feynman said, one ought to look at what it was *doing*. Richard Feynman said that this was one of the most important lessons of his life.

The article had made a deep impression on me and left me feeling oddly envious. Thinking about all that my own father had taught me, I wished he'd had more to say about bugs and birds. I would have been happy just to know their names. It seemed to me the Feynmans got this wrong. Scientific realists that they were, they underestimated the power of naming. For a child, naming can bring the world into sharper focus, make it less alien and inscrutable, more concrete and intelligible. Even without a Melville Feynman to instruct me on their properties and functions, knowing the names of certain things would have brought them into clearer view. Of course, I knew from personal experience how words could also do the opposite, how they could get in the way, how they could obscure and eclipse and stop perception short. "Hydrangea," one says, and the hydrangea disappears; matter melts into sound and mind squanders itself in what it names. As adults we look about us and say *tree, flower, river, bridge, church* like cartographers. But for a child, only beginning to see and understand, words can make the world manifest, less opaque; they can bring into view what hides in shadow. Or so it seemed to me.

At the Chalet on the summit we bought cold drinks and gazed over the city. On our way down, I thought Laura might press me to visit my house, but it was late and she was tired. We took a cab to the hotel. We made plans to meet for a late lunch the next day. Laura wanted to try a restaurant not far from my place.

The next day being Sunday, I spent the morning at church with my mother. Afterward, I headed to Park Avenue on my own for groceries. I had told my mother I was having lunch with my friend from Toronto and would be leaving after I dropped off the bags. Entering the apartment on my return, I could hear my mother's voice in the living room and assumed she was on the phone. Then, hearing that she was speaking in English, I hastened my step as I thought the call might be for me. But through the living room entrance, I could see the phone on its table, and then I could see my mother in the armchair by the kitchen doorway. Someone was in the living room with her. A second later, I saw it was Laura.

She was seated on the sofa, gazing intently at my mother in an effort to follow her broken English. On the coffee table was a misted tumbler of water and my aunt Christina's old confection carousel, its cut-glass bowls filled with the stale nuts, chips, cookies, and candied almonds my mother kept in stow for theoretical visitors. As Laura turned toward me, my mother interrupted herself and said in Greek, "Your visitor from Toronto dropped in to say hello." Her tone was cool. I turned and looked at Laura.

"Odd coincidence," she said, smiling. "I was just walking by and your mother and I bumped into each other on the street." She was wearing her orange halter top and tight denim cutoffs, but at the moment all I could see were vast expanses of gleaming flesh and the row of hoops that crowned her left ear, which suddenly looked five times their usual size. To judge by the position of the spaghetti straps of her top, her spider tattoo was surely visible. I was dressed in my schoolboy church clothes: grey cotton pants and blue dress shirt, sleeves rolled up against the heat, black patent leather shoes. All that was missing was a clip-on bowtie.

"I was standing on the sidewalk admiring the house," Laura continued, "and all of a sudden there's your mother next to me and we started talking and after a while she very kindly invited me to come upstairs."

I could barely hear through the roar in my ears. "I need to put these things away," I said and headed to the kitchen.

My mother got up, and, coming up beside me, helped me empty the shopping bags on the kitchen table. After a few seconds, I turned around and went back to the living room. Laura was eating nuts from her palm.

"We need to go," I said.

She frowned. "Wouldn't that be rude?" she said in a stage whisper.

"We need to go."

She tossed the remaining nuts into her mouth and wiped her palms on her cutoffs.

I turned and said in Greek, "We're going."

My mother emerged from the kitchen. "When are you coming back?"

"I don't know."

Laura came over and I saw she was wearing a pair of my mother's slippers. She tried on different smiles as she gazed back and forth between my mother and me. As I headed to the front door, she shook my mother's hand. "It was very nice to meet you, Mrs. Doukas."

"Me too," I could hear my mother reply stolidly.

I waited on the sidewalk while Laura changed back into her sandals. As she came down the stairs, my mother observed us from the doorway. We walked toward Fairmount in silence. From the corner of my eye, I could see Laura looking at me. When I turned, she flashed the coy, contrite expression of a mischievous child caught with her hand in the cookie jar.

"You know I didn't plan this. I hope that's not what you're thinking."

I didn't trust myself to speak.

"Honestly," she said. "I had no idea anyone would be around. I thought you were at church. And since I was in the neighbourhood, I thought I'd make a detour and go by your place, just to take a look. And the next thing, there's this woman standing next to me asking me who I am."

I could see Laura looking at me.

"She's the one who spoke first. And when I mentioned I was a friend of yours from Toronto, she asked me in. What was I supposed to do? Say no? That would be rude, right? You wouldn't want me to be rude."

"Two things," I said as we turned down St. Laurent. "One...please don't play innocent."

"Excuse me?"

"There are any number of ways you could have declined the invitation."

"Okay, Alex, don't—"

"Two, you could have minded your own fucking business. What the fuck were doing snooping around my place?"

"Excuse me! I was not snooping!"

"You knew perfectly well we were coming back from church."

"I didn't know *when*. I had no idea—"

"Don't play innocent!"

"Don't shout at me."

"I don't buy it. Especially from you. Who's the one who keeps saying there's no such thing as an accident? If the roles were reversed here, how would you be interpreting what just happened?"

"Alex, don't turn this into a thing. I went by to see where you lived. I thought you were at church. That's it. I never imagined your mother would suddenly appear and interrogate me. And, anyway, what's the drama? So I bumped into your mother. So I went inside your house—which by the way I think is charming. I don't know why you're so embarrassed. It's the apartment of a little old Greek lady."

"Don't condescend to me."

"I am not condescending, you idiot. What is your problem? You create these bogeymen, but they're all in your head."

"That's rich coming from you."

We were approaching Laurier. On a different occasion I would have drawn Laura's attention to the fire station resembling a medieval chateau. I would have pointed out the church behind the park, and maybe told her about Duddy Kravitz. But we now passed these in silence.

After a while, Laura said, "Alex, could you do me a favour? Could you run a little experiment and see what happens if you let this drop and not turn it into something?"

"But it *is* something."

She grabbed my arm and brought us to a stop. "Alex, it's my last day here. In a few hours I'm getting on a plane for Paris, and after that...who knows when we'll see each other. Could we just try to enjoy what remains of our time together?"

I resumed walking. When she caught up with me, I said, "You crossed a line today. And you know it. Because you did it deliberately. You know how I feel about these things. However crazy or irrational or *childish* you might think they are—"

"They *are* childish."

"—I would hope you'd have the decency to respect my wishes. But, no, you needed to see how far you could push things, to teach me some kind of lesson. And, to tell you the truth...I don't know if I can forgive you."

Again Laura grabbed me and turned me to face her. She glared at me, then she gave me the finger. "Fuck you." She stormed away. A passing couple exchanged amused glances. I stood motionless, watching her stalk down St. Laurent; then, turning, I walked in the direction we'd come.

At Fairmount, I kept going north. I hadn't been on this stretch of St. Laurent in a while and I barely recognized it. I passed boutiques, restaurants, and galleries I couldn't remember seeing before. Not long ago this part of St. Laurent consisted of boarded-up storefronts and abandoned warehouses and factories. I continued north past the railway tracks and up into Little Italy. Near St. Zotique, I stopped at a café and sat at a table by the window. Some ginos were at the bar watching a gladiatorial spectacle on a gargantuan screen. I ordered a coffee and tried to figure things out. I wasn't sure how to read Laura's parting words. Was it over between us? She had said worse in the past. I wagered I wouldn't hear from her the entire time she was in France. But you couldn't predict: she might call in a day or two full of apologies. One thing was sure: I wasn't going to call her.

When I got home, I went straight to my study and sat at my desk. I opened one of my notebooks, knowing full well I wouldn't get far. Within a couple of minutes, I could hear my mother come out of her bedroom. I heard her settle into the armchair behind me. I pretended to keep reading.

"Who is that woman?"

I said, without turning, "First of all, it's none of your business. But if you must know, she's a friend from Toronto."

"You told me your friend was a man."

I swivelled my chair to face her. "Let's get something clear. I'm almost forty years old. Are you aware of that? I just turned thirty-eight. Who my friends are, and who that woman is, is none of your business. Do you understand? Can you get it through your fat head that what I do with my life, who I see, how I spend my time, is none of your business? If I told you it was a man, it's because you leave me no choice. I didn't want to deal with your stupid meddling and hysterics. She's a friend from Toronto. And that's all there is to it. All right?" I faced my desk again and there was a long silence.

"That's not what she told me."

I was doodling spirals.

"She said the two of you are living together."

I kept doodling.

"You told me you were living in an apartment in the university. She said you are living together in her house, and that you met last summer."

I put my pen down and swivelled around. In a slow, even pace, I said, "As I mentioned, it's none of your business. Yes, I rent a room in her father's house. We share the kitchen. That's it. And the reason I didn't tell you is that I knew you would react the way you are now."

"So it's true. You're living with this woman?"

"I just explained to you. I have my own room. I rent it from her father. That's how it works in Toronto. Rents are high and most people rent rooms in shared houses. There are houses with five and six students living together, men and women. That's how the world is these days. When I was looking for a place last summer, this was the best I could find. But I knew that if I told you, you would do what you're doing now."

She gave a snort and one of her knowing smirks. "So this is why you moved to Toronto. To sleep around with whores."

It was such a ridiculous, laughable comment that it should have taken the steam out of the situation. And yet with those ridiculous words, something took hold of me, a kind of blinding rage, and without any thought, without foresight or will, I was suddenly on my feet and storming into my bedroom. A moment later, my mother came in and saw me pulling clothes out of the closet and tossing them on the bed. "What are you doing?" she said, coming closer. I shoved past her and marched to the back of the house. When I returned with my suitcase, she tried to grab it from me, but I pushed her away. "Stand back!" I roared. "Do not touch me!" I lay the suitcase open on the bed. "Do not come near me!"

"I'm the one who should be angry," she said gently.

I spun around. "Get the fuck out of here!" I screeched in English.

"Calm yourself."

In Greek: "Get out of this room now or I don't know what I will do!"

"Alex, you lied to me."

"Get out!"

"The neighbours."

"Get the fuck out!" I said, again in English.

She shuffled back but didn't leave. "I don't want you lying to me, Alex, that's all."

Composing myself, I said, "Listen to me. Get out now, or I may kill you."

"Alex, I just want you to tell me the truth. You mustn't lie to me."

"You make it impossible. It's impossible to speak honestly with you. It's impossible to tell you anything, with your constant, exhausting, suffocating meddling and interfering in my life."

"What are you talking about? When have I ever interfered in your life? You have always been free to do whatever you want. Since you were a boy. You were free to come and go as you pleased. Make friends with anyone you pleased. I accepted everything. If anything, I have been too lenient."

I kept filling my suitcase.

"In university, you wanted to go to law school, you went to law school. You wanted to quit law school, you quit law school. You wanted to study philosophy, you studied philosophy. You wanted to work at the pool hall, you worked at the pool hall. Did I want any of this? Did you ask my permission? You wanted to go to Toronto, you went to Toronto. I have never stopped you from doing anything you wanted. When we were on Esplanade, you came and went as you pleased. You roamed the park freely. You went downtown on your bicycle. Other parents wouldn't let their children leave the front yard, but you went where you wanted without constraint. While your father and I were at work, you were free to do whatever you wished. You've had a life of complete freedom. With no father to rule you, and with me indulging and coddling you, you've had a freedom unknown to most children." She tried coming closer. "All I've ever wanted is what's best for you. What do I have in this world except you? You are everything. I live only for you."

"Then die!"

"You think I don't want to? There's nothing I want more." I took more clothes out of the closet. "I pray for it every night. Every night when I go to bed, I pray that God won't let me see the morning."

"Me too."

"You're all I have in this world. You're all I live for."

"Fuck you!" I shouted. Then in Greek: "Who wants such a thing?"

"But that's how it is. I can't do anything about it. I wish I could. I love you. I love you more than life itself. I love you...may He forgive me..." She reached a hand toward me. "I love you more than God."

"Do not come near me!" I shouted, slapping her arm away.

But she wouldn't retreat. "Please put away the suitcase. Put your clothes back."

"Don't you dare," I said, as she groped for the suitcase. I pushed her. "Don't make me do something." She eyed me beseechingly. "I should have abandoned you a long time ago." I continued packing. "Lived my life."

All at once, her face crumpled like an infant's and she began to sob. "Alex, I beg you. Don't do this. Please, Alex, stop. You can't leave. You can't leave me. You promised we'd have the summer together."

As a boy, I could not bear to see my mother cry. The sight of her tears would prompt my own, even when I didn't know their cause. And where I was it, I would be overcome with remorse and would throw my arms around her and kiss her and beg her forgiveness. Now I said, "The summer? We have about another ten minutes together. If there's anything you have to say, you better say it now, because this is the last you'll be seeing me. I'm done here."

She dropped to her knees and clasped her hands in supplication. "Alex, I beg you. I beg you. You are my all!"

With these words, something again took hold of me, and, turning, I gazed down at her several seconds. I tried to conquer it, but it wouldn't give. It pushed me on, and as she looked up at me pleadingly, I stepped toward her, bent down, and spat on her face. Putting her hands over her eyes, she doubled over and began to bawl and howl. I bent lower. "Shhh,"

I said, "the neighbours." While I stood over her, I envisioned what else I might do. I felt a galvanizing exaltation at the horrors flashing in my head. So this is how it happens, I thought. This is how the grisly newspaper headlines get made. And how quickly and easily it comes, how rapidly one goes from a regular Joe to a tabloid psycho. Such a quiet, polite boy. So loving and devoted. A model son and neighbour. He was the last person you would ever expect to do such a thing.

But I tore myself away. I got back to packing. And after I was done, and I'd made a final tour of the apartment to make sure I had everything, and I'd hoisted on my knapsack, I headed toward the door to find my mother standing at the vestibule, hands up against the doorjamb in an effort to block my path.

Calmly, I said, "Get out of the way."

"You can't do this. My darling, please."

Calmly, I let go my suitcase and, grabbing her by the hair, pulled her down the corridor and threw her to the floor. As I returned toward the door, she came at me on all fours and clung to my right leg. I grabbed my suitcase and, kicking her away, swung open the door, banged it shut behind me, and lumbered down the stairs. I was surprised when I looked up from the sidewalk to see the door was still closed. I was sure my mother would burst out and create a scene, but she didn't. I looked for a taxi and, seeing none, headed for Fairmount.

The sun shone bright in a blue sky, to all appearances a perfect summer's day. I kept my head down going past the neighbours on the porches and balconies. At Fairmount, I heard a shout from across the street. "Professori!" Luigi the butcher was in his bloodied apron, heaving boxes into the back of a van. "Are you back in Montreal?"

"Just visiting. I'm on my way to Toronto right now."

"And you no even come say hello."

"I did. You weren't there. Say hello to Tony and Vito for me."

Up ahead, I spotted two wavering ink blots in the sunlight. It was Kyra Fotoula and Kyra Despina. I put on my neighbourly smile.

"*Yiássou* Aleko."

"Where are you going with those bags?"

They came to a stop, so I had to pause. "I have to go back to Toronto."

"I thought you were here for the summer."

"Something came up."

"And mamá?"

"I have no choice."

"The poor thing. How happy she was to have you back. It was all she could talk about. Oh my, you should have seen her."

"I'll be back soon."

"This time for good, I hope."

"We'll see."

"You can't leave mamá alone."

"Keep well," I said, pulling away.

"Go to the good."

"To the good."

Continuing up Fairmount, I imagined their talk. What a nice boy. So polite, so dedicated. But unlucky. What a shame, a nice boy like that a yerontopalíkaro. Well, what can you expect, with that poor mother? She's lucky to have a boy like that.

I caught the next train to Toronto and arrived as a baseball game was letting out. Union Station was a sea of blue and white, adult men and women dressed in Blue Jays caps and jerseys. They roamed in packs, shouting, pumping their fists. There were more crowds outside, chanting slogans at the passing cars. Drivers honked back, including my own cabbie. I was channelling Pascal again. Who were these people? What was I doing here? How did I end up in this place? Thinking about the empty house awaiting me, I felt sick to my stomach. Perhaps I should call someone. But almost everyone I knew in Toronto was a friend of Laura's.

I checked my voicemail the moment I got in and was startled to find no messages. I was sure there would be several, begging me to come home. But there was not even a hangup. This was unnerving. But I wasn't going to call. Let her stew. She needed to believe I had meant what I said. As I unpacked, I kept listening for the phone to ring, staring at it, *willing* it to ring. In bed, I listened. I barely slept. In the morning, I checked my voicemail even though I knew there would be nothing. This was not like her.

Going out, I picked up the *Star* and *Now* and went to a café. I ordered a coffee and went through the listings for shared accommodations. Things hadn't improved. I jotted down some prospects and moved on to another place for lunch. Needing a distraction, I went to the movies. I sat through two films, seeing little of either, the images on the screen eclipsed by those playing relentlessly in my head. On my way home, I stopped at a payphone and found my voicemail still blank. Again that night I couldn't sleep. I also had to take some Imodium I found in Laura's medicine cabinet.

The next day I visited a couple of boarding houses so awful I sank further into despair. In the evening, I tried to work at Robarts Library, but I could barely stay focused the length of a sentence. The morning after that, I saw more apartments, and in the evening more movies.

On Thursday I jumped at the hiccup ring of a long-distance call. I stood by the phone and let it go three times before answering. The voice was my uncle's. He was phoning from the Victoria Hospital. My mother was dead. He had found her that morning on our kitchen floor. She had taken an overdose of pills. He would have tried me at this number earlier, but he didn't know I was in Toronto, and he'd been tangled up with police and medical staff. What was I doing in Toronto, anyway? He had tried me here out of sheer desperation. I told him there had been urgent business at school. I said I would get a flight out that night. He gave me the names of some people I might need to contact. One was a police sergeant. He ended the call with unnerving abruptness.

Even before I'd hung up, a sense of unreality descended upon me. I felt in a kind of dream state and literally kept hoping I might wake up and find myself in bed. The lack of sleep didn't help. I could imagine my mother doing all kinds of rash and unpredictable things, but this had never been one of them. I would have thought she was incapable of taking her own life. For my mother, there was no graver sin, no greater effrontery before our Maker. I knew this because she had told me. She believed we did not have title to our existence: it was ours on loan, a gift from God, and therefore only He had the authority to rescind it. Our duty was to endure. No matter how bad things might get, to give up on the effort was a mortal sin. Suffering was a test. Anyway, life had dealt her far worse than this. What was this stupid squabble compared to what she had suffered in the past? With this one senseless, implausible act, she had overturned the prevailing order and rendered the universe unintelligible. If even such certainties were illusory, what was there to stand on? Could there be a mistake? An administrative error? Had my uncle been misinformed? Was it possible he was lying? Was this a ruse, something concocted between him and my mother to get me back to Montreal? This was easier to believe than that my mother had killed herself.

I flew to Montreal that evening. I'd reloaded my large suitcase, again packing my books and notes. I thought they might help me retain my sanity. Making my way up St. Urbain Street, I lifted the suitcase to silence its wheels. The street was dead quiet and I didn't want to draw attention to myself. In my youth, it would have been hopping at this hour, full of children and teenagers, in the yards and on the balconies, men in their undershirts smoking cigarettes and drinking beer, women in dusters and slippers talking and laughing across the railings. Now there wasn't a person in sight, not a sound apart from the traffic. For which I was grateful.

I glanced up at the windows, wondering what the neighbours had heard, what they had seen. In the past, news like this would have been all over the neighbourhood by now. The windows of our place were dark, but I climbed the stairs as quietly as I could. Gently setting down my suitcase, I envisioned the empty apartment, the empty bedroom, the empty bed. I tried to imagine the kitchen. What state would it be in? My uncle said he'd found her in a pool of urine and vomit.

I couldn't face it. I turned and went back down the stairs. I walked to Fairmount and then over to Park Avenue. I went to the closest hotel I knew of, a fleabag near Mont Royal. There was a room available. Dank and dingy, it was preferable to the haunted house on St. Urbain. Collapsing on the bed, I began sobbing again. I had slept so little the last few days that I quickly fell unconscious, waking up with a start to hoots and bursting bottles at three in the morning. Somehow I kept full consciousness at bay, remaining for the next few hours in a kind of liminal state, a hypnagogic hag-ridden purgatory of baiting demons and phantasms that left me anything but rested when I dragged myself out of bed around seven.

I looked at the names and numbers my uncle had given me. Ever since his call, I'd been fretting about what the police might know or suspect. What would he have told them? His call had been short and uninformative, but his very reticence suggested he was keeping something from me. Had he spoken with my mother since my departure? She called him every day. What would she have told him? But he'd had no idea I was in Toronto. It would have been like her to speak with him yet say nothing. She was not one to air her dirty laundry. Still, the police were involved. I assumed they'd been to the house. Had they found clues? Had my mother left a note? Wouldn't my uncle have mentioned that? Maybe that was one of the things he hadn't disclosed. Yet again I went over events, trying to recall every detail, every word and blow. But so much was a blur. Could there have been marks or bruises on her? Had the neighbours heard? Were they home? Had they spoken with the police? What questions might the police put to me? Should I tell them what happened? How could I account for my return to Toronto? But you told your uncle you would be in Montreal for the summer. Why did you leave so suddenly? How did you travel? When did you buy your ticket? Why didn't you call home? Your uncle tells us you speak with your mother every day.

I was panicking. Was I criminally liable? Could this be pinned on me? By the time I checked out of the hotel, I was in a frenzy. Now I was anxious to see the apartment. I should not give the police more cause for suspicion. If they were to question me, I should not let on that I hadn't been to the apartment. Would they understand my reasons for spending the night at a hotel? Maybe. But better that I not have to provide such details.

I went to my room first and sat on my bed to collect myself. It was ten minutes before I made it to the kitchen. Passing my mother's bedroom, I glanced in. The bed was made up. No doubt my uncle's doing. The bed was rarely made at any hour, unless we were expecting visitors. My uncle had said he'd found her in her nightgown, but that didn't signify anything. She could spend entire days in her nightgown.

To my relief, the kitchen was in its usual state. The table was a few inches closer to the counter than normal, and next to the washing machine stood the mop and bucket. Otherwise I saw nothing out of the ordinary. I returned the mop and bucket to the shed and examined the bathroom. Here too I was spared any grisly surprises. I went to the bedroom and looked in from the doorway. The room had barely changed since my uncle was still living with us. On the vanity were still many of my aunt's discarded gimcracks and personal belongings—her combs and brushes, the cracked mirror, the green terra cotta atomizer with tasselled pump ball, the music box, the Jergens milk-glass hand-lotion dispenser, empty since the mid-seventies but preserved from the trashcan because of its decorative appearance, and more. My mother's main contribution to the room was the shrine of icons and crucifixes that covered both walls of one corner. But it was the very ordinariness and unruffled sameness of the room that made it so hard to bear, its bland indifference to its sudden disoccupancy. In the bed's headboard cabinet stood my mother's water glass, a quondam mustard jar now half-full and lidded, as always, by a cork coaster. The mere sight of it sent me into shivers of tears. I could barely look inside the closet, shutting the door as soon as I'd opened it. The scents were unendurable. I would have to confront and sort through this bleak residuum, endure its effusions and emanations, but I wasn't ready. Would I ever be?

I lay on the sofa and ran through my story again. I went over the facts, all the foreseeable questions. I knew I must stick as close to the truth as possible. I had nothing to hide, I had done nothing wrong. I looked over my uncle's list of numbers. I decided I would not call the police. Let them call me. Instead, I dialled the hospital. I was shunted from one extension to another, speaking to four different people, the last telling me that I should drop by the hospital Monday morning to pick up some documents and my mother's personal effects. I was asked what sort of service the family was planning and advised to arrange with a funeral home for timely delivery of the body. When I hung up, I felt a little calmer. Then I remembered I still hadn't called my uncle. I went over my story one more time.

My aunt answered. She asked where I was.

"I'm at the house. I'm here in Montreal."

"Tasso's at the store." There was a long, ambiguous silence. "What happened, Alex?" she said in an unencouraging tone.

"I was hoping you could tell *me*."

There was another long silence. "I only know what your uncle told me." I waited.

"And what was that?" I asked.

"Why were you in Toronto?"

"Things came up at school. There was an announcement for a teaching job in the fall, and I had to meet with some people and sign papers, which had to be done right away in person."

I heard my aunt sigh. "Well...as I said...your uncle's not here. If you want, you can try him at the store. Though...I don't know...maybe that's not such a good idea."

"Why not?"

"No, never mind. Call him."

"Why did you say it's not a good idea?"

"No reason. Go ahead, call him."

When I dialled the Galaxy, my uncle asked where I was and gave me another number. He wanted me to call him on his cell phone, I assumed for privacy.

From his cell, he asked, "When did you get in?"

"Last night. Late."

"And what's going on? What's happened?" Behind his voice was a dim hum, and both kept coming in and out. When he stopped speaking, it sounded as though the signal had dropped.

"I spoke with the hospital and they told me to come by on Monday. This afternoon I'm going by Stamatides."

I listened. The line sounded dead. "Hello?" I said.

"I'm here." I waited. "Can you explain to me what happened?"

My ears throbbed. "With what?"

"Why were you in Toronto?"

"I had to go back to take care of some things for work for September. I had to do some paperwork and an interview for a teaching job. It all came up last minute."

"And why didn't you call home?"

I paused. "What do you mean?"

"Why didn't you call home? From Toronto?"

How would my uncle know whether I had called home or not?

"The police told me your mother had been lying dead for two days."

My blood froze. He hadn't mentioned this before.

"I was so busy," I said. "I called but there was no answer and I assumed she was out. And I was so busy...I didn't call again."

"The two of you spoke every day."

"No, not every day," I lied. There was a long silence. Again the line seemed to have gone dead. "Hello?"

"You told me you were going to be in Montreal for the summer."

"Yes...but as I just explained...I had to go back without warning. The job offer came up suddenly."

"Alex, I don't understand how your mother could lie dead on the kitchen floor for over two days. This is what I keep asking myself."

"What do you mean? What are you asking yourself?"

There was no answer.

"Hello?"

"Yes."

"As I said, I called, but she didn't answer. Which happens. And I was in a such a rush to get things done so I could get back, and which she knew, right? She knew I was coming back, so I didn't feel any urgency to call."

"I don't know," my uncle muttered. "I've been trying to make sense of..." The line was breaking up again. "And I have to...I don't...I don't understand."

"I don't know what to tell you." I scoured my brain for reassuring words. "How do you think *I* feel? I don't understand it either. I had hoped *you* would have some answers."

The reception seemed to have dropped out again.

"Hello?"

This time there was no answer. I returned the phone to its cradle and waited but he didn't call back. I assumed he'd hung up. Perhaps he'd said goodbye and I hadn't heard him.

For the next few days, I remained in a kind of fugue state. I went by Stamatides and Ouellette to make arrangements and pick out a casket. Monday afternoon I went to the hospital, where there were no nasty surprises. An administrator went over some records and documents with me and provided more details about my mother's death.

The viewing at Stamatides was scheduled for Thursday. As I expected, there was not much of a turnout. My aunt and uncle were there, along with my cousins and their husbands. Greeting me with a sombre, silent handshake, my uncle avoided me the rest of the evening. Most of my friends came, as did some of the women from church. There were a few people I didn't recognize who said they had known my parents before I was born. They told me stories I'd never heard. Some of the factory women showed up. I hadn't seen them since I was eight or nine but I recognized them even with time's ravages. Everyone said nice things and treated me with due sympathy, yet I couldn't stop wondering what they were thinking, what rumours were going around. I was tempted to ask Mimi and Terry what they'd heard, but I didn't dare. When, late in the evening, our upstairs and downstairs neighbours arrived, I felt a mild panic. But if they'd heard or suspected anything, they didn't let on. Their condolences seemed sincere.

I couldn't predict whether my father would come. He didn't. I felt relieved, but I was also furious. What a thoughtless, selfish boor! I thought I might see him at the funeral, but he didn't attend that either. There were fifteen people. The weather was beautiful, making the ceremony feel even smaller and sadder. Reluctantly, I had decided to skip the *makaría*, the mercy meal that traditionally follows the burial. I feared my aunt and uncle would protest, but neither said a word. They probably didn't wish to prolong the proceedings any more than I did.

That evening I had dinner with Perry. It was his idea and I was grateful. His company over the last few days had brought home to me what friendship was about, and how much I had undervalued ours. He'd suggested Schwartz's, but there was a huge lineup. Lately there was a lineup outside Schwartz's from morning till night. I assumed it was featured in every travel guide to the city. The people in line looked like tourists. All the city's historic and iconic restaurants and bars were turning into simulacra of themselves. The Main, across the street, was also crowded, but there was a table near the entrance. The city was buzzing in the summer heat. There we all were, the living, going on with our lives, eating, drinking, laughing, planning, the removal of one among us having made no dent.

Perry protested when I ordered latkes. "What's the matter with you? Have a steak. Have the smoked meat." He was treating. "Give him a rib steak," he said to the waitress.

"No, don't do that," I said. I hated when Greeks pushed food on you. It was a mark of our famous hospitality, but there was also something aggressive and controlling in it. "I'm going to have the latkes." I said that I didn't have much of an appetite, which was true. But it was one of my mother's tenets that one must not eat meat or fish for forty days after the death of someone close. I wasn't going to ask Perry if he was familiar with this practice. My mother's take was that if you ate meat during this period, you were consuming the flesh of the deceased. Not that I believed this. Nonetheless, I knew that for the next forty days I would not be having any meat. The thought made me nauseous.

"My uncle's acting funny," I told Perry after the waitress left. "I think he holds me responsible."

"For what?"

"My mother."

"That's ridiculous. Why would he hold you responsible?"

"He thinks I abandoned her. And that's why she tried to kill herself."

Perry grimaced. "That's ridiculous. You had a fight. Jesus. If my parents went and killed themselves every time there was a fight in my house.... What you did was the best thing under the circumstances." Perry had an imperfect understanding of what had happened. I hadn't gone into all the details. "He's just angry," he said. "He's grieving. He lost his sister. It's one of the stages, anger. It's one of the first. It has nothing to do with you."

"Except that I *did* abandon her."

"You did not *abandon* her. And why do you keep saying *tried* to kill herself? You said it earlier too. She *tried* to kill herself."

I gazed at him.

"What?" he said.

"If I tell you something, you have to promise to keep it to yourself."

"Yeah, of course."

"You can't even tell your parents. Nobody. Not even my uncle knows what I'm about to tell you."

"Come on, man. You know me. What is it?"

"My mother didn't die from an overdose. She didn't die from the pills."

"So how did she then?"

It was so ludicrous I was reluctant to put it into words. I feared it would trivialize her death. The pills my mother had taken could not have killed her. But they had probably made her nauseous, and, according to the medical examiner's report, she had choked on her vomit. My mother died like a rock star. It was too grotesque. But I felt a need to talk about it.

"They think really it was just a cry for help," I said after explaining it all to Perry. "She never actually intended to kill herself."

"Who's *they*?"

"The doctors. The medical examiner. I don't know. Look, this is what the woman at the hospital told me."

"Like your mother knew what was in those pills."

"Apparently she had all these sedatives, but instead she took a mix of stuff that would not have killed her."

"And your mother has a degree in pharmacology?"

There was a complicating factor, which I didn't mention. Reviewing my mother's medical records, I had discovered that a couple of months earlier she'd been put on Prozac. I'd known nothing about this and didn't know what to make of it now. The drug and its alleged connection to suicide had been much in the news, and knowing Perry's attitude to doctors and big pharma, I decided not to go into the matter. He would have badgered me to launch a lawsuit or something, and I wasn't in the mood to argue.

The next day I tried my uncle's cell several times, but there was no answer. I called his home number and got my aunt.

"I don't know what's up with him. He's upset right now."

"Is he at work?"

"Yes, but it's better you don't call him just now. He's being irrational. He's probably not answering because he knows he's being irrational and doesn't trust himself. Give it time. He'll soften up with time."

"Soften up about what? What's he being irrational about?"

"I don't know. You have to ask *him*."

"But how can I do that if he won't talk to me?"

"You have to give him some time. That's how he is."

"But I need to talk to him. There's all these things I need to take care of right away. Like the apartment."

"What about it?"

"Well, I can't keep it."

I was hoping to clear out the place before the end of summer. Tenants were required to give at least three months' notice before expiration of their lease, but my mother didn't have a lease, and I didn't know how my uncle would feel about my giving up the apartment at the end of August. In Quebec, the vast majority of leases expired at the end of June, and he might resent having to look for a tenant outside the standard period. My aunt couldn't answer my questions and said she would get back to me.

I called her again two days later. She'd spoken with my uncle and said I was free to do whatever I wanted.

"You know most of the things in the place are still yours," I said. "My mother didn't throw away anything. Even some of the little figurines that fell and broke, she glued them together. Do you want anything?"

"God forfend!"

"Do you want to come by and have a look?"

"No, no! I don't want any of that stuff. That's not ours anymore."

"Okay, but just so you know, I'm probably going to throw most of the things out or give them away."

"Can't you sell them?"

"I don't know. But, whatever I do, I'm not going to be keeping much."

"Aren't you coming back to Montreal?"

"You mean for good?"

"Yes, for good. What are you going to do, live in Toronto?"

"I don't know what the future holds."

"What about your father?"

My aunt and uncle knew nothing about how things stood between me and my father. "He'll be fine," I said.

"You're going to leave him here alone?"

"He can take care of himself."

I had so much to do, yet for the next three days I did nothing. Unable to stay in the apartment, I walked the streets or lounged in cafés or theatres. I wished I could hire someone to empty the place. I dreaded having to sort through its contents. All my life I'd anticipated this moment. As a boy, I would lie in bed imagining my parents' deaths, sometimes driving myself to tears. My own death scared me less. It seemed more abstract. In recent years, I would still think of my parents' deaths, but now almost longingly. It felt despicable, but there was no denying it. Contemplating their absence, I would feel my being expand wide as the world itself, the walls around me dissolving. It felt like freedom. Yet now that my mother was gone, I felt destitute and unmoored. It was I who was dissolving. Walking the streets, I was assailed by memories everywhere, but they didn't feel like mine. It was as though I were recalling someone else's life. Was that really me? Did those things really happen? The city itself seemed unreal and remote, as though it might be a hologram. What did I have to do with this place, these people? I was the ghost in a haunted house. I might lift off the ground, like a helium balloon unloosed from the fist of a five-year-old, but I was both the balloon and the five-year-old, lungs primed for a crying fit. I roamed the streets like an errant dog dragging its leash. My mother would say, "I can endure anything but loneliness. I'll take whatever life throws at me as long as I'm not alone." Now I understood what she meant. "Loneliness the murderess," she would say.

My thoughts kept returning to Laura. She would be back from France by now, but I hadn't heard from her. I wasn't sure where we stood. But I didn't have the strength for another showdown, another loss. I needed understanding and sympathy, someone to listen to me. I couldn't bear Laura being against me at this moment. I needed her. I needed her tenderness and acceptance. Whatever had happened between us, whatever decision she may have made, I had to get back to Toronto as soon as possible.

9

My father has been moved again. Finding his bed unoccupied and stripped, I make enquiries at the nurses station, where I learn he has been transferred to another wing. Tracking him down, I'm surprised to see him in a wheelchair. He's gazing out the window, his back to me. There are three other patients in the room, elderly men. Two are sleeping. One is sitting up in bed and watches me suspiciously as I cross the room. My father keeps staring out the window even after I greet him. I repeat my kaliméra more loudly and there's a few seconds' lag before he turns toward me. Without a word or a sign of recognition, he turns back toward the window. The doctors assure me he knows who I am. I glance outside to see what he might be looking at, but there's nothing there—a parking lot four storeys down, some nondescript buildings the other side, a movement of traffic visible through a narrow gap.

"How did you get in the chair? Did you do it yourself?"

I get no answer.

"It's a beautiful day."

Continuing silence. I don't know what else to say. It seems pointless, even with all the professional assurances it isn't. I've been urged to engage him in conversation, force him to listen, to think, recall, concentrate. Even if he doesn't respond, there's value in it. It helps with his recovery. So I'm told.

"Did you have breakfast?" I give him time. I repeat the question and am heartened by a nod. "What did you have?"

His hand twitches in what appears to be a dismissive gesture. I wait, hoping he might speak. His mouth is collapsed, undentured, his chin jutting up near his nose. I've been instructed to make sure he's always got his teeth in, but I lost that battle ages ago. I turn to lean against the window ledge and see the patient in bed still staring at me.

I gaze down at my father. "What did you have for breakfast?" I ask again. I notice his nose hairs need trimming, and there's some crusted goop in the corner of one eye. "Is the food good here?"

I've asked him about the food before, but I don't know what else to say. He gives me a look that, under different circumstances, I would interpret as sarcasm. Now I don't know what it means. It's not much different from any of his other looks. It's possible he didn't even hear or understand me.

I consider telling him about Leftheris Asikis and Stelios Maniatis. The two died, apparently just a day apart, while I was in Greece. Perry learned about it a couple of days ago when he bumped into Euripides at Provigo. Euripides doesn't look so good himself, Perry said. Apart from Dzonakis, we hardly see any of the old guys. Even the ones who are still alive stopped coming by the Symposium ages ago. Many have left the area and are living with their kids in the suburbs. Walking the neighbourhood these days, I hardly recognize anyone, unless they're our customers. It's all poodles now. This doesn't feel like home anymore. I've begun to give serious thought to selling Perry my share of the business and leaving the city. But what would I do? Where would I go? And what would I do about my father? I fantasize about going back to university, maybe moving to a college town with cheap rents, living in a studio apartment, earning money as a teaching assistant or some such thing. I have some ideas about what I would study.

Watching my father, I come close to blurting out the news about Leftheris and Stelios, just to break the silence. But I stop myself. What would be the point? He'll learn about them from Dzonakis. Which reminds me, I should call him. I haven't seen Dzonakis since I got back from Greece and I'm eager to tell him about the trip.

I can't believe I was in Greece a week ago. Actually, I can't believe the trip lasted as long as it did. I was sure I'd be summoned back far sooner. Every day I expected a call from Perry, but it only came a few days before I was set to return. The doctors were saying it didn't look like my father was going to make it. But yet again he would prove the experts wrong. I was the only one who wasn't surprised. I'm convinced he's made it his mission not to go until I do; the two of us will end our days together in the same nursing home. Selfishly, I try to see this latest setback as a blessing: if he won't talk to me, then he can't badger and bully me, he can't pry into my affairs. But now he gets to me with his silence, which feels wilful and punitive. It's his new way of thwarting and tormenting me. The social worker suggested he's ashamed and frightened and that he'll grow more vocal with time, that I need to be patient. This is what everybody tells me: Be patient. They say I must engage him and encourage him. But how can I do that when he refuses to talk to me? He will barely *look* at me.

Maybe his notebooks would engage him. Even after he'd abandoned the roulette wheel because of his deteriorating motor skills, he continued to peruse his notebooks, examining the wavering columns of figures on each page like an archaeologist deciphering the carvings on some ancient tablet. What was so fascinating? What memories and meanings were contained in those random ciphers? Was he still working on a system? I wondered whether he would even recognize the notebooks now, whether their contents held any significance. I'm still not clear on the state of his memory and reasoning. I was told he will not recover sufficiently to return to his old room. His floor at St. Paul's isn't equipped for the level of care he'll need. I put in a request to have him transferred, but it's unlikely a space will be found any time soon. With the help of the social worker, I've been shopping around for a new place. It's a dismal, exhausting undertaking.

"When did they move you here?" I ask. "Do you remember? Was it this morning?"

He looks at me as though he doesn't understand the question.

"You know you're in a different part of the hospital from yesterday. You were in a different room. Do you remember that?"

He gazes down at the floor, as if he's thinking or trying to recall.

"Did anyone say anything to you about why they moved you?"

He glances out the window, steadfast in his silence. My hands are balled into tight fists. "I'm going to go talk to someone," I say with forced calm, "find out what's been happening. Are you all right here? Do you want me to move you?"

He keeps staring out the window. I might as well be talking to a mannequin.

"Do you want me to get you anything?"

To my astonishment, he shakes his head. This alone loosens the tension in my arms and shoulders.

"You sure? A drink?"

He shakes his head again. This is progress. Maybe the doctors and social worker are right.

"I'll be back in a minute."

At the desk, I learn we are in the stroke rehabilitation unit. My father was in the previous room because of a shortage of beds. I am told he's been assigned a speech-language therapist and that she wishes to meet. My father has been put on a rigorous recovery regimen and my support is crucial. I tell the woman how my father has dealt with therapy and therapists in the past and how he currently refuses to talk to me. She says it's still early days. These things take time and can change from moment to moment, and sometimes suddenly and surprisingly. I need to be patient. There are also special techniques and strategies that facilitate interaction and recovery, which is one of the things the speech therapist wishes to speak about. When would I be available for an appointment?

I leave the desk feeling oddly annoyed. Why does everyone assume they can count on my support and participation? Why am I expected to help in my father's rehabilitation when he won't make any effort himself? I feel guilty about feeling this way, but what support and participation did I ever get? What appreciation or gratitude?

But I mustn't fall into this sort of "self-talk." Things without remedy should be without regard. You're not a child anymore, I tell myself. And he's not your father. He's just a person, a human being in need. I must be compassionate but detached. The trick now is to forget. There's no other way. What's gone and what's past help should be past grief. Forget the past, forget that he's your father. He's just a person like other people. Be kind, be kind, be kind...

A passing orderly looks at me. I'm talking to myself again.

He never said so explicitly, but I knew my father didn't want me to go to Greece. From the moment I announced my plans, he began to sulk. I'd thought he would be pleased. His son was finally visiting his fabled homeland. But he acted as though I were abandoning him. I can't help feeling that his silence now is his way of punishing me. "It's only for a month," I'd explained. "And I'll have my phone. You can call whenever you want." It was like dealing with my mother all over again.

Given how all my past travel schemes had worked out, I had no confidence this time would be any different. Even as I boarded the plane, I expected to be called back. Something would go wrong and keep me grounded. When the plane took off, I stared out the window in disbelief. I marvelled at the blasé attitudes of the other passengers. Most were staring at their devices or reading. Some glanced out the window indifferently. I wanted to ape their nonchalance, yet for the first hour or two I could barely pull my face out of my porthole. Some of the noises and movements on takeoff spooked me, and the sight of the ground dropping away was both exhilarating and nerve-wracking. I couldn't believe how quickly we attained the clouds. They weren't nearly as high as they appeared from the ground. Indeed, they seemed further away below me than they did overhead. According to the pamphlet in the seat pocket, the plane had a cruising speed of 540 miles an hour, but when you weren't looking out the window you could barely tell it was moving. Now and then the plane would drop suddenly or shake and I would grip the armrests and scan the faces around me for clues to the seriousness of the situation. But no one else ever looked concerned. Everyone kept staring at their screens and magazines, and the flight attendants went about their business unperturbed. On our descent into Heathrow, there were more disturbing noises and some alarming activity on the wing that it took me a moment to realize was a routine part of the plane's landing functions.

I spent three days each in London, Paris, and Rome and was surprised by how smoothly everything went. Getting from place to place, finding my way around, dealing with locals—it was all so much easier than I had expected. It helped that in two of the three cities I spoke the language. In Athens it felt surreal to be surrounded by Greeks. They were everywhere—in the airport, on the metro, the buses, the streets. Even the police were Greek. But these Greeks were home-grown, locally sourced. Greeks who weren't immigrants. This took some getting used to. People seemed simultaneously familiar and alien. It was strange to be immersed in the language, to hear it on PA systems, televisions, radios. It covered the land-scape. It was on the street signs, billboards, newspapers. There was Greek graffiti—towering, elaborate illustrations and murals, crude drawings, pol-itical symbols and insignia, slogans, curses, threats. *Life to us, death to the IMF. Fear feeds fascism. Greece cannot be killed.*

From the moment I arrived in Athens, I felt as though I'd left Europe, or was somewhere on its margins. The city was a reminder that the dis-tance between East and West was not a matter of mere meridians and that the past is more fractured and unintelligible than we admit. You were never quite sure where you were in Athens. Where in London and Paris you had a sense, or illusion, of continuity and evolution, each epoch or stratum of the city's history lying atop the other like sedimentary rock, in Athens there was only the crumbling luminous ancient past and the grimy noisy chaotic present, the vast space in between filled by myth, fantasy, and confusion. At the Byzantine and Christian Museum, I confronted yet again the conundrum of Byzantium. All my life I'd been hearing about the Byzantines, yet I never understood who they were. According to my father, we could trace our own lineage back to Byzantine nobility, the Doukas name having belonged to emperors and military leaders directly descended from Constantine. But who was Constantine? Was he a Greek? He called himself Emperor of Rome. Recently I had read somewhere that the Byzantines would not have known of a Byzantine Empire, the term having only been invented in the sixteenth century. They thought of them-selves as Romans. Yet they were also Christians. And they spoke Greek— or some of them did, anyway. So what were they? What makes a people? What makes an ethnos? What is the difference between the two?

Athens turned out to be even uglier and shabbier than I'd expected. Athenians kept assuring me that it hadn't always been this bad, the city wasn't always so grim and run-down. I should have seen it just a few years earlier, during the Olympics, or when Greece won the European Cup. People spoke of these recent events as if they belonged to a remote golden age. This was the reverse of what I was used to. The usual habit was to recall the ancient past as if it were yesterday.

Yet, even with all its warts and bruises, the city could move me, some-times in unexpected ways. My first evening, searching the streets for a place to eat, I came upon a row of restaurants offering a distant view of the Acropolis and, taking a seat at one of the outdoor tables, I gazed at the Parthenon glowing ethereally against the reddening sky. Barely aware of the music coming over the outdoor speakers, I suddenly recognized the opening *taxími* of a Tsitsanis song and felt a pressure of tears. That same moment, a waiter approached with a menu, and as he handed it to me, he hesitated, as if about to ask whether I was all right. But then he turned and retreated without a word. That evening I might have been inclined to attribute my behaviour to a lack of sleep, but such emotional outbursts would punctuate the rest of the trip, often coming at the most surprising and inopportune moments. It was astonishing what trifles could set me off—the plucking of a bouzouki, the raspy wail of an old *rebéti*, the smells from a kitchen, a trinket in a souvenir shop. The crassest piece of kitsch could send me into convulsions of mawkishness. I had not realized just how gooey a sentimentalist I was.

In public, I would eavesdrop on conversations, often inadvertently. As I lacked typically Greek features and dressed like a tourist (T-shirt, cargo shorts, knapsack), the locals assumed I was a foreigner and would freely discuss the most personal matters in my proximity. When I told people of my background, they reacted with surprise and wanted to know more. Everywhere I went, I struck up conversations with strangers. It was so much easier to approach people here than in Canada. Was the difference in them or in me? I gathered the locals took a dim view of us heterochthonous hyphenated types. They regarded us as dull and uninformed money-grubbers. And they could be blunt about it. The Greeks here were no less rude or aggressive than the ones back home. One Athens taxi driver said to me, "I read in the paper that in America they're putting out books that say the Greeks didn't invent the alphabet. Is this true?" Glancing at me in his rear-view mirror, he gave me no chance to respond. "They're saying the gods of Olympus came from Egypt or Africa or somewhere. Do you know about any of this?" He leaned to one side to get a better look at me. Outside, sooty bone-coloured Athens seethed under the Attic sun, the streets a concerto grosso of squawking klaxons, squealing tires, growling engines. A mass protest had snarled traffic worse than usual, and there were distant shouts and drumbeats. On the car radio, a caller on a phone-in show was complaining about the salaries of soccer players. My cabbie shouted over him: "They're now saying it wasn't

Pythagoras who invented the Pythagorean theorem but the Babylonians, and that the Babylonians also invented astronomy." He glared at me in the mirror as if I myself had said these things. "You see what we're up against? They have it in for us and will get us any way they can. You know they want our islands now? Soon they'll want the Parthenon. Or what's left of it. We used to think that, no matter what happens to us, no matter how poor we might be, we have our history. The fact is we Greeks have the most glorious history of any nation, and that's something no one can take from us. But now—" He pushed on his horn. "Now they want that too. They want to take it or to wipe it out. Because they resent our glory. They took our marbles, they took our resources, our money, our freedom, now they want to take away our past. They say we're lazy and backward, but I ask you: What would the world be without us? What would the world be without the Greeks?" I nodded keenly so that he would return his attention to the road. "Without us, they'd still be swinging in the trees."

I'd heard such talk all my life and I didn't react well to it. I tended to adopt the role of a modern-day Jakob Fallmerayer, asking, "Who exactly do you mean by the Greeks?" "Who is us?" I would mention the Minoans and Phoenicians, talk about Mohenjo-Daro, Confucius, the Ramayana. Depending on how cocky I was feeling, I might suggest that, if the classical legacy survived today, it was to be found in the US and Western Europe, that it was the British, Germans, French, and Americans who were its true heirs and custodians. What were we modern Greeks but the bastard spawn of the Ottomans, an invention of the Turks? We were squatters in a derelict castle strutting about in dead men's robes, who had about as much in common with Plato and Pericles as Hosni Mubarak did with Tutankhamen. These were the sort of things I would normally be tempted to say to someone like my cabbie. But these were not normal times. And I wasn't one to kick a people when they were down.

"And the Germans," the cabbie went on, "the Germans are the worst of all!" He shifted gears as I davened in the back seat. "The biggest hypocrites!" He swerved and leaned on his horn. "In the war...." He glared out his side window at a motorcyclist. "In the war, they plunder Europe, kill millions, and what happens? The people they tried to destroy help them back to their feet, forgive their debts, give them money and resources to rebuild. Which, don't get me wrong, I don't begrudge." He checked on me again in his mirror. "That was the right thing to do, the smart thing. That was when America was still smart. But you'd think they would have learned. You'd think they'd remember how they themselves were treated after the first war, how the French stomped on them, beat them to the ground, squeezed out every ounce of blood. Yet what are they doing now to us? It's exactly the same. And why? Because they know we're small and weak and we don't pose a threat. Even if we produced a Hitler, what could he do? What could a little Greek Hitler do? They don't fear us. So they stomp on us like roaches. Like the French did to them a hundred years ago. And what came of that? The bastards. But Greece will not be killed!" He twisted around to look at me. I stared out the windshield, jaw clenched. He faced forward just in time to hit the brakes and turn the wheel. "Greece will not be killed!" he hollered again as I uncurled myself.

I'd seen this slogan on walls, often in English. It appeared to be a wide-spread view that there was a death warrant out on the country, that the outside world had it in for Greece. There was nothing new in this. What had changed was that now I was sympathetic; I was on the Greeks' side. I had begun to share their anger and paranoia. Having sneered all my life at their persecutory obsessions, the talk of hidden agendas and secret machinations, I had begun to think they'd been right all along. Or was it that the world had caught up with their theories? If anything, things appeared to be even worse than they'd claimed. It worried me how far I'd come around to their way of thinking.

From Athens I travelled north toward my father's village, making stops in Delphi, Vergina, and Thessaloniki. On my second day in Thessaloniki, I strolled around Navarino Square, stopping in the afternoon at a relatively uncrowded café. I found a seat on the patio. At the table next to mine sat a heavyset man in a green polo shirt and blue jeans. It seemed Greek men never wore shorts, however hot the weather. As I sipped my coffee and read my book, the stranger kept glancing my way. Catching my eye, he said in accented English, "That is a rather provocative book to be reading publicly in these parts."

"Uh-oh," I said only half-mockingly. "You know this book?"

I wasn't sure how to interpret the stranger's tone. I was astonished, as well as a little disturbed, that he should have recognized the book in my hands. A mix of history and ethnography, it examined the political and

cultural tactics by which Greece had assimilated the heterogeneous popu-
lations of the northern territories it acquired after the war. When it came
out in the early nineties, the book had been roundly denounced in both
the Greek and diaspora press, and its author had received death threats.
Before leaving Montreal, I had wondered whether this was the sort of
reading I should be packing for where I was going, but given how many
years had passed since its publication and that my copy was the original
English version, I reckoned the risks were negligible. Besides, apart from
some academics and a few jingoistic sociopaths, how many Greeks would
have even heard of it?

"I have met the author in person," said my neighbour. "I saw her give a
talk in New York."

I nodded noncommittally. I wasn't sure I wanted this conversation to
continue.

"She's a very knowledgeable and intelligent woman."

"Oh?" I said, surprised by the remark.

"She's just wrong."

"Ah."

"You don't agree?"

"I don't know enough about the subject."

"Ah, please...don't hide behind false modesty."

"It's not false. I honestly know nothing. That's why I'm reading this."

I didn't know this man, but he made me nervous. With his grizzled
beard, long lank hair, and dark sunken eyes, he was the picture of the
Balkan intellectual. There seemed also something menacing about him.
Whatever his show of learnedness and civility, I didn't know his intentions, and these were tense times. According to news reports, random acts
of politically motivated violence were on the rise throughout the country.

"Even when she gets the facts right," said my neighbour, "she's wrong in
her premises."

I nodded silently. I was curious to hear more but thought it safer not to
pursue the subject.

"Have you spent much time in the US?" I asked.

"I have spent much time in many places. The US, the UK, France, Germany...most of Europe in fact. Australia. Africa."

I nodded, duly impressed. I wondered where my neighbour had learned his English. His accent was unmistakably Greek, but he also sounded vaguely British, like my father doing an imitation of Prince Charles.

"But you're from here?" I said.

"Literally," he replied. "I was born a few streets away." He turned in his seat and pointed. "Just behind that building. I still live in the house where I was born." He seemed proud of this fact. "And you?" he said, turning to face me again. "Where are you from? If I may ask."

"Canada. Montreal."

"Ah. I have spent some time there too. I like Montreal." He pronounced *Montreal* in the manner of my parents, the vowels more French than English and the *t* voiced like a *d*. "I have much respect for the Quebecois. I like their survival instinct. They are an example to the rest of us."

I must have betrayed my surprise.

"You don't think so? They will prevail, the Quebecois. What you have in Canada is an aberration. It can't last." He paused and watched a group of Chinese tourists going by. "One day the Quebecois will have their country," he said, turning again to me with a pointed look.

I didn't bite.

"You don't agree?"

"I don't know."

"Really? You have no opinion?"

"I try not to predict the future."

"But you live there. You must have a sense."

"Frankly, I don't know what's happening anywhere anymore. Actually, that's not true. I never understood. But I seem to be growing more confused as I get older."

"Oh?" he said, clearly intrigued. But I didn't go on. "Please," he said, "you must explain."

I remained silent, trying to get a read on his expression.

"Please," he said again, "I'm very curious. Truly."

"Well, it's just, since the financial collapse...I don't understand what's going on in the world. At first I didn't pay much attention. Being Canadian, names like Fannie Mae and Freddie Mac and Bear Stearns meant nothing to me. They sounded like cartoon characters. But then, with Lehman brothers and AIG, I began to take notice, I guess like everyone. And as the dominoes fell, I thought...Oh my god, this is it! This is the moment!

This is the moment I've been bracing for my whole life, the moment the historical materialists and Spenglerians and all the other doomsayers and millenarians have been warning about. This is when the crowds storm the barricades and the streets run with blood. This is when heads finally roll. And how could they not, given the obscene enormity of it? But every morning, I would go to my window, and I would be shocked to see everything looking normal. There they were, people on the street, going to work, shopping, sitting in cafés. There were the buses and taxis, and the electricity, the water in the pipes, the banks, the government. Everything running as usual. But how could this be? Where were the crowds, the pikes and guillotines? Here was all this shit coming down and yet, outside my window, everything continued as if nothing had happened."

My neighbour leaned in closer, a look of amused fascination on his face. Why was I opening up to this man? I didn't know who he was or what he was after. Why was I revealing myself to a stranger like a penitent at confession?

"But something *had* happened," I continued, "something momentous, unprecedented. Yet, somehow, against all logic, the commonwealth doth stand. But how is it being done? I follow the news, I listen to the experts, but I don't understand. I don't know who to believe. I regret I never studied economics. If I could do it all again, I'd become an economist. Marx and James Carvelle had it right. It's all about the economy. It's all about numbers. If you want to understand the world, if you want to understand the universe, you need to know numbers. You know how we keep being told we're living in a digital world? It's always been a digital world. It's digital in its very essence. Galileo said it over four hundred years ago: the language of the universe is mathematics."

"Pythagoras said it two thousand years before him."

"Fine. That underscores my point. Pythagoras was right. The universe subsists in numbers and code. The rulers of the world today are not the politicians. It's the numbers men. The accountants and engineers and scientists. These are the *real* rulers. Do you know that Wall Street now hires mathematicians and physicists to devise their strategies and algorithms?"

But my neighbour appeared to have stopped listening. He had his back to me and was waving a hand in an effort to get the waiter's attention. Hearing his name, the waiter came over and, bending his head, nodded while my neighbour whispered in his ear. When the waiter left, my neighbour turned to face me again.

"Please. You were saying."

"No," I replied, feeling exposed and ridiculous. "There's nothing else." What had got into me, ranting like that, revealing my foolishness to this person I'd just met?

"No, please," my neighbour said. "I find what you are saying profoundly fascinating." He clutched the back of one of the chairs at my table. "I trust you don't mind," he said, rising.

"Oh...no," I said, pushing back my chair and moving the table to make more room.

"I am very interested in this." He adjusted his chair to face me more squarely. "But I hope you will not take offense if I may point out to you a crucial error you are making."

"Just one?"

On closer view, he looked younger than I'd thought. The hair and beard were misleading and I now reckoned he was about my own age, maybe even a couple of years younger. "It's a very common error," he continued, "perhaps the defining error of our age. Like most people today, you are confusing truth and accuracy. But contrary to popular opinion, science does not offer truth. It does not even purport to offer truth. That is not the goal of science, and any scientist who tells you otherwise is not a true scientist. He is a charlatan." *Sarlatan* he pronounced it. "Science only gives us *accuracy*. Now, accuracy is extremely important. But it is not truth. And we have lost sight of this crucial difference. We have been persuaded, en masse, that truth exists in, as you say, numbers and code. This is the great modern myth. But it's ridiculous. I'm sorry. It is a lie, pure and simple. My friend, you should be *grateful* you never studied economics. They call it the dismal science, but it is really a pseudo-science. The economists are the biggest charlatans of all. They are quacks. Left, right, centre. Yet they have succeeded in fooling everyone. When Adam Smith was writing *The Wealth of Nations*, his subject was politics and moral philosophy. But then the economists came along and quantified all social relations and claimed they had created a science. If it wasn't quantifiable, it didn't count, pardon my pun. But this is a form of moral stupidity. When you reduce social relations to mathematical models, the result is bad politics. So that's the first thing, okay? Second...my friend...look around. Do you know where you are? Do you not see? Are the water and electricity running as usual here? Are the stores and restaurants running as usual? Are the hospitals running as usual? Do you think the banks and the government are running as usual? *Nothing* is running as usual. Here in Greece and in Europe the illusion is broken. The game is over. Maybe it continues outside of your window in Montreal, I don't know, but even there, don't worry...it's just..."

The waiter was approaching with a large tray loaded with food and drinks and, noticing him, my neighbour paused and shifted his seat.

"I hope you are hungry," he said as he helped the waiter unload the tray. "I took the liberty to order us some refreshments."

"You really shouldn't."

"Please, don't start with your American niceties," he said, arranging the plates and vessels on the table so that there was enough space for all of them. There were numerous mezéthes, a large bottle of water, some empty glasses, a tumbler of ice cubes, and a small bottle of ouzo. When the waiter left, my neighbour twisted off the cap. "Ice or no ice?"

"Ice."

"Me too," he said, pouring two glasses. He touched my glass with his. "To the future." He took a sip and sighed contentedly. "Please," he said, gesturing at the mezéthes.

"I will...thanks."

He sat back and for a lengthy interval seemed to be absorbed in the passing scene. The street was crowded and he gazed for a while at the passersby. Leaning forward, he surveyed the items on the table. He popped an olive into his mouth. "I was thinking of a movie," he said. "I think it's from the sixties. A movie called *Charlie*." *Tsarlie*. "Do you know this movie?"

"It's based on a book called *Flowers for Algernon*. We read it in school."

"What is it? Flowers...?"

"*Flowers for Algernon*."

"Algernon." *Aldzer known*. "Well, so you know the story. I believe that Greece is like Charlie. We had this period of...*flourishing*, you might say... but it was only the drugs. The easy credit and phony money. But that could only last so long, and then..." He snapped his fingers. "We are back to where we were. We are back to reality. It was like a dream. Like in that movie." He chewed on some sausage. "And the sad thing is we believed it. We all did. Even I believed it. For a few years, it looked like we had joined the modern world. But the fact is, the problem is not Greece. It never was. They say Greece is the sick man of Europe, but you know who is really the sick man of Europe? It is *Europe*. Europe is the sick man of Europe. It was sick from the day it was born. Some people knew this. Some people spoke up. But no one listened. The doctors, the experts, they told us, oh no, don't worry, everything is okay. The patient is healthy and strong. And we believed them. We *needed* to believe them. We were *desperate* to believe them. But, ever since, all we have been doing is managing the disease, confining the symptoms to individual parts of the body. A rash over here, a little bit of numbness there, some aches and pains, okay, but all the time the doctors, the experts—the numbers men, as you put it—they tell us everything is fine. The patient is healthy. Some of them are still saying this, except now no one believes them. Not even they believe themselves, I think, if they ever did. And I'm not just talking about economics, about the financial crisis. You see what is happening in places like Idomeni and Lesvos, and on the border just a few kilometres from here. And in Italy and Paris and the UK. How are we going to manage this? It is like the last days of Rome. The *Völkerwanderung*. You know this word? The period of the migrations I think you say in English. You know what this is?"

I took a moment to swallow some cheese. "If I hadn't before, I do now. It's not the first time I've heard this analogy since I got to Greece."

"Small peoples have long memories. And look around. Look where you are." My neighbour spread his arms out. "You know what all this is, I think, no?" He was referring to the crumbling monuments and antiquities that surrounded us, the vast brown pits of rubble and ruin that gave parts of the area the appearance of a bombed-out war zone.

"I have some idea," I said.

"The parallels are instructive," said my neighbour. After a sip of ouzo, he gave me a summary history of late antiquity. I couldn't count how many such impromptu lectures I'd been delivered since my arrival in Greece. This one was especially convoluted and esoteric, touching on the reforms of Diocletian, the incursions of the foederati, the collapse of the Tetrarchy, and the barbarian invasions of the fourth and fifth centuries. I had difficulty following parts of it, but I was happy to sit quietly and listen. I had slipped into a cheerful and receptive mood, partly no doubt because of the ouzo. I felt like a boy again, sitting with the men in Fletcher's Field.

When my neighbour was done, he seemed to expect a response. Rousing myself, I said, "I don't know. How long have we been hearing this whole decline-of-Rome thing? There was that movie in the eighties, *The Decline of the American Empire*." I felt groggy and was slurring my words a little. "But it goes back further. I've been hearing this narrative of decline my whole life."

"Maybe it's because it's been happening your whole life. You know how they say Rome was not built in a day? It also didn't fall in a day. It happened over decades, over centuries. People think the Vandals and Visigoths stormed in one evening and burned the place down, but it's a slow process. So, yes, it has been happening since probably even before you and I were born. But we have been too distracted by the bread and circuses. By the Olympics and European Cup, by the easy money and endless asset price inflation. But we need to remember that this is not just about economics. Marx was wrong about this. It doesn't all come down to economics. This was one of Marx's crucial failings, that he did not make sufficient allowance for human nature, for the needs of the soul. Marx said some important things about alienation, but he also left some things out."

My neighbour paused, as though he wished me to weigh in on this. But I remained silent. I'd found his reference to the "soul" unsettling. Was he some religious fundamentalist looking for recruits?

"I believe it was D.H. Lawrence who said the past is a foreign country—you must know this saying. But today I think the real tragedy, the bigger tragedy, is that it is the *present* that is the foreign country. Today, everywhere in the world, it is one's homeland that is the foreign country. People are alienated from their own times, from their homes and communities. We live in a perennial and constantly renewable now, a present cut off from any past. Homelessness is the destiny of the world. Everything is about novelty and innovation, about disruption and destruction—creative destruction of course. But no one ever asks what is being destroyed. Certainly not those making the profits. Because there are enormous profits to be made from the wreckage. So it is that in the last fifty years we have had more disruption and destruction than in the previous five hundred. For the first time in history, every generation is obliged to adapt to a world

unknown to the preceding one. Civilization itself has a built-in obsoles-
cence. Everything is disposable, to be replaced every few years, like a car or
a laptop. This is a form of systematized nihilism, no? Culture and tradition
are preserved nowadays only as the commodities of the tourism industry.
I'm sure you've seen it here in Greece—the dances and costumes and all
the other bullshit we bring out for the tourists, so that they can experience the real, the *authentic*, Greece, a Greece which does not exist except
in these stupid displays. But we are to *embrace* all this. We are to celebrate
it in the name of prosperity and democracy and freedom. It is amazing
how we accept these slogans as articles of faith, repeating them like the old
ladies in church, chanting the words with no understanding of what they
mean. Meanwhile, we have a left that has its head in cloudy abstractions
and fairy-tales that no one believes anymore, except the preachers, if even
them. The left is like the Americans, *les grand enfants*. It is only interested
in aerial campaigns. Though it claims to speak for the common man, it
does not want to listen to him. The left today will fight for the common
man as long as it doesn't have to mix with him. But this is trench warfare.
You have to put boots on the ground. But the left isn't interested in real
people. Because it's not interested in reality. And if we don't align our politics with reality, both will fail us horribly."

My neighbour gave me another of his inscrutable smiles. He was making me nervous again. I was also beginning to feel nauseous.

"But reality today, as you pointed out, has been reduced to numbers
and code. It is about algorithms and gene sequences and the S&P Index.
Everything comes down to the bottom line. But there are some things
you cannot put a price on. This is what your secular liberal cosmopolites
don't understand. There are some things that people will not give up for
any amount of money, even today. They will give up their lives first. Why
don't we just tear down the Parthenon, build some luxury condos, or a
mall? It's the perfect location. What a view! Or sell it to the Germans or
the Chinese. Let them run it. They will do a better job. But who would
dare to propose such a thing? And yet to point out these things today, the
persistence of the sacred and the tenacity of cultural memory, is to be a
reactionary. It is to be called a fascist. Am I right? Perhaps this is what you
are thinking, I don't know what you think. We have just met. But explain
to me why when a Navajo or a Chechen or an African protests about his

loss of culture and identity, liberals applaud. They make speeches about cultural genocide. But when a Greek or a Pole or a Serbian expresses the same concerns, he is a fascist. Ask our liberal crusaders how these groups fit into their 'white' postcolonial metanarrative, they have no clue what you're talking about. With all their shouting about historic injustices, they have zero understanding of history. And I love when you Americans preach to everyone about plurality and inclusivity. It's easy to keep your door unlocked when there is nothing inside to steal. But some of us have a legacy we value and wish to preserve. The idea that everything can be left to the open market is dangerous nonsense. Politics is not just about markets and efficiency, or even about what these days is called freedom. True freedom, genuine freedom, does not exist outside a collective social order. In English, you talk about a nation-state. In your language, it is literally in this word where nation and state coincide. But in Greek we don't have this conceptual problem, this self-division. We don't have these different words—nation and state—that we need to bring together to make a new word. Because they are *already* together in the concept of ethnos. The Greek does not distinguish between race, nation, people, nation-state, and so on. These divisions are an Anglo-Saxon invention, which they have tried to impose on everyone else, as though they are natural law.

"Oh, I know what you are thinking. You are thinking I am a nationalist, I am a jingoist, I am a fascist. I see it. Go ahead. Call me whatever you like. Call me a racist, call me a bigot, call me a fascist. But I deny it. I deny it categorically. Of course then you will deny my denial, and so on and so forth, and we will go on playing this game. Because you have been programmed. I'm sorry, I don't want to be rude, but that is the truth. You have been programmed to think in this narrow, utopian, and dangerous manner. You are blinded by superstitions. You see yourself as an enlightened thinker—open-minded, tolerant, pluralistic, inclusive. Yes? You are a good person, a rational person. And me, I am a narrow-minded, intolerant, reactionary bigot. Am I right? You can speak honestly. I will not be insulted. I have heard it all before. I am used to it."

I was feeling weary and unwell and wanted nothing more than to get into bed. I feared I might throw up. Was it the ouzo? I had been chugging it back and my neighbour was quick with refills. Might he have slipped me something?

"But you will say I am a fascist no matter what. You will say I am a fascist because I reject your secular pluralism and abstract universalism. How dare I? Such a rejection is the great blasphemy today. Lock him up! He has no right to speak such words in a free and democratic society. Take him away! Thus the empire of freedom spreads democracy and human rights at the point of a gun. Thus it rains bombs on Belgrade and Bosnia and Iraq, and renditions and assassinates all enemies of freedom. All in the name of democracy and human rights. But, oh no, I am the criminal. No matter how accurate or rational what I say is, because some fascists said it in the past, or say it even today, I am also ipso facto a fascist. But for goodness sake, we are thinking people. We must be able to think. We must be able to reason clearly and honestly and independently, without worrying about what people will think of us or what labels they will attach to us. Are we children? Believe me, I am no friend of the fascists. That is the truth. But I am prepared—indeed, I am *obliged*—to concede where they are correct. When we find truth, when it stares us in the face, does it matter where it comes from? This is the self-sabotage of the left. But I reject all these categories. They have become meaningless. We must liberate our thought from these confused labels and outmoded ways of thought. The fact, my friend, is that I am the *opposite* of a racist. You look at me...but yes!"

I had no sense of what "look" my neighbour was referring to; I was simply trying not to throw up.

"The *opposite*. I am for the freedom and self-determination of all the races of the world. I have no ill will against any nationality. I believe all peoples should be guaranteed the freedom to control their own destinies. So who is the real democrat? Who is the real pluralist, the true defender of diversity? Go today anywhere in the world and what do you see of our great transnational liberal utopia? It is a cultural and spiritual desolation. It has made of every place a no place. No, my friend, the globalists and cosmopolites are the true enemies of diversity and difference, the raceless and rootless elites who have no attachments, affiliations, or loyalty to anyone or anything except the bottom line. They are the hollow men, the Davos men. They are part of the same cabal, no matter what their nationality. Tell me your enemy and I will tell you who you are. Well, *this* is my enemy. This is public enemy number one, the enemy of all the world. But, oh no, they care about human rights. They are spreading democracy and the open society. They care about the rights of gays and the people of colour and the refugees. Oh, yes, they care very much about the refugees."

My neighbour scrutinized me, as if trying to gauge what I made of what he was saying. I continued to monitor the tumult in my stomach.

"Do you remember how everyone thought capitalism was the winner when the Soviet Union collapsed? I thought this too. It looked like capitalism had won. Remember Fukuyama? But no. They are both losers. It just happened that one fell before the other. What is collapsing in fact is internationalism—or, as I prefer to call it, political transcendentalism. Communism and capitalism were built on transcendental impossibilities. One collapsed before the other. But both go against reality and human nature. You know how they say communism necessarily leads to the gulag? So global capitalism leads to Brussels or Beijing, take your pick. In the end, it doesn't matter if you call it socialism or capitalism, left or right, if it's the Soviet Union or the European Union. All such transcendentalist projects lead inevitably to technocratic authoritarianism. These universalist dreams are a kind of secular religion. As was communism, so is neoliberalism. They are both ridiculous fantasies. I don't know, maybe in Canada you can sustain the dream a little longer, where you are not tied by a common culture and tradition. Maybe there everything can exist in an infinite nexus of exchange value, being nothing in itself. But, no, even in Canada, look at Quebec. Or the aborigines. Look at the African-Americans and the Latinos and all the other groups in the US. Everyone belongs to a persecuted group, or aspires to. Why do you think that is?

"It reminds me of a story about Giacometti. You know Giacometti, the sculptor? One day, crossing the street, Giacometti is hit by a car and as he falls on the ground in terrible pain, just before he becomes unconscious, he thinks, At last something has happened to me." Here, my neighbour leaned back in his chair and laughed heartily. "This is an excellent story, don't you think?" He paused to laugh some more. "It can be interpreted in many ways, but for me it is about the nature of freedom, or what today we *call* freedom. Because what we are really talking about is *anomie*. Do you know this word, anomie? It is a fine word, from the Greek. To be free or detached from the law. To be removed from social norms. This is the freedom we have. But this is an empty, soulless freedom. It is a freedom that does not release but *crushes* the human spirit. It is *individualist* freedom, which is the great myth of modernity. This is not freedom but isolation.

"The fact is we all need something bigger than ourselves, we all require something that not only encompasses but nourishes and defines us, that gives us our existence precisely as individuals. Otherwise we are nothing but animals. Lower than animals. If this is freedom, one would rather be dead. One would rather be hit by a car, just to feel alive. All over Europe and in America young people are going to Syria and Afghanistan to fight for Islam. Some are not even Muslim. They are converting. White kids. Even girls. Why? Young people abandoning their safe comfortable Western lives with all its freedoms and opportunities to go to the desert to become jihadists. How do you explain this? Is it not precisely because they wish to *escape* their so-called freedom? Because they desperately crave something more than their own minuscule atomistic drives and cravings? I think most people understand this, even if only intuitively. We all feel it. The paradox of our human existence is that for our life to have meaning, there must be something more meaningful than our life. There must be something for which indeed we are prepared to *give up* our life. Like one's children, for instance. And if we don't have such a thing, we will invent it. Otherwise we have nothing. We suffocate in our freedom. It may be the devil, or it may the Lord, but you have to serve somebody.

"Do you know the word idiot?" my neighbour asked. "I know you know this word, but do you know where it comes from, what it actually means?"

I assumed this was another rhetorical question and remained silent.

"Do you know?" my neighbour asked again.

Why didn't I just get up and leave? Why did I worry about offending this stranger? Did he worry about my feelings?

"Do you know where this word comes from?" he asked me yet again.

I straightened myself up a little. "It's from the Greek," I said. "*Ithiótis*. Denoting something like the private individual, the person apart from society, from the polis. One concerned only with his own affairs."

My neighbour gave me a puzzled look. "I'm impressed," he said. "And your pronunciation..." He studied me a moment. Creasing his brow, he leaned in closer. "Are you Greek?"

Was it that lone word, idiot, that gave me away?

More than ever I wanted to flee, but I was still nauseous and dizzy. It

I remained in my seat, it was because I didn't trust my legs. Answering truthfully would only draw me in deeper and I considered lying.

"My parents are Greek," I said.

He continued to scrutinize me silently. "Your *parents* are Greek."

"Yes."

"*Both* of them?"

"Yes."

"They were *born* here?"

"Yes."

"So you are Greek."

"I was born in Montreal."

"But you are Greek."

"That seems to be the thinking."

"Do you *speak* Greek?" he asked me in Greek.

"Not very well. I can get by if the conversation is simple."

"You speak it perfectly."

"No, I don't, believe me."

"Hearing you now, I wouldn't know you're not from here."

"You're just being polite," I said in English.

"Not at all," he said, switching back as well.

"In any case, my main language is English. I think in English."

"But your mother tongue is Greek."

"Actually, I'm a resident alien in both languages." I looked at my watch. "I really should be going."

"What? Why?" my neighbour said as I slowly got to my feet. "Please. It's early. Why must you go?"

"I have to get back," I said, clutching the table to steady myself.

"Where? Why?"

There was a grinding in my head.

"Are you okay?"

I noticed a young bearded musician in the nearby square. He was singing into a microphone and playing electric guitar, the sound of his voice and instrument echoing and colliding against each other. The racket had probably been going on for a while but I'd only now become aware of it.

"I'm fine," I said. "I just have to go."

"But why? Please." My neighbour looked genuinely concerned, even alarmed. "I have so much I want to ask you. I wish you had told me before that you are Greek."

"Why?" I said, remaining where I was. I still felt woozy and didn't trust myself to move. I felt a pressure on my forearm.

"I beg you," said my neighbour, tugging on me. "If you go now, I will be certain I said something to offend you."

"You didn't offend me."

"Then please sit down. You don't look well."

Standing up had made me dizzier. Reluctantly, I sat back down.

"What is it? Is it something I said?"

"I'm just feeling a little ill."

"It's maybe the ouzo. And the heat. You drank too fast on an empty stomach. I told you to eat more. Here..." He nudged some plates toward me, like my mother. The gesture infuriated me.

"No," I said with a limp wave.

"Something," he said, proffering a cube of cheese on a toothpick. I wanted to smack it out of his hand. "You will feel better."

"No...thank you."

I slumped back in my chair and closed my eyes. When I opened them again after what felt about two minutes but may have been two hours, I saw my neighbour speaking with a scrawny boy. The boy appeared to be South Asian, maybe nine or ten. He was dressed in shorts and a white undershirt and carrying a tray full of CDs and assorted trinkets. My neighbour asked the boy in Greek what his name was. I couldn't hear the answer.

"Who are you selling these for?"

"For me," the boy said with an accent.

"Don't lie." My neighbour leaned over and examined the items on the tray. "This is all junk." He reached into a pocket and handed the boy some coins. "That's for you—but only for you. You understand? You keep it for yourself."

The boy pocketed the money and walked over to another table. What was this about? Was it for my benefit? Was my neighbour trying to prove something to me? The whole scene felt like a dream.

"There goes your modern European," my neighbour said. "That boy has more in common with our bourgeoisie than you might realize."

I contemplated the passing crowd, but I could feel my neighbour staring at me. He put his elbows on the table. "I have an idea," he said. "Let me show you around. No one knows this city like I do. I will show you a Thessaloniki not even the locals know. Then I will take you for some Greek food you cannot find anywhere else in Greece."

"It's very nice of you, but I'm not feeling well."

"What's wrong?"

"I don't know. I just feel... I really should get back to my hotel."

"What about tomorrow? Tomorrow would be better. We will have more time. There is much to see in Thessaloniki. We have a very rich history. It's more interesting than Athens. And it would be my pleasure."

"I'm leaving tomorrow."

"Then it *must* be this evening."

"I don't think so. I need to lie down."

"Where is your hotel?"

Why did he want to know this?

"It's far from here," I lied.

"Well, the more reason you should not go. Wait until you feel better. Eat something." He started pushing plates at me again. I retrieved my knapsack from under my chair. "What are you doing? No. Oh no, I will not accept your money."

"I'm paying for my share."

"Please. Don't be an American. You insult me."

With all his talk of sovereignty and self-determination, I was tempted to point out that some people might take exception to his habitually lumping Canadians and Americans together.

I managed to get to my feet. "I'm at least paying for my coffee."

"You are paying for nothing," my neighbour said sternly. "If you will not take my offer to show you the city, at least I can treat you to a coffee."

I was too tired to argue. "As you wish." I put away my wallet and held out my hand. "It was very nice to meet you. And thank you for everything."

The stranger stood up. We were silent for a moment.

"If I may ask," said the stranger. "What do you do?"

"I run a billiard hall."

The stranger frowned. It occurred to me we didn't even know each other's name. I wished to keep it that way. He seemed to be studying me, as if trying to determine whether I was joking. Before he could speak further, I left.

I headed in the direction of the busker. There were a few people gathered around him, most of them tourists. His microphone and guitar were hooked up to a small amp, which was also playing a drum track. He was strumming his guitar percussively and doing some kind of Greek rap, though I couldn't make out the words. When the song came to an end, there was light applause, and as I exited the square, I could hear him address the audience in what sounded like English.

Every few seconds, I turned to see whether the stranger was following me. I replayed our encounter, trying to understand what had so discomposed me. I never did learn what the stranger did for a living. I assumed he was some kind of academic, perhaps at the nearby university. At first there had seemed something Mephistophelean about him, but with time I had warmed to him. I even agreed with much of what he said. But then I'd grown confused again. Might he really be a fascist? If he was, this was a retooled and rebranded fascism for the new century. Was this what the European right sounded like these days? Or had I overreacted? Had I been too quick to jump to conclusions? I went over all the stranger had said, trying to identify precisely what I'd found so disturbing. In some ways, he reminded me of my old friends in Toronto. It seemed to me he had much in common with them. Of course they would have been outraged by this. They wouldn't have understood what I meant. I recalled how they too had dismissed the old political labels as obsolete, and how I'd regarded them as glib and callow. But they'd been right after all, though probably not in the way they'd intended. These days, the old terms—that classical geometry of left and right, progressive and reactionary—were not just meaningless but misleading, even pernicious. What passed for one now would have been seen as the other just a few years ago. That whole decrepit nomenclature needed to be dismantled and reconceived. The stranger seemed to me proof of this. Still, I had no doubt that, even with their disdain for the old labels, my Toronto friends would not have hesitated in labelling him a fascist. This was one of the old terms they clung to tenaciously. They would have labelled me one as well for giving him the benefit of the doubt. Meanwhile, he would have seen them as the sort of pampered, out-of-touch elites he called public enemy number one. I recalled how they themselves had branded me an "elitist." That still amused me and stuck in my craw. I regretted that I had never asked them if they saw a distinction between "elitists" and "elites."

I had told the stranger I was leaving Thessaloniki, but that was a lie. Having arrived the previous afternoon, I planned to remain a few days. The next morning, I avoided Navarino Square and headed for the *Áno Póli*, the upper town, keeping an eye out for the stranger. On Akropoleos, I thought I spotted him stepping out of a car and almost knocked over an old woman as I bolted into a doorway. The man emerging from the car turned out to be yet another lookalike. The city was full of them.

That afternoon, I went to the Jewish Museum. I wasn't likely to find many locals there. This was a part of their history most Greeks had little interest in. For centuries Thessaloniki had had a large Jewish population, but you wouldn't know it these days, although the current mayor was taking some controversial and courageous steps to change that. There were few monuments or memorials to the city's Jewish past, apart from the faded Hebrew or Ladino inscriptions you might see etched in a stone block of a building or sidewalk, or even of a church. These were fragments of headstones that, following the destruction of the city's Jewish cemetery during the war, had been recycled as construction materials. I could hardly think of better testament to Renan's contention that all nations were built on historical amnesia and error. Making the rounds of the museum, I wondered what my father knew of this history. Had there been any Jews in his village? Surely he would have known about the Jews of Thessaloniki. Did he know what had happened to them during the war? What had he known at the time? Why had I waited until now to start asking such questions?

After leaving the museum, I had an early dinner and returned to my hotel. I had intended to spend another two days in Thessaloniki, but I was too antsy. It wasn't just the stranger; I had also become impatient to get to my father's village. I gave notice at the front desk that I would be checking out early, and in the morning I hopped on the first bus and was in my father's village before noon.

The bus dropped me off at the edge of the agora, and as I made my way toward the main square, I saw a group of old men watching me. They were gathered beneath a pair of chestnut trees, the tables before them covered with coffee cups, glasses of beer, and water bottles. Several were in caps and suit jackets despite the heat. A few clutched wooden canes. Opposite them, on the other side of the square, stood a white building with a porticoed façade and a pair of flags above the entrance. One was the blue-and-white cross and stripes, the other the Sun of Vergina. Gazing at the old men beneath their sheltering foliage and blazonry, I couldn't help thinking of the kobolóya. What had I achieved in the end?

Greeting the old men, I enquired how I might find a room.

"Are you alone?" one of them asked, twirling his amber worry beads.

"Yes," I said.

From a doorway behind him emerged a short man with a walrus moustache. He looked about my age and was dressed in a yellow short-sleeved shirt, beige cotton pants, and brown leather sandals. He gave me the once-over and said, "You're looking for a room?"

"He's alone," said one of the old men.

"Where are you from?" the younger man asked.

"Canada. Montreal."

"Montreal," echoed an elder in a fisherman's cap. "My brother-in-law lived in Montreal. Now he's in Ottawa. Parahoritis the surname."

I shook my head. "I don't know him."

"Why would you?" he said dryly.

The flagpoles pinged and rattled behind me in the breeze, and I turned and looked up.

"Do you know what that is?" someone asked, seeing me gazing at the Sun of Vergina.

"Oh yes," I said, turning back toward the men. "My father's from here."

"Who's your father?" someone asked.

"Andreas Doukas."

"Kyra Sophia's son?" said a man smoking a cigarette.

"That's right," I answered excitedly. "Did you know him?"

"He was older, but...I remember him."

"You're Alexander Doukas's grandson?" asked another man.

"Yes."

"What's your name?"

"Alexander. Alexander Doukas."

Some of the old men exchanged glances.

"*Kalossórises, paithí mou*," one of them said. Welcome, my child. "Kalossórises," echoed the others.

I gave the ritual reply, expressing gratitude to find myself in their company.

"How long are you staying?" asked the younger man.

"I was thinking maybe six, seven days."

"You can stay here," he said. "I have a nice room for you. And as a native son, you get a discount. Come, let me show you."

I twisted out of my backpack and followed him inside. "I'm Stratos," he said as we stepped into a small taverna. The place was unfussy, with seven or eight tables. On one wall was a flat-screen TV, the sound muted. Three middle-aged men in suits and a couple of garish bosomy women who reminded me of Soula sat behind a shiny curved desk gesticulating fiercely at one another. To one side of the taverna was a steam table, where a slim young man stirred the contents of a small plastic tub. He was in his early twenties and had vaguely Slavic features. Glancing at me, he smiled and wished me a good day with what sounded to me like a foreign accent.

The room was on the second floor and was small and sparsely furnished. There was a bureau with a small TV on it, a double bed with an old-fashioned iron frame, and some small simple watercolours on the bright white walls. The window faced the square. The toilet and shower were down the hall. Stratos informed me that there were two other guest rooms on the floor but were both unoccupied. "You also have a balcony," he said, and parted the sheer curtain. Through the open French doors, I could see the flags on the other side of the square. I checked the doors' angle to the bed. I gauged I'd be able to see the Sun of Vergina lying in it.

"What are you smiling about?" Stratos asked.

"Nothing," I replied, still smiling.

He informed me that he owned another house where I could stay. It was on a nearby farm and he could drive me there to have a look if I was interested in something more "ecological." I said this room suited me perfectly.

When I returned downstairs, I was disappointed to find some of the men gone. The ones remaining invited me to join them and asked about my travels. They wanted to know when I had arrived, where I had been, who I had met, and what I thought of everything. The conversation turned to my father. I had many questions, as did they, and I ordered mezéthes and drinks. More men arrived and sat with us, and I ordered more food and beverages. Everyone was pleasant and welcoming, and some of the old men even invited me to their homes. Over the coming days I would meet their wives and children and extended families. Life in the village turned out to be much better than I'd imagined. The homes I visited were modest but clean and well-maintained, and the village generally was in fine shape, the buildings, roads, and infrastructure having been kept in good repair during the boom years. Back home, I had read that the Greek countryside was experiencing something of a revival, with people returning to their ancestral homes to reclaim derelict farms and orchards. In the city you couldn't survive without money, but with a plot of land you could at least feed yourself. I saw little evidence of such a resurgence here, though there were a few younger people who had come back to take advantage of free room and board. The vast majority of the villagers were pensioners. The local economy remained largely agricultural, with some people working at a ceramics factory or in one of the villages on the coast, where there were more tourists. There was only so much work to be had on the farms, and much of it was being done by foreigners. Nonetheless, the situation here, I was told, was better than in other parts of the country.

Unfortunately, I found few people who had first-hand acquaintance with my father or grandparents. And even they didn't seem terribly reliable. They were old, their minds and memories frail. Others had tales and anecdotes to relate, but they were based on hearsay. Even the oldest of the villagers had barely been teenagers when my father left the village, so how much could they know or remember? I was told again and again that the person I needed was old Dimitri. Old Dimitri, I gathered, was the village bard and the leading authority on the region's history, but he had passed away a month earlier, two days short of a hundred. Till the end, everyone told me, his mind was clear as a bell. I wished I could have said the same for the people I spoke with. Much of what I heard was not just patchy and muddled but contradictory. People contradicted not just one another but even themselves. Occasionally, I had the sense they were making things up, whether to impress me or amuse me or for other reasons, I couldn't tell. A couple of people cautioned me not to believe what certain villagers told me because they were habitual liars and concerned only about protecting their families' reputations. It was like talking with the kobolóya.

One of the more interesting discoveries I made was that my grandfather bore little resemblance to the creative genius and dashing war hero described to me by my father. The Alexander Doukas of village lore was a lout and a liar. He was a spendthrift, schemer, gambler, womanizer, and all-around scoundrel. But why should I be surprised? Why did I never learn? I wanted to kick myself that I hadn't seen this coming. One thing that remained unclear was what my grandfather had done for a living. He had been a kind of odd-jobs man, working at one time or another as a field hand, a goatherd, a carpenter, a waiter, and a few other things. He was mixed up in all kinds of shady activities and would sometimes disappear from the village for weeks at a time. Mostly he had sponged off his wife, who came from a fairly well-to-do merchant family and, before the war, had a bit of money and property.

Before leaving Montreal, I had loaded some of my father's old monochrome photos onto my tablet, but none of the villagers could shed much light on these. Few were even able to identify my father, who was of adult age in the photos. Some guessed that the beautiful Levantine woman in wire rim glasses was my father's sister, and I had to point out how this was impossible given that my father's sister had never reached this woman's age. One old man insisted nonetheless. I asked several people whether she might be my father's mother, and the few who remembered my grandmother declared categorically that the woman in the photo looked nothing like her. One old woman was able to confirm that the inscription on the back was Vlach, which I'd already learned from Steve Kaldaras, Mikos's son. One afternoon, he had dropped by the pool hall and not only identified the language but also translated the inscription as saying something like: "Proof I once was young."

One thing my father seemed to have been right about was his father's musical talent. A few villagers remembered my grandfather playing the fiddle or the lyra or both, though no one could recall him composing his own songs or poems. One old man broke into laughter at the suggestion. "Alex Doukas could no more write poetry than a donkey could sing," he wheezed. A woman present, embarrassed on my behalf, reminded the old man of who I was, but I said I appreciated the honesty and explained again that I wanted the truth, no matter how unflattering or unpleasant. I kept having to emphasize this, as I often got the impression people were holding back or skirting my questions.

Eventually, I figured out why. My grandfather was not a local. On this, there was a consensus. He had not been born in the village. But where he'd come from, or when, no one could say for sure. Some people said he had arrived with the refugees in 1922, others that he was Romanian or Vlach. One couple remembered him as Bulgarian. No one could tell me how he had met my grandmother, though they were keen to speculate. Nor could anyone tell me where he had gone. When I mentioned his joining the andártes in the mountains, I got sneers and snickers. Not a single person could recall him having anything to do with the resistance, though a few claimed he'd been involved with YDIP. This was an agency the Germans created during the war to oversee the expropriation and administration of Jewish property, ranging from simple personal belongings to large businesses. Though created by the Germans, the outfit was devised as an arm of the Greek state and run by local state bureaucrats and functionaries. Among these were one or two my grandfather had an in with, and through them he involved himself in the gathering and disbursing of confiscated property, at some profit to himself. He did well in the war, though he also made enemies. The thinking among the villagers was that, if my grandfather had fled to the mountains, it was not to fight the Germans but to escape the Greeks. Some also were under the impression he had fallen in with the Bulgarophiles and secessionist *Makedontsi*. Where these notions came from, I was unable to determine. It all seemed like rumour and hearsay. Was this how folktales were made? If a village is a hive of gossip, then are legends and folktales simply gossip transmitted across generations?

But how could these stories not have reached my father? And where did his own come from? Had he just made them up? For whose benefit? Was it possible he'd heard these rumours but had kept them to himself? I had to remind myself that my father was only ten when he'd left the village, so it was perfectly plausible he'd never heard the stories I was hearing now. But shouldn't he have had some inkling? He knew what his father was like, and he must have known something of his reputation, even at that age, and especially in a village setting. But then, what had I known about my father's character and reputation at ten? And where I had grown up was very much like a village. I could only assume the source of my father's tales was his mother. On the run with two frightened orphaned children, what was she going to do? Tell them what a rogue and a traitor their father was? To console them and to bolster their spirit and resolve, she told them epic tales of his ingenuity and valour. If they must be without a father, she would at least provide them with an inspiring and sustaining memory of him. That was my postulate.

But where did this leave me? I'd travelled all these miles hoping to shed some light on my father's past only to learn that I was even more in the dark than I'd realized. And would remain so. After a lifetime of wilful ignorance, now that I longed to know about my father's history, most of it was forever irrecoverable. It was a painful irony and a hard fact to swallow. Already I had given up on the blonde woman and the boy in the Polaroids. I'd had to admit that Dzonakis and the kobolóya were right, that the boy was very likely a child from a prior marriage and the rumours of his being my father's were a product of my mother's delusions and vindictiveness. All the evidence was on their side. And yet... What I would have given to be able to speak to the parties themselves. I was still nagged by doubts and continued to hope I might track them down one day and question them directly. I reckoned the boy would now be in his late forties. He may have even lived in the neighbourhood. Perhaps we had crossed paths. Perhaps we had even spoken. A few weeks before leaving for Greece, I had spotted a clerk at Home Depot who seemed to me the adult imago of the boy in the photos. He was exactly the right age. Getting closer to him, I was startled to see the name *André* on his tag. I couldn't decide whether this increased or diminished the odds. For fifteen minutes I shadowed him around the store, trying to settle on a plan of attack. Finally, I enquired about some smoke alarms I pretended to be interested in. I asked him a few questions, and after that I was at a loss. As he turned to leave, I asked him, perhaps a little abruptly, whether his mother's name was Chantal. He gave me a wary look at first; but then, his expression softening, he informed me that his mother's name was Joanne. I apologized for my forwardness and he assured me there was no offense taken.

I was surprised by how crushed I felt. At one time, the thought of my father having had a child with another woman had appalled and sickened me. Now I felt a kind of bereavement and yearning. I had developed a strange attachment to the boy in the photographs. I experienced an odd thrill at the thought that somewhere out there I might have a half-brother. I wondered what he himself knew about me, or about his father. What did he remember of him? What had he been told? Did he recall that day when he'd posed for those photographs? Had he and my father kept in touch? When had they last seen each other? I kept imagining this stranger showing up one day at St. Paul's and the two of us sitting down and trading memories and stories and developing a lifelong brotherly relationship. It was a preposterous, juvenile fantasy, the fantasy perhaps of an only child.

Nearing the end of my stay in the village, I realized what a mess I'd made of things. Once more I'd failed to plan properly. I would need more than five or six days to get the kind of information I was after. I should have known that it would not be enough merely to interview a few senescent villagers. I would have to do some real research, dig through archival documents, civil registries, church records. I would have to do the work of a real historian, the kind of work I had dreaded when doing my PhD. If I wanted answers, I would have to come back. I felt demoralized. Why did it always take me so long to figure things out?

I decided that, with the little time remaining, I should try to speak with the village priest. I'd been told he was young and had arrived only recently, but I figured he could still be helpful. He could give me access to records and other documents, maybe even advise me on who to consult, where else to go, how to proceed generally. I would drop by the church and see if I could arrange a meeting with him.

That was when I got the call that my father had had another stroke. "It doesn't look good," Perry told me. "The doctors are saying he's probably not going to make it." How many times had I heard this? "I think this time it's for real," Perry said. I made my way back to Montreal fast as I could.

Returning to my father's room, I discover he's not there. I search the ward and find him in a lounge at the end of a corridor. He's watching television, or at least performing a pantomime thereof. In a corner, next to the TV set, an elderly man in striped pyjamas is slumped in a chair, sleeping.

"How did you get here?" I ask my father. "Did someone bring you?" He stares at the TV. It's tuned to the news. I pull up a chair. "Did you bring yourself here by yourself?" I'm genuinely curious, as I'm still not clear about his physical capabilities. But he doesn't answer. "Did you push yourself here by yourself?"

He raises a hand and grunts. I don't understand.

"Sorry?"

He points at the television, then up at the ceiling.

I glance up but see nothing. "I don't understand."

He raises his hand again and makes a twisting gesture.

"You want it louder?"

He grunts.

Delighted at this successful exchange, I spring to my feet. The guy in the corner is snoring. I pick up the remote and increase the volume. "Is that okay?

I get a nod. I'm shocked. This is the most we've communicated all week. Hanging on to the remote, I return to my chair.

"Thank you," I say.

My father continues to stare at the TV without acknowledgment. But that's fine. He probably doesn't understand why I'm thanking him.

"Is it okay where it is? Do you want me to change channels?"

He shakes his head. This is good.

"Do you want the buttons?" I ask, holding out the remote to him. He stares at it a moment and again shakes his head.

I flash back to the two of us on the couch on Esplanade, watching the six o'clock news. Black-and-white footage unspools in my head—Richard Nixon in China, the Peking streets thick with bicycles; Nixon and Trudeau posing outdoors somewhere, both stiff and smiling uncomfortably; Trudeau arm in arm with a begowned Barbara Streisand; Leonid Brezhnev in a long coat applauding a parade of tanks and soldiers. I remember the gorillas, the slaps to the head. I remember the plastic gondola and porcelain figurines atop the TV cabinet, the decorative porcelain plates on the wall, my mother in the kitchen.

But all at once I'm pulled back by the images on the screen. I see familiar sights, shots of Athens. I turn to my father.

"Can you hear? Do you understand?" No answer. "They're talking about Greece." The Greek prime minister is shaking hands with EU dignitaries. "Do you know who that is?" I ask. "Do you recognize him?"

My father turns and gives me what appears to be a meaningful look, but

I can't decipher it. Is he miffed, angry, confused? He turns back to the TV. I peek at him intermittently but can't tell what he makes of what he sees. What does he know about the situation in Greece? What does he know about anything?

On screen, there are more shots of Athens. A marketplace. A merchant giving his opinion, with voiceover translation. A pedestrian mall.

"That's where I was," I say, pointing. "That's near where I stayed."

My father stares at the TV impassively.

"Do you remember that I was just in Greece? Just a week ago?"

He gives me another inscrutable look. Have I insulted him? Why do I care? He hasn't asked me a single question about the trip since my return. And the few times I've mentioned it, he has shown no interest—even when I told him I went to his village. I ache to tell him about that experience, about the people I met, what they told me; I want to see his reaction. But I know it's childish spite. And to what end? It would only make me feel worse. Still, I'm desperate to tell him all I heard.

As the newscast shifts to another story and another part of the world, my father keeps staring at the TV. Another war somewhere. I watch him, wondering what he sees, how much he understands. But, then, do I see or understand much more? I reach down and, unzipping my knapsack, pull out my tablet. I turn it on and the photo of the woman in the wire rim glasses comes up. I've made it my wallpaper. The original sits on my desk, set inside a mahogany frame I found in an antique shop in Thessaloniki. I've grown extremely fond of this photograph, partly for aesthetic reasons, but also because there's something deeply beguiling about the woman in it. I still don't know who she is, but I've developed a theory about her. In fact, it's hardened into something like a conviction.

I turn down the volume on the TV and scroll through my albums. A few days earlier, I loaded pictures from my trip, and I browse through them. Shifting closer to my father, I hold the tablet before him and he gazes at it as if trying to figure out what it is. I give him a few seconds.

"Can you see?"

He doesn't answer.

"Should I bring your glasses?"

He shakes his head.

"Should I hold it closer? Or farther?"

He doesn't respond.

"Do you recognize the location? You recognize where that is?"

He stares.

"It's Athens. Not far from the hotel where I stayed. It's in Monastiraki. You must recognize it."

I get no answer. I swipe to the next photo. "You recognize that?" I keep swiping. "I took all these. Do you remember that I was just in Greece?"

No answer. But he's looking. Something in the images holds his interest. I keep swiping, and offer brief explanations. When we get to the village, I don't comment. I watch for a reaction. There isn't one.

"Do you recognize any of these places?"

I show him a series of portraits, shots of the villagers, some in groups, some alone.

"That's Yiorgos Zagorakis. He says he knew you in school. He's a little younger than you. Do you remember him?"

No answer.

"He told me some stories about you, about when you were a kid. He told me some things about your mother. And your father."

How far am I prepared to push this?

I move on to another photo. "You know who that is?"

My father's mouth is slack, drool collecting in a corner.

"That's Kyra Olga's daughter. Do you remember Olga Dimitriou?"

Silence.

"You can just nod or shake your head. You can do that, can't you? Do you remember Olga Dimitriou?"

Nothing.

I roll through more pictures. "This is Miltiades Karakatsanis."

I swipe quickly through several more pictures and stop at one that shows a plain two-storey house. Parked before it is a red Toyota Corolla.

"They told me this is where your house used to be. The original building was torn down in the seventies. But this was where your house stood. That's what they told me. Do you remember it? Do you remember your house?"

Silence.

I swipe through a series of photos showing the same building from different angles. Glancing up, I notice a thin streak of moisture on my father's cheek. At first I think it's perspiration, but then, with a shock, I realize he's crying.

I shut the tablet. "Are you all right?"

He's gazing into the distance, eyes brimming. I don't think I've ever seen my father cry.

"What's going on?"

He's staring at the floor but he's clearly focused on something internal.

"Are you okay?" I'm beginning to panic. "Are you in pain? Should I call a nurse?"

He turns and looks at me, but he doesn't speak. Even with the tears, his expression is as impassive and inscrutable as always. It's more like he's leaking than weeping.

"Should I call a nurse?"

He parts his lips and mumbles something.

"What?" I lean in closer. "What did you say?" He mumbles again but I can't make sense of what he's saying. It's partly a physical problem: without his dentures, much of what comes from his mouth is even at the best of times a gummy phonetic mush. I now discern occasional words and names—*stone, watermelon, Manolis, cold*. Less frequently, I make out complete phrases, but they don't meld into anything coherent. The words seem to be detached not just from one another but from their own semantic footing. I hear *dog, pants, Levesque, mosquitoes, artichokes*, but do these sounds have the same meaning for my father that they do for me? And what's he doing anyway? What is this? A confession, a lament, a complaint?

Suddenly I am a child again, as when I used to see my mother cry. I can't help myself: I start crying too in a kind of sympathetic response. I can't seem to stop it. I don't know whether my father notices. He's still looking at me, but I don't know whether he sees the tears. He gives no indication of what he's seeing or thinking. I don't know whether he even knows who I am.

I take his hand unwittingly, and the tears come even harder. His hand feels cold and bony and unfamiliar. I can't remember the last time I held my father's hand, but I retain some sense memory of it and this isn't it. As he continues his murmuring, I check to see if there's anyone around. I don't wish to be on display at a moment like this. But there's no one in sight, and I face forward again. Across from us, the TV flickers dumbly, the old man in pyjamas sits slumped in the corner, snoring. I look at my father, watching his lips. Still holding his hand, I lean in, trying to hear, the both of us soundlessly weeping as he continues talking his gibberish.

Acknowledgements

My thanks to Julia Dryer, Smaro Kamboureli, and Mark Finkelstein for their comments on early drafts of this novel. Special thanks to David Hull for his editorial acumen and tactful and tireless diligence, which have not just improved the writing in this book but improved me as a writer.

About the author

Fotios Sarris was born in Montreal and grew up in the Mile End district. He did his undergraduate degree at Concordia while working as a stage-hand in one of the last of the city's burlesque theatres. After completing his doctorate at the University of Toronto, he joined the faculty of Ryerson University, where he is a lecturer in the School of Professional Communication. *A Foreign Country* is his first novel.

Printed by Imprimerie Gauvin
Gatineau, Québec